TABOO TREE

ISBN-13: 9780982978177

Printed in USA by CreateSpace (www.createspace.com)

Alphonso, Carolyn, Wanda, Todd, Masee and Ahmad. I couldn't ask for a better support system. I love you all very much.

THE GWALTNEYS
Jason & Minerva Gwaltney

Tavares   Demetria   JJ   Sanford   Cecelia

THE AUGUSTINES
Charles "Chick" & Ophelia Augustine

CJ   Stephanie   Derric   Cameo   Huron

PART ONE

WHAT HAS PASSED...

Taboo Tree

ONE

Virginia 1968

The pond was sparkling clear, almost translucent in its appearance. Perfectly round, it connected two vast properties. The estates were breathtaking to say the least. The grass was a vibrant green and spread out over scores of hilly acres. Towering, leafy trees offered a grand expanse of shade while cooling the area surrounding them. Travelers often stopped to take a closer look at the incredible outlay of land. Aside from its exquisite, raw beauty, the most unique aspect of the territory was its owners.

For generations, the land had been cultivated by the Gwaltneys and the Augustines. In addition to working the rich property, the two black families also defended their possession with great enthusiasm, pride and fierceness. Financial strife, inclement weather and, of course, man-made threats each played a role in those days especially.

Still, aside from the threats which often drew them together, nothing else seemed to unite the families. The Gwaltney-Augustine feud had outlasted three generations and was at work on a fourth. The battle had gone on so long many wondered if the feuding clans really remembered what started it. Some speculated that the unrest had to do with land disputes others thought it was simply competition for wealth and status.

Still, there were those who felt the feud rose from more 'intimate' reasons.

Whatever the motivation that fueled the on-going unrest, one thing was certain: the quarrel showed no signs of ending.

Four year old Jonas Josiah Gwaltney scurried past the towering trees, past the heads of cattle grazing in the distant pasture. JJ's short, stocky legs carried him over the rolling hills and the lush greenery beyond the line which divided his family's property from the Augustine's. Of course, the adorable, chocolate skinned little boy was unaware of the fierce squabbles that existed between his family and their neighbors. What mattered to little JJ was that he was a free man. His parents were home and the field workers and house staff were all about their business. He was at liberty to do whatever he pleased and he intended to enjoy it.

The child found his way to the edge of the Gwaltney property. JJ stared out and saw acres of new play land. The heated debates and fights over the pond's rightful owners were unimportant to the innocent boy. There was no big person there to shoo him away or scold him for having ventured so far from home. He inched closer, his small, sneaker-shod feet bringing him nearer to the crystal-like pond. A breathless giggle escaped his tiny mouth as the calm, cool water soaked his jeans and the hem of his T-shirt. Soon, he was splashing around like a wild fish. His carefree laughter filled the air.

Acres from where young JJ savored his freedom, there sat a gorgeous three story red brick home. A tiny man-made stream ran through the huge front yard, which was dotted by large, hanging-moss trees. Bushes bearing sweet berries and flowers skirted the base of the trees. Toward the back of the mansion, workers toiled beneath the afternoon sun. Those closest to the house pruned bushes, watered plants and maintained other areas of the front and back yard. Far off in the distance, the field workers tended the horses, cattle and crops. The men's wide

Taboo Tree

chests and backs glistened with sweat as they completed the last of their chores and prepared to end another day's work.

Inside the main house, almost every room was bathed in silence. Per instructions from the mistress, the home was kept in pristine condition at all times. The furniture was polished each day, the cushions tossed and all rugs were vacuumed or swept. The frames of the portraits lining the halls were polished as were the banisters and doorknobs. Despite the extravagant efforts to maintain the untouched, elegant look, the place still retained its cozy, inviting appeal. The kitchen had to be the most tempting area, with a half dozen cooks bustling about, clattering pans and utensils in preparation for that evening's supper.

The second floor of the Gwaltney home housed the room of the eldest son, Tavares. There were at least six more lovely rooms, though they were unused at the present. The bed sheets were changed each week and the rooms were cleaned every other day. The home's third floor carried the grand master suite and playrooms. These were the only two rooms on the floor-each at opposite ends of the long hallway.

With JJs absence, the master bedroom suite was the only occupied room. Rising past the imposing, double mahogany doors, were the unmistakable sounds of pleasure. Inside, a man and woman enjoyed the spacious four poster maple bed that sat catty-cornered in the chamber. The woman was small, yet quite voluptuous. Her complexion was an even molasses color that almost blended with her shoulder-length onyx tresses.

A giant, dark man was hunched behind the woman. His skin tone was as dark and smooth as his partner's. His head was shaved bald and shiny with sweat. Clearly, he had been so impatient to bed the lovely woman; he hadn't taken time to remove his clothes. He wore a pair of dusty gray overalls which sagged around his thrusting hips. A beige linen shirt was cut off at the sleeves to reveal his massive forearms and biceps.

The small woman clung to one of the tall bedposts. The bed shook from each thrust. She was leaning against the carved headboard as the man took her from behind. Her lilting cries only seemed to encourage him, causing him to increase the force of his movements. His big hands curved over his partner's slender hips and his perfect teeth gnawed the soft flesh of her shoulder. He withdrew after a while and his dimples flashed when he smiled in response to her moan of disappointment. He settled to his back and lifted her as though she were weightless. When she straddled his massive dark frame and eased down over his stiff manhood, they moaned in unison. The woman's long nails grazed the man's wide chest and flat abdomen. Her dark eyes sparkled wickedly when he gripped her hips and increased the speed of his upward thrusts. Soon, overwhelming waves of pleasure drenched them as they simultaneously reached a powerful climax.

In minutes, the tiny woman had collapsed over her huge partner. At once, they began to laugh.

"Woman, your husband know you spend all day laid up in bed?"

The woman smiled and raised her head from her lover's chest. "He don't mind as long as I'm...ready when he calls me."

"You a bad woman Minerva Gwaltney."

Minerva inched closer to the handsome man lying beneath her. "And don't you forget it, Mr. Gwaltney." She cooed, smiling when her husband pulled her into another kiss.

Jason and Minerva were about to slip into another round of lovemaking, when a tentative knock sounded on the door.

"Lonnie." They guessed. The cooks always sent the timid, housemaid upstairs to fetch Minerva when dinner was nearing completion. Lonnie was somewhat dimwitted and innocent to the ways between men and women. The cooks believed an intrusion by the girl would be less embarrassing for their employers, should they be bothered during one of their many afternoon rendezvous.

"Coming Lonnie!" Minerva called, easing away from her husband. "You'll just have to hold on until tonight, Baby." She teased.

Instead, Jason pulled her back onto the bed and pinned her beneath his heavy frame.

"Baby, I have to go check on dinner with the cooks."

"Hush." Jason whispered, cupping Minerva's chin to hold her in place for his kiss.

Minerva surrendered, her fingers curling around Jason's neck as his tongue stroked the even ridge of her teeth before delving into the sweet recesses of her mouth.

"Alright, go on and check on my dinner." Jason suddenly ordered, slapping his wife's bare bottom as he sent her on her way. He lounged back on the huge bed, watching her through narrowed eyes. Love and desire radiated from his deep-set onyx gaze, as he reflected on how far they had come.

As a young married couple, they had opted to work the land left to Jason and his brothers when their parents passed away. The brothers set off for parts unknown, leaving their elder brother behind. Jason had no complaints. In fact, he had secretly dreamed of being king of the vast property and populating it with crops and children. His sexually enthusiastic wife raised no protests about helping him accomplish the second task.

Minerva was buttoning a light blue frock as she made her way down the stairs. The smile on her lips was a mixture of pride and satisfaction. She glanced at the lovely artwork and rugs lining the grand hall and stairways. Her life was just as she would have it. With their son Tavares, daughter Demetria and now their youngest, JJ, even more joy was added to their already full lives. There would be more children, but JJ was such a bundle of energy and excitement, Minerva and Jason decided to wait a while before adding to the family.

"Miss Minerva, you just in time!"

"What's in store for tonight, Gladys?"

Head cook Gladys Wickers, beamed with pride as she stood near the huge, nine burner stove. An iron pot simmered on each eye. "I think you'll be pleased, Miss."

Minerva waved her hands in the air. "Please, I know I will be. What have we got?"

"Slow-cooked baby lima beans with ham hocks, we got fried okra with onions, pineapple glazed ham and stew beef with rice and cornbread. The girls are putting the pumpkin pies in the oven now."

"I hope my plate is ready." Minerva sighed. Her mouth watered from the list of items mentioned.

Gladys chuckled as she loaded a side of the plate with a generous helping of the seasoned baby limas. Although the Gwaltneys immediate family only consisted of four people, Minerva always made sure dinner included everyone. Even though the majority of the staff felt their employers spent too much time 'indisposed', they loved Jason and Minerva for the respect they always showed every employee. The couple had enough food prepared to feed the entire staff if they chose to dine. Otherwise, the leftover untouched food was packaged and shipped to the local mission.

"Oh goodness..." Minerva drawled, as she closed her eyes. "Another success ladies." She complimented, marveling at the tender stewed beef that practically melted on her tongue. The cook staff always prepared a plate of the main course for Minerva. She rarely, if ever, had a complaint.

"Willett, where in the world, did you find these huge sweet potatoes?"

Another cook, Willett Mannis, smiled and tossed one of the big potatoes in her hand. "These are from Mr. Jason's store."

Minerva's eyes widened. "They're growin' that big out there?" She gasped.

"Mmm hmm, Mr. Jason's got the best produce selection in town." Willett declared. "Lotta white folks mad 'cause he's gettin' all the business from black *and* white customers."

"Well, well that's always good to hear." Minerva admitted, brushing Willett's plump shoulder with hers. She and the tall, middle-aged woman stood talking a while longer. Then, Minerva strolled out the back screen door. She stood on the wide brick steps and gazed up at the late evening skies. For several minutes, her dark gaze was held captive by the comforting shades of purple, blue and orange fusing together.

"Evenin' Miss Minerva."

"Evenin' Charles," Minerva called, waving to the head gardener as she smiled. "Charles you seen JJ around here?" She asked.

Charles pulled the worn, gray cap from his head and wiped his brow. "Saw him runnin' around here earlier, but I can't say how long ago it was."

"That lil' boy..." Minerva groaned, propping one hand to her hip.

"Aw Miss Minerva, he's probably gettin' in some mischief 'round here someplace." Charles determined.

"Yeah..." Minerva sighed. "Thanks Charles." She called, smiling from the door as the man walked on. The assurances could have been true enough. For some reason, they did nothing to calm her.

Minerva stopped a few of the gardeners and asked if they had seen her son playing around the house. Few could remember having seen the child. Eventually, she was pulling aside the field workers as they headed towards the main house. Panic began to rise in her luminous deep brown eyes.

Jason was on his way outdoors when he spotted his wife heading into the kitchen. His double-dimpled smile faded, when he noticed Minerva wringing her hands. He could see the nervous look in her eyes when she approached him.

"What?" He demanded, his large hands curving over her small ones in an effort to stop their shaking.

Minerva shook her head, sending several curls bouncing into her face. "JJ...I don't know where he is."

Jason's soft, deep chuckle rushed forth. "That all Minnie?" He queried, pulling her into a light embrace. "Girl, you know how that boy is. He's probably gettin' in some devilment 'round here somewhere."

Minerva shook her head against Jason's chest. "I talked to everybody. I asked all the field hands. Being that far out, surely they would've seen him."

Jason grimaced, when he looked down into Minerva's upturned face. Her eyes glistened with tears and her lips trembled. "Baby, he is fine. You know he's done this mess before-"

"But, no one has seen him Jason and I have a bad feeling!" She blared, just as the tears burst forth.

A low, frustrated growl rose in the depths of Jason's wide chest. He pulled Minerva into his arms and carried her the short distance to one of the chairs at the kitchen table.

"I'm goin' outside to round up some hands to go look for the boy." He told the staff, who watched him and Minerva with wide eyes, "Get her upstairs and into bed." He ordered and stormed outside. The screened door slammed shut in his wake.

Before anyone could touch Minerva, she was out of the chair. "Y'all forget about me and this dinner and search this damned house for my baby!"

***

Before an hour passed, everyone on the estate shared Minerva's concern: Little JJ was definitely missing and had ventured far from the main house and property. Several interested neighbors helped with the search. Some brought dogs to the Gwaltney estate and, due to the hour, torches had been lit.

"JJ! JJ Gwaltney!" Minerva called, running like a banshee across the lush property. She carried no torch, but some unseen force was certainly directing her. She opened her mouth to call out again and realized her throat had become too dry to form the words. Her frantic gait slowed, and soon she was wandering-despair filled her eyes. She had reached the edge of the land and there was no sight of her son.

Then, she saw it: The pond-The pond which separated the Gwaltney and Augustine properties. It was an incredible body of water, twinkling and glittering beneath the silvery glow of moonlight. Minerva smoothed both hands across her face and strolled closer to the inviting pool. After a quick glance across her shoulder, she decided to rest her aching feet.

Easing down on the grassy bank, she removed her hard sandals and drew her knees up to her chest. After a while, the sound of the water's gentle ripple began to calm her raging nerves. Unable to resist any longer, she gave into the desire to soak her feet. She stood and sauntered to the edge of the water and trailed her big toe against its translucent surface.

A tiny shiver raced up her spine when the coolness touched her skin. She walked further into the pond, until the water just reached her calves.

"Mmm..." She sighed, brushing both hands across her arms and smiling at the simple treat. When she glanced down at the darkened body of water, she could just make out a figure beneath the thin steam of moonlight.

Minerva peered closer, certain that the shadow was a turtle, duck or some other animal. The figure traveled closer to the pond's edge and bumped right next to her against the bank. Something brushed her foot and her mouth fell open as the tears returned. She knelt closer-closer to the tiny hand brushing her ankle. Slowly, she reached down and pulled the tiny body into her arms. Minutes passed as Minerva knelt there on the bank and rocked her dead son in her arms. The pained sobs rose like a terrible bile in the back of her throat. In seconds, her voice had returned and her wounded cries filled the air.

"Julius, I want you and your group to start searching in them woods skirtin' the pasture. Corvell, you Montez and Rico take your group and go up the trail leading into that mess of hills behind the barn."

"Mr. Jason! Mr. Jason!"

Jason raised his hand towards the group of men who raced towards him. He finished delegating duties to the search groups, and was about to send them on their way, when he heard the cries.

"Mr. Jason-"

"Hush!" He ordered, his hands poised in the air. "Minerva." He whispered.

The group made way for Jason, lest they be trampled. The man broke into a frantic run, headed in the direction of his wife's wailing. Somehow, he knew where to go. His heavy steps carried him to the hilltop overlooking the valley where the Augustine pond was located. There, beneath the moonlight, he could make out the form of his wife and son huddled together.

"My boy is dead." Jason muttered, as though he couldn't quite believe it. He broke into a sprint once again and headed for the pond. By now, a crowd had gathered around Minerva and JJ. Jason cut through the mass of bodies and pulled the boy's limp body from his wife's arms.

Minerva gasped and jumped to her feet the instant JJ was taken from her. The sight of her powerful husband crying profusely shocked her only for a moment. Those in the crowd prayed for the child. Minerva sobbed against JJ's back, while Jason squeezed him and cried out into the night.

***

On the opposite side of the Gwaltney property, Ophelia Augustine was tossing a dishcloth to the counter.

"Dammit." She hissed, a small furrow forming between her sleek, black brows. "Gumbo don't taste the same when it's cool. Where the devil are they?" She muttered.

Seven year old Charles Henry Augustine Jr. ambled into the kitchen. There was an over exaggerated look of aggravation on his cute chocolate-toned face.

"Mama, can we eat yet?" CJ whined, leaning his slender form against the rectangular mahogany kitchen table.

"As soon as I find out where your Daddy and Sister are." Ophelia told her first born child.

"Daddy's on the back porch with Steph." CJ supplied.

Ophelia frowned and leaned over the double sided porcelain sink. She saw no trace of her husband or daughter when she peered out the window. "They must be out in the yard."

"I'll go get 'em!" CJ volunteered.

"Oh no!" Ophelia decided, catching her energetic little boy before he got too far. "Uh uh, Mista. I got one of you in here and I'm keeping you."

"Aw Ma..." CJ whined, when his mother placed him in his usual chair at the table.

Ophelia removed the apron that covered her pink and white pedal pushers and matching short-sleeved blouse. She ventured outside. Her waist-length jet black hair lifted around her face the instant it was touched by the evening breeze.

Ophelia Augustine was independence personified. She held her tongue for no one, except her husband whom she loved dearly. Her striking features left most people staring. Huge expressive dark brown eyes, a tall lithe body and a sense of intelligence, produced a strong woman, firm mother and incredible wife.

"Don't y'all smell that gumbo out here?" She called, spotting her husband and daughter standing in the middle of the huge back yard. Charles "Chick" Sr. and Stephanie Karina Augustine seemed to be transfixed on something in the distance. Wondering what held their attention so reverently, Ophelia walked closer to the quiet twosome.

"Hey," she whispered, setting her chin against her husband's broad shoulder.

"Something's goin' on at the Gwaltneys." Chick noted, his thick dark brows drawn together as he stood with his arms folded across his wide chest.

"Maybe it's a party, Daddy." Stephanie shared from her leaning stance against her father's long legs.

Chick's deep set ebony gaze twinkled with love when he looked down at his six year old daughter. "I don't think so, Babygirl." He disagreed with a smile.

"What are you thinking?" Ophelia asked, intrigued as she caught sight of the flickering firelight in the distance.

Chick shook his head and smoothed one hand over the soft crop of curly hair covering his head. "I don't have a good feeling about it, whatever it is." He whispered and slipped an arm around his wife's small waist.

Chick, Ophelia and Stephanie stood in silence a few moments longer. The firelight illuminated the otherwise black expanse of land. The effect of the glow was as hypnotic as it was eerie.

"Well, let's get inside for dinner before CJ has a fit." Ophelia decided, turning her family towards their home. "I'm sure the commotion'll be over soon." She added, casting an uncertain glance across her shoulder.

The gumbo was still piping hot and perfectly seasoned. The four Augustines ate heartily and quietly. With the exception of grace, dinner usually passed in silence. Ophelia had to smile as she watched her family concentrate on the food. They cleared their plates after each refill and it made her proud to take care of them and to ensure their safety and well-being.

Her gaze slid down to the head of the table to her husband. In ten years of marriage, they had been through a lot. Still, Ophelia knew she wouldn't have traded a minute of her life with Chick Augustine. He was an incredible man; mentally and physically. Standing over six feet, his skin was a flawless, rich brown. Heavy black brows lay in a sleek line over his midnight eyes. A beard and mustache covered the bottom of his handsome face. Though Chick lacked nothing in the brawn department, he was more of a thinking man. Still, he was revered as a no-nonsense type of man. When he spoke, people listened.

Charles and Ophelia met and fell in love during their college years in North Carolina. Chick wasn't about to let the devastating beauty get away and asked her to marry him after they graduated. Their families were quite comfortable financially, but the couple was determined to make it on their own. They moved to Virginia after Chick's grandmother passed and left the family estate to his care. Chick was no farmer and preferred a job that would allow him to use brains instead of muscles.

With a degree in accounting, Chick did the books for a sewing factory. He quickly caught the eye of his superiors. Ophelia made use of her teaching degree and worked as a seamstress to bring in extra money.

The young couple thrived in the struggle and they were determined to show their families they could really make it. When the owner of the factory died, Chick was working as the man's first assistant-an incredible accomplishment for a twenty-something black man. It proved to be just the break the newlyweds needed. Ophelia quit teaching and went to work with her husband. Through their combined efforts and seemingly endless hours the factory acquired several jobs from the new businesses rising in town. The factory had been commissioned to produce uniforms for the local black hospital and hotel. The money and recognition began to pour in. Of course, it was only the beginning.

Ophelia shook back to the present. A soft smile clung to her lips. "Has anyone saved room for dessert?" She asked.

"Meeee!" CJ and Steph both squealed.

"Baby?" Ophelia whispered, watching Chick expectantly.

"Nah, thanks Fe, but I'm gonna go sit in the front room for a while."

Ophelia's expressive brown gaze followed her husband, until he left the kitchen. She cut slices of the homemade sweet potato pie and served the kids.

"Are you gonna eat some pie, Mama?" Stephanie asked her dark gaze focused on her mother.

Ophelia smiled and smoothed her daughter's sleek hair pulled back into a ponytail. "Just going to talk to Daddy a minute, Babypie." She promised.

The Augustine home matched the Gwaltneys in size, but there the similarity ended. The Gwaltney's fabulous mansion carried the appearance of some grand plantation. The Augustine home was just that, a home. Ophelia's presence could be felt in each room. She had placed a loving effect on each of the large, comfortably furnished rooms. The color scheme was a relaxing mix of earth tones. The furniture was finely crafted, but remained unpretentious in its appearance. The gleaming hardwoods in the upstairs bedrooms and hallways were covered by the loveliest rugs. Portraits of family and friends lined the walls and decorated all the rooms.

Ophelia's steps slowed when she neared the arched doorway leading to the sitting room. She folded her arms across her chest and watched Chick intently. He had the evening paper perched on his lap, but it was clear that he wasn't looking at it.

"Baby?" Ophelia called, waiting for Chick's midnight eyes to move to her face. "Honey what is it?" She asked, walking further into the room. "What has you so upset tonight?" She whispered.

Chick massaged his temple and leaned his head back against his favorite burgundy armchair. "I wish I knew what was goin' on over there." He admitted.

"This is about the Gwaltneys?" Ophelia asked, her slightly husky voice holding a trace of disbelief. "Baby please don't waste your time worryin' about them people." She said and rolled her eyes towards the chandelier in the ceiling.

"Fe..." Chick sighed.

"Honey, they are not worth it. Do you really think Jason or Minerva would be sitting around worrying about you?"

"Ophelia." Chick called again. This time, he pushed himself out of the armchair and fixed her with a hard glare.

Of course, Ophelia rarely hesitated to reveal there was no love lost between her family and their neighbors. Chick usually listened to her ravings about the Gwaltneys with little more than a raised brow. That night, he was unusually on edge and Ophelia advised herself to curb her tongue.

Instead, she closed the distance between them and linked her arms around his lean waist. "Why are you so upset about what's goin' on over there?" She whispered, smoothing her mouth along his jaw, while toying with the empty belt loops on his jeans.

Chick bowed his head and inhaled the soft scent of his wife's perfume. "I wish I knew, Fe. I wish I knew."

TWO

"Here, let's sit you down." Ophelia whispered, guiding Chick
back to his chair. She was very concerned by the expression on
his face and prayed it would pass. In all the years of marriage she
had seen the look more than once. This time, the look seemed
more haunting.

"How's that?" She cooed, rubbing his neck and shoulders
in brisk fashion.

Chick closed his eyes and allowed his head to slope
forward. "Mmm..." He replied.

Ten minutes later, a quick, hard knock sounded on the
front door. Ophelia smothered a curse over the interruption,
when Chick went to answer the door. She took a seat on the arm
of the chair and waited.

Out in the night, three men waited. Chick recognized
each of them and nodded towards George Mooney, Felix Durant
and Jesse Simpson.

"Y'all come in." He invited, stepping aside so they could
enter.

"Hey y'all." Ophelia called, standing when she saw the men walk into the sitting room. "Can I bring in something to drink?"

"Oh no, Miss Ophelia we don't need anything." Felix Durant spoke for his friends.

The sitting room was bathed in silence for several moments, it seemed. Finally, Chick cleared his throat and looked down at each man's dirtied clothing.

"You boys look like y'all been fightin' a fire." He noted.

"Chick man, I wish to Sweet Lord we had been fightin' a fire." Felix told him, the smile on his face a cross between faint humor and terrible sadness.

"What happened?" Ophelia asked when she stood next to Chick.

George Mooney twisted the brim of his brown hat in his hand. "It's somethin' terrible, Miss Ophelia."

"Is it Minerva or Jason?" Chick asked leaning against the maple paneled wall as his three guests took their places on the long, forest green sofa.

"It's there youngest boy." Jesse Simpson informed them, shaking his head as the words left his mouth.

"JJ?" Ophelia whispered, resuming her seat on the arm of Chick's chair.

"The boy ran off...sometime in the afternoon." George Mooney explained, his saddened expression matching the look in his eyes. "He was dead when they found him."

"Dead?" Ophelia gasped.

"Drowned." George clarified his round wide gaze solemn.

The Augustines absorbed the information with growing horror. The circumstances of the child's death struck them like a blow to the face.

"Where'd they find him, Jess?" Chick asked his onyx stare riveted on the man seated closest to him.

Jesse glanced at Ophelia and his friends before responding. "They found him in your pond." He revealed, becoming flushed beneath his vanilla complexion.

Taboo Tree

"My Lord." Ophelia cried, her warm gaze pooling with tears. Her heart began to ache as she imagined the couple's grief over such a loss.

The rumbling sound of sneaker-shod feet, racing across the hardwood floor, caught the adults' attention. CJ and Stephanie ran into the sitting room, unaware of the serious moment they had just interrupted.

"Hey Mr. Simpson, hey Mr. Mooney, hey Mr. Durant!" They bellowed.

"Have you two finished that pie?" Ophelia called, hurrying towards her children. "Did you rinse those plates?" She asked when they nodded. "Well, let's get upstairs and let Daddy talk." She said, hustling the boy and girl from the room.

"How did he get all the way out to that pond? Was he alone?" Chick asked, once his family had left the room.

Each man appeared reluctant to answer.

"It appears he was there alone." George said after a while.

Chick was baffled and angry. "How the hell did he get all the way out there with no body noticing?"

George, Felix and Jesse exchanged glances. "We were wondering that ourselves."

"You'd think with all those hands they have over there, somebody would've seen something." Chick remarked, massaging his light beard.

The men went back and forth over the incident. None of them could believe such a terrible thing could happen. Moreover, no one could fathom how the incident would affect the two most powerful black families in their community.

Ophelia returned downstairs after getting CJ and Steph settled. The look on her lovely face still appeared haunting. Chick noticed and extended his hand.

"Are you all sure the baby is dead? I mean, had the doctor even been called?" Ophelia asked when she sat perched on the arm of her husband's chair.

The three men nodded.

AlTonya Washington

"We're sure Miss Ophelia." Jesse confirmed. "It took a while to get Miss Minerva to let the boy go, but before we left, they were making plans to carry him into town."

"They should be announcing the funeral any day." George added.

The room was silent, with the exception of Ophelia's shuddery breaths. Further conversation seemed unnecessary then. After about three minutes, Felix reached for his hat and stood.

"We better be gettin' on." He said, offering Ophelia a small, sympathetic smile.

Ophelia could not return the gesture but managed a shaky nod for the tall, dark man and his friends. "Thank you all for coming." She whispered.

"I'll show y'all out." Chick offered, watching the men head for the front. He stood and moved closer to his wife. "You alright?" He asked, his big hands cupping her flawless caramel-toned face.

"Mmm hmm," She lied her lashes fluttering madly when he pressed the softest kiss to her mouth.

Ophelia waited until Chick left the house with the other men. She tried to focus on clearing the table, but her thoughts got the better of her. It was as though a recorder had been switched to play in her mind. She could recall every nasty event that had occurred between herself and Minerva Gwaltney. She also heard every evil thing she'd wished on the woman. Despite all that; however, despite all the anger and dislike, she had never wished for something so terrible. Tears of sorrow and regret formed in her eyes, then. Soft sobs worked their way through her chest and up her throat. She was crying heavily by the time Chick walked back into the house.

"Fe?" He called, seeing his wife at the kitchen table with her hands covering her face.

"Mmm. Hey baby," Ophelia whispered, faking a light tone of voice. She quickly brushed the wetness from her face and left the table.

"You alright?" Chick asked, already knowing the answer. He folded his arms over his chest and tilted his head a bit as he stepped further into the kitchen.

Ophelia was running dishwater and had her back turned. "Yeah, I'm fine. Did you change your mind about some pie? I'm surprised CJ and Steph didn't gobble down the whole thing." She rambled.

"Hey." Chick whispered, covering Ophelia's hands. Beneath the running water pelting their skin, he could feel her shaking.

Ophelia turned and raised her sad eyes to his face. "Chick all the things I've said about those people. I've wished for the most horrible things. Chick is this my fault? Did I bring this on them?"

"Shh..." Chick commanded softly. His heavy black brows drew close as he pressed a kiss to her forehead. "Stop this. You know that's crazy."

"Is it?" Ophelia snapped, sniffling loudly as she blinked tears from her eyes.

Chick leaned back and watched her in disbelief. "You know it is. You didn't drown that child, Fe."

"I know that, but..."

"But what?"

"He died in our pond." Ophelia whispered, so low, she could barely be heard.

Chick didn't need her to repeat the statement, though. The same words had replayed themselves in his mind more than once.

***

The heavy, back screened door slammed and drew the attention of everyone in the kitchen. Jason Gwaltney stormed through the house and upstairs. The cooks and housemaids all flinched when the man walked past, but they would not look at him.

Jason had been in the most evil mood since his son's death, and no one could fault him for his attitude. Still, with Jason it was more than that. The man had never experienced such intense hurt and feared he would never recover. More importantly, he feared his wife would never be the same.

Minerva had been in a trancelike state since the night she found JJ in the pond. The doctor saw no need to give her sedatives or anything to help her sleep. She didn't appear unsettled or upset at all. Still, Dr. Farius Byers left the sleep medication. Minerva took it faithfully. Unfortunately, her mood appeared unchanged no matter how much she rested.

Jason slowed his steps as he approached the closed door to his bedchamber. He twisted the knob and entered the room quietly. The heady scent of Minerva's perfume brought a smile to his dark face. He closed his eyes and uttered a brief prayer that he would find his wife trying on some decadent article of lingerie she'd purchased to surprise him with.

No such treat, met his eyes, but he was pleased to find that she was out of bed. The last couple of days had been murder on his mind, not to mention other areas of his anatomy. Minerva slept well past the crack of dawn when Jason woke. When he returned to bed after sundown, he found her asleep as well.

"Minnie!" Jason called, scanning the large bedroom suite. Silence met his greeting and his steps led him to the bathroom. There, he was favored with the familiar, yet missed sight of Minerva lounging in the white porcelain claw foot bathtub.

"Want some company, woman?" He playfully bellowed, going to his knees next to the tub. He watched Minerva fight to produce a smile that just wouldn't blossom. He loved her all the more for trying.

"Talk to me Minnie." He whispered, cupping her round, dark face in his massive hands.

Tears appeared instead. Minerva covered her face in her hands and deep sobs shook her small frame. Jason reached into the bubbly water and pulled her close. They held each other for the longest time.

The day of the wake finally arrived and Minerva appeared to be a changed woman. She was out of bed, dressed and downstairs before Jason even turned over. The house staff felt as though they were caught in a whirlwind. Minerva Gwaltney always demanded her home be kept in nothing less than spotless condition. On this day, the furniture in all the ground level rooms had been moved aside so that the hardwoods could be scrubbed and polished. Long buffet tables were moved into the ballroom and all the windows were opened to allow the house to "breathe".

"Jana make sure to tell Miss Gladys to use my white China casserole dishes from the top cupboard!"

"Yes, Ms. Minerva!" Jana called over the wind whipping around their heads.

Minerva turned back to her chore of hanging table and bed linens on the clothesline. She was completely involved with her task and didn't notice her husband approaching her until he had grabbed her around the waist.

"Jason!" She gasped, her fingers stilling on the line.

"Come with me." He whispered against her hair.

Minerva struggled against the unbreakable hold. "Come where?"

"Shh...don't ask questions." He ordered, pulling her away from the clothes.

"Where are you taking me?" She asked, already noticing that they were headed for the woodshed. "Jason?"

"Do you know how many nights I've done without you?"

Minerva's lashes almost fluttered close in response to the suggestive question. "This isn't the time." She softly reminded him.

"I'll make it the time." Jason decided his big hands folded over Minerva's waist as he guided her inside the deserted shed.

"And this is hardly the place." Minerva criticized, eyeing her dirty surroundings with clear distaste.

Jason chuckled. "You never had a problem with it before." He reminded her, a smug grin triggering his deep dimples.

Minerva turned to watch him when he released her. "We got almost the whole town comin' over here in a few hours."

"I thank you for your compliment Ma'am." Jason purposefully misunderstood and bowed his head. "I promise not to take quite that long."

Minerva raised her hand to offer more resistance, but she never had the chance. Jason took her hand and hauled her against his massive frame. He dipped his head and gnawed the side of her neck while his fingers found the zipper in back of her plain burgundy dress and eased it down.

Minerva began to struggle, but it was useless against Jason's superior strength. Her dress was unzipped to her waist and he was at work on the lacy bra she wore.

"Jason don't." She demanded.

The plea fell on deaf ears. Jason was so hungry for his wife, his handsome face practically buried in her lush buxom. His big hands fondled and squeezed the dark mounds possessively and he growled at the missed sensations firing his arousal.

"Jason..." Minerva called again. She felt herself being lowered to one of the wooden tables in the shed. She tried to move Jason aside with her knees. That was an impossible task with her legs apart and his heavy frame situated between.

Jason found a rigid nipple and his lips closed over it. He could feel Minerva pounding against his back as her passion awakened. His arms encircled her small frame as he intensified the motions of his lips and tongue.

"I can't." Minerva groaned, though she felt herself weakening beneath her husband's powerful persuasions. When she felt his hand slip beneath the hem of her dress, her ineffective pounding against his back, grew stronger.

A few moments passed, before Jason raised his head. A frown came to his face when he realized the blows to his back were not an outlet of his wife's passion, but resistance. With a low growl of frustration, he braced himself on massive forearms and glared down at her.

"Dammit, what the hell is the matter with you?" He demanded.

Minerva was not intimidated. She shoved at Jason's chest with one hand and clutched her dress to her bare chest with the other. "This is all you think about, isn't it?!" She spat while inching off the table.

Jason smoothed one hand across his shaved head. "What the devil are you talkin' 'bout?"

"Sex! Sex Jason. Lord, we just lost our baby. Why don't you act like you remember that?!"

Realization flashed in Jason's dark eyes. Slowly, he took a seat on the edge of the table. "What are you sayin' Minerva? Are you sayin' that I don't care that my son is dead? Are you sayin' that I don't think about how my baby looked comin' out of that pond?"

"Jason-"

"Hell no!" The big man snapped, pushing himself off the heavy table with such force it inched back. "What the hell kind of man do you think I am, Minerva? I miss my boy like hell, but I miss you too. I miss havin' my wife in my arms-lovin' me."

Minerva squeezed her eyes shut and turned away. "Jason, I can't talk about this now."

"Then when, dammit?!"

Minerva could offer no response and only shook her head. Seconds later, she had run from the dark shed.

***

The elegant glass chandelier bathed the spacious kitchen in soft, golden light. Ophelia Augustine stood at the hardwood counter and grated the fifth and final block of cheddar cheese.

Stephanie arrived in the kitchen and strolled over to watch her mother work. After about two minutes of studious gazing, she looked up at her mother. "When can we eat dinner, Mommy?"

Ophelia smiled and tapped the cheese grater against the side of the blue and yellow ceramic mixing bowl. "Dinner will be early tonight, but I'm not making this for us."

"Oh." Steph whispered, taking a closer look at the mound of cheese in the huge bowl. "What's it gonna be?"

"Macaroni Casserole."

"Mmm...who are you making it for?"

"The Gwaltneys," Ophelia replied, setting the bowl aside.

Stephanie watched her mother pull eggs and milk from the icebox. "Why?" She called.

"It's for the wake tonight."

"A wake?" Steph queried, clearly confused.

Ophelia smoothed both hands across her apron and returned the dairy products to the icebox. She predicted her daughter would soon be bubbling over with questions. Ophelia, who believed in explaining everything to her children, prepared to explain just what a wake was.

"Is somebody waking up, Mommy?" Steph asked, twisting her sneakers on their sides as she frowned.

"Not exactly, Baby." Ophelia sighed, trying to decide the best way to discuss the situation with her little girl. She removed the green apron protecting her black and gray striped sundress. Then, she waved towards Stephanie. "Come sit on Mommy's lap, Baby." She instructed.

Steph skipped across the polished floor and moved up to share the high backed kitchen chair with her mom.

"Now, a wake is when a group of people who know someone get together to remember that person."

A tiny frown marred Stephanie's cute, flawless brown face. "Remember them?"

"Mmm hmm, because they've gone on."

"Are they taking a trip?" Steph inquired.

Ophelia's brows rose a bit. "Sort of. But, it's a trip they never come back from."

Stephanie's brown eyes grew wide. "Ever?" She gasped.

"Afraid not, Sweetie."

"Why aren't they coming back?"

"Well...Sweetie, they can't come back."

"Why?"

Taboo Tree

Ophelia patted her hand against Steph's tummy pushing against her pink cotton T-shirt. She couldn't help but smile at the child's inquisitive nature. Steph had gotten it honest.

"Honey, remember when Chester...went away?"

Steph's eyes registered recognition when she heard the name of her beloved cat. After a moment, she managed a nod.

Ophelia nodded as well. "Remember what we told you about him?"

Stephanie rested her head against her mother's chest and nodded. "You said Chester was living with God and he wouldn't be back."

"Mmm hmm...well that's where Mr. and Mrs. Gwaltney's little boy is."

"JJ." Stephanie whispered, looking up into her mother's face.

"That's right, Sweetie." Ophelia confirmed, hoping the child wouldn't be too upset by the reality.

"JJ's dead?"

"Yes Baby."

Stephanie looked out over the kitchen as she absorbed the news. She remembered the little boy, remembered seeing him in the distance. Though he always played alone, he seemed to have the most fun.

"Mommy? Why didn't I ever get to play with him?"

Ophelia never expected the question and was at a loss for words. She turned grateful eyes on the back screened door when Chick and CJ returned from the morning of fishing. "Look Baby, dinner's here." She whispered, pressing her forehead against Stephanie's.

The question was forgotten as Steph's brown gaze brightened. Fish was her favorite meal and she scrambled off Ophelia's lap to inspect the catch her father and brother brought home.

Chick noticed the solemn expression on his wife's face and strolled over to the table. "What's wrong?" He asked, taking her by the hands and pulling her up to stand before him.

Ophelia shrugged and tossed her head back. "Steph wanted to know what a wake was and why she never got to play with JJ."

A single tear slid down Ophelia's cheek and Chick kissed it away. "Shh...stop it now." He urged, pulling her into a protective embrace. "You in any shape to go to that thing tonight?"

Ophelia almost melted in the man's arms. "How do you do that? Always read my mind like that?" She marveled, tugging on the hem of his black shirt.

Chick brushed her lips with his thumb. "I guess I have a thing for reading pretty faces." He whispered and pressed a kiss to the tip of Ophelia's nose.

"I'm making a Macaroni Casserole." She said, a sniffle following her words.

"I'll make sure it gets there in one piece." Chick promised, his gorgeous smile appearing.

Arm in arm, they strolled out of the kitchen. "Anybody still messin' with that fish is gonna be in charge of cleaning 'em!" He warned CJ and Stephanie.

***

The front and side yard of the Gwaltney home was filled with cars. The wake began just before sunset and there were as many people outside as there were inside. Most of the attendants held plates or glasses as they held low-volume conversations.

Chick arrived about a half hour after the gathering was underway. Everyone greeted him warmly as he made his way inside the house.

"Chick, where's Ophelia?" Marci Henry asked, her round brown face showing concern.

Chick handed the casserole to one of the maids near the buffet and turned to face his wife's secretary. "She's feelin' sort of down, so she stayed home."

Marci nodded and patted Chick's arm. "Tell her, I hope she feels better."

Chick only nodded as the woman walked away. Several people questioned his wife's absence and he gave the same excuse. Of course, they all assumed Ophelia was sick. He didn't correct them.

One of the maids served him a glass of lemon iced-tea. Chick took the cold drink and headed further into the house. He found Jason Gwaltney greeting a few new guests and walked over to pat the man's shoulder.

Jason turned and fixed his neighbor with a slow smile. "Chick." He whispered.

"I'm sorry man." Chick whispered back, shaking Jason's hand as he nodded.

"Thanks man. Thanks for coming." Jason replied, his robust voice sounding tired and hollow. His dark eyes narrowed when he glanced past Jason's shoulder. "Where's Ophelia?" He asked.

Chick shrugged. "She wasn't feelin' up to it. How's Minerva?"

The drawn look on Jason's face grew more haggard. "I don't know Chick...I don't know. One day she's runnin' around here like a banshee-cleanin', makin' sure everything's in its place. The next day, she won't even leave the room. I don't see an end to it."

Chick clapped the man's shoulder. "She's hurtin' man."

"I know." Jason softly acknowledged pushing his big hands into the pockets of his black trousers. "I just wish I knew how to handle it," he confided, dropping the strong demeanor for Chick, "she was up at the crack of dawn getting this place together and now-"

"Jason! Jason!"

All conversation silenced when Minerva Gwaltney appeared in the huge ballroom-hands on her hips and feet spread. Since the wake began, she had remained out of sight. People had begun to wonder if she would even make an appearance.

"Oh Lord." Jason groaned, spotting the fierce glare on his wife's dark face.

"Give her my best, man." Chick urged, taking note of Minerva's confrontational stance. Of course, he was sure she wouldn't want his heartfelt condolences. Chick always believed the Gwaltney-Augustine feud could have ended had it not been for his wife and Minerva. He and Jason had always been close despite the tension between their families. The closeness had always come easily between the two men. Ironically, it was that bond which fueled the anger for so many years.

Minerva waited for Jason at the doorway of his office- the only secluded room downstairs. When he stepped into the room, she slammed the heavy maple door shut behind them.

"What the hell were you telling Chick?" She demanded.

Jason turned to stare at his wife. His mouth formed a perfect O and his expression was one of stunned disbelief. "Is this what that foolishness out there was about?"

"I hope you weren't puttin' him in our business, Jason?!"

Suddenly overheated, Jason whipped the black suit coat off his back. "I don't believe you havin' a fit over that. Hell, the man was offering condolences like everyone else in the room!" He snapped, tossing his tie to the big pine desk in the corner.

"Condolences my behind." Minerva retorted.

"What the devil is it, Min?!" Jason roared, fast approaching the end of his patience. "You run around here all day, getting this place in order and when folks start to arrive, you disappear. What is it gonna take to get you out of this mood?!"

"Certainly not any condolences from Chick Augustine!"

"Min!"

"Nosy bastard!"

Losing the last restraint on his temper, Jason stormed across the room and grabbed Minerva's shoulders. "Dammit woman," he growled, shaking her fiercely in hopes that it would bring her back to him, "we just lost out boy and all you can do is hang onto this blasted hate!"

Minerva was not intimidated by her husband's anger and refused to heed his warnings. "I don't need Chick Augustine or anyone from his damned family comin' over here offering apologies for what happened. They could never do anything to make up for that!"

"What in God's name are you talkin' about Min?" Jason whispered, looking as though he didn't recognize his own wife.

"You know what I'm talking about, but you so damned close to Chick Augustine, you won't see it!"

Jason's long lashes closed over his pitch black eyes in a brief gesture. He could never remember being so angry with Minerva. His palm actually ached with the need to strike her. Muffling a savage curse below his breath, he turned away. He had never hit Minerva in all the years he'd known her and he wasn't about to start.

"I'm goin' to find the doctor." He decided, smoothing one hand over his bald head as he turned toward the door.

"I don't need no damned doctor!" Minerva raged. Her ample buxom heaved beneath the demure white blouse she wore with the black pinstriped coat of her skirt suit. She followed Jason out the office, like the devil was at her back.

Conversation in the ballroom had silenced again. Most of the guests could hear the raised voices. Everyone tried to avoid the argument, but it was impossible to dismiss Minerva's high-pitched ranting and Jason's powerful bellowing.

When the couple stormed into the ballroom, the crowd stood in awe of the tiny woman who fought to get past her husband.

"Let go of me, dammit!" Minerva ordered, when Jason held her waist in his iron grip.

Chick was halfway through his plate off collard greens, macaroni, chicken, biscuits, dressing and yams. The commotion near the front of the room pulled his attention away from the delicious meal.

"Get off me Jason!" Minerva demanded, still struggling against the man's overpowering hold. "Get off me and let me go tell this nigga what to do with his phony condolences!"

Someone gasped. Then as if on cue, everyone turned to look at Chick.

"I don't know what gave you the notion to come over here! You and your damned family done enough already!"

"Minnie!" Jason roared.

"Jason please! You know damn well what I'm talkin' about. You know if it wasn't for them JJ wouldn't be dead!"

Chick tilted his head to one side, his dark eyes registering shock at Minerva's accusation. Slowly, he turned and set his plate aside. "Jason." He said, with a curt nod before turning to leave.

Jason's hold around Minerva's waist loosened, giving her the opportunity to scramble out of his embrace. She rushed over to the buffet and picked up the dish of macaroni. "And take this shit with you!" She cried, and threw the heavy white China bowl across the room.

THREE

"**A**re you sure it's okay for the kids to stay at your house today, Vonda?" Ophelia switched the phone to her other ear.

Ravonda Cornell chuckled over her friend's question. "Honey, you know it is. I've got my neighbor's teen-age daughter watching my two and the girl can certainly handle two more. She's very responsible."

Ophelia smiled and finished placing the last few items in her black strapless clutch purse. "That's good. I really didn't want them going with us to the funeral. I can just imagine how emotional it will be."

"Ophelia..."

"Hmm?...What Vonda?" Ophelia prompted, setting her bag to the nightstand. She could hear the unease in the woman's voice.

"Um...did Chick tell you about the wake yesterday?"

Ophelia slipped her feet into the black patent leather heels and frowned. She remembered how rattled Chick seemed when he returned home. "I didn't ask him about it. He didn't seem to be in the mood to discuss anything when he got back." She finally replied.

Ravonda had attended the wake and witnessed the awful scene at the Gwaltney home. Still, she decided it would be best to remain silent and she prayed Minerva had calmed down from the day before.

"Ravonda? Is there anything I should know?" Ophelia was asking.

"Oh no!" Ravonda quickly replied, grimacing at the anxious tone to her words. "It's nothing like that. I was only asking. Um, I'll be looking forward to seeing CJ and Steph."

"Oh yeah, we'll be by soon." Ophelia said, already forgetting her suspicions. "The two of them can't wait to get over there."

"Well, I'll see you then."

"Alright and thanks."

"Where are you takin' the babies?" Chick asked, the moment Ophelia set the brown phone receiver to its cradle.

Ophelia jumped at the sound of her husband's deep voice. "I um, arranged for the kids to go the Ravonda Cornell's while we're at the funeral." She explained her brown eyes wide as she watched him from the bed.

Chick dropped the log books he carried to the desk which sat in the rear of the spacious sun-drenched bedroom. "No need for you to take them over there."

"No need? Why?"

"We're not going to the funeral."

Ophelia turned on the bed in order to face her husband more fully. "What are you saying? We have to go."

"No Fe, we don't."

"Chick-"

"Ophelia." He snapped, turned his mellowed black stare towards her. "I said we won't be going and I meant it. I don't want to discuss it anymore."

Ophelia swallowed past the huge lump in her throat and chewed her bottom lip. "Don't you think I deserve to know why?" She probed, using her softest voice.

"Don't you think I mean it when I say I don't want to discuss it?"

Ophelia took heed that her husband's mood was steadily worsening. Still, she had to know what was going on. His mood was completely changed when he returned home the night before and curiosity had gotten the better of her.

"Baby, what happened at the wake yesterday?"

Chick's fingers paused over the record books. "What happened?" He parroted. "It was a wake, Fe." He replied, faking a light tone of voice.

"I know something happened." Ophelia told him, moving off the bed to check her appearance in the floor length mirror. "Ravonda didn't go into details, but I know there was something she was just itching to tell me."

Suddenly, Chick slammed his fists to the desk with such force the furniture squeaked. "Dammit woman, I don't want to go. Can't you leave it at that?"

Ophelia ignored her heart's fierce pounding and forced herself to meet Chick's angry glare. "That's fine, Baby. You certainly don't have to go. I'll go." She coolly decided, giving one last look at her stylish ankle-length black button down dress. Satisfied with her appearance, she headed out the bedroom.

"Ophelia."

"Chick," she groaned, bracing her hand against the doorjamb and bowing her head. "I didn't go to the wake. You can't ask me not to go to the funeral."

"I'm not asking Fe Fe."

There it was. He'd said it. Ophelia turned to watch her husband. She hated when he pulled the overbearing husband-my word is law-act on her. There was more going on besides that, though. She couldn't put her finger on it and since Chick wasn't talking, she would have to find out on her own.

"I'll be leaving with the kids in another hour." She informed him, clasping her hands tightly as she prayed for courage. Chick rarely lost his temper, but when he did it was best to be as far away as possible. She turned towards the door and began to walk out of the room again. When he called out to her again, she closed her eyes. She turned and he was standing right

AlTonya Washington

before her. She prayed he couldn't detect how much he intimidated her then.

Chick stepped even closer a dimple appeared in his cheek when he smiled at the look on Ophelia's face. "Don't leave without me." He whispered, squeezing her hip before he stepped past.

***

Jason grimaced as he tugged on the navy blue and black tie around his neck. He was on the way downstairs when he met cook Cora Dealy on the last step.

"How is she Mr. Jason?" Cora asked, her soulful brown eyes turned towards the upper level of the house.

Jason patted the woman's small hand. "It's hard to say." He whispered, glancing toward the ceiling as well. "At least she's up, getting dressed for...the funeral."

Cora bowed her head and nodded once. "Did she sleep?"

Jason breathed deeply. "Thank God Doctor Byers was here yesterday." He said, remembering the horrid scene. Minerva seemed to calm a bit once Chick Augustine had gone. Jason carried her to the bedroom with the doctor close behind. "The doc gave her something to make her sleep and since she woke up she's been real quiet." He confided.

"She's grievin' hard for that baby, Mr. Jason." Cora said, pressing one of the man's massive hands in both of hers.

Jason pulled the older woman close and they hugged. "I'm grievin' too Cora." He whispered, his eyes closing.

"Mr. Jason, the car's all washed and gassed up!"

Jason kept one arm around Cora's shoulders as he smiled at the field hand who called up from the kitchen. "Thanks Fred!" He replied, waving towards the slender dark man. "I guess we better head on out." He told Cora.

"I'll see y'all at the church." She whispered, patting his arm with quick soft taps.

Jason watched Cora waddle off. Then, he dropped his head and went back upstairs. His steps slowed, and then halted completely when he stood before the bedroom door. Walking inside, he found Minerva seated on the window sill that

overlooked the grand, rear expanse of the estate. He stepped
behind her and massaged her shoulders through the satin
material of her black dress. When he pressed his face against her
wild curls and kissed the top of her head, she moved away.

Jason balled a fist and pressed it against the sill. His
patience was past its end and he didn't know how much longer he
could allow Minerva to shut him out. He ached for her physically
yes, but also emotionally. After all, he had lost his child too.

"You ready?" He called, finally turning from the
window. He watched Minerva take a sweater from the closet as
she nodded in response to his question. When she brushed past
him, he caught her arm and pulled her back against his chest.

"Why are you doin' this to me?" He groaned into her
hair, his huge hands lowering to massage her hips.

Minerva wrenched herself from the sensuous embrace
and rushed to the door. Jason took several deep breaths, but they
did nothing to calm down. Instead, his fist connected with the
huge vase on the mahogany stand next to the door. The burgundy
vase shattered into countless pieces. Shards of glass glittered
amongst the vibrant petals of the flowers.

***

The front and side yard of New Bethel Church was
filling with cars. JJ Gwaltney's body arrived at the church in a
white and gold horse drawn carriage. The massive crowd made a
pathway as the carriage drew closer. Sniffles and soft prayers
could be heard as the pall bearers removed the tiny, silver casket
from the rear of the carriage.

Ophelia and Chick were leaving their car as the
procession began to move inside the church. Blindly, Ophelia
reached for her husband's hand. Of course, Chick was right there
to offer his support. He knew his wife would surely need it
before the end of the day.

Ophelia smoothed her other hand over the perfect
chignon she wore and managed a smile and nod for the familiar
faces she spotted. Her intuition told her they all knew what
Ravonda Cornell had been unable to confide. She squeezed
Chick's hand even tighter.

AlTonya Washington

Inside the church, Chick took hold of her upper arms and moved her into a pew near the middle of the church. The exquisite house of worship was complete with beautiful stained-glass windows, red-velvet cushioned pews and red carpeting throughout. The soft, melodic voices of the sixty person choir provided a relaxing mood as they performed *Blessed Assurance*.

Several minutes passed before Pastor James C. McClendon began the eulogy. His strong, heartfelt words of encouragement drew cries into the air and sent heads nodding. When the beautiful speech reached its end, no eye was dry.

The announcement was made that the body would be committed at the nearby cemetery where all the Gwaltneys were buried. The pews began to empty as people made their way to the front of the church. They viewed the body and bestowed their sympathies to the bereaved parents.

Ophelia was headed that way, when she was pulled back into an unbreakable embrace. "Chick please." She whispered, squirming out of his hold in order to continue her trek towards the front.

Minerva's sad, teary brown gaze narrowed when she spotted Ophelia and Charles Augustine making their way forward. The sadness left and was replaced by something cold.

Ophelia held her hands clasped tightly and waited her turn. When the grieving mother looked up, Ophelia mistook the harsh look for one of pain, not hatred.

"Minerva, I don't know what I can say to tell you how sorry I am," she began, a gentle smile touching her full lips, "JJ was a lovely child and he'll be missed-"

"How dare you bring her here?" Minerva spat, staring past Ophelia's shoulder and into Chick's dark eyes.

"Excuse me?" Ophelia whispered.

Minerva's eyes were still on Chick. "I thought I made it clear. I don't want anything from you...or her."

"What is she talking about Chick?" Ophelia asked, her gaze turning hard and never leaving Minerva's face. Her attempt at being humble was quickly draining and her temper was coming to a slow simmer.

"Chick?" Ophelia called again. Her husband didn't have a chance to respond.

"I'm talkin' about you and your husband." Minerva supplied, moving off the pew to bring her face almost eye level with Ophelia's. "I told this nigga yesterday I didn't want any of your phony apologies or nothin' else! Now why don't y'all get the hell out!"

"Minnie." Jason whispered, rubbing the woman's back.

Minerva threw her husband a scathing look. "Get your damned hands off me." She softly commanded, dismissing the hurt which flashed in Jason's dark eyes. "My baby would still be alive if it weren't for you." She declared, without blinking an eye at the Augustines.

"What are you talkin' about?" Ophelia's voice grated and shook with hate.

Minerva wasn't intimidated by the taller woman. "I'm talkin' about that damned pond."

"What?" Ophelia sneered, stepping closer only to have Chick's arm slip around her waist.

Minerva couldn't wait to elaborate. "If the Gwaltney's were in charge of that pond, as it should be, it would've been taken care of-properly. Instead it's nothin' but a deserted, shitty piece of trash!"

"That's enough Min!"

Minerva waved off Jason's warning. "You Augustines bickered and schemed to get it and look at it now! My baby never would've been out there alone if the place were watched by Gwaltneys!"

Despite her anger and the renewed hatred she felt for Minerva, Ophelia could not dismiss the hurt surging through her. Tears pooled in her voluminous brown eyes and she could never remember being so angry and terribly sad at once.

"We should go." Chick said, giving Ophelia's waist a gentle nudge.

Ophelia only nodded and turned to leave with her husband.

"Stuck up, educated bitch. Why don't you and Chick use some of them brains and learn how to take care of that piece of crap land?"

Minerva's parting shot drained Ophelia of her sadness and fired her anger to an explosive state. She wrenched her arm out of Chick's grasp and turned to face her nemesis. "Well since we're lettin' everything out, Minerva let's talk about how your baby wandered out to my piece of crap land in the first place."

"Fe Fe-"

"What the hell were y'all doin' while he was out there alone?" Ophelia queried.

Something flickered in Minerva's eyes and a smile came to Ophelia's face.

"Mmm hmm..." She breathed her lovely face a picture of satisfaction. "As if I needed to ask when everybody probably heard what y'all were doing."

"Ophelia please don't. Not here." Jason urged as he stepped a bit closer.

"No Jason. Your wife started this." Ophelia snapped, too far gone to exercise tact. "Let's hear it Minerva. Isn't it true that you and Jason were up in that house fuckin' the afternoon away while your boy was drowning?"

"Bitch." Minerva whispered, her lashes fluttering beneath the weight of heavy tears.

"That's enough Fe." Chick ordered, taking Ophelia's arm and practically dragging her to his side.

Ophelia didn't pull away, but she was far from silenced. "What? It's true, Chick! Ask any of their hundreds of servants. Not a one of 'em could tell you I'm not speakin' truth."

"You get out!" Minerva screamed and buried her face in Jason's chest.

Ophelia had no sympathy. "Hmph. At least she was screwing her husband. I remember when she used to take anything with a cock to bed."

The church was still filled with people. Once the argument began, many waited to view the outcome. Ophelia's last remark sent a solid gasp through the church. Stunned onlookers turned and began to whisper amongst themselves. Many agreed that Ophelia Augustine had been speaking the truth.

Head held high, Ophelia turned to leave with her husband. Minerva wasn't about to let her go so easily and reached for the thick chignon Ophelia sported. Her fingers just grazed the silky ball, when Ophelia turned and laid a stinging slap to her cheek.

Minerva retaliated with a blow of her own. Before the exchange could explode into a brawl, Jason and Chick separated their wives. All conversation ceased as the crowd watched the two couples part ways.

***

Minerva was still in a raving mood when she and Jason returned from the cemetery. She'd managed to keep her composure, but her husband could tell her nerves were like a twig about to snap. Jason could certainly relate. He had been on edge since the ordeal began.

Minerva left the car, slamming the door behind her. Jason had given everyone the day off, so the estate was bathed in silence. Minerva ran into the house and disappeared before Jason got out of the car.

"Not today." He growled, slamming the door with such force, the entire car shook. "Minerva!" He bellowed, bounding up the long, brick front porch steps.

Silence met his calls when he stepped past the front door. "Minerva!" He called again. A murderous glare gave his handsome features a more sinful appearance.

Minerva was in the kitchen. She held a glass in one shaking hand and poured water with the other. "I don't want to be bothered now." She told her husband when he found her.

Jason didn't bother with a verbal reply. He closed the distance between he and Minerva and slapped the glass from her hand.

Minerva gasped, but didn't have time to dwell on the shattered glass littering the polished wood floor. Jason placed her none too gently on the kitchen table and towered above her. Eyes wide, Minerva studied the look on Jason's face. She had never seen him so angry.

"Jason?" She whispered.

He didn't respond. He was much too focused on Minerva's dress. His big hands ripped the delicate material like paper. If possible, his dark eyes narrowed further as they roamed the pair of full breasts spilling from the lacy black bra. Jason didn't bother unfastening the wispy piece of lingerie. Instead, his fingers curled around the front and he ripped it off. Minerva cried out, her hands flexing as she watched her husband lean closer.

Jason kept Minerva pressed firmly against the table. His head bowed to her buxom and he inhaled the scent of perfume and sweat clinging to her skin. His lips parted and Minerva could feel his breath next to her nipples. They stiffened in response. When he took one of the rigid buds into his mouth, she squeezed her eyes shut and tried to block out the effect of his touch.

Jason's low growl sounded deep in his chest as his tongue stroked and suckled. He could feel Minerva soften beneath his hands and released her hips. His fingers slid over the tattered material of her dress and beneath the hem. In seconds, he was stroking her womanhood through the middle of her panties.

Suddenly, Minerva cried out and slapped Jason hard across his face. They both froze, watching each other with wide eyes. Minerva had never behaved that way and was just as shocked by the action as Jason. A moment later, she was racing from the kitchen and upstairs.

After closing and bolting the heavy bedroom door, she began to remove the ruined dress. The door flew open under the pressure of a mighty kick from Jason's boot. Minerva let out a terrified scream and clutched the dress to her chest. It was no protection against Jason's wrath. He was too angry to take heed to her fright.

Minerva stood watching him come closer. The dress slipped from her weak hands, just as his hands closed around her arms. He pulled her to the bed and pushed her down. Minerva didn't try to move away, she simply watched as Jason's clothing fell to the floor. When he stood naked before her, Minerva's breathing had noticeably increased. Still, she remained lifeless when he went to work on removing her half-slip and panties.

"Jason, please no...I can't." Minerva moaned, even though her inner thighs were moist with need.

Jason noticed. "Don't make me force you, Min." He whispered, tugging her earlobe between his perfect teeth. He felt her go pliant beneath his body and he settled himself between her silken legs...

"I really appreciate this, Vonda."

Ravonda Cornell chuckled and rolled her eyes. "Girl, after what you went through today, I certainly understand. Besides, my three are havin' the best time with CJ and Steph."

Ophelia smiled and closed her eyes resignedly. "I still appreciate it anyway. We'll be by to collect the kids before lunch tomorrow, okay?"

"No problem, Honey."

"Thanks Vonda, bye bye."

Ophelia set the phone aside and tapped her fingers against the maple message desk near the rear of the living room. When she turned, Chick was leaning against the doorjamb.

"The kids are gonna spend the night at Ravonda's." She called.

"You must've been reading my mind." Chick replied, a tiny smile touching the curve of his mouth.

Ophelia could only manage a tiny shrug. *Yes, I suppose you wouldn't want the kids around when you blast me for this afternoon*, she silently predicted, trying to interpret Chick's easy expression.

When he pushed himself off the doorjamb, she unconsciously retreated. She cursed herself for being such a coward. To hide her nervousness, she headed out of the living room and up the wide staircase which branched off to opposite wings of the house.

"I'm sorry about today. I just couldn't take any more of that woman. I tried to let it go, but when she made that last

.

comment, I-something just snapped." Ophelia rambled, when she realized her husband was following her up the carpeted stairwell.

Chick hadn't said a word. He walked into the bedroom behind Ophelia and began to remove his black suit.

"...I mean she had some nerve accusing us of killing her child. I admit I could've chosen my words differently, but she knew I was on the mark about what she and Jason were doing. I could see it in her eyes."

Ophelia had been turning down the bed amidst her lengthy explanation. After a while, she realized Chick hadn't responded since she began to speak. She turned to see if he was even in the room and found him standing right behind her. A startled gasp escaped her lips, giving Chick the opportunity he needed. His head dipped and he thrust his tongue deep inside her mouth.

Ophelia moaned and eagerly participated in the satisfying kiss. Her arms slid around Chick's neck when he lifted her off her feet and placed her on the bed. Using an expert's touch, Chick reached behind Ophelia and unzipped her dress. He broke the kiss to trail his mouth down her temple and past her earlobe, tugging the soft flesh between his even white teeth and suckling gently. Ophelia's tiny helpless groan fueled his desire and sent a shudder through his athletic frame.

"Chick please..." Ophelia sighed, nudging her hips against his.

A soft chuckle filled the room. Chick realized his wife's anxiousness. After all, they rarely had the house to themselves. He intended to see that they took advantage of every moment.

Ophelia threw her hands above her head when Chick slid the dress and her under things along her lithe, dark body. He grasped her thighs and buried his handsome face in the valley between. Ophelia's hips arched off the bed at the feel of his breath against her womanhood.

Chick pleasured her unashamedly. His tongue delved deeply inside her and slowly rotated. Ophelia began to tremble. She pushed her fingers through his soft hair to hold him close.

Chick increased the circular movements of his tongue as the shuddery gasps overhead spurred him onward. Mercilessly, he increased the pressure of the act. His hands tightened around Ophelia's thighs and her soft gasps became wanton cries.

"Does this mean you're not mad?" Ophelia whispered, when Chick finished plying her with his devastating treat.

"I will be if you don't shut up." He growled, thrusting his tongue past her full lips in the same manner that his manhood thrust into her body.

***

Almost a month had passed since the funeral and the fiasco that followed. Jason Gwaltney hoped the passion he and Minerva enjoyed on the day of the funeral, would bring them closer. If anything, Minerva seemed to withdraw more deeply. She spent even more time in bed and was just rising many evenings when Jason returned from the fields.

Jason was used to being in control of any situation. Now, he was at his wits end. "Dammit." He groaned, eyeing the beaming sunlight with a dismal look. For the first time in a long time, he actually dreaded beginning another day. Still, he shook the heavy thoughts from his mind and moved to get out of bed. It was then that he realized he was alone in the massive four poster.

"Minerva?"

There was no answer and it appeared she had left the bed chamber. Jason whipped back the covers and reached for his robe. He was about to leave the room, when strange sounds caught his ears. They seemed to be originating from the private bathroom. His steps slowed as he listened for a few seconds. He was prepared to kick the door in, but tried the knob first. It gave and he found Minerva crouched before the toilet bowl.

"Minnie?" Jason called, horror filling his dark eyes as he watched her vomiting profusely. In an instant, he was on his knees next to her.

After several minutes, the vomiting turned into dry heaves. Minerva had been in the throes of nausea so long, she was completely limp. Jason pressed a kiss to her temple and carried her back to bed.

AlTonya Washington

"What the hell is wrong with her, Doc?" Jason demanded of Dr. Farius Byers' partner Dr. Irving Nance.

Dr. Nance appeared uneasy as he fidgeted with the stethoscope around his neck. "Have her eating habits or anything else seemed out of the ordinary?"

"Are you serious?" Jason asked, a look of humorous disbelief appearing on his handsome face.

Dr. Nance closed his eyes and nodded. "Crazy question." He admitted, realizing how the question sounded in light of all that had happened.

Both men noticed Minerva tossing in bed and they stepped closer. Dr. Nance pressed one hand to Jason's shoulder.

"Would you mind if I had a moment alone with her?" He asked.

Jason studied the older man's weather-beaten vanilla-complexioned face and, after a moment, he nodded.

Minerva raised her head from the pillow when the door shut behind her husband. "What's wrong with me?" She whispered, her wide voluminous eyes appeared weak and sunken.

Dr. Nance stepped closer to the bed and patted Minerva's hand. "If I'm not mistaken, Miss Lady, you already know."

Minerva closed her eyes and turned her head towards the curtained window. "No..." she sighed.

"Minerva?"

"I'm pregnant?" She whispered, turning back to the doctor who nodded and smiled.

***

Ophelia was certain Chick would come down on her about the things she'd said at the funeral. He never did. Of course it was the talk of the town. The Augustines and the Gwaltneys were always on someone's lips.

As a result, Ophelia kept her social appearances to a minimum. Her outings were limited to the grocery store, the kid's school and Chick's business.

Minerva Gwaltney was even less visible. Aside from Jason, the house employees and Dr. Nance, no one had seen her.

News of the pregnancy had been bittersweet for the young couple. It filled them with twin emotions of grief for the child they lost and guilt that they'd been creating one child while losing another.

No one could be certain that the new baby had been conceived that day, but Minerva knew. She nor Jason could dismiss Ophelia Augustine's remarks on the day of JJ's funeral. They had been enjoying the pleasures of lovemaking while their child fought for his life.

***

Chick stroked his beard as his eyes narrowed over the contract he viewed. The document labeled the terms of the agreement between Augustine Seams and a new retirement home which had been established for the black elderly.

Members of the management team began to trickle in for the staff meeting. Chick's mood over the last several weeks had been friendlier than he ever expected. Needless to say, his staff was delighted by his mood and eager to discuss the newest contract they'd acquired.

Lamar Robinson, one of Chick's vice-presidents, was usually among the last to arrive. Today, he hurried into the noisy meeting room and took his place next to Chick.

"Did you hear the news?" He whispered.

"No." Chick replied, with a grimace and without looking up from his paperwork. Lamar was always coming to him with some form of gossip which usually concerned the employees.

Lamar straightened his wide gray pin-striped tie and cleared his throat. "It's about your neighbors." He smugly supplied, smiling when Chick pinned him with a questioning look.

"Minerva Gwaltney's pregnant." Lamar went on to announce.

Chick nodded. He could understand why Lamar thought he should know. The pregnancy confirmed-more or less-what Ophelia said at the funeral.

"Your wife hit it right on the mark, Charles." Lamar raved, chuckling the entire time.

Chick ignored the rest of the man's speech. He knew this upheaval, like all the rest, would pass after a while. No one in town would frown upon his wife for speaking what she felt as true because no one held the Augustines or Gwaltneys responsible for anything they said or did.

That didn't hold true for Chick as his easy mood began to fade into something more heated. He managed to conduct the business meeting with the staff. Afterwards he headed home.

***

Ophelia pulled the wide-brimmed straw hat from her head and smiled. For the last hour, she had been pruning the green bushes decorating the front of the house. She dusted her hands against the back of her jeans and prepared to head inside the house, when Chick's shiny, black Ford truck sped into horseshoe driveway. It was an unexpected treat to have him for lunch, especially when they could enjoy it alone.

Ophelia was about to tell her husband that, when his terrible frown came into view. Before she could back away, he caught her upper arm.

"Chick, what-"

"Shut up." He whispered, squeezing her arm so tight a tiny cry slipped past Ophelia's lips.

"Dammit Chick, what is wrong with you?!" She cried, when he pushed her into the house.

"I don't want to hear another damn word about anything else you have to say against the Gwaltneys!" He roared, slamming the front door so hard, the flower vases and picture frames shook.

"What?" Ophelia whispered, massaging her sore arm. The outburst had her shocked and confused, especially since she hadn't said anything to anyone in weeks.

Chick shrugged out of his navy blue suit coat and threw it to the burgundy high-back sofa. "I'm sick of this bickering and sniping back and forth. It's you and Minerva who's kept this thing goin' for so long!"

"Me and Minerva?" Ophelia snapped, becoming angry as well. "She was the one who started it with me at that funeral!"

"I don't care."

"Well, you should!" Ophelia retorted, her almond-shaped brown eyes blazing with fury. "After the way they've always treated you, you should care most of all."

Chick ran one hand over his soft hair. "I never had any problems with Jason."

"Hell, you didn't have to Chick. Minerva's more than enough to handle. Besides, I've never seen Jason come to your defense when his wife was talkin' shit."

By now, Ophelia and Chick had taken their 'discussion' to the kitchen. Chick selected a can of beer from the fridge, popped the top and took a long swig of the brew.

"Did you know she was pregnant?" He asked, after taking several sips of the drink. His back was turned to Ophelia and his voice was low. "Now everybody will know you were right about what you said." He continued, finally looking at his wife.

"But...she could've been pregnant before JJ."

"But you know they won't think that? Jason and Minerva are probably feelin' guilty as hell because they're thinking the same thing."

"Dammit Chick, that woman accused us of killing her child!" Ophelia reminded him, her eyes sparkling with renewed anger.

Chick finished his beer and threw the can into the sink. He stepped right up to Ophelia and held his index finger inches from her small nose. "Not another word Fe-Fe." He ordered, his voice sounding harsh and rough.

Ophelia swallowed past the lump in her throat, when Chick brushed against her on his way out of the kitchen. She knew that was the end of the discussion. Forever.

The heated feud cooled after decades of unrest. Years; however, only provided time for the hatred to simmer until, once again it was ready to explode.

FOUR

Virginia- 1978

"I didn't expect this to get so tedious, CJ." Stephanie Augustine moaned, tossing a pen to her white student desk.

Charles Augustine Jr. only shrugged. He was much more interested in his sister's growing album collection. "You were the one who wanted to trace the family tree for our Senior Project, remember?" He absently remarked, his deep-set dark eyes scanning the album covers.

Steph rolled her eyes and pulled her slender fingers through her straight, shoulder length tresses. "I'm beginning to think this was a bad idea."

"Well, it's too late to turn back now." CJ decided, turning to pin his usually responsible sister with a knowing glare.

"Wait a minute." Steph drawled. "Is this you tryin' to sound sensible?"

CJ went back to the red record player and set the Parliament Funkadelic album to play. "I just want all this mess finished, before the parties get started."

"I should've known." Stephanie sighed, knowing her older brother had an ulterior motive. "But, you're right." She conceded, reclining in her desk chair to study the Jacksons poster before her eyes. "This is no time to decide on a new project with graduation right around the corner."

CJ and Steph were born a year apart, but the smart young woman quickly caught up with her brother. Her parents couldn't have been more proud when she was chosen to skip a grade level. It was a good thing, too. Stephanie had inherited her mother's strong will and intelligence. She kept her laid back, fun-loving brother on his toes.

"If you can tear yourself away from all your engagements," Steph began, waiting for her brother to stop bobbing to the music and pay attention, "we need to set up a time to go to the Hall of Records for more research."

CJ grimaced and waved his hand. "Don't start with that crap, Steph. I know you and Sweet got plenty of parties to go to."

"Which is why we need to get on the ball with this." Steph reiterated.

Groaning, CJ took a seat on the chair next to the desk. "We already got a shit load of info," he said, rifling through the papers cluttering the desk, "I didn't think we'd find this much."

"Well, our family goes back a long way in this town." Stephanie reminded CJ as her lovely brown eyes scanned all the information they'd gathered. She knew CJ would never agree, but she'd found it extremely interesting-piecing together their family history. "I still can't wait until we're done." She admitted.

"Amen." CJ confirmed, standing from the chair. He went to peer past the white ruffled curtains shielding Steph's bedroom window. From there, he had an incredible view of the huge back lawn.

Many changes had taken place during the last ten years. Chick Augustine had a basketball court constructed when his son expressed an interest in the game. The Augustine pond was off limits, so a huge in-ground pool had been installed. Ophelia's impressive flower garden sat a couple of acres away from the recreational area, along with a stately vine-covered gazebo.

CJ's intense, dark gaze traveled farther into the distance, toward the overgrown pathway which led to the pond.

"CJ? CJ? CJ!"

"Huh? What?"

"Boy, what's got you so stoned?" Steph demanded, a frown marring her lovely caramel-toned face.

CJ shrugged off the question and turned away from the window. "When do you want to finish this research?"

Steph frowned towards the calendar on the back of her bedroom door. "Sometime early next week. I want to hurry up and get this done."

"How much more are you gonna do today?"

Steph's arched brows raised a notch and she shrugged. "Just a little more. Then, I'm taking a nap and then I'm gonna enjoy what's left of this weekend."

"I heard that!" CJ bellowed, already on his way to the door. "I'm goin' for a swim!" He called.

Stephanie slammed her hands to her desk. Papers flew everywhere in the wake of her brother's departure.

Ophelia Augustine's melodic laughter filled the lower level of the house. She was seated at the huge kitchen table that was always set for the next meal. Now a mother of four, the years had been wonderful to her and she was lovelier than ever. Her brown eyes sparkled more merrily and her waist length onyx hair seemed even more full and healthy.

"Girl, you are too crazy!" Ophelia cried, laughing hysterically with her first cousin, who lived in Columbus, Ohio.

"Honey, it's true!" Dyna Davidson retorted through her breathless laughter. "That girl has been worrying me senseless about going to visit her cousins in VA."

Ophelia laughed again. "Well, I can't wait to see Amina. I know she's got to be a beauty."

Dyna whistled. "Honey child, she is. She got that skin tone and hair just like you, Grandma and Stephanie."

"And you know that devilish girl done chopped hers to her shoulders." Ophelia lamented, referring to her daughter.

"Stop."

"Mmm hmm. Talkin' about it's easier to manage." Ophelia replied, faking her daughter's sometimes haughty tone of voice.

"I know she's still a fine sista." Dyna predicted.

Ophelia shook her head over her strong-willed daughter. "She is." She couldn't help but agree.

The cousins carried on their lively conversation, discussing everything from their children in their family. Ophelia became distracted a while later when her husband walked into the kitchen. Of course, the years had been just as kind to Chick Augustine. His rich chocolate-brown skin was still flawless, but he had removed the beard years earlier. His intense black eyes could still penetrate with startling effectiveness.

Chick blew a kiss to his wife, and then went to inspect the chicken pot pies baking for lunch. When Ophelia leaned over to swat his behind with her dishcloth, he closed the oven door and took an oatmeal cookie from atop the stove.

"Who's on the phone?" He asked, through a mouthful of cookies.

"Dyna."

"Hey, girl!" Chick called, before pressing a loud smack to his wife's cheek. "I'll see you later. I'm goin' to take Steph to do some research at the record hall."

Ophelia puckered her lips for another kiss, which Chick happily delivered. "I love you." She called.

"Oh brother." Dyna playfully complained. "Do y'all ever argue?"

"Ha! Baby don't be fooled." Ophelia shared. "Me and Chick have had some wild ones. Especially when the Gwaltneys were causing such an uproar."

"Is that mess finally over?"

Ophelia leaned back in her chair and toyed with the heavy braid dangling from her ponytail. "I would say it's over, but that's only because we don't cross paths."

"What about the kids? Don't they all go to the same school?"

Taboo Tree

"Mmm hmm, but they never say anything about them. They don't socialize."

"How many kids do they have?"

"Two who are school age-a girl and boy and I think there are another girl and boy, but they're only babies." Ophelia explained, pulling a crumb from her snug white T-shirt.

"Hmph, big families." Dyna noted.

"Yeah, but Chick forbids me to say anything negative about them."

"Is that difficult?"

"It is when my intuition keeps callin' to me."

"And what's it telling you?"

"That this whole thing is far from over."

***

CJ raced out of his parent's immaculate home like the devil was at his heels. He passed the basketball court, barbeque pit and the pool. His final destination would prove to be far more enjoyable. He had discovered the treat several weeks earlier, while taking a break from the dreaded senior project.

For years, CJ's parents had demanded he never go near the pond. He had heeded their warnings...to an extent. The crystalline body of water beckoned him, but CJ took position behind the heavy mass of trees shielding the pond. He chose his usual spot and settled down for a show that was strictly taboo.

A striking young woman lay spread along the grassy bank of the pond. Her slender, molasses-toned frame was scantily clad in a white bikini. A mass of thick, black curls surrounded her angelic face like a dark cloud. Her eyes were closed, but their smoky-brown color and sensuous intensity were stamped onto CJ's brain.

Demetria Monique Gwaltney wiggled her toes in the cool, delightful water. Her long lashes flew open and she stared up at the partly cloudy sky. Since she could remember, the pond had been forbidden territory.

Now, at age fifteen, she had discovered the comforting power of the area. The fact that no one ventured out there, gave her a feeling of decadence and mystery. The pond was the one place where Demetria felt she could be herself. There was no one around to constantly remind her to watch her posture, smile more or talk louder.

A rustle from the cluster of trees behind her, pulled Demetria back to the present. She knew it wasn't the wind and a smile came to her face. CJ Augustine, she thought. She wasn't frightened by the presence of her silent admirer, who was also the son of her family's enemies. She was excited.

Demetria realized she was being watched some time ago. One day, she hid on the opposite side of the pond-closest to her property. There, she could see handsome, CJ Augustine walk out to the bank as though he were looking for something or someone. Demetria made a noise in the bushes and emerged from her hiding spot. CJ made a fast escape, but Demetria had the best time taunting the young man. Secretly, she hoped he would make his presence known.

CJ watched Demetria intently. He berated himself for becoming so infatuated with a girl who would enter high school later that year as a Freshman. Unfortunately, he could not help himself when she was so incredible to look at. His heart pounded in the back of his throat, as anticipation set in. He wondered how long he'd have to wait that day before seeing more of her.

CJ wouldn't have long to wait. Demetria, who knew he was there, pulled her feet from the water and stood. Slow; tormentingly slow for CJ's benefit, she untied the flimsy strings holding the bikini top to her chest.

CJ gripped the tree trunk so tightly bits of bark loosened and fell to the ground. His dark lashes fluttered as a wave of male desire overcame his senses. When Demetria wriggled out of the matching bikini bottom, he uttered a soft grunt and leaned against the tree. His gaze traced every inch of her body as she turned to and fro inspecting her nude form. The inspection lasted about five minutes before she walked into the water and immersed himself in its coolness.

Leaves crunched beneath CJ's blue and white Converse when his strong legs weakened beneath him. He sat there, his eyes focused on the pond. He could not look away...

***

"You want a soda or something before diving into all that work?" Chick asked, pulling the sleek gray LTD to a stop in front of the Cantone Market.

Stephanie shook her head and smiled for her father. "I'd never finish it in time and they don't allow drinks in the Hall of Records."

Chick raised his hands in a playful, defensive gesture. "Well they allow drinks at Augustine Seams, so I'm gonna go grab somethin'. Be right back."

"Okay, Daddy." Steph called, giggling when the man tugged on a lock of her hair. She uttered a tiny sigh, happy for the chance to change the radio from her father's preferred Blues tunes to a more up tempo station. She was tapping her fingers to the latest O'Jays tune, when the market's screened front door opened. A tall, muscular young man walked out with the owner's son.

Stephanie's lovely brown eyes widened and she waved to her boyfriend from the car window. Samuel "Sweet" Kensie's double dimples appeared the instant his spotted Steph.

"Oh hell, I know you about to tell me to split." Nikos Cantone teased, his deep voice laden with an unmistakable northern accent.

Sweet's long brows drew close. "Why?"

When Nikos nodded towards Chick Augustine's car, a smile spread across Sweet's handsome, honey-toned face.

"Later, man." Nikos was saying, chuckling as he shook his head. "Hey, Steph!" He called, throwing up one hand.

Stephanie waved back. "Hey, Nikos!"

Sweet strolled over to the car. His gait was an over pronounced "pimp" which sent Stephanie into peals of laughter.

"What's so funny, girl?" He queried, pretending to be confused.

"You know why." She accused through her laughter.

Sweet joined in briefly, before leaning inside the car window and pressing a kiss to Steph's mouth. She trailed her fingers along the side of his smooth face and savored the sweet gesture. Sweet uttered a low sound and increased the intensity of the kiss. Stephanie gasped, giving him more room to explore. She moaned and eagerly participated. After a moment or two she remembered where they were and pulled back.

"My dad's right inside the store."

Sweet chuckled and trailed his wide fingers across Steph's pretty face. "He's talkin' to Mr. C." He assured her and prepared to lean in for another kiss.

"Stop." Stephanie playfully resisted, pressing her hand against one of Sweet's broad shoulders. "He won't be in there long. He's takin' me to the Hall of Records to get some work done."

Recognition dawned in Sweet's deep brown eyes. "Damn, y'all puttin' a lot of effort in that thing." He noted.

Steph shrugged. "Cause we want an A." She told him. "Plus, we've been finding so much information it hasn't been too hard piecing it together."

"Well, as long as it don't keep you too busy." Sweet decided, reaching inside the car to toy with the strap of Steph's bra, visible at the scoop collar of her snug green T-shirt. "We only got a few more weeks before we graduate."

"I know." Steph sighed, sadness dimming the sparkle in her eyes. "We still haven't talked about what we're gonna do afterwards." She reminded her boyfriend.

Sweet kissed a lock of her hair. "We'll think of somethin'." He promised.

Chick emerged from Canton's Market and spotted the young couple. He smiled, before clearing his throat and forcing a stern, 'fatherly' look to his face.

Sweet heard Chick approaching and stood straight. "Hey, Mr. Augustine." He greeted, moving around the car to shake hands with his girlfriend's father.

"What's happenin', man?" Chick replied, returning the hearty handshake.

"Not much, Sir. Just tryin' to keep Steph from workin' herself to death."

"I heard that." Chick agreed. "Y'all got plans for later?"

Sweet's shoulders rose in a lazy shrug beneath the black and gray football tee he sported. "I hope so." He whispered.

Chick clapped the boy's shoulder. "Hang in there, man." He advised, before heading to the driver's side of the car. "Isn't CJ supposed to be helpin' you with the project, Baby?" He asked when he settled in behind the wheel.

Steph waved to Sweet, before rolling her eyes. "He sure is Daddy!" She drawled, matter-of-factly.

Chick laughed. "Don't let him pull that jive on you, girl." He told her.

Stephanie burst into uncontrollable giggles at her father's use of the slang term. The car was filled with laughter as it sped down Main Street.

***

Tavares Johnson Gwaltney had organized a gritty football game in his parent's backyard. The players were in their element as they raced back and forth across the lawn in their pursuit of the cherished pigskin.

Tav had devised his teams between high school buddies and his father's field workers. No one got any work done. Those who weren't participating in the game, were happy spectators.

"That damned boy." Jason Gwaltney growled, spotting his son at the center of the recreation. He tossed the remainder of his coffee into the sink and headed outside.

The cooks jumped in unison, when the back door slammed shut behind the man.

"Tav!" Jason bellowed and play ceased instantly. "Get over here, Boy!" He ordered.

Onlookers were intrigued when Tav went to stand before his father. They were almost mirror images. Tav was just as tall as Jason, only not quite as massive. Of course, he was well on his way. He had his father's gorgeous, dark features and physical nature. Aside from all the brawn, he was an intelligent young man who would one day take control of his father's thriving business.

"Boy, what the hell is on your mind?" Jason whispered, clapping his hands to his son's shoulders.

Tav gazed innocently into the frowning face that appeared almost as youthful as his own. "Just lettin' off some steam, Poppa."

Jason shook his head. "How about lettin' it off after the men get off work, hmm?"

Tav nodded, having no desire to incite his father's considerable temper. He sent his friends home and told the workers they would resume the game some other time.

Jason waited on the hilltop overlooking the small valley where the game was held. "Pick a better time for play next time, alright?" He suggested when his son joined him.

Tav debated, before deciding to issue a reply. "Poppa, I figured these cats could use a break instead of workin' all the time."

Jason ran one hand over his bald head. He couldn't help but chuckle at his son's smooth talk. "I appreciate what you're sayin', man, but I need you to be more responsible. Especially when it comes to the people who work for us. You'll be running this place one day and if the men see you as a runnin' buddy before seein' you as the boss man, you won't have an ounce of control. Think about it." He urged, slapping one hand to the middle of Tav's chest before walking off.

Tav let his skepticism show once his father moved on. He waited until the man was absorbed in conversation with the field men, before racing off towards the front of the estate.

Of course, Tav knew better than to disagree with his overpowering father. Still, he had no aspirations to run the estate...at least not right away. At that point, the handsome high school senior was interested in two things: sex and sports.

Tav raced by his mother in his quest for the shiny black Impala parked in the front yard. Minerva Gwaltney, like her husband, had grown older in years, but not in appearance. She was as lovely as ever despite the fact that she had given birth to five children.

"Where're you off too?" Minerva called, watching Tav stop in his tracks and walk back to the porch.

"I got some things to do in town, Ma."

Minerva's brown eyes narrowed. She was far from being fooled. "Don't push your father too far, Baby. You're already skating on thin ice with him as it is."

Tav's grin brought his dimples to life. "Me and Poppa got an understanding." He assured his mother.

"Mmm hmm..." Minerva replied, as she bounced her third son Sanford, on her hip.

Tav sprinted up the brick steps and pressed a kiss to the top of his little brother's head. Then, he kissed his mother before jogging off to his car.

Minerva looked out across the field and saw Jason standing with his hands pushed into the pockets of his black overalls. He had been watching their son as well. "Enjoy your playtime, Boy." Minerva whispered.

***

Tav left home quickly to avoid another lecture by his father. He knew his mother was right. Sooner or later Jason would demand he spend more time learning the family business. That would be especially true after graduation in a few weeks.

Tavares wasn't against being a part of it all. He admired his father's success and prayed, one day, he could be as dedicated and hardworking. Still, at the present, Tav was more interested in savoring the fringe benefits of being Jason Gwaltney's son: money, popularity, girls...He had plenty of time to be a businessman.

Tav drove to the playground, where a pickup basketball game was in progress. The court teamed with young men waiting to get into the game and girls waiting to be noticed by a cute boy. Most of the guys hoarding the court were upperclassmen-members of the basketball team.

When Tav arrived, they quickly opened a spot for him. The boy had a charisma no one could deny. His powerful build

and fantastic looks made him first pick for any games and almost
every girl vied for his attention.

"What it is, black?" Tav greeted Sweet when they met at
the edge of the court.

"You ready for this ass whippin' on the court, man?"
Sweet taunted as he and Tav shook hands.

"Give it all ya got, blood." Tav insisted, heading over to
the packed, wooden bleachers.

"Can I hold your shirt, Tav?" One of the young women
asked, when the navy blue garment was discarded.

Of course, Tav granted her the privilege. He tossed the
shirt over his shoulder and flexed the muscles that rippled in his
chest, arms, back and abdomen.

"You think she'd go out with me?" Nikos Cantone was
asking.

Sweet shrugged as he watched Joselle Wallace across
the court with Tav. "She's a fast one, man." He warned, tossing
an empty water cup into a nearby wastebasket.

Nikos' pensive, dark stare narrowed as he continued to
stare at the dark slender young woman. "It's a front." He decided.
"She's in a lot of my classes. She seems real cool."

"I'll bet." Sweet replied in his most sarcastic tone. "Man
why don't you go after one of them Italianas?" He teased.

Nikos looked over at his friend. "You got a problem with
me goin' after the sistahs, brotha?" He playfully drawled.

"No." Sweet answered with a shrug. "But someone
might."

Nikos' bronzed face softened with a knowing look. "I
ain't had no complaints yet."

Sweet retied his black Converse and shook his head.
"Yeah, right. Man, let's get this game started."

Hours later, the court was becoming more deserted as
players and spectators ventured off for more enjoyment during
the warm Saturday afternoon.

Nikos had seen Joselle leave several minutes earlier. She was headed in the direction of one of the walking paths. He had never approached her before, but decided now was as good a time as any.

"Yo! Nik, man! You comin'?!" Sweet called.

The two, tall young men met at center court and shook hands.

"Nah man, I got some stuff to do, but I'll catch up wit'cha later."

Sweet pulled the pick from his hair and began to fix his afro. "You goin' back to the store?"

"Hell no!" Nikos replied, with a laugh. His double dimples appearing as an even white smile broke through. "It ain't every day Pops gives us both the same day off."

"I heard that!" Sweet bellowed, reaching out to shake hands with his co-worker. "See ya later, man."

Nikos watched his friend walk off. He turned in the direction he saw Joselle headed. Fanning the Knicks jersey from his torso, he set off to find her.

Obviously, Joselle and Nikos weren't the only two interested in taking a stroll in the park. Nikos had been walking a while, when he happened upon a couple sharing an intimate rendezvous.

They were braced against a tree. Distinct moans and breathless cries filled the air surrounding them. The boy was huge and hunched over the girl, whose hand shook against the tree trunk. Her lover took her savagely from behind, but she didn't seem to mind.

Tavares Gwaltney urged his partner with crass statements; calling her demeaning names as he satisfied himself. His large hands cupped the girl's breasts as his hips thrust forward in rapid succession.

Nikos watched, but not out of voyeurism. He had to know the girl's identity.

"Mmm..." Tav groaned his thrusts slowing as he reached satisfaction. When he pulled away, Joselle Wallace's limp, nude body was revealed.

Tav pulled on his loose gray jogging pants and reached for his T-shirt. "Later." He called leaving the girl slumped against the tree.

Nikos retreated behind some heavy brush and remained there until Joselle had gathered her things from the ground and left. Afterwards, he pulled both hands through his thick, wavy black hair and tried to burn her image from his mind.

FIVE

Cardman G. Wainright High school was a massive four-story structure located along the outskirts of town. The school's student body consisted of the town's entire "minority" teenage population. The ten minutes between classes gave students a chance to socialize in the halls or on the huge school yard. The well-manicured green lawn teemed with talkative students, cars and motorcycles.

Samuel "Sweet" Kensie's deep-set gaze narrowed with skepticism. "You sure it was her, man?"

Nikos leaned against the wide, stone banister leading into the school. He had been telling Sweet about the 'lover's tryst' he'd walked in on. "I'm positive it was her." He declared, folding his arms across the orange T-shirt he sported.

"He was fuckin' her right there on the tree?" Sweet asked, disbelief clouding his words. He whistled when Nikos nodded.

"And I'd just seen that muthafucka with some other girl a couple of days ago." Nikos recalled.

Sweet shook his head at his friend's naïveté,. "My man, Tav Gwaltney ain't no 'one chick dude'." He informed the boy.

"I'm beginning to see that." Nikos sighed, his stomach churning as he remembered the way Tav left Joselle after they 'made love'. "I'm surprised he ain't made no moves on your girl." Nikos teased, his perfect, even smile appearing.

"Steph?!" Sweet bellowed, his robust laughter spilling forward. "Man, believe me, that chick has zero tolerance for the Romeo or his family."

"I heard that!" Nikos replied, smacking palms with Sweet. "And speaking of family, here comes your future brother-in-law."

"What's happenin', y'all?" CJ greeted, slapping palms with Nikos and Sweet.

"What's goin' on, man? You comin' to play ball with us after school?" Sweet asked bending to tie his sneakers.

CJ grimaced and shook his head. "Gotta pass today, brotha. My Ma's got me goin' to pick up my cousin from the train station. She's staying with us for the summer."

"Daaaamn, they already out of school?" Nikos marveled.

CJ waved one hand in the air and shoved the other into his jean pocket. "She's one of them smarty pants, takin' advanced classes and stuff like that."

"She sounds just like Steph." Sweet mentioned.

"Mmm hmm." CJ agreed. "Anyway, they already got out for summer up in Ohio."

"Is she going to graduation?" Nikos asked.

A rueful smirk crossed CJ's wide mouth. "Man, I hope *I'll* be going to graduation. That senior project is so damned complex." He lamented.

"Problems?" Sweet asked.

CJ shook his head. "Not really. We got a lot of information. It's just a lot to piece together and I don't know if we'll get it all done in time."

"Man, do you know how hard your sister's been workin'?" Sweet asked, giving his friend a reassuring clap on the back. "She'll make sure y'all don't miss the deadline."

"Hmph. Well, as much time as I've been givin' Steph, she probably won't even let me put my name on the damn thing." CJ mused, joining in with Nikos and Sweet when they laughed. A while later he said his goodbyes and left for the train station.

Sweet decided he had to get going as well and told Nikos they'd meet at the ball court. Nikos was headed for his truck, when he bumped into Joselle Wallace. The girl had always been kind to him and that day was no exception.

"Hey Nikos." She greeted, with a radiant smile brightening her round, pretty face.

Nikos was tongue-tied. He had no idea what to say after what he'd seen. His image of Joselle as a sweet innocent girl was still there, but that image was now mingled with something else.

"Are you okay, Nikos?" Joselle asked her words soft and unhurried as she noticed the closed look on his handsome, olive-toned face.

Nikos forced a slight shrug. "Just um...just got a lot goin' on...you know?"

"Mmm..." Joselle replied her brown gaze faltering as the lull in conversation lengthened.

"Jo! Hey Josie! Eh Girl!"

Joselle and Nikos were strolling across the parking lot in silence, when Joselle heard her name. Tavares Gwaltney stood across the wide, gravel parking lot. He was leaning against his black Impala surrounded by a group of his friends.

"Eh Joselle, tell Mister Italiano, his crew is down at the spaghetti shop!"

Several other students in the parking lot heard the crude remark. Of course, everyone loved Nikos, so the only laughter came from Tav and his gang.

"What a bastard." Joselle whispered, her voice shaking with hate. "I'm sorry." She added.

Nikos waved it off. "That mess don't faze me." He sighed.

Joselle reacted as though the insult were directed at her. "Stupid, stupid..." She chanted.

Nikos didn't ask what the problem was. He already knew. A moment later Joselle was asking him to excuse her and disappeared across the parking lot.

***

AlTonya Washington

"Steph. Girl get those books off the table!" Ophelia cried, when she flew into the kitchen.

Stephanie frowned and watched her mother checking the simmering pots. "I can't believe you're goin' to all this trouble for a family member-a teenager at that."

"It's not just a family member, little girl." Ophelia retorted, mocking Steph's haughty tone. "Amina is my favorite cousin's only child and Dyna asked me to take care of her. She's never been away from home before."

"So what's she like?" Steph asked, as she began to clear away her books.

Ophelia stirred the pot of black-eye peas simmering in onions and ham hocks. "Amina is a very smart young woman. Extremely smart-book wise. She's also very quiet-a graceful, poised sort of child. Dyna says some people may think she's stuck on herself, but it's just her way. She's a lovely girl and quite sociable once you get to know her. So be nice." Ophelia warned, tweaking her daughter's nose when she walked by.

Silence settled over the kitchen as Steph cleared the table under her mother's watchful eye.

"Are you getting enough help from your partner?" Ophelia asked referring to CJ as Steph shuffled papers.

The girl flipped a lock of her hair from her face. "Not as much as I'd like to, Ma." She admitted. "CJ acts like he's in some kind of daze half the time. Especially when we're trying to work on the weekends."

Ophelia leaned against the counter and pushed her hands into the pockets of her form-fitting bell-bottoms. "What do you mean dazed?" She queried.

Steph shrugged. "I can't say for sure and I really don't know how else to describe it. He just acts like he's in another world sometimes."

"Well do you think the project will be finished in time?"

Steph's weary expression quickly turned confident. "I'll be finished with it. There is no way I'm spending any more time than necessary at Cardman G. Wainright High."

Ophelia's laughter filled the room.

***

CJ parked his mother's sleek red Cadillac near one of the overhead speakers at the station. The sounds of Ike and Tina Turner resounded from the state-of-the-art 8-track tape deck. He closed his eyes and leaned against the black leather headrest.

His thoughts took him away from the crowd of travelers to the previous weekend.

He could live forever off the sight of Demetria Gwaltney. Realistically, he had to admit it would be impossible to accept sight without touch. The time would come when he would either make his presence known or stop going to the forbidden pond.

"Number 6063 from Columbus, Ohio on Track Seven. Again, number 6063 from Columbus..."

"Damn!" CJ hissed, jumping out of the car to race inside the terminal. He headed right to the ticket window and asked for directions to the track.

"CJ?"

It took a moment before CJ tuned into the soft voice calling his name. When he turned and looked down, an incredibly lovely cinnamon-skinned girl looked back at him.

"Amina?" He whispered.

Amina Celeste Davidson's long lashes fluttered over her eyes in relief. "I was hoping it was you." She sighed.

"How'd you get off the train so fast?" CJ was asking, as he moved away from the ticket window.

Amina's hazel almond-shaped eyes actually seemed to sparkle when she laughed. "They've been announcing the train for a while now. I've been in here almost ten minutes."

CJ cleared his throat, realizing his daydreaming had completely taken over and he'd forgotten where he was. "Well, let's get your stuff and get outta here." He suggested.

Amina let out a yelp when CJ turned on the car. "I see why you couldn't hear the announcement!" She called over the music blaring from the speakers.

CJ grinned and adjusted the volume. "Sorry. Do you listen to Parliament?"

"I do." Amina replied, sliding a lock of her waist-length wavy hair behind her ear. "Mostly, I listen to the O'Jays, Mavis Staples, Rose Royce, The Fifth Dimension and the Jacksons."

"Just like Steph." CJ said, shaking his head in amusement. "So what grade are you goin' to next year?" He asked.

Amina giggled. "No grade. I just graduated this year."

"Get the hell outta here!" CJ ordered, flashing his cousin a quick look of disbelief. "Damn you are just like my sister. Y'all should get along big time."

The light in Amina's eyes faded a bit. "I hope so. It'll be so nice. I don't really have any girlfriend's up in Ohio."

CJ came to a stop at the red light and turned to face her. "That's hard to believe."

Amina fiddled with the hem of her ruffled neck, blue blouse and shrugged. "I could never get them to accept me."

"Not even your smart friends?"

"There weren't many my age." Amina explained her expression sad. "Besides, people tend to frown on you for being 'smart' and then...I had other things against me too."

"Like what?" CJ probed, pushing the accelerator when the light changed.

Amina leaned back against the headrest and closed her eyes. "Most of the girls I went to school with thought I was after their boyfriend's when it was really the other way around."

CJ nodded, but did not respond. He could hear the hurt in Amina's soft voice even though she tried to mask it with laughter. He understood her plight. Despite the fact she was his cousin, there was no denying her beauty. Amina had the look of his mother and sister, but there was an added gentleness- something sweetly graceful. Instantly, he felt a need to protect her.

***

Although it was mid-week, the basketball court was packed. Middle and High school students finished homework, while others socialized or watched the game. Sweet and Nikos were on the same team that day. The two friends were dynamic partners, much to the dislike of Tavares Gwaltney.

Tav and his crew made up the opposing team and didn't like being bested by anyone. Especially a team, which included someone they deemed 'beneath' them.

"Time!" Tav called, after a few plays added 8 more points to the opposing teams staggering lead.

"We gotta stop these muthas." He practically growled, when his team met in a huddle. "Marcus, let me guard that greasy headed Nikos."

"I knew it wouldn't be long." Nikos mused, when the huddle broke.

Sweet frowned. "What you talkin' bout, Man?"

Nikos's grin sparked his deep dimples. "I'll bet Tav's gonna guard me."

"Just concentrate on whippin' these fools, man." Sweet suggested, fanning his sweat-drenched white tank top.

Unfortunately, the 'game' wasn't on Tavares Gwaltney's mind. The game that had always existed between he and Nikos Cantone reached a fevered pitch that day. The supposed "guarding", lead to a shoving battle which resulted in punches being thrown. Nikos could handle himself, but against Tav's rage, his skills wore thin. Tav seemed close to killing Nikos, when the fight was stopped.

"What the hell is wrong with you, fool?!" Sweet raged, pulling Nikos limp body off the pavement.

"It's just a fight Sweet, man. Be cool." Tav replied, a broad grin crossing his face.

"Fuck cool, man. You almost killed him!" Sweet roared, as his teammates carried Nikos from the court.

Tav felt no remorse. "Maybe he should play ball someplace where he'll feel safer!"

Sweet waved his hand and turned away. "Fuck you, Man!" He called.

Tav only laughed. "Y'all do Italians even play ball?!" He inquired of his teammates who all laughed at the remark.

AlTonya Washington

Sweet caught up with his friends who were escorting Nikos to his blue Toyota truck. "We gotta get you home, man!" He decided, pulling Nikos' keys from the back pocket of the boy's jean shorts. They settle Nikos into the passenger side while Sweet got behind the wheel.

"Damn Gwaltneys!" Sweet raged, slamming his fist against the steering while his friend moaned in pain.

***

"Oh, you look just like Dyna!" Ophelia raved, pulling Amina close for another hug.

Everyone was in high spirits, having another member of the family beneath the roof. Amina was especially delighted by the warm reception she'd received from the Augustine clan.

"I hope you're hungry!" Ophelia warned, when she went to the oven and removed the broccoli and cheese cornbread.

"I am!" Chick and CJ called, as they stormed into the kitchen.

"CJ put these mittens on and take the cornbread out to the dining room." Ophelia instructed, and then pressed a quick kiss to her husband's cheek. "Baby, I already fed Derric and Cameo. They should be asleep. Would you go check?"

"No problem." Chick replied, giving his wife a light salute before he disappeared upstairs to see to the youngest Augustines.

"Steph, get the drinks, alright?"

"I'm on it, Ma." Stephanie called, already pouring fresh lemonade into tall glasses.

Amina stood in awe. "Aunt Ophelia, you've got it together." She complimented.

"Amina, pleeease don't let her think she's bad." Steph playfully scolded.

Ophelia removed the apron from her floor length floral print sundress and smacked Steph's bottom. "Let the girl speak, child. Yes baby, I'll admit it takes a lot to keep these people on schedule."

Steph mocked her mother's flamboyant gestures when the woman went on about how difficult it was raising such a large family. Ophelia turned to give her daughter another smack on her derriere, just as Chick returned to the kitchen.

"You expecting your beau tonight, Babygirl?" He asked.

Steph nudged her father's shoulder at his use of the old-fashioned term. "He said he'd stop by after he left the court."

"The court?" Amina queried, taking a seat at the kitchen table.

Steph nodded and took a seat in the chair at her cousin's left. "Mmm hmm. The basketball court. Everybody hangs out there."

"What's it like?" Amina questioned, her light eyes sparkling as Steph explained about the park and basketball games that grabbed all the kid's interest.

A knock sounded on the backdoor, amidst Stephanie's speech. Chick went to answer and smiled when he saw his daughter's boyfriend on the porch.

"What's goin' on, man?" Chick greeted stepping aside to allow the young man entrance.

"Hey Mr. Augustine." Sweet replied, weariness evident in his deep voice as he stepped in from the evening shadows.

"Sweet!" Steph cried, being the first to spot the blood red streaks on the boy's white tank top.

Sweet closed his eyes and grimaced, having realized he hadn't changed his shirt. "I'm fine. I'm alright." He assured his girlfriend and her family when they gathered around him.

"Man, what happened?!" CJ asked when he returned to the kitchen and saw his friend's bloodstained clothes.

Steph pulled Sweet over to the kitchen table as he spoke. "That nig-sorry Mr. and Mrs. Augustine. Tav Gwaltney happened. Got all up in Nikos face during the game. Started shovin' him, one thing led to another, then they were brawlin'. I thought that fool was gonna kill Nik."

"Rank bastard." Stephanie sneered.

"Dumb ass." CJ whispered.

"Hey! Hey!" Chick reprimanded when he heard his son and daughter's remarks.

"Sorry Pop, but that fool ain't nothin' but a-"

"A nuisance." Stephanie finished for her brother.

"Who is he?" Amina asked, her light voice resounding in the now silent kitchen.

Ophelia practically bubbled to give her second cousin the real deal on the Gwaltney's. One glimpse of the warning look in Chick's dark eyes changed her mind.

"Tav and his family are our next door neighbors, Baby." She replied, the tone of finality telling everyone else that the conversation had reached its end.

Several acres away at the Gwaltney estate, Demetria was applying liniment to Tav's busted knuckles. "Daddy do you think he needs a doctor?" She asked, frowning at the horrid cuts on her big brother's hands.

"I don't need a thing." Tav replied, before his father could say a word.

"You need a whippin' in my wood shed!" Jason bellowed, slapping the back of Tav's head. "What the hell were you thinkin' about fightin' like some damned hoodlum over what?! I should take you outside and show you what a real fight is!"

Tav looked up at Jason, who appeared ready to bust from the confines of his dusty gray work shirt. Tav shuddered and prayed the huge man would not carry out his threats.

"I got somethin' better in mind, though." Jason muttered, helping himself to a drumstick from the platter of fried chicken. "Because of this blasted fight, you have forfeited your summer of fun, boy. Your black ass will be learning the business instead of traipsin' over town all time of the day and night."

Demetria finished her doctoring and left the table. She could feel Tav's hand shaking against hers as their father passed his sentence. Clearing her throat, she pushed the Band-Aids and gauze into the pockets of her green sundress and left the kitchen.

Tav knew it would be foolish to argue, but the idea of losing an entire summer, made him want to scream. "Day and night? What can I learn about the market at night?"

"I'll think of somethin'." Jason promised.

Tav pushed his chair away with enough force to knock it to the floor. "Poppa you can't do this to me, man! This is my last summer before college."

Less than a second seemed to pass, before Jason laid a powerful backhand to his son's face. "Enjoy these weeks until your graduation, boy. After that, your ass belongs to me."

Tav was motionless and speechless as he clutched his flaming cheek. Defeated, he watched his father stroll from the room.

***

Dinner at the Augustine home was an enjoyable affair, despite its rocky start. CJ and Steph were delighted by Amina's company. They were even more pleased by her presence, when Ophelia allowed them to forgo helping her with the dishes in order to entertain their cousin.

"I wish you had changed your shirt." Steph whispered to Sweet, as they all watched "Baby I'm Back."

He shrugged. "After I took Nik home, I didn't feel like goin' home and havin' my dad give me the third degree about what happened."

"How was Nikos when you left him?" Steph asked.

"In pain, but he's tough. Bruises'll probably be the only way to tell he was in a fight." Sweet decided.

"That fool's gonna tangle with the wrong person one day." CJ predicted, his handsome face hard with anger.

"Why don't you all get along?" Amina asked, after she'd listened in for a few moments.

"It's a long story." Sweet warned.

"She still needs to know." Steph decided. "His entire family has been a pain in our side for years, right CJ?"

CJ nodded, though he couldn't bring himself to demean everyone in the Gwaltney family.

"But Tav has got to be the worst of 'em," Stephanie was saying, "he's crude, arrogant, stuck on himself, foul-mouthed, nasty, no respect for women..."

"He probably has respect for his Mama." Sweet teased.

78

"And she'd be the only one." Steph retorted.

Amina smoothed her hands across her burgundy sweater. "Y'all make him sound so scary."

"You just stay away from him." CJ cautioned.

Steph rolled her eyes. "Please, once he sees Amina y'all know he's gonna try to run them same pickup lines on her."

The conversation continued, becoming more heated by the minute. When Chick passed the den doorway, the discussion was silenced.

SIX

During the next couple of weeks, things were relatively silent. The fight between Nikos and Tav was almost forgotten. Forgotten, that is, by everyone except Nikos, Tav and Jason Gwaltney. The bruises faded, but Nikos Cantone was left with an even deeper hatred of Tavares.

Of course, Tav had greater concerns. His father had remained true to his word, making Tav attend meetings and offer input on marketing ideas for the store. Tav hated it, or so he thought. His ideas for Gwaltney Produce were quite insightful with the potential to net substantial profits. Slowly, but certainly, he was gaining the respect of his father's top people.

Amina Davidson had also been pulling attention. She had already turned the heads of several of CJ's male friends. Everyone wanted to know more about her. Amina; however, was content shopping with Ophelia and helping Stephanie with her senior project. Only to herself could Amina admit there was one person she wanted to meet. His identity, she dared not reveal.

Soft streams of sunlight fought past the lavender curtains in Amina's bedroom. It didn't take long to awaken, especially with the loud voices on the other side of the wall.

"What the?..." She whispered, slowly pushing the covers away. Pulling a pink chenille robe over her green thin-strapped nightgown, she left the room and went to investigate.

"It's Saturday mornin' and your butt ain't out of bed yet!"

"That's because it's Saturday mornin'."

Steph rolled her eyes as her small hands clenched into fists. "This is it! I ain't overlookin' your laziness no more!"

"Damn Steph, I ain't get to bed 'til-"

"I don't care when you got to bed!" Steph roared, her arched brows meeting to form a fierce frown. "CJ, I can't believe you haven't finished the research you promised to have for me by this morning."

CJ groaned and pulled the ends of the pillow up to cover his ears. "I'll get it done." He grumbled.

"When CJ?" Steph persisted, stepping closer to her brother's bed. "The project is due Friday and I wanted to get it finished this weekend."

CJ sucked his teeth and rolled onto his side. "Aw Steph, we gonna pass whether we turn that mess in or not. Our grades are good enough."

CJ's lax response only enraged Stephanie further. Nostrils flaring, she jumped on the bed and reached for a pillow. Her anger and frustration spewed forth as she pounded her brother's face, back and chest with heavy blows. CJ laughed, until the blows grew harsher and he realized his sister was really angry.

"Steph!" He cried, becoming breathless as the pillow landed across his face in rapid succession. "Steph, alright! Alright, damn!"

"Alright what?" Steph demanded, holding the pillow poised for another hit.

CJ took a moment to catch his breath. "I'll finish my part of the research today and piece it all together. We can work all day and night if we have to."

Steph eased back and smiled. "That's more than acceptable." She coolly replied, smoothing her glossy hair back into place. "But you'll be working alone, since I'm goin' out with

Amina." She announced, sending CJ an expectant look-daring him to complain. When he nodded, she moved off the bed with the dignity of a queen and strolled from the room.

Amina watched the scene from the doorway. When Steph passed, they slapped palms.

"That's cold!" CJ called from bed.

***

As usual, the Gwaltney household was already up for the day. The family was enjoying a hearty breakfast of grits with sausage links with gravy, biscuits with jam, scrambled eggs with cheese, milk and coffee. Today would be an important day for business as Jason was meeting with a new market from the next county. He hoped to have his produce stocked there.

"I can't believe you're finally looking to sell your wares outside the county, Baby."

Jason managed a soft smile for his wife, before he shook his head. "I still don't know, Minnie. You know I ain't too high on doin' business with whitey."

Minerva nodded, forking a mound of the seasoned grits into her mouth. "Well, that's a small price to pay to bring more money in, right?"

"That's the best reason." Jason agreed. "That, and the fact that it was my boy's idea for me to broaden my horizons."

"So, how does it feel to be a decision maker, Baby?" Minerva asked her son.

Tav's expression was a mixture of anxiety and weariness. "We're having lunch with them today, Ma. So I'll let you know after they sign the papers."

Minerva and Jason exchanged glances, before bursting into laughter.

"At least he's confident!" Minerva raved.

"That's my boy!" Jason bellowed through his roaring laughter.

Minerva noticed that Demetria had not said much, despite the lively conversation. "What do you have planned for today, Honey?" She asked, tapping her fingers on the navy blue tablecloth to get her daughter's attention.

"Not much." Demetria replied, looking up from her plate for the first time since breakfast began.

Minerva propped her fist beneath her chin and smiled into the face which resembled her own. "I don't like you spending so much time alone, Sweetie." She whispered.

Jason pushed his chair from the table and took a quick swig of his coffee. "We should get going." He said to Tav. The two well-dressed men left the table after kissing Minerva and Demetria.

When the dining room was silent, Minerva inched her chair closer to her daughter's. "So, do you have anything exciting planned for the weekend?" She probed again.

"Like I said, Ma, 'not much'." Demetria reiterated, folding her arms across the front of her purple silk robe.

Though there was nothing strange about a young woman enjoying long walks and finding quiet places to read, it set Minerva on edge. She had always thought Demetria would be more like her-take charge, lively, outgoing. Unfortunately, all mother and daughter shared were looks. There, the similarity ended. Minerva forced herself to be gentle with Demetria because she sensed how fragile the girl was.

"Baby, are there any girls you'd like to invite out here?" Minerva suggested, hoping to spark interest with the idea. "You know, summer's coming up," she continued, "and maybe you'd like to have a slumber party or something like that."

Demetria's huge brown eyes drifted downward. She showed no excitement.

Minerva caught her lower lip between her teeth to ward off the frustration bubbling inside her. "You wouldn't have to worry about Tav butting in on the party, you know? Your Daddy's wearing him out every day." She teased.

Demetria managed a smile, hoping to soothe the unease she heard in her mother's voice. Still, it was clear that she was disinterested. "Could I be excused?" She softly requested.

Minerva realized she'd been holding her breath and finally nodded. Demetria left the table like a flash, leaving her mother looking after her in confusion and concern.

Demetria raced upstairs and ripped her nightclothes from her back. She changed into the revealing red, string bikini she had chosen for the pond that day. She covered the skimpy outfit with a pair of yellow shorts and a matching top. She made her way out of the house, taking care not to run into her mother along the way.

Demetria left through the back door, as though she were running for her life. The girl did not stop until she was far away from the workers. Her sprints slowed to a stroll and soon she had reached the pond. Burying her face in her hands, she took a deep breath, inhaling the clean air which seemed exclusive to the pond.

Lectures from Minerva always produced the same results. Demetria realized long ago that her mother would never understand her. Minerva Gwaltney wanted a daughter to follow in her footsteps. Demetria knew she would never be able to meet those expectations. She had no desire to. She was a different type of person. A person who found excitement in ways her mother would never understand.

The tree leaves rustled against the wind and Demetria's heart raced. CJ Augustine would arrive anytime, but she had plenty of time before he got there. Setting down to the bank, she leaned against a rock and opened a thick book.

***

Later that afternoon, Ophelia stood frowning over one of the dozens of cookbooks that filled her kitchen. CJ had requested a special meal that night for Nikos Cantone, who he had invited for dinner. Nikos's father was satisfied that his son had healed enough to venture out socially and had no problem with his visiting the Augustines.

Chick walked into the kitchen and found his wife leaning against the counter. "What you doin, Girl?" He whispered against her neck.

Ophelia nuzzled against her husband and smiled. "CJ's inviting Nikos for dinner and wants something special." She explained.

AlTonya Washington

"And where's everybody else?" He asked, crossing his arms over the black cotton top he sported with blue jeans and sneakers.

"Derric and Cameo are playing out back," Ophelia replied, her fingers tapping against an interesting recipe she'd located, "and Steph finally laid down the law with her brother about getting on their project."

Chick laughed over his son's plight. "Poor man." He mused.

"Hmph, he's still in better shape than Tav Gwaltney, or so I hear."

"Really?" Chick replied his interest peaked.

Ophelia closed her eyes. "Sorry." She groaned, remembering their agreement of not discussing the Gwaltneys.

Chick was intrigued. "It's alright. What'd you mean?"

"Well, word is Jason put his foot down after that fight. He's got Tav learning the business to keep him out of trouble."

Chick stroked the smooth line of his jaw. "That's not a half bad idea. I've been wondering when I should talk to CJ about spending more time down at the office."

"Well, you better catch him quick before his calendar fills up with party dates." Ophelia warned, pulling a chair to the counter to help her reach the top cupboards. She was checking for an ingredient, when the room slanted crazily and she felt faint.

Chick had been appreciating his wife's curves, when he saw her grip the back of the chair. The weak expression on her face caused him to frown.

"What is it?" He whispered, pulling her from the chair and into his arms.

Ophelia hesitated for a moment, before answering. "I'm fine now. I think I just lost my balance for a minute." She explained, though her heart raced frantically.

Chick held her even closer, his mouth brushing the smattering of hair at her temple.

Ophelia eased out of the comforting embrace. "I'm fine." She assured him, patting his arm before turning back to the cookbook.

Chick didn't press the issue, but he was far from reassured. Luckily, the tension was interrupted when Steph waltzed into the kitchen.

"Ma, do we have anymore soda?" She called, already headed for the refrigerator.

"Just look Honey. I'm sure there's some in there." Ophelia called, waving her hand without bothering to turn around.

"Y'all okay?" Steph asked, noticing the expressions on her parent's faces.

Chick nodded and moved away from the counter. "We're cool. Who's the soda for?"

"For me, Amina and CJ." Steph replied, already refocused on what she'd come to collect from the kitchen.

"You three have any preferences for lunch?" Ophelia asked.

Steph tossed her head, her heavy ponytail swinging merrily. "CJ might, but I'm taking Amina into town. We're gonna do some shopping and have lunch out somewhere."

"More shopping?" Chick cried, in pretend disgust. He walked over to his daughter and kissed her forehead. "Be careful and have fun." He whispered, pressing a few bills into her hand.

Steph's lovely brown eyes sparkled even more. "Oh we will!" She promised, her fingers closing around the wad of cash. "Thanks Daddy! Bye Ma!" She called, racing from the kitchen.

Chick turned back to Ophelia, the confusion returning to his dark, deep-set gaze. He closed the distance between them and patted her waist. "I'll see you later, hmm?" He whispered, pressing a soft peck to the shell of her ear.

Ophelia leaned into the kiss and nodded. When she was alone in the kitchen, she slumped against the counter and held her head in her hands. "Oh hey!" She called, before the girls could get too far. "Be back in time for dinner. Nikos is coming over."

"We'll be here. I'll be sure to tell Sweet if I see him."
Steph promised.

"Nikos?" Amina asked on their way upstairs.

"He got into a fight with that bastard Tav Gwaltney,
remember?"

"Mmm..." Amina replied, with a nod before she
disappeared into the bedroom.

***

Demetria was growing restless, despite her love for the
pond. She'd received none of her usual warnings to let her know
CJ was in her midst. At one point, she had gone so far as to
venture behind the brush to see if he was there. He wasn't and the
realization was so disturbing, she almost cried. She couldn't help
but wonder if he'd lost interest. After all, he was a graduating
senior and she was just starting high school.

Voices on the other side of the pond reached her ears
then. Demetria checked to make sure she was presentable, and
then pulled the book back onto her lap.

Two Gwaltney employees: Julius and Kathy Bismarck
emerged from behind the green brush surrounding the pond.
Their conversation ceased when they spotted Demetria.

"Are you okay, Sweetie?" Kathy asked, her strong voice
softened by concern.

Demetria looked into the woman's plump, dark face and
smiled. "I'm fine, Miss Kathy."

Kathy and Julius exchanged glances, and then focused
their attention out over the pond. Even the cool loveliness could
not stop their minds from wandering back to that terrible day so
long ago.

Julius cleared his throat to catch his wife's attention.
"We're gonna be sayin' goodbye, Miss Deme. You be careful out
here, alright?"

Demetria clutched the book to her chest and smiled up at
the thin, light-complexioned man. "Yes sir." She told her father's
foreman.

Kathy waited until she and her husband were out of earshot. "I thought Ms. Gwaltney told the kids to stay away from there?"

Julius only shrugged.

When the Bismarcks were gone, Demetria tossed her book aside and pouted. She toyed with a bouncy curl and began to think. Gradually, the pout faded and was replaced by a cunning smile. The next time CJ was there, and she knew there would be a next time she would give him every reason to stay...and keep coming back.

***

Jason and Tavares Gwaltney met at The Kirby Steakhouse for their afternoon meeting. As usual, Tav had dazzled their potential business associates. As a result, they were most interested in his proposal. Jason only had to sit back, look proud and enjoy his meal.

"All this talk of contract negotiations and profits is makin' me want to go to the bathroom." Roy Samms groaned, pushing his chair from the table.

"I'll take a Bourbon straight, Honey." Cordell Holmes of Holmes Fish and Produce, told the smiling waitress. "Roy, wait up!" He called to his Vice-President.

"I could stand a trip to the head, myself." Jason decided, but let the other two men go on ahead.

Tav could feel his father's eyes boring into him and prayed he wasn't in for another tongue-lashing. When he worked up the nerve to look up, he found the man grinning.

"I want to congratulate you, son." Jason told him, clapping one hand to the sleeve of Tav's navy blue suit coat. "You're doin' a fine job." He added.

Tav let out a relieved sigh. "Thanks Poppa. I'm actually enjoying myself, but I do realize it's work. I want you to feel confident putting the business in my hands."

Jason gave his son a playful slap. He had no doubt Tav would make a fine successor. Of course, he decided to keep that to himself.

When Jason left for the restroom, Tav remained at the table enjoying his beer. Though he was no stranger to alcohol; sharing a drink with his father and their associates had him feeling quite grownup. Today was just the beginning, he thought. He had big plans for Gwaltney Produce. Before he was done, the name would be recognized nationwide.

The waitress returned with fresh drinks for the table of businessmen. She fluffed her shoulder length honey-brown tresses and made her smile more radiant for the handsome young man at the table.

"Will you be needing...or wanting anything else over here, Mr. Gwaltney?" She asked, adding a bit more sugar to her words.

The girl's blatant suggestive tone, not to mention her mannerisms, brought Tav's gorgeous dimpled smile to view. Before he could take the brown-skinned beauty up on her obvious offer, two more lovely young women walked into the dining room. One, held Tav in speechless fascination.

"That was some sale." Amina whispered, as she took a seat at the table. Her almond-shaped gaze grew wider at the sight of all her purchases.

Steph situated her bags beneath one of the vacant chairs at the table. "I know the place was a tad on the expensive side, but all the extra cash Daddy gave up, really came in handy." She said, brushing lint from the bellbottom denim jumpsuit she sported.

"For real." Amina agreed.

"Besides, all that hard work we've been puttin' in on that project the last two weeks... we deserve it." Steph declared.

"Amen." Amina agreed, just as the waiter arrived to take their drink orders.

The girls accepted menus and scanned the wide selection, trying to decide on their orders.

"Amina?" Steph whispered, after a few moments of silence.

Amina was frowning over her menu. "Hmm?"

"I just wanted to apologize."

Amina set her menu aside and looked up. "Apologize?"

Steph toyed with one of the thick curls from her high ponytail. "Me and CJ have been spending so much time on that damn project, while you've been doin' nothing but shopping with Ma for the most part. I really appreciate all the help you gave me with the work, but I know you've been bored to death."

Amina giggled and shook her head. "Steph, please. I have been havin' the best time helping you with the project and shopping with Ophelia."

Steph's bright smile reappeared. "I'm glad you weren't pissed."

Amina folded her arms across the snug-fitting gray top she wore with white bellbottoms. Her naturally arched brows raised a few notches. "Believe me, Girl. After wearing all those Sunday school dresses to school every day, I'm havin' too much fun buying the snazzy stuff."

"Looks like we'll finally get a chance to sport our new threads on Friday." Steph announced, after the waiter walked away with their orders.

Amina fiddled with a few wavy tendrils which dangled outside the thick braid around her head. "What's Friday?"

"The parties, Girl!" Steph replied, beginning to dance in her chair. "And then there's summer. With a lot of people leaving for college, this is gonna be one for the books." She predicted.

Amina closed her eyes and smiled. "I can't wait."

"You?!" Steph bellowed, appearing more than ready.

"What's happenin', Steph?"

Both girls looked up, when the deep voice reached their ears. Stephanie's happy expression disappeared instantly.

"What the fuck do you want?"

Amina almost choked on her tea when she heard her cousin snap. Her eyes were wide as they rose to the person who had spoken so politely. Her heart thundered against her chest when she saw the incredible looking young man at the table. He was very tall, massively built-perhaps a football player, Amina thought. His head of wavy black hair was worn in a low cut afro,

AlTonya Washington

the eyes were dark and deep-set, the nose long and slightly wide and the fantastic mouth was curved into a smile.

Tav tried to mask his aggravation. "I just came by to speak, Steph." He slowly explained.

Steph was not pleased. "Speak about what?"

Tav pushed one hand into his trouser pocket. "I'm here helping my Pop close a business deal." He said, leaning against the table.

Unimpressed, Stephanie sent him a scathing glare. "How nice for you. Now would you leave? We're about to eat and I can't digest my food with you around."

"Steph!" Amina leaned across the table and whispered.

Tav's probing dark eyes slid to the sweet, caramel-toned beauty across from Stephanie. "It's okay." He told her, extending his hand. "I'm Tavares Gwaltney."

Before Amina could accept his hand, Steph stood and slapped it out of the way. "You stay away from her." She practically snarled.

Tav's jaw tightened as he allowed his anger to show. "You know, Steph, everybody ain't as anti-social and stank actin' as the Augustines."

"News for you jackass, she *is* an Augustine." Steph spat, loving it when Tav winced. "Now get away from this table." She ordered, pointing behind him. "Go on!"

Tav rolled his eyes away from Steph and back to Amina. His dimples faintly appeared when he smiled at the soft look she sent him.

SEVEN

"I told CJ and them Tav would be tryin' to run his jive on Amina when he saw her."

Steph was still in an uproar when she and Amina returned home. She was telling her mother what happened at lunch. Since Chick was gone, Ophelia didn't mind being vocal about her own feelings toward the Gwaltney clan.

"Baby, are you okay?" Ophelia asked Amina, who had been very quiet. "Tav didn't upset you, did he?"

"Oh no, I'm fine." Amina assured her cousins, but said nothing more.

Ophelia and Steph hardly noticed. They had plenty to say where the Gwaltneys were concerned.

While mother and daughter ranted, Amina thought back to her 'meeting' with Tavares Gwaltney. She wouldn't dare breathe it to her family, but she thought he was incredible. He was even more handsome than she expected, with the flawless, molasses-toned skin. Tav didn't seem anything like the monster her family portrayed him as. Naïveté would not let her think first impressions were often false.

"Hey, what's with all the loud talkin'?" CJ called, when he walked into the kitchen.

"I had a run-in with Tav when we were out at lunch." Steph explained.

"A run-in?" CJ questioned, his heavy brows drawing closer.

Steph raised both hands, sensing her brother's anger. "It was nothin'. I handled it. He was just tryin' to get in Amina's face with his pickup lines."

"Mmm." CJ replied, his frown fading. "Ma, what's up with dinner?" He asked.

Ophelia sent him a smug smile and focused on smoothing non-existent wrinkles from her yellow sundress. "Baby everything is under control. It'll all be ready in time." She promised.

CJ nodded his satisfaction, and then wiggled a finger toward his sister. "Can I talk to you a minute?" He asked.

"I tell you, that boy always brings it out in me." Steph rambled as she followed CJ out of the kitchen. "I mean, he had a bunch of nerve comin' over to our table like that. I swear-"

"Steph, would you hush?!" CJ snapped, his handsome face twisting into a sinister frown. "I got somethin' I need to show you."

Steph figured her brother was in one of his strange moods. She followed quietly, as he led the way to her bedroom. Her eyes lit up like beacons when she walked through the doorway. Gratitude and relief shone on her face and she threw her arms around CJ's neck while jumping up and down.

The report was typed and stacked on top of the research log. Next to it, on the bed, was a layout of their family tree.

"I didn't finish inserting all the names." CJ explained, watching Steph scan the work. He leaned against one of the pink bedroom walls and pushed his hands into the side pockets of his black and white gym shorts.

"CJ this is good." Stephanie marveled at the neatness of the layout.

"You really need to read the thing Steph and then tell me what you think."

"Why do you sound so down about it? Looks like we're in the home stretch now." Steph decided, turning to pin her brother with a frown.

"Just tell me what you think Steph, damn." CJ muttered, as he headed to the bedroom window.

"Ohhhhh...I know what's wrong with you." Steph sighed, tapping one brown polished nail to her chin. "You couldn't run out to where ever you go every Saturday afternoon and you're over here pouting."

"And you don't even know what the hell you talkin' about Steph." CJ snapped, before storming out of the room.

Stephanie forgot her confusion, when the phone rang. "I got it!" She called, snatching up the receiver. "Augustine residence."

"Hey girl, you ready to get down?"

"More than you know, since we're a half hour from finishing our project." Steph replied, laughter filtering through the announcement when she heard Sweet clapping on the other end of the phone.

"Congratulations! So when do you want me to pick you up?"

Steph turned and began to scan the project. "Well, we're all having dinner with Nikos tonight at the house, so I guess after that...Amina'll probably ride with us."

"Cool. Well, I'll try to make it for dinner. Otherwise, I'll see you later tonight."

"Talk to you later, Baby." Steph whispered, blowing a kiss through the receiver.

***

Dusk was approaching and Demetria had not returned home. Minerva was either standing on the back porch or peeking out the window every ten minutes for any signs of her daughter.

Jason, on the other hand, had arrived home in high spirits. The wide grin of a proud father practically encompassed the entire lower portion of his attractive dark face.

"Minerva! Minnie?!" Jason called, when he stormed in through the front door.

A second or two passed before Minerva emerged from the corridor leading to the kitchen. "What is it?" She whispered, her hushed words carrying a hint of anxiety.

"You should've seen our boy takin' care of business today!" Jason relayed, his big hands spreading wide as he paced the sitting room. "All I had to do was sit back and let him handle it all. He closed the deal, we got the papers signed and the ball is rollin'."

Minerva couldn't help but smile at her husband's excitement. "That sounds good, Baby. Where is he?"

Jason began tugging at his necktie. "Should be here any minute. He was following me in his car. What's wrong with you?" He asked, beginning to frown at the unease on his wife's lovely face.

"Nothing...it's probably nothing." Minerva replied, fighting to keep her tone unaffected.

Before Jason could question his wife, Tav bounded into the house. If possible, his grin was even broader than his father's. He was basking in the glow of his stellar performance and had decided to use it to his benefit.

"Poppa can I go to Calvin Hammerson's party tonight?" He asked, praying the request sounded humble and unassuming. "Everybody's gonna be there you know? With graduation and all."

Jason waved his hand, urging silence. "Go on and have a good time. You earned it." He told his son, partly because it was true, mostly because he wanted to know what had Minerva so unsettled.

Tav raced out of the cozy, room before his father could change his mind. Jason walked over to Minerva, who stood staring out the window.

"What's goin' on, Min?" He whispered, slipping his long, strong arms around her waist.

Minerva savored the embrace and leaned back into Jason's unyielding body. "Deme's been actin' so strange...she left this morning right after you and Tav. I haven't seen her since."

"Well, that don't mean something's wrong, Baby." Jason comforted, kissing Minerva's cheek.

"I just don't like the way she keeps to herself. I tried to get her to think about having some girls over, she acted like I'd just told her to go jump out of a window."

Jason chuckled. "Baby, you know how our girl is, how quiet she always is."

Minerva turned away from the window and began to stroll out the room. Jason followed.

"Deme's going to high school this year. I want her to have a good experience. I don't want people to see her as some... outcast."

"Minnie, stop this now." Jason ordered his baritone voice soft and deep. "Don't worry yourself about that."

"I can't help it." Minerva sighed, as she and Jason walked into the kitchen.

Kathy Bismarck was across the room at the huge stove. She was checking on a batch of corn muffins, when she overheard the Gwaltneys discussing their daughter.

"Jason, I just want the girl to be more outgoing, more talkative. She keeps to herself so much...I can't think of one friend she has."

"Well, maybe that's a good thing Minnie." Jason decided, leaning back in his chair at the head of the small rectangular table. "Deme don't need none of them fast girls corruptin' her."

Minerva wore a snug fitting orange knit sweater and still, she shivered. "It's more than that Jason." She snapped. "She runs off every Saturday. If she has no friends, where's she going, what's so doing?"

Kathy rose to her full height and closed the oven door. She hadn't meant to eavesdrop, but couldn't stop herself. After what the parents had been through in the past, she couldn't bear to see them upset over another one of their children. Smoothing both hands over her brown uniform dress, she was about to head over to them.

At that moment, Demetria walked in through the back door. Kathy closed her eyes and uttered a soft prayer as Jason and Minerva rushed over to their child.

"Where have you been all day?" Minerva questioned, brushing her hands over Demetria's face and clothing as though she were making inspection.

"I'm fine, Mama." Demetria sighed, grimacing a bit at the fuss her mother was making. "I just lost track of time." She explained to her father who stood looking concerned.

"Where were you, Babygirl?" Jason asked.

Demetria sought Kathy Bismarck's dark gaze briefly, before looking back at her father. "Just walking...I found a quiet place to read."

Jason appeared satisfied. "That's a good girl." He whispered, pressing a kiss to Demetria's temple.

"May I be excused to my room?" Demetria softly requested. She avoided looking at her mother, unnerved by the look in the woman's eyes.

"That's fine, Baby." Jason allowed, watching Demetria run from the kitchen. "You know Min, I just don't know...Maybe the child just likes being alone."

Minerva's gaze remained suspicious.

***

"I'll get it!" Amina called, jogging past the front sitting room when the doorbell rang later that evening. She tossed her wavy locks over her shoulders and quickly inspected the capped-sleeved gray cotton dress, before opening the door.

Nikos Cantone's pitch black stare narrowed the second the door opened. The small, confused frown which had formed between his sleek brows disappeared as he found his voice.

"I'm Nikos...Cantone. CJ's friend?" He slowly announced, becoming more intrigued by the young woman who had pulled the door open.

Amina's smile widened as she began to nod. "Right, come on in. I'm Amina Davidson. CJ's cousin." She explained, stepping aside to allow the tall young man past the doorway.

Nikos closed his eyes as realization dawned. "Oh yeah, CJ said you were coming to visit. How do you like VA so far?" He asked, watching Amina close and lock the door.

"I love it." She promptly responded. "I've only been here a few weeks and I'm already havin' the best time."

Nikos waited until Amina took a seat on the burgundy loveseat in the sitting room. He joined her there. "Well, CJ and Steph are cool and they always know how to have a cool time."

Amina nodded her agreement, her hazel stare narrowing from curiosity. "You know, you don't sound like CJ and Steph at all." She noted.

Nikos leaned forward, bracing his elbows on his black jeans. "I don't get it."

"What I mean is, you don't sound like you're from Virginia."

"Well, originally I'm from New York."

Amina's eyes widened. "New York?"

"Mmm hmm." Nikos confirmed, with a nod. "I moved here when I was eleven."

Amina settled back against the sofa and braced her elbow along the back. "Tell me what it's like." She urged and settled in to listen to Nikos talk.

***

"So what do you think?" CJ was asking Steph as he pushed her bedroom door shut and leaned against it.

Steph paced the square Oriental rug in the center of her room. "I think we should take your suggestion from this morning."

CJ massaged his temple. "Remind me, Steph."

"We'll pass anyway, right?" Steph challenged, reaching for a red leather belt to loop around her stylish, black polyester jumpsuit. "Whether we turn anything in or not."

"What do we tell Ma and Pop?"

"Nothing." Steph replied, with a shrug. "As long as we graduate, that's all that matters."

CJ folded his arms across the multi-colored shirt he wore outside a pair of hunter green slacks. His uneasy expression matched the sound of his voice. "So, what about the project?"

Steph fluffed out her hot-curled hair and turned away from the window. "We'll just put it up somewhere. We'll never finish it now." She decided, eyeing the project on the bed with a foreboding glare.

"I've only seen pictures, but I've always wanted to live there. I never thought I'd meet someone who came from there."

Nikos chuckled over Amina's excitement about New York. He had never met anyone so interested in his stories about his hometown. "I suppose it's okay if you've never been there, but I prefer VA to New York any day."

"That's hard to believe." Amina sighed, propping her fist beneath her chin. "I mean, I've had a lot of fun here, but after living in a small area of Columbus, Ohio all my life, New York sounds like a dream."

Nikos rolled his eyes toward the chandelier in the ceiling. "A dream, huh?"

"Why'd you and your dad leave?"

Nikos hesitated and the easy, open expression on his handsome face disappeared for the first time that evening. "My mom's family made it hard to stay."

Amina's probing gaze narrowed. "How?" She asked.

"Ever heard of the mafia?"

"The mafia?" Amina whispered, leaning closer as though she were being told a big secret. "I learned about it in school... seen movies about it."

"Well, it's very real, lemme tell ya. Anyway, my dad didn't want anything to do with it and they made it hard for him to stay after my mom died."

"What about his family? Couldn't he go to them?"

Nikos pushed one hand through his glossy black waves and shook his head. "That was the last thing he wanted to do, especially when they're connected too. Stuff like that could start a war."

"My God." Amina breathed, her mouth falling open.

Nikos shrugged beneath his gray, nylon shirt. "Anyway, my dad didn't want me growing up in that life. So we left. Only a few people know where we are now."

"That's incredible."

"My pop just did what he thought he had to and I'm proud of him. He left New York with only a little money and now he's got a successful store."

Amina shook her head. "Haven't you ever wondered? You know...what it might've been like?"

Nikos brows rose, but he offered no response. He could never admit to anyone, especially his father, that he had always been curious and more than a little interested.

***

"Why Sweet! We didn't think we'd see you tonight." Ophelia cried, pulling her daughter's boyfriend off the front porch.

Sweet's dark eyes sparkled as he walked inside. "Sorry, Mrs. A. I told Steph I'd probably be late. Is all the dinner gone?" He asked.

Ophelia threw her head back and laughed. "I'm afraid so, Baby." She informed Sweet, patting her hand against his back. "And don't look so down. I know your Mama cooked big today. But, if you saved room, I have two big pieces of sweet potato pie wrapped up on the stove for you."

Chick, Nikos and Amina laughed, when Sweet took off like a rocket in the direction of the kitchen. Their big smiles faded a bit when CJ and Steph walked down stairs.

"Are you two okay?" Ophelia asked, closing the distance between herself and her children. "You've both been so quiet all evening."

Brother and sister nodded.

"We're cool, Ma." CJ replied, squeezing his mother's hand.

Ophelia nodded, though her brown gaze was far from easy. "Well, try not to be out all night. Steph, Sweet's in the kitchen." She announced, stepping past them to check on Derric and Cameo upstairs.

Sweet was on his way out the kitchen, when he saw his girlfriend headed inside. "What's wrong?" He asked, noticing the strained look on her face.

Steph could only rest her head against her boyfriend's shoulder. When Sweet felt her trembling in his arms, he pulled her further into the kitchen. He placed the pie on the table, before leaning back against it.

"What the hell is wrong with you?" He asked, squeezing Steph's hands in his.

"Besides getting an F on my final?" Steph snapped, tears slipping from the corners of her eyes.

"An F? I thought you told me y'all were done with it?"

Steph wiped her eyes with the back of her hand. "There's no way we'll finish it now. We'll just have to take the F."

"I don't get it, Steph."

Steph smiled into her boyfriend's handsome chocolate-toned face. "I don't really feel like talkin' about it now anyway."

"Hey y'all, come on!" Nikos called from the living room.

Sweet kissed Steph's cheek. Then, arm in arm, they left the kitchen.

***

Calvin Hammerson's pre-grad party had the makings of being the biggest and best party of the year. The elm tree lined backyard was already packed with dancing bodies when CJ, Steph, Sweet, Amina and Nikos arrived.

CJ didn't remain dateless for long. One of his many admirers pulled him onto the dance floor. Sweet and Steph followed suit, leaving Amina and Nikos bobbing their heads to the music of Earth, Wind and Fire pulsing through the air.

Nikos turned to Amina and spread his hands. "You mind dancin' with the only white guy at the party?" He teased.

Amina laughed and shook her head. "Come on." She sighed, taking his hand and pulling him to the crowded dance floor.

Tav Gwaltney was in his element, this being his first party in weeks. He was surrounded by his buddies and, of course, several young ladies. Still, remaining true to form, Tav

Taboo Tree

was always on the lookout for someone even more intriguing to occupy his time. His penetrating, deep dark gaze narrowed when he spotted a lovely, familiar face across the yard. When her dance partner came into view, he smirked and his fists clenched. He knew he wasn't out of the woods with his father, and this was no time to rouse the water, but he had to go over...

"Are you up to this?" Amina was asking Nikos as they gyrated to the music. She noticed him wincing each time they bounced to the up tempo beats.

Nikos tried to put up a brave front, but he couldn't mask the pain against his still tender ribs.

"Come on." Amina decided, taking it upon herself to end the dance. "Let's sit down and you can tell me more about New York."

Nikos dimples flashed when he heard the request. "I swear I never met anybody so interested in that place."

Amina shrugged and took a seat across from Nikos at one of the picnic tables along the far edge of the yard. "I just have this crazy dream about owning my own business there one day."

"That's not crazy." Nikos assured her.

Amina waved one hand in the air. "I'll agree with that when I'm sittin' in my top floor office overlooking the city." She replied, joining in when he laughed. The easy going mood, halted abruptly when Nikos looked up and saw Tav at the table.

Tav was about to reintroduce himself to Amina and accept the handshake he was deprived of earlier that day. Before he could make a move, CJ and Sweet were there.

"What's goin' on, Tav?" CJ queried, though his hardened expression proved the question wasn't meant to be social.

Tav raised both hands. "I didn't come over to cause trouble." He swore.

Sweet took a step closer. "Well, then you won't mind leavin' will you, my man?"

Tav nodded and pushed one hand into his dark blue designer jeans. He sent Amina a soft look, before stepping away from the table.

CJ, Sweet and Nikos began to discuss Tav and his actions. Amina's radiant gaze followed the topic of conversation making his way to the other side of the yard.

***

"CJ Augustine can I ask you something?"

CJ smiled down at the seventh young woman he'd had the pleasure of dancing with that evening. "What's on your mind?"

Shelly Evans arched her slender form closer to the tall, handsome young man who held her. "Why don't you have a girlfriend?" She whispered, her slanting black gaze trailing his mouth suggestively. "I mean, you're one of the cutest boys in school. If not *the* cutest."

CJ knew his cheeks would've been red, had his complexion been lighter. "Thanks." He managed.

"It's true." Shelly replied, smiling when CJ's dark eyes slid down to her glossy, red lips. "You've broken a lot of hearts at Cardman with this single brotha routine, you know?"

CJ was intrigued by the conversation which proved to be very enlightening. He had no idea so many young women found him so appealing. Unfortunately, the more Shelly talked about him being single and seemingly disinterested, the more he thought of Demetria Gwaltney.

Amina went to freshen drinks for her and Nikos. They had been seated for most of the party, but she didn't mind. The conversation was incredible. At the refreshment table, Amina noticed a boy about her height, approaching her. She focused on fixing her drinks and waited for him to say something. When he only stood and stared, she turned to face him. For a moment, the boy appeared thunderstruck.

"Um...Chad. My name is Chad Reynolds." He finally revealed. "What's yours?" He slowly, almost timidly, inquired.

"Amina." She replied, smiling at the uneasy young man.

Taboo Tree

Chad nodded. "Sorry to bother you Amina, but I'm um here for my friend Tav. He wants to talk to you, but your family..."

Amina nodded, understanding completely.

"Anyway, he wants to call you."

"Well...I'm staying with my family...the Augustines."

Chad's smile faintly resembled a grimace. "He'll call you tomorrow."

Amina's lashes fluttered like hummingbird wings as she watched Chad walk away. She closed her eyes and willed her heart to beat slow.

EIGHT

A ringing telephone greeted the Augustines when they arrived home from church that Sunday. While everyone else kicked off their shoes and began to get comfortable, Amina's wide eyes were glued to the phone. Her first thought was of the boy from the party who told her to expect Tav Gwaltney's call. Before anyone could make a move to answer, she rushed to the message desk near the back of the sitting room.

"Augustine residence." She whispered.

"Amina?"

"Hi." She replied, her voice just a bit shaky as she greeted Tavares Gwaltney.

"I know you can't talk, but would you meet me somewhere later? Around five?"

Amina cast a quick glance over her shoulder. "Where?" She whispered into the receiver.

"At the edge of your family's property there's a pond on one side and a garden on the other side. Meet me in the garden... Amina? Will you be there?" Tav asked, his deep voice carrying just a hint of anxiety.

"Yes." She told him in a hushed tone and quickly set the receiver back to its hook.

"Who was that, Amina?" Steph asked from the doorway of the room.

"Just Nikos calling to see if I had fun at the party." She replied, following her cousin from the sitting room.

"Fe? You wanna go out instead of cooking?"

Ophelia turned away from the cupboards and sent her husband a strange look. "On Sunday, Chick?" She asked, pushing one hand into the pocket of her stylish, brown polyester zip front frock.

Chick pushed himself from the kitchen doorjamb and stepped inside. "You look drained, you sound weak even though you're trying to sound lively for my sake."

"Chick."

"Admit it."

Ophelia rolled her eyes and leaned against the counter. "Alright, I have been feeling just a little drained lately."

"Mmm hmm." Chick replied, already figuring as much. "I want you to see the doctor." He demanded, slipping his arms about her waist.

Ophelia looked up and pressed her hands against his solid chest. "Chick, before I do that-"

"Fe, don't argue with me now." He said, his onyx gaze flashing with impatience. "You been looking peaked for too long and I don't like it. Please don't argue with me, not about this."

"Shh..." Ophelia requested, smoothing her lips across Chick's strong jaw. "I'm not arguing with you, but I have a theory about what's wrong with me."

Chick leaned back. "Spill it." He ordered.

Ophelia squeezed her husband's muscular forearms before curling her hands around his neck. "I think you're gonna be a daddy again." She whispered, her luminous brown gaze holding a trace of unease.

Ophelia needn't have worried. Chick let out a yelp and hauled his wife's slender frame high against his chest.

"Baby don't say anything until we're sure, alright?" Ophelia gasped, amidst dozens of kisses being pressed to her face.

***

Sunday afternoons were usually the slowest time of the week for the Cantone Market. The store sometimes experienced a small rush just after church, but that was mostly it for the day. With Gwaltney Produce growing bigger every month, the usual business was even more difficult to come by.

Nikos had run upstairs for a bathroom break. On his way out of the apartment, the phone rang.

"Cantone's." He greeted.

"Nikos, boy!" A boisterous, deep voice replied.

Immediately, Nikos began to laugh at the sound of the highly missed thick Brooklyn brogue. "Constantine Bellini, is that you?" He teased.

"Eh, that's Uncle Connie to you, boy!"

"What's happenin' Uncle?"

"Well, if I'm not mistaken, and I never am, you're about to become a graduate."

Nikos shook his head. "You never miss a date, Uncle C."

"And don't you forget it." Connie warned.

Nikos took a seat on the black leather living room sofa and settled in to talk with his favorite uncle. Constantine was his mother's older brother and the man always had hopes of his nephew assuming control over the family's interests.

"So what are your plans after graduation?" Connie asked.

Nikos stared at the Converse logo on the front of his T-shirt. "I really don't know, Uncle."

"No thoughts of comin' back home?" Connie pried.

"I'm not sure yet." Nikos replied, though he'd thought of little else especially since his conversation with Amina.

"You know there's a spot for you here, if you want it."

Nikos leaned back against the sofa and smiled. He wondered when his uncle would get to the point of the call.

Constantine had no children of his own which made him more determined to have his sister's child running his affairs.

Carlos Cantone entered the small, cozy, above-store apartment and heard his son's laughter. The calm, relaxed expression on his dark face disappeared the instant he heard his brother-in-law's name. He strolled into the living room and waited for his son to finish the call.

Nikos choked on his laughter, startled to see his father in the room. "Um...Uncle C, can I um call you back later?" He whispered.

"Old man just walked in, huh?"

"Uh-huh."

"Forget about it. I'll talk to you soon, alright?"

"Thanks, Uncle." Nikos replied, easing the black receiver back to its hook. "Sorry Pop."

Carlos waved both hands in the air as he took a seat on the opposite end of the sofa. "Listen Nikos, I can't forbid you to be interested in your mother's family. You'll be graduating soon and I have a feeling you want to go back to New York."

"Papa-"

"Nikos. I understand." Carlos told his son, reaching over to grasp the boy's shoulder. "I only want you to be careful. To think before you make any decisions."

Nikos sighed and slouched back against the sofa. "It ain't such a big deal, Pop."

"Yes it is, Son." Carlos argued, his round midnight gaze filling with concern. "My boy, once you're in there's no going back."

Nikos kept his face free from expression. As usual, he thought his father was making too much of the situation.

***

CJ had fought the desire to visit the pond for as long as he could. He convinced himself Demetria wouldn't be there-he didn't know if she even went to the pond on Sundays. At any rate, he had much to think about and the solitude of the place would do him good. He set out, bumping into Stephanie on his way down the back stairway.

Taboo Tree

"You alright?" He asked, slowing his steps as he approached his sister. He didn't like the weary look on her face.

At first, Steph could only manage a nod. Then she shrugged, her shoulder nudging the glossy flip of her black hair. "I just can't wait until graduation."

CJ stepped closer. "That's why you're walking around here moping?"

Steph smoothed her hands over the cotton sleeves of her orange and purple striped blouse. "I think it's time to leave Virginia."

"Over this?" CJ asked, finally understanding what had his sister so upset.

"Over everything, CJ." Steph replied, leaning against the polished mahogany banister. "I'm ready to see different things and get away from all the anger and hate around this place." She vented.

"I can understand that."

CJ's solemn reply brought a smile to Stephanie's face and laid a playful slap to his cheek. "You don't even understand. You love it here and will probably end up running Daddy's business. All you need to do is choose between all these chicks chasing after you."

CJ laughed, his dimples appearing. "Shut the hell up, Steph." He ordered, pulling her into a tight hug.

Demetria ventured to the pond right after church, as she usually did. After CJ Augustine's uncharacteristic absence the day before, she prayed he would be there on Sunday. Easing down to the grassy bank, her huge dark eyes mirrored the sparkling water. She promised herself that, after that day, CJ wouldn't think of not showing up again.

The soft look on her dark face faded a bit, when she recalled the scene with her parents. It appeared she had returned home just in time, she thought remembering seeing Kathy Bismarck in the kitchen. Today, she couldn't risk anyone snooping in on her private place. She wanted no onlookers for what she had in mind.

AlTonya Washington

The familiar sound of leaves crunching underfoot sent Demetria's heart pounding. CJ, she thought, preparing to set her plan into action. A cunning smile teased her full mouth as she thought of her mother. If Minerva only knew that her daughter had in fact taken on several of her more ...outgoing characteristics.

Heart racing, Demetria set her book aside. She remained focused on the pages while easing out of the fuchsia shorts set she wore with no underwear.

CJ's long lashes closed briefly as he watched Demetria. He had seen the young woman nude many times, but today was different. After the short set had been discarded, Demetria spread a red beach towel on the ground and relaxed on top of it. Reaching for the book once more, she held it close to her face and pretended to read while her fingers trailed the length of her body.

CJ looked on, becoming both shocked and aroused as he watched Demetria's fingers disappear between her thighs. The girl pleasured herself shamelessly, her slender form writhing as ecstasy claimed her. When she tossed the book aside and moaned into the breeze, CJ's knees weakened beneath him. He dared not blink, fearing he would miss something.

Demetria was not disappointed, when CJ remained hidden behind the brush. She could feel his dark stare past the greenery, focused on her bare body as she enjoyed the intimate treat. It won't be much longer now, she promised herself, bringing a halt to the explicit act. Coolly and very slowly, she pulled on her clothes, collected her things and sauntered away. She dared not look back, lest her admirer see the huge smile brightening her face.

***

Amina was reading in the living room, when the front doorbell rang. "I'll get it!" She called, leaving the airy, elegant room and heading to the double, cherry wood doors.

"Nikos!" She greeted, happy to see her newest friend.

Nikos didn't appear quite so elated. "Hey Amina, CJ around?"

"Mmm...not right now. He should be back soon, though." She informed him, tugging on the sleeve of his black shirt as she urged him inside.

Nikos hesitated. "I can come back, Amina." He decided.

"Well, let's talk for a while first." She suggested, sensing it was what the boy needed. "I was just reading in the living room."

"I gotta tell ya, Amina. I never met anybody who read just for the fun of it." Nikos teased, a wicked grin coming to his face. "Lemme guess, it's a book about New York?"

Amina slapped his shoulder. "Nooo...but I have thought about getting a few from the library."

Nikos slapped his palm to his forehead. "I should've known."

"Boy, I ain't studyin' you." She mumbled, rolling her eyes to the ceiling. "You're gonna regret all these jokes when I open my company there." She predicted, giggling when Nikos exchanged his teasing expression for a more humble one.

"Speaking of New York," he said, joining Amina on the long hunter green sofa, "I had a talk with my favorite uncle who lives there."

Amina turned sideways on the sofa and sent Nikos a knowing look. "I'll bet that was nice?"

"Yes and no."

"Say what?"

"Damn, Amina." Nikos snapped, moving off the sofa to stare out the long windows. "My uncle wants me to move back to New York. I can't do that without tellin' my Pop and I know how he feels about it."

"And how do *you* feel about it?" Amina asked, curling her sandaled feet beneath her stylish denim bellbottoms.

Nikos turned away from the windows and leaned against the wall. "I want to be part of my Uncle Connie's business, but I feel low about it."

Amina fiddled with the French braid dangling from her high ponytail. "So your Uncle Connie's business is...sort of shady?"

AlTonya Washington

Nikos laugh was not a humorous one. "It's so shady, it's pitch black."

"But you still want to be part of it?"

"The power excites me." Nikos admitted, his handsome olive-toned face taking on an unusual gleam. "The power in my uncle's world does something for me that runnin' a small town store could never do."

Amina's hazel stare faltered as she traced the embroidered patterns in the sofa cushions. "Do you really know what kind of world you'd be getting into? I mean, Nikos could you live with...hurting people?"

"I guess I won't know 'til I have to do it."

"Nikos!" Amina gasped, at the nonchalant response.

He walked back to the sofa, palms outstretched. "I know it sounds foul, but Amina...I been foolin' myself a long time that I was just like my Pop. Content with the small town life and being an ordinary Joe fadin' into the crowd. Even though I got my ass beat, that fight with Tav made me see violence is in my blood."

Amina reached for Nikos' hand and gave it a squeeze. "I don't care what you say. I don't see that type of violence in you." She whispered fiercely, her grip on his hand tightening.

They sat that way for the longest time.

Minerva was in the kitchen critiquing dinner, when she spotted Tav on his way out.

"Baby, dinner's about ready. Where are you off to?" She called.

Tav stuck his head inside the kitchen. "I'm goin' for a walk, Ma. I'll be back in plenty of time." He promised, before blowing his mother a kiss and leaving the house.

A few minutes after Tav's departure, Jason arrived in the kitchen. He waited until the cooks were preoccupied across the kitchen, before cornering his wife.

"What's for dinner?" he growled into Minerva's neck. His big hands squeezed her bottom through her silk floral lounging dress.

Taboo Tree

Minerva was pressing lemons for lemonade. "Now that one's acting crazy." She grumbled. "Tav's going for a walk." She announced.

Jason chuckled. "So?"

"Since he learned to drive, that boy never goes anywhere on foot."

"You worry too much, woman." Jason decided, pressing a kiss to his wife's cheek and helping himself to one of the golden biscuits cooling on the counter. "Anyway, I don't care what the boy does as long as he keeps dazzling my business associates."

"Uggh!..." Minerva groaned and threw her hands up in defeat.

Tav prayed Amina would be waiting for him at the edge of the property. He had no idea why he was so fascinated by the girl, but figured it was because she was, in his words, 'fresh meat'. Still, there seemed to be more. He could sense it and he didn't even know her.

The meeting of the Augustine Gwaltney property resembled another world-A place untouched by the anger between the two clans. It sat far on the other side of the pond and was similar to a wild flower garden in its appearance.

For the first time, Amina began to have doubts about meeting Tavares Gwaltney. She remembered all that she'd heard about him. Though he seemed nice and approachable, no one she knew had anything favorable to say. What if he was the mean, disrespectful bully that everyone claimed? Her heart beat more from uncertainty than excitement. Her nerve was draining like water from a sink and all she could think about was leaving. As if on cue, Tav stepped through the brush.

Amina smoothed her hands against her jeans and waited. The smile on Tav's handsome, molasses-toned face was soft but it triggered his dimples just the same.

"Tavares Gwaltney." He quietly announced so he would not frighten her.

"Amina Davidson."

"Amina." He repeated, as though he were reciting a poem.

Tav took a step closer, but retained a healthy distance between himself and the poised beauty in his presence. "How are you related to the Augustines?" He asked, pushing both hands into the front pockets of his snug fitting jeans.

"Ophelia Augustine is my mother's first cousin."

Tav nodded, gnawing his bottom lip before speaking again. "I guess Ms. Augustine didn't waste any time telling you how bad we Gwaltneys are."

Amina couldn't prevent her smile from showing. "I know some of the history. My cousins hate you a lot." She couldn't help but add.

Tav didn't appear angered. "I haven't given 'em much reason not to hate me." He admitted. "I would've thought twice about that if I'd known I was gonna meet you."

Amina threw her head back and laughed, missing the captivated look in Tav's dark eyes.

"Where are you from?" He asked.

"Ohio. Columbus." Amina replied, taking a few steps closer as she spoke.

"Are you in high school yet?" Tav asked, not believing she was even old enough.

"I already graduated high school."

"Stop jivin'."

"I'm not." Amina assured him, with a quick toss of her head. "I skipped a lot of grades and was able to graduate early."

Tav's heavy brows rose. "I'm impressed." He admitted. "You thinkin' about college?"

"Yeah, I can't wait to get in and get out." Amina told him, finding a seat on one of the large, smooth rocks. "I want to have my own business one day."

Tav nodded. "Sounds good. I'm planning on takin' over my Pop's business one day too."

"I'm thinking about starting a cosmetics company for the sistahs." Amina replied, smiling when Tav chuckled. "What?" She asked.

"I just can't believe someone who looks like you, would need makeup." He replied, as though that fact was more than obvious.

Despite her rich cinnamon-toned complexion, Amina was sure she was blushing.

***

Amina and Tav made plans to get together from that first day on. They enjoyed long walks along the deserted outskirts of their family's properties. Tav arranged many private lunches at their special place and they became very close. Still, despite Tav's obvious interest, Amina was uncertain. She was a natural beauty, but couldn't help feeling a bit out of her league-considering the types of girls she had seen with Tav. The fact that he was such a gentleman and never even tried to hold her hand, only made her feel more inadequate.

Amina was on her way to meet Tav one afternoon, when she saw Nikos' blue truck pulling into the driveway.

"Hey!" She cried, running over to envelope the boy in a tight hug.

Nikos laughed, savoring the hug. "It's been a while, Girl!"

"A few days."

"Ha! Weeks!" Nikos argued. "How you doin'?" He asked, staring down into her lovely face.

Amina shrugged. "I'm fine."

Nikos' sleek onyx brows drew close. "That the truth?"

"Yeah." She replied, though her gaze faltered. "Why wouldn't you believe me?"

"Cause I don't. Fess up."

"Nikos, do you think I'm pretty?"

Nikos would've laughed, had it not been for the concern he saw in Amina's hazel eyes. He realized she was serious. "Why the hell would you ask that?"

Amina propped her hands on her hips and stared down at her mauve-polished toes peeking out from her sandals. "Would you just answer me, please?" She whispered.

Nikos couldn't believe anyone so incredible would need to be told they were incredible, but he obliged. Cupping Amina's chin in his palm, he smiled down at her. "Believe me when I say, you're more than pretty. Now what made you ask me that?"

Amina replied with a shrug.

"I won't let up 'til you tell me...Amina..."

"You can't tell anyone, alright?" She urged, stepping close to grab the edge of his Dodgers T-shirt.

A car horn sounded just then. It was Chick and Ophelia who pulled into the opposite end of the gravel driveway.

"Are you happy about this?" Ophelia asked, after she and her husband waved to Amina and Nikos.

Chick shut off the engine and turned to face his wife. "I already told you how I felt." He said, stunned by the question. "I'm more than happy, aren't you?"

Ophelia sighed and looked in the backseat, at the adorable boy and girl who played there. "After Derric and Cameo, I wasn't tryin' to get in the family way again."

Chick cleared his throat, his penetrating midnight stare even more narrowed. "So, what are you sayin'?" He asked, fearing his wife may want to terminate the pregnancy.

Ophelia read his thoughts. "I'd never do that to our child, Chick. This is just gonna take some adjusting, that's all." She assured him, smoothing her hand against his smooth, dark brown cheek.

Chick took her hand and pressed a kiss to her palm.

"I need you to keep this between us, Nikos." Amina demanded, after they'd found privacy beneath one of the elm trees in the front yard.

"Alright, already I promise." Nikos said, though he felt it was a mistake to do so.

Amina cast a quick glance across the yard to make sure her family was out of earshot. "I've been seeing Tav Gwaltney."

"Tav Gwaltney?!"

"Shhh!"

"Tav Gwaltney? Amina are you crazy?" Nikos whispered, his dark eyes sparkling with anger...and hurt.

Amina clasped her hands to her chest. "Don't be like this." She pleaded.

"Be like what, Amina?" Nikos snapped, his hands waving in the air. "Did you forget about how much your family hates Tav or what that muthafucka did to me just because he didn't like the way I looked?"

Amina knew her friend was hurting and her heart went out to him. "Nikos please, don't think I don't care about that. It's just that...I've seen a different side to Tav and-"

"It's a lie, Amina. A big front." Nikos declared, shoving one hand through his wavy, black hair. "Amina, I seen too many nice girls be fooled by that mutha."

Amina wouldn't hear it. She shook her head violently, the ponytail slapping her cheeks. "He's not like that. Not with me. He hardly even touches me."

"Is this why you were asking me if you're pretty or not?"

Amina looked away, pushing one hand into the wide back pocket of her green bellbottom jeans.

Nikos had his answer. He became even more enraged, his concern for Amina fueling his anger. "I can't talk about this..." he muttered.

"Nikos please..." Amina called, her eyes filling with tears as she watched him walk away. "Nikos? You won't say anything, will you?"

Finally, Nikos turned. He stepped back to Amina, his index finger poised in the air. "That fool is only tryin' to get in your pants and once he does he's gonna think he can treat you like gold or like shit-depending on his mood."

"Nikos-"

"You're gonna regret the day you started seein' him." Nikos foreshadowed, the haunted look on his face making him seem far older than his eighteen years.

"Will you tell anyone?" Amina whispered.

AlTonya Washington

Nikos' pitch black stare raked the length of her petite form. Finally, he shook his head. "I won't say anything." He promised, then turned and headed back to his truck.

Amina watched him with uneasy eyes.

"Steph and CJ must be out." Ophelia noted, when she and Chick walked in the house and heard the phone ringing. Chick carried Derric and Cameo to their playpen in the far corner of the kitchen while she answered the call.

"Mrs. Augustine?"

"Yes?"

"Hi Ophelia, this is Margret Dubois."

"Hey Margret." Ophelia replied, smiling when she recognized the voice of CJ and Steph's history teacher.

"I'm so sorry to be calling on the weekend, but I uh...I have some concerns."

"Concerns about CJ and Steph?" Ophelia asked, catching Chick's eyes across the room. "Such as?"

Margret seemed reluctant to respond. "Ophelia, Stephanie and Charles came to me Friday and informed me that they would not be turning in their final project.

"What?" Ophelia replied, her face a picture of surprise.

"I told them they would receive an F and they seemed fine with it. Their only concern was that this not prevent them from graduating. I assured them it wouldn't, but this is not like them at all. I knew they put a lot of time into the work and I can't understand why they wouldn't follow through."

"That is strange." Ophelia agreed, tapping her nails to her chin as she listened. "Margret, I appreciate you calling. Chick and I will talk to the kids as soon as they get home."

"What was that about?" Chick asked when Ophelia ended the call.

Ophelia shook her head. "CJ and Steph told their history teacher they weren't turning in their final project. They told her they'd take the F as long as they graduated."

"Hmph. That is strange." Chick agreed, stroking his jaw as a thoughtful expression came to his face.

"You didn't seem as upset as I thought you'd be." Ophelia noted, removing the sweater she wore over the sleeveless pin-striped straight dress. "But that's okay." She decided, folding the sweater. "I'm angry enough for both of us and I can't wait for those two to get back here."

"Fe." Chick called softly, almost absently. "Lemme handle this, alright?"

Ophelia recognized the hard glint in her husband's eyes and nodded. "I'll let you know the minute they walk through the door."

***

CJ had no plans of changing his weekend ritual, after Demetria's revealing 'show' two weeks earlier. Now, the watching had become almost unbearable and quite difficult on certain parts of his anatomy. Demetria's exploits had become increasingly explicit and CJ found his hands actually aching to touch her.

He realized, of course, that was impossible. Especially when he knew...

The thought went unfinished as the tall grass parted and Demetria appeared. She chose her regular spot and began to undress. CJ saw that she wore a revealing yellow bikini underneath the orange jumpsuit which slid to the ground. He wondered if she'd only be using the pond's privacy that day for swimming or reading.

Swimming and reading were not what Demetria Gwaltney had in mind. In fact, she did something completely out of the ordinary. Blanket in hand, she turned and faced the thick trees and brush where CJ hid.

CJ stood rooted to the spot and could only watch as she moved closer to his hiding place. Everything seemed to move at a snail's pace, but soon they were face to face.

CJ began to clear his throat, desperate to find the voice that had deserted him. Demetria was even lovelier up close. That only added to his nervousness.

Demetria smiled at the handsome, uncertain young man standing before her. When he opened his mouth to speak, she stepped closer and pressed her finger to his lips. Then, she turned and spread the large dark blue blanket upon the ground and stepped to the center. Her huge, deep brown eyes sparkled with practiced innocence when she reached for CJ's hand and placed it across her bikini top.

CJ glanced around to make sure they weren't being watched. His long lashes fluttered once at the sensation surging through his body. His hands slowly contracted over Demetria's breast and he grunted. When she arched against his palm, CJ lost all control and pulled her against him. His hands cupped her lovely dark face as his mouth slanted across hers.

Demetria trembled fiercely as the kiss deepened. She was, at once, an eager participant-returning the kiss with lusty enthusiasm. Her slender arms slipped around CJ's neck and she began to rub herself against the arousal pressing against the zipper of his jeans.

Suddenly, Demetria stepped away and eased out of her skimpy attire. CJ had seen many girls nude, but none affected him as she had.

Demetria tossed her thick, bouncy black locks across her shoulders and stood more erect. CJ slipped his arms about her waist and lowered his handsome face to the crook of her neck. He inhaled the soft fragrance of her perfume and whispered her name as though he were chanting it.

Demetria tugged on the hem of CJ's T-shirt before pulling it over his chest and back. The remainder of his clothes disappeared shortly afterwards.

Naked, they rolled on top of the soft blanket. CJ treated himself to all the pleasures he'd only daydreamed about. He had no idea how experienced Demetria was, but to his delight she was a very willing partner.

They made love until the afternoon sun began to set.

NINE

Stephanie's mood had not improved when she returned home that afternoon. She'd hoped being out with Sweet would lift her spirits, but it hadn't. Her boyfriend was determined to find out what had her so upset.

"Steph?" Ophelia called, when she stepped out of Chick's study. She saw her daughter trudging towards the back stairway. "Steph?" She called again.

"Ma'am?" Steph mumbled.

"Your father wants to have a talk with you and CJ."

Ophelia's tone of voice caused Stephanie to turn and pin her mother with a curious look. "Somethin' wrong, Ma?" She asked.

"He'll talk to you when CJ gets home." Was all Ophelia would reveal.

Steph placed her denim tote to the kitchen counter. "What's wrong, Ma?" She asked, her heart beating a little faster.

"Do you know where CJ is?" Ophelia asked instead.

Steph shook her head. "I haven't seen him." She slowly replied, her expression a mixture of suspicion and unease.

Ophelia only shrugged and headed for the door. "I'll call you when he gets here." She said, leaving Stephanie standing in the kitchen.

CJ and Demetria lounged behind the thick brush, basking in the afterglow of lovemaking. CJ forced himself to block the mild wave of disappointment over the fact that Demetria was not a virgin. Of course, the disappointment was short-lived as the girl's expertise satisfied him more than once. The two, young lovers lay beneath the shady elm trees, enjoying the feel of each other's bodies.

Demetria sighed and flipped onto her stomach. Bracing herself on her elbows, she smiled down into CJ's face. "So, what happens now?" She asked.

CJ couldn't stop the despair from filling his onyx stare. "We can't be together like this again."

Demetria's brown eyes mirrored the look in CJ's gaze. Before she could say anything, he reached for her hand and pressed it to his chest.

"You know this can't happen again." He said, forcing his words to sound convincing.

"I don't understand." Demetria whispered, her gaze faltering.

"Baby, I just committed a felony by sleeping with you. That's a risk I can't take again, no matter how good it was." He explained, forcing himself not to think of the other reason why an involvement with Demetria Gwaltney was impossible.

Demetria wanted to cry, but she realized CJ was right. It could never work between them. What they'd shared had been beautiful and she would treasure it always. Finally, she found her smile and leaned closer to CJ again.

"If this is going to be the only time," she whispered, nudging his jaw with her nose, "do we have time for more?"

CJ's lips curved into a knowing grin and he pulled Demetria's slender form atop his athletic frame and obliged her request.

***

Amina arrived at the secluded garden spot a few moments before Tav. Her heated discussion with Nikos robbed her of energy and she'd opted to take a nap before setting out again. She prayed Tav hadn't already shown up and left. She needn't have worried.

Less than a minute passed when Tav came rushing out to the clearing. His expression seemed harried and he was out of breath.

"Sorry Amina. Sorry I'm late." He gasped, bracing one hand against a tree trunk as he enjoyed deep gulps of air.

"I just got here myself." She replied, managing a small smile.

Tav raked one hand across his head. "My Pop is on the warpath today. I just managed to sneak off while he was talkin' to some of the field hands."

"So I guess we don't have any time together, huh?" Amina was asking. She stood with her arms folded across her snug-fitting green, yellow and white striped T-shirt.

"I'm sorry." Tav whispered, walking closer. "But, I wanna take you out to dinner tonight." He said, settling his big hands to her waist.

"Out to dinner?" Amina repeated, her hazel eyes narrowing. She and Tav had been seeing each other privately for weeks. "Tav...I don't know..."

"What?"

"Are you ready for everybody to know about us? 'Cause I don't think I am."

"Well, I'm tired of sneakin' around." Tav argued, a frown beginning to form on his dark face. "I want everybody to know you're mine."

Amina's uneasiness lifted like mist. Tav's possessive statement sent her heart thudding with excitement. A moment later, she was nodding.

"So how do we meet?" She asked, knowing there was no way she could simply walk out of the Augustine home without questions.

Tav leaned against one of the elm trees, unmindful of the slices of bark clinging to his cream trousers and gray shirt. "Don't worry about that. I plan on driving to the Augustines and knocking on the door."

Amina was horrified. "You can't! Are you serious?" She cried, searching the boy's handsome face for some sign of humor.

Tav wasn't smiling. "This mess between our families has gone on too long and it don't even have a thing to do with us."

Amina's lashes fluttered and she appeared drained. "Tav..." She groaned.

He reached for her hand and squeezed it tight. "I'll see you at seven." He promised.

***

"Hey Pop." CJ called, surprised to find his father sitting on the porch when he returned home around six that evening.

"I want to see you and Steph upstairs." Chick told his son, already pushing himself from the large black rocker.

CJ had planned to take a shower, then adjourn to his room and think about his afternoon with Demetria. One look at his father's face told him those plans would have to wait.

Marvin Gaye's soulful mellow crooning filled Stephanie's room as she relaxed on her bed with a thick Agatha Christie novel. She heard a quick knock on the door, before it opened and CJ walked in with their father.

"Sit down." Chick instructed CJ, pointing to the foot of the twin bed Steph occupied.

The teenagers watched their father turn down the music and take a seat on the opposite bed. They watched him intently as he relaxed on the dainty ruffled fuchsia spread.

"Your mother got a call from Ms. Dubois today." He informed the children.

CJ and Steph exchanged quick glances, but offered no response.

"What are you two thinking about? Letting all that hard work go to waste?"

Finally, Stephanie replied. "It's a long story, Daddy."

Chick shrugged. "I have all night."

"Me and Steph decided it was all for the best not to turn the thing in."

Taboo Tree

"Why?" Chick insisted, frowning into the face which was a younger version of his own. "Do y'all prefer F's to A's these days?" He asked, when his prior question went unanswered.

"Aren't we graduating?" Both kids asked in unison.

"What if Ms. Dubois said you weren't?" Chick challenged, his deep voice softly probing. "Would it make you turn in the work?"

CJ and Steph answered the question without saying a word.

"Did ya'll come across something in your research that upset you?"

"Upset us?!" The siblings cried, looking as though they were horrified.

Chick only shrugged, his onyx gaze sliding from one child to the other.

Suddenly Steph pushed the book from her lap and turned to face her father more directly. "Daddy, could you let it go?" She pleaded, her fingers stretched wide. "We started coming up with too many loose ends on the thing and there was no way we'd have it done before the deadline." She declared, her expressive brown eyes widening with desperation.

"Shh...Baby, it's alright." Chick soothed, raising both hands to calm his daughter. When she leaned back against the headboard and bowed her head, he chuckled. "Lord, you are just like my great aunt sometimes." He sighed, closing his eyes as he envisioned the outspoken, humorous, excitable woman. "Miss Lulabay Augustine Godfrey. Did you come across her name in your research?" Chick asked, nodding when the kids smiled.

Chick grinned and folded his hands across the front of his green, short-sleeved sport shirt. "I remember the day I announced to the family that I was marrying Ophelia. It was very important to Auntie Bay Bay that I was truly happy and in love with your mother. She went on to say that she knew what it was like to want a love you could not have and settle for what you did not want."

"Smart woman." CJ couldn't help but remark, as his own situation came to mind.

"Very smart." Chick confirmed. "And very hurt." He added.

"How?" Steph asked.

Again, Chick closed his eyes and rested his head back against the wall. "Your great great aunt was a strong-willed lady. She always said what was on her mind and you could love it or hate it. She really didn't care. I think it was personality more so than her beauty-which was stunning-that really interested most men."

"But she still got hurt?" Stephanie inquired hanging onto her father's every word.

Chick nodded, without opening his eyes. "She got hurt, when she fell in love with the wrong dude."

"Josiah Gwaltney." CJ provided, easily recalling the name from research.

After a while, Chick looked across the room. "Exactly. You see...in those days, the Augustines and Gwaltney's biggest upset was over the land. When Auntie and Josiah got together...Did you two get past my aunt and her...man?"

Steph looked at her brother, and then shook her head at Chick. "We stopped there...too afraid of what we'd find, I guess."

"Well, lemme finish puttin' the pieces together." Chick decided, reaching over to the bookcase and switching off the record player. "Aunt Lula Bay and Josiah realized it couldn't work. Besides the dislike between the families, Josiah was way older than she was. That didn't stop them from enjoying a brief, but productive relationship. My aunt got pregnant and wanted to keep her son James, but knew it would be impossible. She was a child herself. Josiah took the boy, gave him his name and the Gwaltneys raised him. No one knew about the mother. It was to protect my aunt from anyone knowing she'd had a child out of wedlock."

"Then how were we able to find out about your Aunt and Josiah at all?" CJ asked.

Taboo Tree

Chick shrugged. "The Augustines and Gwaltneys have been powerful families in this town a long time. I honestly can't tell you how this all came to be recorded. I didn't even think you two would get so far in your research."

Steph leaned forward. "There's more, isn't there Daddy?"

Chick sighed. "Ressie Augustine-my mother-grew up and fell in love. She didn't know the man she adored was her cousin."

"She fell in love with her Aunt's son?" CJ remarked, his dark eyes widening.

Chick managed a slow grin. "That's right. Like my Aunt, she got pregnant and had me. The family wanted to disown her, but Auntie Lula Bay refused to let them do it. I never knew my father, but those two women raised me better than if I'd had ten daddies."

"Did your dad know about you?" Steph asked, seeing the hurt beginning to cloud her father's face.

"He knew." Chick responded, his voice close to breaking.

CJ raised his hands. "Well, what'd he do?"

"Married another woman. Lauranetta Samuels. I think my mother died a little every day after she heard the news."

"Did they have any kids?" Steph asked.

"Several." Chick confirmed, pinning the kids with an unwavering dark stare. "You two wouldn't know any of their sons, but one. I have a cousin who is also my brother and he lives not ten minutes away."

"Jason Gwaltney." CJ stated, a heavy lump forming at the base of his throat.

Chick only nodded, watching his son and daughter absorb the incredible details of their family's history. The room was silent for several minutes. CJ and Steph were too in awe to speak the questions filling their heads.

"Do the Gwaltneys know about this, Pop?" CJ finally asked.

"Jason does. I don't know about his brothers. I know he's kept it from his wife and kids."

"What about Ma?" Steph asked.

Chick shook his head. "She has no idea."

"Does this mean you understand why we didn't turn in the project?"

"I do." Chick told his son. "And I hope you two understand why we need to keep this quiet?" He cautioned, watching his son and daughter nod in agreement.

Stephanie was leaning forward to ask another question, when a heavy knock sounded on her bedroom door. The frantic, constant rapping was followed by Ophelia's voice.

"Chick! I need you downstairs, now!"

Chick practically leapt from the bed at the sound of his wife's voice. He raced from the room with Stephanie and CJ at his heels.

Downstairs, Amina stood near the front of the living room. Her hazel eyes sparkled with unshed tears as she wrung her hands in nervous fashion. Tavares Gwaltney stood outside on the front porch. He appeared just as uneasy as he peered into the house through the screened door.

"What the hell?..." Chick breathed, his dark eyes narrowing in disbelief as he stepped closer to the door.

Amina raised her hands and stepped in front of her cousin-in-law. "We have a date. Tav's taking me out to dinner." She explained, grimacing when everyone gasped her name.

Ophelia shook her head in disbelief. "Amina...Honey you don't even know this boy."

"I've been seeing him for weeks." Amina softly informed her cousin.

Chick's grin was far from humorous. "Amina, Baby I don't care if you been seein' him for months, we can't let you do this."

"But Chick-" Amina began, her voice catching on his name as sadness overwhelmed her. The tears rolled down her cheeks and her bottom lip trembled uncontrollably.

Tav looked on and wanted to kick himself for causing such a mess. When Amina began to cry loudly, he stepped closer to the screened door.

"Mr. Augustine, it's just dinner-"

"Boy if you don't get the hell off my property." Chick snapped, raising his index finger in Tav's direction. "I don't want you sniffin' around her another minute. You can cancel whatever you had in mind for this girl."

"It wasn't like that, Sir."

"Just get outta here, Tav!" CJ ordered.

"Stop it! Stop it, all of you!" Amina cried, and then raced from the living room with her hands covering her puffy face.

"What the hell are you up to?" Chick whispered his glare clearly suspicious.

"Nothin' I swear it Mr. Augustine." Tav declared, pressing one hand against his stylish olive-green shirt.

"Well, swear it to somebody else, I don't wanna hear it. I don't want to see you back around here again and if I hear 'bout you bothering that girl, it's gonna be your ass." Chick promised, seeing Tav wince at the threat. He did realize he may have been coming down hard on the young man. Unfortunately, the story he'd just told his children, sparked a lot of the hurt and anger he thought he'd buried.

Tav said nothing further and turned to head down the porch steps. The front door closed with a vicious slam and he flinched from the sound that vibrated through his ears. He couldn't wait to reach the privacy of his car, where he planned to bellow his frustrations.

"Tav?" Amina called, just as he was about to settle into the black Impala.

Tav forgot about his anger and rushed over to pull Amina close. "I'm sorry." He whispered, pressing kisses to the baby fine hair along her temple.

Amina shook her head. "It's not your fault. I should've just met you someplace. I knew they'd act like this."

"I'll remember that next time."

"But I want to go out with you tonight." Amina whispered, pulling away to look at him.

Tav could see the tears in her eyes with the help of the moonlight. "Chick'll have my behind if I put you in this car."

"Just go on to the restaurant. I'll meet you there."

Tav frowned, knowing he'd misheard. "Meet me? How?"

Amina shook her head, her expression becoming more hopeful. "Don't worry about it. Just be there."

Tav studied the pretty face in the line of his gaze. He wanted to kiss her terribly, but decided it would have to wait until later.

Amina watched him settle behind the wheel of the car and waved as the Impala tore out of the driveway.

"Amina, Girl what were you thinkin' agreeing to go on a date with that fool?"

"Forget the date, what have you been doin' with him all these weeks?!"

Amina paused on the bottom step and glared at CJ and Stephanie. "Y'all don't know him. So caught up in hating his family, you always think the worst!"

"That's because he is the worst, Amina."

"Steph-"

"She's right." CJ interrupted his handsome face dark with disgust. "Tav Gwaltney is an evil son of a bitch. He's been that way since we known him. If you don't see it now, you will."

Amina refused to listen. She shook her head, the rich brown waves brushing her shoulders as she did so. "Tav always treats me good. We've talked so much and he's told me a lot. He's a good guy and y'all-"

"You know Amina I really ain't tryin' to hear this bullshit." CJ snapped, leaving his sister and cousin at the stairway.

After a moment, Steph followed her brother. Amina raced upstairs to her bedroom.

"Cantone's?"

"Nikos?"

"Hey Amina."

"I hope you're not still mad?"

Nikos chuckled and reclined against the mahogany headboard. "Forget about it. What's happenin'?"

"I need a favor."

"What's goin' on, Amina?" Nikos probed, finally hearing the anxiety in her voice.

Amina smoothed a shaky hand across the red mini-skirt she wore with knee socks and white platforms. Her other hand clutched the receiver so tightly, her palm had turned beet red. "I need to get out of this house. Can you come get me?"

"Amina, what's the problem?"

"Nikos, please!" Amina snapped, almost to the brink of tears again. "Just come get me and I'll explain when you get here."

Nikos was already off the sofa, searching his pockets for keys. "Calm down, alright? I'll be there in a minute."

CJ smiled when he slipped between the bed linens. After his shower, he was finally able to indulge in focusing on the scandalous memories from earlier that day. Scandalous, he thought. That was the perfect description for the day's events. He'd known well before the enlightening discussion with his father, that his actions with Demetria Gwaltney were strictly taboo-in more ways than one. Still, he had already started to have second thoughts about his decision not to see her again. After the ugly scene with Amina and Tav, he realized that the decision was for the best.

"Amina?"

"It's only Nikos, cousin Ophelia." Amina sighed, her hand poised on the brass front door knob.

Ophelia closed the distance between herself and Amina. "Sweetie, we only want you safe. We've known the Gwaltneys a lot longer than you have and all I've ever heard about Tav has been terrible."

"Yes ma'am." Amina conceded, her lashes fluttering out frustration, when Ophelia pressed a kiss to her temple. "We'll be back soon." She called, before leaving the house.

Nikos leaned across the long front seat of his truck and opened the passenger door. He waved to Ophelia as Amina settled onto the beige leather seat.

"Let's get out of here." She grumbled.

"Damn, what the hell happened in there?" Nikos asked, putting the truck into gear.

"A misunderstanding." Amina sighed, leaning back against the headrest.

Nikos shook his head. "I never thought I'd see the day. Everybody in that house gets along like The Brady Bunch."

Amina rolled her eyes. "Hmph. Not when it comes to Tav Gwaltney." She said, staring out into the darkness.

"What's he got to do with it?"

Finally, Amina turned on the seat and pinned her friend with a needy gaze. "I want you to take me to Franklin's Grill. Tav came to pick me up for dinner and they wouldn't even let him past the door."

Nikos slammed on brakes so hard, both he and Amina had to brace their hands against the dashboard. "Please don't tell me you got me out here takin' you to see Tav?"

"Nikos please-"

"Hell no, Amina! Hell no!"

"If you don't take me, I'll just walk." She threatened, her mouth curving down into a pout.

Nikos slammed his hand against the steering wheel and cursed fiercely. "You too smart to be falling for this, Amina."

"Why does everybody figure he's the worst?"

"Because he is and I ain't gonna let you do this."

Amina reached across the seat and squeezed Nikos fist on the steering wheel. "Please." She whispered. Her voice shook as the tears resurfaced.

Nikos turned to stare out the window. The muscle in his jaw twitched erratically as he debated.

"Nikos please." Amina whispered once again.

"Fuck." Nikos groaned, pressing hard on the accelerator and continuing ahead.

Taboo Tree

The ride to Franklin's Grill didn't last long, but Nikos tried his best to persuade his friend to change her mind. Amina would not be swayed. For every reason Nikos gave not to become involved with Tavares Gwaltney, Amina came back with at least two reasons why she wanted to keep seeing him.

"Thanks Nikos." She whispered, when the truck stopped in the front of the restaurant's entrance. "Tav'll bring me home." She said, pressing a quick kiss to his cheek before leaving the truck.

Nikos's fist remained clenched, as he watched her race inside the restaurant. Before driving away, he silently admitted what he'd known for some time. He was falling in love with Amina Davidson.

Tav stood the moment he saw Amina enter the dining room. He expelled a sigh of relief as she made her way towards him.

"You okay?" He asked, concern touching his dark face.

Amina nodded. "I'm fine." She assured him, smiling when he moved to help her into her seat.

"How'd you get here?"

"Nikos brought me."

"Nikos? Cantone?"

"Mmm hmm..."

Tav's steps were slow as he returned to his seat. "I didn't know you knew him like that."

"Oh yeah." Amina lightly replied, her hazel gaze scanning the simple, laminated menu.

Tav wasn't so reassured. "You trust him?" He queried.

Amina finally looked up. "Very much. Nikos has been the best. We don't always agree, but he never acts like he's looking down on me, because I don't see things his way."

Tav didn't have to ask what 'things' Amina was referring to. He figured she'd told Nikos who she was meeting and Tav didn't relish the idea of Nikos Cantone knowing the details of the relationship. Tav would've asked how much she'd confided to the boy, but Amina was already talking too much about her 'friend' for his taste. When the waiter arrived to take their orders, he uttered a silent prayer of thanks.

"So, what are you doing after summer ends?" Tav asked, once their meal of fried chicken sandwiches, fries, coleslaw and sodas had arrived.

Amina set the ketchup aside and shrugged. "Well, I know I don't want to go back to Ohio. Not right away, anyway. I think I'll travel, see the country. I gotta convince my mom to loan me the money, though."

Tav laughed. "Where do you want to go first?" He asked.

"New York." Amina answered without hesitation.

Tav nodded, biting into the mammoth-sized sandwich. "Big place." He noted, amidst his chewing.

"That's what Nikos says. He used to live there, so he knows everything about the place. We talk about it all the time."

Tav groaned, as the subject returned to Nikos Cantone.

"I had fun." Amina whispered, when Tav shut off the lights and engine just down the road from the Augustine house.

Tav shared the sentiment. Despite the rocky start at conversation, the date turned out just as he'd planned.

"I wish I could take you to the door." He whispered, entwining his fingers with hers. A few moments passed in silence, and then Tav leaned across the seat with intentions of placing a simple kiss to Amina's cheek.

She turned, just as his lips brushed her face. Their lips connected in a flurry of sensation. Amina gasped, giving him the opportunity to thrust his tongue deeply into the dark sweetness of her mouth. Tav could tell she had never been kissed before and felt a rush of possessiveness overcome him. He cupped her supple cheek in his palm and groaned into her mouth. Amina's innocence only excited him further and he was at the brink of laying her flat on the front seat, when he stopped himself. Amina was too fine for a quick toss in his car. Surprising himself, he released her and retreated back to the driver's side.

134

"I'll see you tomorrow." He promised. And the day after that, he added.

Amina smoothed her hands across the long-sleeved white, cotton shirt she wore. "Good night, Tav." She replied, slipping out of the car and into the night.

A few more weeks passed with Tav and Amina managing to keep their relationship secret. Nikos, against his strong disapproval, continued to act as the go-between. Transporting Amina to Tav, was killing him. Still, he couldn't deny how happy and alive she seemed. Unfortunately, the nagging voice kept telling him it wouldn't be long before Amina saw Tav Gwaltney's true colors. He could only pray she'd recover from the devastation.

***

Graduation day arrived at last. The Augustine home was alive with conversation, laughter and family. Many relatives flew into town for the festivities. The front yard was filled with cars and children ran throughout the grand backyard; laughing and playing.

A huge breakfast had been planned before commencement and smells of pancakes, muffins, eggs, ham, sausage and steaks intermingled through the house and outside.

Dyna Davidson, Amina's mother had flown in for the exercises as well. Of course, she was more than interested in her daughter's activities during the last few months. Nikos and his father had been invited to the breakfast and Dyna couldn't help but question her cousin about the young man who seemed so taken by Amina.

"He's a sweet young man," Ophelia was saying as she removed the last batch of apple muffins from the oven, "very respectful and smart. He and Amina are just friends, though."

"Thank goodness." Dyna sighed, smoothing one hand beneath her red lounging dress as she took a seat at the table.

Ophelia sent her cousin a wicked look. "What does that mean?"

"The last thing I need or want is to see my only child hooked up with some white man."

Ophelia wasn't surprised by Dyna's candor. She set the muffins aside to cool and leaned against the counter to watch the woman closely. "I hear what you're saying, but Nikos is a very nice young man and much better than the one, the *black* one Amina had her sights set on a few weeks ago."

Dyna waved her hand, beckoning Ophelia to continue. "Details." She ordered, smiling when her cousin took a seat at the table and happily obliged.

***

The Cardman G. Wainwright graduation proved to be the event of the year. Like the Augustines, the Gwaltneys had just as much family attending to see Tavares accept his diploma. Of course, everyone filling the bleachers and seats in the spacious gymnasium, cheered on the new graduates who marched toward the stage in a sea of hunter green and burgundy robes.

"Amina!"

"Nikos!" She cried, running toward her friend with her arms outstretched. She couldn't have been happier for her cousins or all the friends she'd made during her stay in Virginia. Still, as happy as the occasion was, it was also a highly emotional time.

"So this is it, huh? I guess you'll be setting your sights north, soon?"

Nikos shrugged at Amina's assumption. "Actually, I been thinkin' about staying in Virginia."

Amina folded her arms over the front of the gray and white striped dress with flaring sleeves. "You're not serious?"

"What?"

"I mean, you just seemed so excited about going back to New York, is all."

Nikos tapped a commencement program against his palm. "I don't know if it's the right move for me."

Amina's gaze narrowed. "Nikos Cantone are you scared to leave your Daddy?" She teased, joining in when he laughed.

Taboo Tree

"Seriously Nikos, you should go. I know you really want this. Plus, I'll need somebody to go visit when I go up there."

Nikos was still chuckling, when he pulled Amina close and held her tight.

"And he's already been accepted at Hampton!" Jason Gwaltney bellowed as he and his clan surrounded Tav across the crowded gym lobby.

"How you gonna make it without him, Jase?" Cory Gwaltney, one of the cousins, was asking.

"I'll manage." Jason replied, pushing both hands into the deep pockets of his dark trousers. "He'll be working for the business during summer and ready to take over by the time he graduates." He went on to say, the image of a proud father as he clapped his son on the back.

Tav stood next to his father, beaming just as brightly. He had waited a long time to see the man so pleased with him and he wanted to savor the feeling.

Sadly, Tav's serenity was short-lived, when he spotted Amina with Nikos Cantone. His fists clenched reflexively, the rage beginning to simmer deep inside. Luckily, having so much of his family around offering him their best wishes, helped him keep a lid on the rage...and suspicion. Talk of the big dinner to be held later that day in his honor, eventually captured his interest.

Amina never noticed she was being watched. The day had been so hectic and event-filled, she hadn't even thought of Tav. She and Nikos were soon interrupted by Steph, Sweet and a few others. Everyone was in high spirits as they discussed plans for later that day. They all planned to meet back at the Augustines for the big cookout to be held in honor of the graduates.

CJ was making his way through the crowd, when he saw Demetria Gwaltney watching him from a few feet away. She was an entrancing dark angel in a flowing, white empire-waist dress with capped sleeves. Even in the demure, ankle-length creation, he found her as alluring and tempting as that day at the pond.

She captivated CJ so he wanted to go to her regardless of what would be said.

"CJ! CJ Augustine!"

CJ turned and found himself enveloped in a tight hug. The young woman had clamped herself around him like a limpet as she bestowed her best wishes upon him. CJ reciprocated the well-wishes to his fellow graduate, but his thoughts were wholly focused on Demetria. When he looked around, she was gone.

***

The huge crowd was filing out of the gym much later and Tav knew he was moments away from losing his temper. He had tried to ignore Amina with Nikos, but whenever he looked around, they were either hugging, laughing or smiling at one another.

The happy expression illuminating Amina's face only grew brighter when she heard Tav call her name and saw him heading towards her in the parking lot. Thankful to have a moment alone with him, she waved and rushed over to meet her secret boyfriend. Unfortunately, Tav's mood was far from jovial. His handsome face was twisted into something sinister. The hem of his graduation robe whipped around his long legs as his strides quickened.

"What the hell is goin' on with you and that greasy head muthafucka?" He demanded, wrenching Amina's arm into an overpowering grip.

Amina's smile faded as she looked up into the angry face so close to her own. Anxiety filled her hazel eyes as she searched the parking lot for any sign of her family.

"Did you hear what I said?" Tav persisted, giving her arm a warning tug.

"Ta-Tav, my family...we don't need to have them see-"

"I don't give a fuck!"

Amina tried to smother her fear, but it constantly revived itself. Especially, when Tav stepped before her. His wide body completely blocked her view.

"What the hell you doin' with Cantone?"

"Nikos is my friend. I told you-"

"I know what you told me."

"Then why are you being like this?"

"Why the hell he gotta be all over you like that? Why he gotta be touchin' you and shit?"

"He's a friend, Tav. You do know what that is?!" Amina snapped, growing angry despite the pain shooting up her arm. "Or do you only think a girl is only meant to be screwed?"

In response, Tav squeezed Amina's arm more tightly. His strong fingers bit into the soft flesh as he waited for her reaction. When Amina winced and cried out in pain, he let her go and stomped off into the crowd.

Amina tried to massage the ache from her bones, but only seemed to inflict more pain in doing so. All the negative remarks she'd heard about Tav flooded her mind like a tidal wave. She closed her eyes and prayed she wasn't about to see the monster she had been warned of.

TEN

Minerva stabbed her fork into the mound of fluffy yellow scrambled eggs. Her dark eyes were focused out the window in the master bedroom, where she and Jason decided to enjoy breakfast that morning.

"Well, what do you think is wrong with her?" She asked.

Jason spoke through a mouthful of eggs, steak and buttered toast. "Baby, please. Nothin' goin' on with that girl."

Minerva shook her head. "Sometimes you can be so blind when it comes to those kids." She accused, turning to glare at her husband.

"What's got you so riled? The girl always keeps to herself, she's always quiet." Jason pointed out, wiping his mouth with the gray cloth napkin tucked into the collar of his striped shirt.

Minerva shook her head, the curls in her high ponytail dancing wildly. "Something's different." She pointed out.

"Minnie-"

"Soon as we got home after graduation, she ran upstairs and locked herself in her room. She didn't even come down for Tav's dinner."

Jason leaned across the cozy round table and reached for the silver coffeepot. "You want me to talk to her, Minnie?"

Minerva slapped Jason's hand and poured the coffee instead. "Don't even waste your time. The child will only bat her eyes at you and say 'nothing Daddy' and you'll leave it at that." She predicted, setting the shiny pot aside. "I'll talk to her after breakfast."

***

Amina walked into the kitchen just as the phone rang. She was so on edge from the day before she actually jumped at the sound.

Ophelia was removing a tray of cinnamon toast from the oven and looked over her shoulder. "Baby, would you answer that for me, please?"

Amina took a quick, deep breath before lifting the receiver off the white wall phone. "Augustines." She greeted.

"Amina?"

"Why are you calling me here?!" She whispered panic filling her eyes when she looked to see if Ophelia was near.

"I have to apologize for yesterday." Tav told her, his deep voice sounding strong yet anxious. "Amina?" He called, when she offered no response.

"Go on."

"Baby I'm sorry and I want to tell you that in person."

"I don't think so."

"Amina please. I was way out of line and I can't expect you to believe that, unless I can say it in person...Please?"

Amina's every instinct screamed that she decline Tav's urgent request and write him off as a bad dating choice. Unfortunately, Tav's persistence and the fact that Ophelia was right across the room pushed her to make a quick decision.

"Alright. When and where?"

"Our spot in the garden. Come now."

Amina replaced the receiver, and then rested her forehead against it.

"Honey, have a seat. I'm about to set out breakfast." Ophelia called.

Amina smoothed her hands across her bare arms and shook her head. "I don't really feel like anything right now."

Ophelia propped one hand on her hip. "You okay?"

Dyna walked into the kitchen and heard the question. Immediately, her narrow light brown eyes focused in on her daughter. "You alright, Baby?" She asked, walking over to press the back of her hand against Amina's forehead.

Amina nodded, absently wiping her wet palms against the back of her green shorts. "I think I'm gonna take a walk before I eat anything."

Dyna and Ophelia exchanged glances when Amina practically ran out the back door. They were both more than a little suspicious.

"What's happening', Pop?" CJ greeted, when he caught up with the man headed downstairs.

"Goin' to get some of this breakfast 'fore it's all gone." Chick teased.

"I heard that." CJ replied, also on his way to the kitchen.

"I did want to ask you something, though." Chick called, brushing his son's shoulder.

CJ stopped on the stairway and turned. "Shoot Pop."

Chick propped both hands on his hips, slipping his fingers through the belt loops of his gray tweed trousers. He seemed to be debating on how to approach the subject. "You'll be starting college in the fall and I know this summer's gonna be pretty hectic with all the social events."

"Yeah..." CJ agreed, folding his arms across his Giants T-shirt and watching the man closely.

"I know you'll want to have fun and all that," Chick continued, "but I'd like you to consider spending some time at the business. It's no secret I want you to take over one day."

CJ nodded and tried to hide his smile. He had never seen his father so uneasy and felt proud that the man thought enough of him to want him aboard. "That sounds good, Pop. I been wanting to ask if I could work at the company during the summer, anyway."

"You were?" Chick queried, CJ's interest almost rendering him speechless. "Are you sure you want to work like that this summer? You'll be missin' out on a lot of parties, you know?"

"I appreciate the warnin', Dad. But, I don't really care 'bout that." CJ said, his voice dropping an octave as thoughts of Demetria filtered his mind.

Chick was more than a little impressed by his son's mature attitude. He dared not say anything and embarrass the boy, though. Instead, he patted CJ's shoulder and they continued on downstairs.

Minerva braced herself and knocked lightly on Demetria's door. Lately, she didn't know how to approach her own daughter, but vowed that would not stop her from trying. Over the weeks, she had seen Demetria withdraw into an even tighter shell. Minerva was more than a little afraid of what she would discover. After her knock went unanswered, Minerva tried the doorknob. A smile came to her lips when she found that Demetria hadn't locked it.

"Deme?" She called, finding the room empty.

At first, silence answered her greeting. Then, the sound of coughing and something else rose in the air.

"Deme?" Minerva called again, stepping further into the room. Clutching the hem of her purple floral print lounging dress in one hand, she followed the tortured sounds to the private bathroom. There, she found Demetria hugging the commode amidst an attack of coughing and vomiting.

"Jesus!" Minerva cried, running into the room. She fell to her knees next to Demetria and threaded her fingers through the girl's thick, sweat-drenched hair.

"Let it all out, Baby." She instructed, holding Deme's hair away from her face until the vomiting ceased to dry heaves.

"Thank you, Mama." Demetria whispered her voice barely audible.

"Can you stand?" Minerva asked, feeling Demetria brace against her as she tried. It was useless and the girl settled back to her knees, shaking her head slowly.

Taboo Tree

Minerva pressed a kiss to her daughter's cheek. "Come on." She softly urged, helping Demetria out of the bathroom and back into bed. She watched the child's eyes close the instant her head touched the pillow.

"Sweetie, how long have you been this way?"

"Something I ate." Demetria excused, turning her head into the pillow.

"But you haven't eaten anything. Not today or the day before."

Demetria used the sleeve of her white cotton nightgown to wipe the sweat from her forehead. "That's probably it then, Ma. I didn't eat, that's probably why I'm sick."

Minerva was far from convinced, but could see her daughter wasn't up for discussion. Instead, she cleaned the bathroom and helped Demetria change gowns.

"I'll be back to check on you." Minerva promised, pressing a soft kiss to her daughter's cheek.

Downstairs bustled with activity as usual. Minerva looked around for about ten minutes, until she located Sally Royal the head housekeeper.

"Something you need, Child?" Sally asked her kind brown eyes wide with concern.

Minerva patted the older woman's hand and smiled. "Just a question, Miss Sally. It's about the laundry duties over the last month."

"Yes?" Sally replied, her easy expression growing a bit more serious.

"Who was in charge of laundry then?"

"Has the staff been doing a poor job?" Sally asked, the tone of her voice meaning she was ready to reprimand them.

Minerva began to wave her hands quickly. "It's nothing like that. I only want to know who's been taking care of Demetria's clothes. I want to make sure that child is on time getting dirty things to the staff. She's been very moody lately and you have to stay on these girls, you know?"

"Amen." Sally concurred, tapping her index finger against her chin as she thought. "Let's see...last month...that would have been Kathy Bismarck handling laundry."

"Thanks Miss Sally." Minerva whispered, squeezing the woman's hand once, before she hurried off.

Minerva checked her watch. She knew Kathy usually took a few minutes to speak with her husband Julius around that time. She found the woman waving off her husband as he headed back to the stables.

Kathy smoothed one hand across her sleek chignon and turned. "Miss Minerva!" She gasped, her eyes widening when she saw her boss standing there. "Miss Minerva, I'm sorry. Julius was just-"

"Oh Honey, please." Minerva cut in with a wave of her hand. "You don't need to explain a thing." She assured, pulling the woman aside. "I have something to ask you." She whispered.

"Yes ma'am?"

"Has Demetria been getting her laundry to you on time?"

Kathy took a small step back. "Her laundry?"

"I only want to make sure she's doing what she's supposed to."

"Oh ma'am she is." Kathy quickly replied, her hands clasped across her chest. Slowly though her gaze clouded with the slightest uncertainty.

Minerva saw it. "Something you want to tell me?"

Kathy chewed her bottom lip almost a minute before she answered. "I did wonder about something...Demetria was only giving me her clothes."

"Mmm hmm."

Kathy could see Minerva wasn't grasping her meaning and stepped closer. "Demetria only gave me clothes. I never washed any of her under things. Especially the ones she wears during her menstruation. I usually bleach them, but I haven't done so for going on two months now. I didn't ask her about it, because I thought maybe...she was getting embarrassed over me handling something so personal."

Minerva closed her eyes, fearing that her suspicions were credible.

"Miss? You alright?" Kathy whispered.

Minerva could barely manage a nod as she turned and blindly headed back towards the house.

This is a bad idea girl. A bad idea! Amina began to chant the phrase the closer she came to the secluded garden. It would be best to end things, she knew that. She had been telling herself that very thing since she raced out of the house. Tav's attitude at graduation made her afraid of him for the first time since they'd met. Still, she ignored it. She ignored it, because Tav said he wanted to apologize.

"Oh girl, is it worth it? Is he worth it?" She sighed, wishing there were someone she could completely confide in.

When Amina reached the clearing, all doubts left her mind. She found Tav already waiting. He paced slowly back and forth. His handsome dark face was a picture of concentration. Amina watched him for a while and convinced herself the boy was definitely worth it.

"Tav?" She whispered.

Tav stopped pacing and was by Amina's side in an instant. He cupped her lovely cinnamon-toned face in his huge palms and favored her mouth and neck with soft kisses. "I'm sorry...I'm so sorry. I had no right to treat you that way. I swear I'm sorry."

Amina's heart thudded uncontrollably, her lashes fluttering as kisses showered across her eyes and brow. "Why did you act that way?" She moaned.

Tav pressed his forehead against hers and squeezed his eyes shut. "I go wild when I see you talkin' to other guys," he admitted, "especially Nikos."

Amina squeezed his hands. "But we're just friends. That's all it's ever been. You can't keep doing this." She urged, though in the far corners of her mind, she found it exciting that he was jealous. Emotion ruling her actions, she stood on her toes and kissed him.

Tav was affected at once. His arms slid around Amina's tiny waist and he held her high against his muscular form. His tongue thrust past her lips and he kissed her with explicit thoroughness.

Amina gasped and moaned beneath the possessive kiss. She was so overwhelmed by Tav's expert touch she barely noticed that he had settled her to the soft, sun-bleached grass. She shivered from the sensuous feelings firing through her body, and smoothed her fingers across the collar of his blue shirt.

Tav added more pressure to the kiss as his hand toyed with the hem of the green and blue striped top Amina wore. When his hand slipped beneath the garment to stroke the lacy edge of her bra, she knew it was time to call a halt to the scene.

"Tav...wait..."

"Mmm mmm."

"Yes Tav." Amina softly insisted, trying to ease his hand away from her breasts.

Tav's fingers were already caressing the gentle swell of one breast. His arousal was more than evident as he began to simulate vague thrusting motions with his hips.

"No Tav." Amina resisted, this time using the most firm tone she could muster.

Tav raised his head and looked down into her wide eyes. The innocence and sensuality combined in the stunning hazel gaze urged him to wait. Instinct told him she was a virgin and he knew it would be well worth the wait to indulge in the untested sweetness.

"I'm sorry." Amina whispered, her voice cracking on the last word as she watched him move away.

Tav helped her stand, and then cupped her chin between his fingers. "Don't apologize to me. It's okay." He soothed, brushing his mouth against her temple.

That day, Amina fell a little more in love with Tavares Gwaltney.

***

Stephanie selected another slice of the gooey cheese pizza she shared with Sweet.

"I don't get it, Steph." Sweet admitted, between mouthfuls of pizza. "We're going to college. You know how much freedom that means?"

"But we're going to different schools." Steph reminded her boyfriend, her pretty face a picture of sadness. "How's that gonna affect us?" She asked.

"Why are you worried about this?" Sweet asked, pinning his girlfriend with a confused glare.

"You want Hampton. Obviously, you're not interested in leaving Virginia."

"Well, what do you have in mind?" Sweet asked, folding his arms across the blue and red striped shirt he wore.

Steph's brown gaze faltered. "I want Howard."

"In D.C.?!"

"You know another?"

"Damn." Sweet sighed, his long brows tugged close into a frown. "I didn't think you wanted to go so far."

"It's not that far." Steph replied, her laughter coming forth.

Finally, Sweet shrugged and reached for another slice of pizza. "I guess a change wouldn't be so bad."

Steph's eyes widened. "What are you tryin' to say?" She asked, fiddling with the bamboo earrings dangling from her lobes.

Sweet uttered a short laugh, but didn't bother to look up. "If you think I'm letting you out of my sight Stephanie Augustine, you crazy."

Suddenly, happier than she'd been in weeks, Steph giggled and slid around to Sweet's side of the booth. She threw her arms around his neck and began to shower his neck and face with kisses.

Sweet could only laugh. "Lord girl, is it that big a thing for you to get out of VA?"

Stephanie eased away and sent the boy an exasperated look. "You have no idea how ready I am to get out of this place."

"What the hell for? I mean, hell Steph you got that big house, cool parents, what-"

"I know where you're comin' from." She admitted, moving back to her side of the booth. "But, do you ever have a feeling that no matter how good things are goin', something's about to go down? Something bad? And you want to be as far away from it as possible?"

"Jesus, Steph." Sweet sighed, more than a little concerned by her solemn words and expression.

Stephanie reached across the table and held her boyfriend's hand in a tight grasp.

***

"I appreciate this, Seymour. I know how hard it is to make house calls on such short notice."

Dr. Seymour Robinson smiled as he followed Minerva Gwaltney upstairs. "Don't give it a thought. I'm always happy to help out an old friend. What exactly is wrong with Demetria?" He asked, scratching his balding head.

"You mean, besides the mood swings and the vomiting?" Minerva queried.

Seymour switched his medical bag to the other hand and shrugged. "How's she been eating? Has she been getting enough sleep?"

"There hasn't been anything out of the normal on that end. She usually eats quite good and she spends so much time in her room that I'm sure she's getting more than enough rest."

"Have her cycles been regular?"

The simple question made Minerva halt her ascent up the stairs. "I honestly don't know." She admitted, bowing her head.

Seymour touched her arm. "Minerva?" He called, fixing her with a pointed look.

"Oh Seymour, I really don't know." Minerva cried, slapping her hands to her thighs. "I began to suspect when I found her vomiting. I even checked with my maid who told me Demetria hasn't been putting her under things-her menstrual things especially-in with everything else to be washed."

Seymour could see how affected Minerva was becoming. He decided against asking any more questions. Instead, he patted Minerva's hand and they continued upstairs.

Demetria could barely lift her head from the pillow, when her mother walked into the bedroom with Dr. Robinson. The dizziness and foul bile rose in the back of her throat the instant she moved.

"Hello Demetria!" Seymour greeted, setting his hat and bag to the white and gold nightstand next to the brass canopy bed. "I hear you're feeling a little under the weather. Can't have a pretty girl like you cooped up in her room all day, can we?"

"Do you need anything, Seymour?" Minerva called, still standing just inside the room.

Seymour smiled his kind brown eyes warm and reassuring. "We're fine, Minerva. Just give me and this young lady a few minutes alone."

"She didn't have to bother you with this." Demetria told the doctor when the door closed behind Minerva.

"Your mama's concerned Demetria and she wasn't bothering me. I'm a doctor, you know?"

Demetria couldn't manage a smile over the doctor's teasing remark.

"It'll pass soon. I just have to give it a while." She told him.

Surprised by her words, Seymour chuckled. "And how can you be so sure?"

Demetria closed her eyes. "It always passes after a while."

"Have you seen another doctor?" Seymour asked, intrigued by her confidence.

"No."

"Then, how do you-"

"I read, Doctor Robinson." She replied, her voice sounding firm for the first time that day.

Seymour unbuttoned his white, cotton suit coat and folded his arms over his chest. "And what has your reading told you?"

AlTonya Washington

"That this is common...and temporary."
"This?"
"Morning sickness."
"Demetria-"
"Doctor Robinson, I'm pregnant."

ELEVEN

"**B**oy! You keep on like this, I'm gonna be retirin' early!" Jason bellowed, as he and Tav walked in the house later that evening.

Father and son brought life into the unusually quiet house. They talked loudly and laughed boisterously. Unfortunately, the lightheartedness was about to fade.

"Jason!" Minerva roared, as she ran out into the living room.

Jason tossed his suit coat to the white high-backed sofa. "Woman, lemme tell you about our boy today."

"Jason, I can't discuss that now." Minerva interrupted, raising one hand alongside her face. "Tav Baby, excuse your Daddy and me a minute, alright?"

"'Kay Ma." Tav replied, his expression suspicious as he watched his mother pull his father out to the porch.

Jason was frowning furiously. "Jesus Min-"

"I called Doctor Robinson today to see Demetria." She announced.

Jason pointed his index finger towards his wife's dark, lovely face. "You keep on botherin' that girl she's gonna end up resenting you." He predicted.

Minerva caught Jason's index finger and squeezed it. "She's pregnant."

"Woman are you touched?" Jason snapped, watching Minerva as though she were a stranger. "You said Seymour came out here? He didn't take the girl to his office to check her out, so how do you-"

"She told him from her own lips." Minerva replied, her gaze unwavering while she looked up to judge Jason's reaction. "Of course, we need to take her in for the proper tests, but-"

"What?!" Jason roared, as though the full meaning of Minerva's words had finally hit him.

Minerva ended her recount of the day's events as Jason's voice vibrated in her ears. He looked ready to murder someone.

"Who's responsible for this?" He growled.

"I haven't had a chance to talk to her yet. Seymour gave her something to help her sleep."

The screen door hit the outside of the house with a loud thwack when Jason stormed inside. Minerva was upset, but her mood was no match to her husband's.

"Baby, be easy with her." She urged.

"Easy?!" Jason thundered.

Upstairs, the den door opened a crack and Tav peeked out. "What's happenin', y'all?"

"Get back in there!" Jason ordered and his son wasted no time obeying.

Jason could vaguely imagine the intimidating sight he made storming through the house bellowing like a mad man. He rarely raised his voice or appeared upset. However, this was different. He had two daughters and the reality of a man spoiling either of them, had him blindly enraged.

Jason and Minerva stopped before the closed door of their daughter's bedroom. The clenched fist Jason held, relaxed and he laid his palm flat against the door, before entering. The moment he saw Demetria lying sprawled in her bed, he covered his face with both hands-his emotions taking over.

Minerva steeled herself from comforting her husband. She decided it was best to remain in the shadows for the time being.

"Deme?" Jason called his baritone voice surprisingly soft.

Demetria turned onto her back and managed a watery smile. "Hey Daddy."

The innocent tone melted Jason's anger towards his little girl. In a few short strides, he closed the distance between them and sat on the edge of the bed.

"Who did this to you?" He whispered, gathering Demetria's pliant form in his arms.

"I don't know."

"What do you mean you don't know?" Minerva blurted, turning away when Jason glared at her.

Demetria looked away, burying her face more deeply into her father's chest. "I was raped."

Despite their daughter's muffled voice, her parents heard every word.

***

"I can't believe you got all this done by nine thirty AM."

Dyna's smile reflected pure pride. "With the way these people eat around here, I knew I had to get in here and get down to business. Besides, I had to give you a chance to rest yourself." She told her pregnant cousin.

Ophelia braced her elbow against the table and smoothed her hand across the multi-colored silk scarf covering her head. "I really appreciate it, then. I sure can't get none of these folk to crack out the pots and pans."

"Hey." A wounded Stephanie argued from her position at one end of the table where she fed Derric and Cameo.

Someone knocked on the back door then and everyone called for them to come in.

"Trouble at the Gwaltneys!" Nikos announced, when he stepped past the door.

Chick and CJ looked up from their business conversation. "What happened?" Chick asked.

"Roy, one of their field guys, had his truck to breakdown in front of the store. I gave him a ride to this side, this morning." Nikos explained. "When we got there, the fuzz was everywhere and one of Roy's co-workers told him to step right 'cause Jason Gwaltney was actin' like a crazy man."

Chick was standing now. His arms were folded over his silver blue suit coat, his feet spread in a confrontational stance. "Nikos, what happened?" He asked again.

"His daughter, Demetria, got raped."

CJ dropped the folder he held. The only sound in the kitchen were the pages slipping to the floor.

"When?" Steph asked.

"Who did it?" Ophelia wanted to know.

"Have the police arrested anybody?" Chick queried.

"I can't believe this," Steph sighed, taking the cereal bowls to the sink, "Demetria Gwaltney never goes anywhere. Did somebody grab her last night?"

"Hold up, Steph. Hold up." Nikos urged, waving his hands around his head. "This mess happened a while back. The girl is pregnant. When her father found out she told 'em she was raped."

The kitchen grew noisy at once, as everyone began talking. CJ could do nothing but close his eyes and hold his head in his shaking hands. His heart threatened to beat from his chest, as he listened to the conversation.

"...I tell ya, the man wants some heads to roll." Nikos was saying."

"They have any suspects?" Chick asked.

Nikos accepted a glass of orange juice from Dyna and leaned against the counter. "Since Demetria never goes out anywhere, they're thinkin' maybe one of the field hands or somebody close to the property. Nobody's said anything."

Conversation rose again as everyone relayed their own ideas about what happened. No one noticed CJ leaving the room. He raced upstairs to his bathroom and placed his head beneath the cold water faucet.

***

Sheriff Marvin Tennyson and his deputy Leroy Childers sat clutching their glasses of lemonade-afraid to move. Their eyes were trained on the huge man who paced the living room.

"I want blood, dammit!" Jason raged, his dark face twisted into a sinister scowl.

"Jason, why don't you calm down here?" Deputy Childers suggested.

"I want every man in this town questioned!" Jason demanded.

Sheriff Tennyson cleared his throat. "That list includin' your own men?"

"Especially them." Jason growled.

Tennyson removed his gray wide-brimmed hat and wiped his bald red scalp with a handkerchief. "Jason, ain't it jus' possible the girl coulda been molested by one of her schoolmates. Maybe there's a boyfriend-someone she don't want y'all to know 'bout?"

"My daughter ain't no slut." Jason whispered, his dark eyes narrowing towards the Sheriff's red, weather beaten face.

"Jason, I didn't mean-"

"Just get off your white asses and find the muthafucka who did this!"

The Sheriff and Deputy exchanged quick glances, before setting their glasses aside and standing.

"We'll be back with someone to take the child's statement." Sheriff Tennyson decided. "We'll find the bastard, Jason." He promised.

Tav had waited until the policemen left, before he went into the dining room. "Poppa?" He called, unused to seeing his father slumped over when he sat down. "You alright?"

Jason shook his head. "I just don't understand how this could happen. Deme is a good girl. She never goes anywhere, she ain't flirtatious." His fist hit his palm with a loud smack. "The man who did this pays for it...with his life."

In the kitchen, the cooks were huddled together discussing the morning's events. No one could believe it had happened and everyone speculated as to who the culprit was. Kathy Bismarck was quiet, her round dark eyes focused out towards the pond.

Minerva moved back and forth in the huge white rocking chair facing Demetria's bed. She prayed her daughter's rapist would be brought to justice, but there was still a nagging suspicion that something didn't calculate.

The covers moved as Demetria turned over in bed. Minerva could hear her groan softly as she awakened. When the girl looked into her eyes, she scooted the rocking chair closer.

"Demetria, we need to talk, Honey."

"Mommy...I'm too tired."

"Well, I'm sorry about that, but you've been asleep since yesterday afternoon." Minerva pointed out, rolling up the sleeves to her green blouse. "Now, I need you to tell me what happened. When and how and where."

Demetria rolled her head across the pillow. "I can't...I don't remember."

"Well, you better start trying." Minerva advised, leaning back in the rocking chair again. "The police are gonna be back here soon to take a statement from you."

"The police?" Demetria gasped, pushing herself up in the tangled bed. "A statement?"

"Baby, I hope you didn't just expect us to let this go?"

"Well, no...but-"

"Your Daddy's having everybody questioned over this."

Demetria began to rub her hands across her arms as though she were chilled. The long-sleeves of the pink cotton nightgown were no use against the cold rushing through her.

Minerva could see her daughter was shaken and it only made her more suspicious. It made her sick to think her own child would lie about something so horrid.

"Demetria, why? Why didn't you come to us the day this happened? Or why didn't you at least tell Tav about it?"

In response, Deme bowed her head and traced the raised pattern in her bedspread.

Minerva shook her head and stood. "You know Deme, I've known women who've been raped." She said, pushing the chair back to its corner. "The last thing many of them want is to hide it, especially if a child is in the picture. Nine times out of ten, they want to get rid of it. You were determined to keep this from us and I can't understand why? If you had no consent."

Demetria finally raised her head. "What are you trying to say?" She asked, her dark eyes narrowing to the thinnest slits.

Minerva headed to the bedroom door. "Just an observation, Dear." She replied, her hand curved around the doorknob. "I pray to God you're telling the truth about this."

Demetria watched her mother leave. Then, alone in the room, she drew her knees to her chin and hugged herself.

"'He grabbed me while I was walking home from the library. I didn't recognize him. He told me he wasn't from here when I asked if he knew who my father was. He said he was from out of town. That's all I remember.'"

"And that's it." The secretary announced, placing the clipboard across her lap.

Sheriff Tennyson frowned toward the perky, blonde woman before looking over at Jason and Minerva.

"She couldn't remember what he looked like?" Jason asked, a confused frown plastered to his face.

Michelle Kenny nodded once, looking confused as well. "That was it, Mr. Gwaltney. She couldn't even tell me if he'd worn a mask. When I asked her where it happened, she said 'in the woods'."

"Is any of this enough to go on?" Minerva asked.

The Sheriff's expression was not hopeful. "It's highly unlikely that we'll find the guy after so long a time. Especially with such sketchy details."

"Dammit!" Jason bellowed, slamming his fist the mahogany coffee table. "Look here Marvin, I don't care what y'all got to go on. I want somebody's head and I want it fast!"

Marvin knew that was a long-shot, but he chose to keep silent in light of Jason's temper. Instead, he and his staff said their goodnights and left. Minerva showed them out of the house, and then turned to watch her husband with concerned eyes.

In the days that followed, the police did their best to investigate the mysterious crime. Needless to say, their efforts went unrewarded. They did their best to question employees of the estate as well as people in the vicinity of the library.

In that time, Jason Gwaltney grew to be more of a tyrant. Gone was the gentle giant his employees loved. The staff practically walked on eggshells when the man was around. Even the relationship with his wife was strained.

***

"And a tuna sandwich on wheat with heavy mayo. Can I bring y'all anything else?"

Kathy Bismarck looked expectant as she turned her gaze toward her husband. When he shook his head, she smiled and waved toward the waitress. "Thanks, Nicole."

"Kat, why you puttin' yourself through this?" Julius asked, once the waitress walked away from their booth.

Kathy shook her head while cutting into the sandwich. "I just think that little girl had more goin' on down there by that pond than reading and enjoying the view."

"She's a quiet girl. Maybe that is all she was doin'." Julius decided, speaking through a mouthful of his cheeseburger.

"I don't think Minerva believes she was raped, either."

"How do you know?" Jason asked, eyeing his wife closely.

Kathy's plump shoulders rose beneath her plum shirt. "Minerva came to me one day, asking about the laundry. Whether Demetria was getting her things to me."

"So?"

"I think she wanted to know if the girl was having her periods."

"Kaaat..." Julius groaned, acting as though he were disgusted.

"Shh.." She admonished, unable to hide the smile from the round face. "Anyway, I think the woman believes Demetria was doing something...disrespectful that got her in that condition."

Julius' handsome face registered interest, his wide dark eyes growing a bit narrowed.

"I think I should tell 'em about the pond."

"You think it'll do any good?" Julius asked his tone skeptical.

Kathy leaned back against the booth, disbelief filling her eyes. "You must've forgotten how tense things have been at the Gwaltneys. Hell Julius, what we know could shed some light...on the truth."

***

"Hey Boy!" Steph called, sticking her head just inside CJ's room. She forced the concern from her eyes and tried to put on a happy face. "What'cha doin' cooped up in here?" She probed, waltzing into the spacious poster-lined room. "You're usually out playing ball or somethin'." She added.

In response, CJ gave a heavy sigh and moved out of the black armchair next to the stereo. Obviously, he wanted to be alone.

Stephanie ignored it of course, and plopped down onto his four poster maple bed. "Please talk to me, C. You're going through something and I wanna help."

"Damn Steph, just cause I ain't talkin' to your ass, you think somethin's up?" CJ snapped, folding his arms over his chest as he glared out the window.

"Well, you haven't talked to Nikos and Sweet either and they're concerned too."

CJ offered only a shrug and nothing more.

Steph refused to give up. She turned onto her back and relaxed in the middle of the bed. "Well since you're so grouchy, maybe my news can cheer you up. Sweet said he was gonna try getting into Howard too. That way we can be together. I think it'll work since his grades are so good. He's already applied, so all we have to do is watch the mail and-"

"Demetria Gwaltney wasn't raped."

The lone statement sounded hollow amidst Steph's rambling, but she heard every word. Still, she asked CJ to repeat himself.

"She wasn't raped."

"CJ-"

"I got her pregnant."

"CJ what the hell are you saying?" Steph gasped, kneeling in the center of her brother's bed.

"I used to go out and watch her on the weekends. That's why I was never around to help much with the project." He said, turning to pin Steph with a rueful dark stare. "I wanted her for weeks and then, one day...we did it."

Steph toyed with the wide white belt around her yellow jumpsuit. She could barely think with all the questions running through her mind.

"CJ, why would she cause all this commotion telling everybody she was raped?"

The look in CJ's deep-set eyes changed to something much more solemn and Steph closed her eyes.

"Does she know about our families?"

"She doesn't know about all that. We were only together that one day, but I know the kid is mine. When I told her we couldn't have sex again, I know she took it hard."

"Hard enough to sleep with somebody else?" Steph asked in a tiny voice.

CJ rubbed his hand over his soft hair. "I don't think so. The times I seen her since, I could tell she was still hung up on me."

"CJ do you know what a big chance you took?"

"Damn Steph, I know." CJ snapped, taking a seat on the far corner of the bed. "But I think she wants to keep it a secret as much as I do."

Steph fiddled with a lock of her glossy hair and chewed her bottom lip. "Are you sure nobody say y'all together?" She finally asked.

CJ scratched his head, his wide mouth curving into a grimace. "We were careful enough." He sighed.

Steph lowered her eyes to the black bedspread. Careful, maybe. But, stuff like this always comes out. She silently added.

***

"Baby are you comin' to bed soon?" Minerva called to Jason who sat in his rocker overlooking the estate from their bedroom balcony. When he offered no response to her question, she pushed herself off the doorjamb and went to him.

"What is it?" She whispered, pressing a soft kiss against his shaved head. He didn't need to answer, really. Minerva knew what happened to Demetria was killing him. It broke her heart too because she knew he believed he was a failure for not protecting his own daughter against such a horror. She stood behind the chair, massaging his broad shoulders, until the phone interrupted the moment. Reluctantly, she went to answer.

"Yes? Minerva Gwaltney here."

"Ms. Minerva? This is Kathy Bismarck."

Taboo Tree

TWELVE

"**A**re you sure?" Minerva whispered, once Kathy had cleared her conscience.

"Yes ma'am." Was the soft reply, followed by a silence which lasted almost three minutes. "I hope I'm not out of line, Miss." Kathy added, before clearing her throat.

Minerva shook her head after a moment's hesitation. "It's no problem, Sweetie. Thanks for calling. Goodnight."

"Who was that?" Jason asked, walking into the bedroom a few minutes after Minerva hung up the phone.

"Kathy Bismarck."

"Mmm." Jason absently replied, as he got comfortable beneath the crisp, green sheets on the four poster maple bed.

Minerva removed her powder blue chenille robe and slipped between the sheets. "She wanted to talk about Deme."

"What about her?" Jason asked his eyes closed.

Minerva inhaled deeply before continuing. She twisted the frilled edge of the sheet as she anticipated Jason's reaction. "She told me that she and Julius have seen Deme at the pond. They didn't know if she was meeting someone or just enjoying the view. Kathy thought it might help to mention they'd seen her there."

"Minnie..." Jason groaned and covered his face with his hands. "Why does that blasted pond always wind up hurtin' our babies?"

"So you believe Kathy?" Minerva asked, flipping onto her stomach to stare down at her husband.

"It would fit." Jason admitted, pulling his hands from his face. "I still can't accept Deme would lie about something like that."

Minerva's dark eyes grew darker with suspicion. "She might lie if she was expecting a man to meet her."

"You think the girl's that convincing, Minnie?" Jason asked, his deep voice filled with disbelief.

"I hate to think that way, Baby. But, I admit I suspected something foul long before she cried rape."

Jason couldn't admit to his wife that same concern had crossed his mind once. He and Minerva discussed their troubled daughter for the better part of the night. They decided to confront the child first thing the next morning.

***

Nikos honked his truck horn around 7AM the next morning. He and Sweet waited until they saw Steph come to her door and wave at them. The group had decided to take a daylong trip to the beach.

"Where's CJ?" Sweet asked his girlfriend when he and Nikos stepped into the Augustine home.

"Upstairs." Steph replied, casting an anxious look towards the ceiling. She had suggested the outing in hopes of drawing her older brother out of his mood. "I hope he won't back out." She whispered.

Nikos walked on ahead to the kitchen where he found Amina sitting the table for breakfast. His pitch black gaze lit up when he saw her. His heart soared at the fact that she would be joining them that day.

"Hey Nikos." Amina greeted, when she looked up from her task and found him approaching the table.

"How you doin', Amina?" Nikos asked, her vibrant expression already providing him with an answer.

"Can't you guess?" She replied, practically gliding to the refrigerator for orange juice.

Nikos managed to keep the weak smile plastered to his face. Deep down, he hoped Amina's excitement had a little to do with him, but he knew better.

"What's happenin' y'all?!" CJ bellowed, when he arrived downstairs and found the group in the kitchen.

"You cool?" Steph queried when she pulled CJ aside.

CJ nodded. "Thanks for doin' this, Steph."

"Believe me I didn't do it just for you." Steph playfully replied, tossing her hair with more flamboyance than necessary. "We're gonna have some fun! Right y'all?!" She called, laughing at the group's enthusiastic confirmation.

***

Tav sat on the edge of his sister's bed and squeezed her hand between both of his. He had avoided talking with her until some of the commotion settled.

"I couldn't tell anyone, Tav. I wish you could understand that." Demetria whispered. She knew Tav was hurting by her secrecy. It was very important for him to be the great protector.

"Did you think I'd look down on you or somethin'?" Tav asked, his brows drawn close in confusion.

Demetria shook her head and covered Tav's hand with her own. "I was ashamed."

Tav nodded, realizing how much his sister must still be hurting. "You remember anything else...about it?" He asked, watching Deme shake her head.

The bedroom door opened then, drawing an end to the conversation.

"We need to talk to your sister alone, Boy." Jason announced, when he and Minerva walked into the room.

Deme didn't like the look on her parent's faces and squeezed her brother's hand. "Can he stay?" She meekly requested.

"I don't mind." Tav replied.

Jason's expression did not soften. "Out, Boy." He ordered, without looking in his son's direction.

Tav cast a quick glance at Minerva, but she said nothing. Rolling his eyes toward the ceiling, he stomped from the bedroom. Deme's wide dark gaze followed him and she wished she were leaving as well. She watched her father take a seat on one side of the bed, her mother occupying the other side.

"Deme, have you been going out to the Augustine pond?"

"The...pond?"

Minerva leaned a bit closer to her daughter. "That's what I said." She whispered.

"We already know the truth." Jason announced, when he saw the girl's gaze falter. "Don't make it worse by lying." He advised.

"Do you remember us forbidding you kids from going out there?" Minerva asked, her pretty face twisted by a frown, when Deme offered no explanation. "Have you been meeting somebody out there? A man?" She persisted.

"Mama!" Deme gasped.

Minerva took the girl's wrist in an unbreakable hold. "You start giving me the truth or I'll beat it out of you." She threatened with the softest tone of voice.

Deme broke into a fit of nervous sobs, even as her mind raced for an explanation. "He used to watch me every day," she began, the story rolling off her tongue as she glared at her bedspread through an abundance of tears, "he told me that, when he...grabbed me. He must've been living in the woods around the pond." She revealed, her soft weeping giving way to stronger sobs. "I didn't know he was back there, until that day. He...he-he said he was tired of just watching."

"Who was he?" Minerva asked, barely able to hear the question above her own pounding heart.

Deme shook her head, sending a slew of curls into her dark face. "He looked like some hobo. He was black, but his face was so dirty, he looked even darker-if that's possible...He had a scraggly beard and it almost went to his waist..."

Jason and Minerva listened in horror as Demetria added more embellishments to her false account. She told them how the attacker had his way with her all afternoon-deep in the woods surrounding the Augustine pond.

"...when he...finished, he told me not to tell because he knew where I lived and he'd be back. That was a lie," she said, finally meeting her parents' unwavering gazes, "I think he left that same day. I didn't tell 'cause I knew I was in trouble for going to the pond in the first place."

"Baby, if you thought you were pregnant, why would you hide it?" Minerva asked.

Jason pulled both Deme's hands into his. "Why would you want this monster's baby?"

"Because it's a part of me and you." Demetria replied without hesitation.

Deme's soft words, worked on Jason and Minerva's emotions, tugging at their hearts. They were overwhelmed with sorrow and love for their daughter. Not to mention gratefulness and relief that another one of their children had not been lost to the pond.

"Everything'll be fine." Minerva finally whispered, as both she and Jason pulled the girl into a hug.

Demetria kept her headed buried between her parents' bodies, lest they see the triumphant smile brightening her face.

***

A soft hymn filled the air as Charlotte Skylar hummed during her morning dusting. The tiny, middle-aged housekeeper was the only domestic employee for the Augustine home. She was mostly called in to baby sit for Derric and Cameo-the youngest members of the family.

Charlotte's melodic humming was interrupted when the phone rang. "The concert will continue in a minute, you two." She told Derric and Cameo, who dozed in a huge bassinet out in the living room.

"Hello? Augustine residence."

"May I speak to Amina?"

Charlotte smiled. "The kids have already left for the beach. They should be gone all day. Is there a message I can take?" She offered, only to hear the phone click in her ear.

Tav stroked his square jaw, tapping his fingers against the receiver. "The beach, huh?" He said, a slow smile creeping across his face.

***

The trip to Virginia Beach only took a few hours. The group leaped from Nikos' truck before he could even shut off the engine. The beach, parking lot and boardwalk were packed with scantily clad bodies. Everyone was eager to enjoy the warm, sunny day.

Sweet and Stephanie went off for a swim and it wasn't long before an adoring young woman snatched CJ away.

"You think you and Steph packed enough food?" Nikos teased, his even white grin contrasting sharply against his bronzed complexion.

Amina waved her hand and continued to set the feast on the green pallet spread on the white sand. "We had to if we expected to get a bite with you, Sweet and CJ eating."

"Well since we're on the subject," Nikos sighed, dropping to his knees, "how long I gotta wait before tasting this stuff?"

Amina's thick, wavy brown hair slapped her arms as she shook her head at her friend. "Go on and dig in." She sighed, checking the huge, wicker basket for the drinks. "Oh no," She groaned.

"What?" Nikos called, his dark eyes focused on the platter of fried chicken.

"We packed all this food and forgot the sodas."

Nikos set the plate aside and wiped his hands. "No sweat, I'll go to the concession stand and get some."

"Thanks." Amina smiled, looking up as Nikos wiped his hand against his black swim trunks.

Alone, she stood and looked down over the pallet. Everything appeared cozy and inviting with the huge platter of chicken, an equal sized platter of biscuits, cole slaw, homemade

Taboo Tree

fries and oatmeal cookies for dessert. A shiver of excitement raced down her spine as she gazed out over the beach. All the people running along the white sand and frolicking in the blue water brought a contented smile to her face.

Suddenly, she felt herself being whirled around and drawn into a kiss. Before her lashes drifted close over her eyes, she saw Tav. His mouth captured hers possessively, his tongue delving deeply, his hands massaging her bare back revealed by her skimpy orange bikini top.

"Stop!" She hissed, breaking the kiss and managing to hold him only a few inches away. "Tav, my family is here." She whispered, when he moved to pull her back.

"Come with me." He growled.

"I can't. I gotta watch this." Amina was saying, looking back at the pallet.

Tav gnawed the inside of his jaw. "Meet me in the parking lot when they get back." He told her, pressing a quick kiss to her cheek before he sprinted away.

Amina couldn't think of refusing. She waited impatiently at the pallet, her vibrant gaze wide as she searched for someone to watch the food. When Steph and Sweet returned, she raced off the find Tav.

***

"I want it burned down, dammit! It's past time, don't you think Chick?"

"Amen." Minerva Gwaltney whispered, in full agreement with her husband.

The couple had driven to the Augustine estate after talking with Demetria. The fact that she had been molested on that particular piece of property had them both highly enraged. Thoughts of their dead son ran rampant.

"Chick?" Ophelia called, making her way down the long staircase.

"Go back to bed, Fe." Chick called, without bothering to look back.

Even in her pregnant condition, Ophelia was determined to make it down to the living room. She'd heard the raised voices and wasn't about to let the Gwaltneys 'double-team' her husband.

"What the hell are these bastards doing in our house?" Ophelia demanded, clutching the banister as she strolled down the carpeted staircase.

Chick closed his eyes. "Fe..."

"No Chick. What's going on?" Ophelia persisted, casting a distasteful look towards Minerva Gwaltney.

"They want the woods around the pond burned down." Chick finally announced, pushing both hands into the back pockets of his jeans.

"Burned down?" Ophelia gasped, crossing her arms over the green lounging robe. "As usual, y'all have some nerve."

"Save it, Ophelia. We got more than enough reason to want this." Minerva snapped, ready to do battle. "Maybe you forgot that unkempt pond is the reason my JJ died?"

"When are you gonna let that mess go?" Ophelia blurted.

Minerva was stunned. "Let it go? Woman that was my child-"

"Who you let run wild while you tended to other things," Ophelia pointed replied.

Minerva stepped closer. "Bitch," She sneered.

"Cunt," Ophelia retorted.

"Alright, y'all," Chick interrupted, stepping between the two angry women. He didn't see his wife mouth the obscene insult the second time. "Is all this necessary?" He asked.

"I want all the woods around that damned pond burned to the ground." Jason obstinately replied, refusing to bend even a little.

"You're asking us to destroy property that's been there for years." Chick argued.

Jason moved his hands into his beige trousers and focused his dark gaze on the pattern in the rug. "I think you should be lucky I don't demand the pond be drained. A man raped my little girl in those woods, Chick! I'll be damned if I sit around and do nothing'!"

"She could be lying again." Ophelia pointed out. "You Gwaltneys latch on to any reason to make trouble for us!"

"Make trouble for *you*, Ophelia?" Jason whispered.

Chick turned and patted his wife's back, until she calmed. "I'll get somebody out there today." He promised.

***

Amina found Tav standing near his car parked under a gathering of tall elm trees. The trees provided a good portion of the lot with shade from the blazing sun. Amina wasted no time hurrying to meet her boyfriend.

Tav had no words. His onyx eyes were focused on the bikini Amina wore. The stretchy orange fabric of the top, adored her small, yet full breasts and the denim cut-offs hung low across her slender hips.

When Amina was just inches away, Tav reached out and pulled her into a tight embrace. Her soft gasp, allowed him access to the dark recess of her mouth. Taking full advantage of her scant attire, his hands roamed every expanse of exposed skin. All the while, he urged her back towards the car which sat parked less than three feet away.

Amina heard the back door open and felt herself being settled against the Impala's black suede seats. She didn't dwell on her surroundings long, when Tav's nose nuzzled the cleft between her breasts. His big hands rose to cup both mounds as his tongue traced the firm nipples through the material of the bikini.

"Tav...wait, wait." She whispered, although the sensations created by his touch were incredible.

Tav didn't hear the soft resistance as he nuzzled his face deeper into Amina's chest. He massaged the top drawn over her breasts and soon had one of the nipples between his lips.

A deep shudder ripped through Amina's body as she reacted to the caress. As wonderful as it felt though, she wasn't ready for what Tav had in mind. When her shoves against his chest grew more persistent, he finally looked up into her eyes.

"What?" He whispered, anger and irritation combined in his expression.

Amina tried to brace on her elbows, but it was impossible beneath Tav's weight. "I don't wanna do this." She said.

Tav's expression grew darker. "Why? I don't make you feel good?"

Amina rolled her eyes. "That's not even it, Tav. Look around, this is the backseat of a car."

"So?"

Amina's temper rose to a slow simmer, her hazel eyes glittering with anger. "Can you just get off me, please?"

Tav thought back to when the idea of trying to bed Amina in his car disgusted him. He obliged her request and retreated to the opposite side of the back seat. "How long you expect me to wait for it?" He asked, watching as she fixed her clothes.

"Until I'm ready," Amina retorted, never looking up.

Tav raked one hand through his thick hair and nodded. "I never have to wait on gettin' a piece, Amina. I ain't used to that."

Amina didn't need to be reminded of that. "I don't care what you're used to. I'm not like that and if you can't accept it, too bad." She decided, fumbling for the door handle while she spoke.

Tav watched her scramble out of the car. He exited as well, but did not try stopping her as she ran away. His hand curled into a fist and he pounded the roof of the car. The blow left the smallest dent in the frame.

"Hey y'all, where's Amina?" Nikos asked Steph and Sweet when he returned to the pallet along with CJ and his friend Sara Franklin.

Sweet glanced up, before returning his attention to the full plate he'd prepared. "She's right behind you, blood."

Nikos turned, his dark eyes brightening when he saw her. Amina forgot her encounter with Tav. The meal was delicious. Afterwards, everyone lounged on the pallet-laughing, talking, telling jokes and enjoying the lazy Saturday afternoon. Much later, the boys issued a challenge for a water fight. The girls eagerly accepted and, soon, everyone was out playing in the ocean.

Tav remained at the beach as well, after meeting up with some friends. He and the group strolled out to the beach to take in all the lovely young women in scandalously skimpy bikinis and bathing suits. When Tav spotted the three happy couples in the water, a horrid frown added something sinister to his gorgeous face.

***

"What in the world?..." Demetria whispered, scooting down in her bed; closer to the window. She had been lounging in her room, when the smell of smoke drifted inside. A peek past the frilly white curtains allowed her to see many people rushing over the green hillside.

Unable to control her curiosity, she jumped from the bed, pulled on a blouse and jeans and scurried out.

"I'm surprised Mr. Jason ain't ask 'em to burn it down before."

"Every man got his breakin' point."

Demetria heard the remarks and several more like them as she raced along with the crowd. Panic filled her mind and her eyes as she neared the hilltop closest to the outskirts of the Gwaltney land.

"Nooo!" She cried, her fingers covering her lips when she saw the fire blazing in the distance. She stopped there, while everyone headed onward.

Alone on the high hilltop, Demetria witnessed the burning of her escape-her oasis. Tears filled her eyes and streamed down her cheeks as the vibrant brush and trees withered against the orange flames.

"What the hell?" Nikos said, sticking his head out the driver's side window. "Hey y'all!" He called, getting the attention of his four passengers riding in the flat bed.

CJ's, Steph's, Sweet's and Sara Franklin's gazes were instantly riveted on the pitch black cloud of smoke that rose against the reddish-blue late evening sky.

Nikos' truck arrived in the Augustine front yard like a cannon. He left it parked at an angle close to the bricked mailbox. The group jumped out and raced to the back of the house. The girls screamed when they saw the fire raging high against the sky. It blazed above the area where the pond was located. The kids wasted no time running in that direction.

Chick turned just in time to see CJ and Steph bounding towards him. He mouthed the word "whoa" as his arms stretched out to halt the kid's progress toward the flame.

"Daddy what is this!" Stephanie cried, her face shining with tears and sweat.

"Shhh..." Chick soothed, pulling his children close. "The Gwaltney's wanted it burned down-"

"Burned? Why? Pop, what-"

"CJ" Chick called, squeezing the boy's shoulder until he quieted. "Demetria says she was raped out here. Her parents are real upset and I can't blame 'em after what happened...before."

CJ and Stephanie exchanged glances-their questions hushed. All conversation, in fact, was silenced as the huge crowd viewed the demolition. Only three people knew it was all for nothing. Beauty destroyed for no reason.

CJ's onyx stare narrowed as he peered through the translucent waves of heat dancing in the atmosphere. He could see Demetria through the water looking, white-hot waves. She stood alone, high atop the wide hill overlooking the pond. Her dark tresses blew wildly against the smoky wind and CJ was almost mesmerized as he watched her. Somehow he knew. He knew he would never see her again.

THIRTEEN

The episode with the pond set everyone on edge in the Augustine household. After almost five days of little or no conversation amongst the family, Chick suggested everyone get out for a big family gathering.

Spirits were high at The Kowtow Umbrella; the town's new Chinese restaurant. The group feasted and enjoyed conversation which steered clear of the Gwaltneys. Even CJ appeared to be in a great mood as he basked in the admiration of his family. The soon-to-be college freshman had decided to work with his father while attending Chick's Alma Mater in North Carolina. The family was just as proud of Stephanie who planned to attend school in Washington DC and Amina with her choice to attend Bennett.

"Baby? Everything okay?" Dyna asked her daughter, noticing how far away the child seemed.

Amina fidgeted with a curl hanging from the high ball atop her head. She managed a slight nod and smile which did nothing to convince her mother. Unfortunately, Amina was too preoccupied by the phone call she'd received before leaving for the restaurant.

"*...I ain't seen you in a week. Why can't you meet me?*"

"*I already told you, Tav. Chick is takin' us out for a family dinner.*"

"*Fuck that. You could get out of it if you tried.*"

"*Well, maybe I don't want to!*"

"*I ain't surprised. You probably goin' to meet that grease ball anyway.*"

"*What?*"

"*He gonna be there Amina? Huh?*"

"*Who?*"

"*You know who. Nikos?*"

"*I don't believe this mess! I already told you I can't meet you. We can try to get together, but it won't be tonight! Goodbye!*"

The conversation ended with Amina slamming the phone in Tav's ear. The scene placed a damper on the lovely evening. She hated herself for letting Tavares Gwaltney affect her so. It was as though he had some invisible thread and barely had to tug in order to get her to come to him.

"Y'all I'm gonna run to the restroom right quick. I'll be back." Amina told her family, hoping she sounded cheerful enough.

Dyna leaned back in her chair, folding her arms over the red silk blouse she wore with matching bellbottoms. She studied her daughter who moved away from the table and left the dining room. Dyna's face was a picture of concern.

Amina allowed her steps to quicken when she rounded the corner from the dining room. She was so involved in her thoughts as she hurried down the hall, she didn't notice Nikos Cantone headed right towards her.

"Whoa!" He called, when she barreled right into him. "Amina? What you doin' here, Girl?"

A genuine smile came to Amina's pretty face for the first time that night. "Chick brought the whole family out for dinner." She explained.

Taboo Tree

Nikos midnight eyes narrowed as he looked over Amina's head. "I'll go speak in a minute."

"Well, what are *you* doing here?" Amina asked, her fingers curling around the lapels of his three piece black suit. "You look nice." She complimented.

"Thanks." Nikos sighed. "I'm having dinner with my Pop and my Uncle Connie from New York."

"For real?" Amina gushed, her hazel eyes growing wide. "Is he talkin' to your Dad about you going to New York?"

Nikos shrugged. "Probably."

"Well? What's the problem? I thought you wanted to go?"

"I mean, I'm curious about it and I want to spend some time with my other family, but...I know my Pop won't like it."

Amina took Nikos' hands and pulled him down the hall to share the red velvet bench. "Talk to him. Tell him how you feel." She advised. "It's not like you have a thing to keep you here."

Except you. Nikos silently corrected.

Conversation ceased after Amina's 'pep talk' and, after a while, Nikos noticed the sad, faraway look in her sparkling eyes.

"So what's wrong with you?" He asked.

Immediately, Amina began to shake her head. "Nothing, why?"

Nikos pointed across his shoulder. "I saw how you looked comin' down the hall. Something's up."

"No. Not really." She lied.

"This is me, Girl. Spill it." Nikos insisted.

Amina massaged her eyes and grimaced. "Tav called, wanting me to meet him. I told him I couldn't tonight and he...got so mad. I can't even enjoy tonight, thinkin' about how mad he acted."

Nikos' soft expression disappeared at the mention of Tav's name. "Amina, dammit! When you gonna stop lettin' that son of a bitch do this shit to you?"

"Nikos." Amina whispered, urging him to do the same.

"Nah, Amina." Nikos groaned, shaking his head. "You too smart for this mess. You know that."

"I don't know what it is." She admitted, her voice trembling terribly. "I don't know why I let him get to me like this." She said, her eyes welling with tears.

"Hey." Nikos soothed, drawing her close. He pressed a soft kiss to Amina's temple, when she rested her head against his shoulder. "You're too good for him and you deserve better..." He declared, smiling when he felt her nod against his chest. "...somebody who'll treat you like you should be, like you're special and fine and all he wants. That's how I'd treat you, if you were mine."

The sweet words, coming straight from Nikos' heart touched Amina's emotions. She looked up into his darkly handsome face, her exquisite gaze wide with curiosity.

"I'm sorry." Nikos whispered, squeezing his eyes shut as he shook his head once.

Amina's fingers rose to his bronzed cheek. "Don't be sorry." She whispered, inching closer to replace her fingers with her lips.

Nikos turned and the innocent kiss to his cheek, landed on his mouth. His body temperature rose instantly, even though the kiss ended as suddenly as it began.

"I better get back to the table." Amina whispered, brushing her fingers to her lips while Nikos cleared his throat.

Across from where the Augustines enjoyed their spicy, Chinese feast, two handsome middle-aged Italian men occupied a cozy table near the back of the dining room. They spoke in hushed tones, their raspy brogues rising ever so often in their native tongue.

"You know I don't like this shit, Connie."

"What's not to like, the boy's my sister's child."

"He's my child too."

"And you've had him all his life. He should know his other family."

Carlos Cantone clenched his jaw in effort to remain calm. "Look Connie, I got no beef with Nik knowin' his family. But I think you and I are talkin' about two different families."

Constance Bellini did not attempt to feign misunderstanding. "Nikos should have the right to decide whether he wants to know or be a part of that."

"Fuck that, Connie!" Carlos snapped, the longer tendrils of his close cut dark hair falling across his forehead. "I don't want him involved with that shit."

"You always been a self-righteous bastard 'Los." Connie grumbled, his bushy black and gray brows drawing close to add a sinister element to his round, dark face.

Carlos grinned at the remark. "I'll take that any day over bein' a murderer."

Constance shook his head, turning his attention back to the mound of Shrimp Chow Mein on his plate. "Nikos is a grown man. We'll let him decide."

That suggestion didn't make Carlos feel any better, but he grudgingly admitted it was for the best.

***

The evening at the Chinese restaurant was a helpful tonic for almost all who attended. After that night, everyone went on with their lives-preparing for new events in their futures.

CJ spent more time with Chick who taught him everything about running Augustine Seams. Stephanie prepared to attend college in the fall while Ophelia Augustine prepared for another addition to her family.

Even Amina tried to get her life and emotions in order. She started by convincing herself to get over Tavares Gwaltney. It had been three weeks since their paths crossed and she prayed he had given up hope on their relationship. She couldn't have been more wrong.

Tav was simply biding his time. He decided to wait-knowing there would be a time when Amina would be alone.

Checking the mail had become a daily ritual for everyone in the Augustine home. Information, regarding freshman orientations, scholarship award letters and other college paperwork, frequently arrived for the soon-to-be college students.

Amina strolled down the cobblestone path leading to the mailbox. She, Stephanie and CJ each took turns checking the box sometimes more than once in the event something had been overlooked.

The sound of screeching tires caught Amina's ears, just as she reached the box. Her hazel eyes widened to the size of saucers when the familiar, black Impala pulled alongside her.

"Get in." Tav ordered, when he slowed the car and leaned across the passenger side of the long, front seat.

Later, Amina realized she never thought to refuse. The fierce look on Tav's handsome face and his possessive tone of voice overruled her good sense and she obeyed the request.

Two seconds after the car began to move, Amina realized she had made a terrible mistake. Tav drove the car hard and fast for about fifteen minutes. To Amina, he appeared to be heading toward town, when he made a sharp turn off the main road.

"Tav!" Amina cried, covering her face with both hands. The car's speed did not decrease and she lowered her hands. She saw that they were on some back woods path a few miles from town.

"Where are you taking me?" Amina whispered, though she still managed to sound firm.

"Here." Tav replied, pulling the car to a halt in a clearing amidst towering trees. "Why you been avoiding me?"

"Tav-"

"We supposed to be goin' together and you won't even see me or call me." He ranted frowning at her from across the long seat.

Amina turned, her hands raised in a pleading gesture. "A lot of stuff's been happening with school and all," she explained, " we have all this information coming in and it's got to be sent back before-"

180

Taboo Tree

"Fuck that!" Tav roared, his deep voice vibrating inside the confines of the car. "We supposed to have somethin' goin' Amina. You supposed to be my girl and I got to watch you actin' like a slut with that greasy Nikos Cantone!"

Amina's hand started to burn and she laid a vicious slap to Tav's face. He immediately retaliated with a more vicious backhand blow, which sent her reeling back against the door.

"Tav!" She cried, kicking out at him with her small sneaker shod feet. Her fingers curled around the polished, chrome door handle, but he caught her waist and prevented her escape. The rough hold ripped both sleeves of the delicate peach blouse she wore with black denim cutoffs.

"What's wrong with you?!" Amina hissed, the terror in her light eyes a perfect match to the tone of her voice.

Tav behaved like a man possessed. "You shouldn't have made me wait. We supposed to be goin' together." He reasoned, flipping Amina to her back and dropping his weight across her petite form.

Amina continued to fight, though her efforts seemed useless against Tav's superior strength. His face once handsome, was now twisted with sinister intent. His dark eyes focused on her breasts heaving rapidly beneath the black lace of her bra. At last, Amina triumphed when her elbow connected with his jaw and his hold slackened. She kicked out against his chest, then scrambled out of the car and raced towards town.

***

Late afternoon, sent a cool breeze through the air. Nikos carried garbage out behind his father's store and made sure the can was properly sealed. The wind stirred above his head and faintly, he swore he heard his name.

"Nikos?"

He stumbled into the tin can, when he whirled around. "Who's there?" He demanded, raising the short wooden board he'd grabbed. When Amina emerged from the shadows in the far corner of the alley, he couldn't have been more surprised. "What you doin' back there?" He whispered, his attractive features taking on a horrified glean when he noticed her appearance. "Tav." He stated, extending his arms as he approached her.

Amina fell against his chest and let her tears rush forth. "He wouldn't stop." She repeated several times, her breathing coming in short hiccupping spurts.

"Come inside with me." Nikos said, taking her arms in a gentle hold. The slight grasp only inflicted more pain and he cursed Tavares Gwaltney's soul to hell. "Shh..." he comforted, when he and Amina began to take short steps towards the chrome back door.

On the way inside, Amina began to recount her terrible ordeal. She could barely speak for crying and shaking as she remembered Tav's cruelty.

I'll kill him, Nikos chanted as he guided Amina to the upstairs apartment. Right now, she was his top priority and he was determined to take care of her.

"Come on." He whispered, ushering her past the oak front door, past the living room and down the long corridor. "I'm gonna get you a drink," he said, looking into his bottom bureau drawer for a fresh washcloth, towel and T-shirt. "You can get cleaned up, and then I'll take you home."

Amina's lovely bright eyes widened as she began to shake her head. "You can't! I can't! I can't...go home, not-not now. I-they'll ask all these questions that I don't wanna answer."

"Okay, okay." Nikos whispered, kneeling before Amina where she sat perched on his bed. "I won't take you home until you're ready, but I am going to get you a drink while you get yourself together."

Amina nodded and managed an unsteady smile. "Thanks." She whispered, smoothing her palm against his cheek.

Nikos pressed a kiss to the center of her palm, and then left the room. When he returned with a tall glass of iced tea, Amina was just easing off the bed. He knew he should have looked away when she began to pull the ripped blouse from her body. His dark eyes were riveted, though. He couldn't look anywhere else. When he saw the ugly, burgundy/purple bruises marring her once flawless cinnamon skin, his entire body shook. The tea sloshed around the mouth of the glass.

"That muthafucka's ass is mine." He growled, slamming the glass to his dresser.

Amina whirled around, easing the shirt back over her shoulders. "Nikos-"

"When I see him...Amina, when I see that...he's dead."

"Nikos stop." Amina soothed, closing the distance between them. She smoothed her hands across the front of his burgundy T-shirt and pressed soft kisses to his cheek.

Nikos' anger made his torso heave against Amina's hands where they pressed against his chest. His long, silky dark lashes fluttered over his eyes as he struggled to contain his rage.

"Shh..." Amina soothed, her kisses to his cheek lowering to the strong line of his jaw.

Nikos' heavy breathing slowed, though his expression was still fierce. Amina looked up into his face and brought her fingers to the furrow between his brows. She massaged the area, until the frown disappeared.

"Amina...stop."

"What?"

"You don't know what you're doing."

"Tell me."

Nikos pushed Amina's hand from his face and kissed her fingers. "You know how I feel. You have to."

Amina's eyes never strayed from his. "I know...I know."

A heavy silence covered the room for several seconds. Finally, Nikos' fist uncurled at his side and his hands slipped around Amina's small waist. Slowly, he began to massage her there.

"Nikos." Amina gasped, taking a few baby steps closer to the tall, dark gorgeous young man who held her so gently.

Suddenly, Nikos closed his eyes and shook his head. "You need to change, Amina. I'll be in the living room, okay?"

"No." Amina decided her soft voice surprisingly firm. On impulse, she stood on her toes and pressed her lips to his.

Nikos felt his knees weaken the instant she kissed him. "You don't need this. Not tonight, Amina-"

"Especially tonight, Nikos. Especially from you." She corrected, sliding her hands over his chest and around his neck.

The words were like a magical phrase that released the pent up tension from Nikos's entire body. His hands caressed the small of Amina's back, bared by the torn blouse. His touch was feather soft, so as not to aggravate her bruised skin.

"Amina..." He sighed, just as his mouth covered hers. Tentatively, his tongue sought and stroked hers. When she responded in the same manner, he added the slightest pressure to the kiss.

Amina melted. Instinctively, she arched into Nikos' hard frame. This was the last place she expected to be when she left the house to check the mail that afternoon. Now, she couldn't imagine being anywhere else.

Nikos broke the kiss for only a moment in order to reach down and swing Amina into his arms. He held her as though she might dissolve in his embrace.

"Are you sure, Amina?" He asked when he'd placed her in the center of the green and black cotton spread covering his bed.

Amina nodded against the pillows. Her innocent gaze was focused on his penetrating dark one. "I'm sure."

Nikos closed his eyes as though he were saying a prayer of thanks. Then, his lips lowered to her collarbone and he stroked her satiny, cinnamon-toned skin with his mouth. Though raging, youthful male desire commanded he take what he'd dreamed of for so long, Nikos restrained himself. He wanted to remember every detail of that night-a night he wished would never end.

***

The next morning, Nikos drove Amina home. She wore one of his sweatshirts in place of her tattered blouse. He parked the truck but left the engine running.

"I don't think I better stay." He said, sending Amina a lopsided grin as he watched her across the seat.

Amina's heart broke as she looked his way. Her one wish was that they be able to enjoy what they discovered with one another. Unfortunately, that could never be. "Nikos-"

He waved one hand to silence her. "I know." He assured her, knowing he couldn't bear to hear her say what they were both thinking.

Amina inched across the seat and took his hand in both of hers. "I don't regret it, Nikos. I don't regret it one bit." She fiercely whispered, lacing her fingers between his.

Nikos smiled and nudged his hand against her thigh. "I know." He told her again. Their eyes held for several moments, before Amina turned and left the truck.

"Thank God." Dyna whispered, clasping her hands together against the front of her mauve housecoat. She watched her daughter approach the house and knew she had never been so relieved. No one in the house had gotten much sleep the night before, after Amina disappeared.

"She's back!" Dyna called, holding the front screened door open for her girl.

Amina prepared herself for the slew of questions sure to hit her in the face. She was pleasantly surprised when her mother simply pulled her into a soft, simple hug.

Members of the family began to trickle in from different areas of the house. The dreaded questions rose and were combined with tight, long hugs. In the midst of it all, Amina couldn't hide her physical pain. She cried out when her mother pulled her close for another embrace. Before anyone could ask what the problem was, she was racing upstairs.

"Wait y'all." Dyna called, when both Chick and CJ moved to follow Amina. "I'll go see to my baby." She whispered.

"Yeah?" Amina sighed, when she heard the knock on her bedroom door.

"Mina?" Dyna called, sticking her head just inside the room.

AlTonya Washington

"Hmmm?" Amina replied, pretending to be busy looking for something in the dresser.

"Honey, what's happening with you? Where were you all night?"

Amina pulled one hand through her tousled wavy hair. "It's nothing." She groaned.

Dyna clasped her hands behind her back and looked around the bedroom. She caught sight of the blouse Amina had worn the day before.

"You were wearing this yesterday," Dyna absently recalled, giving the blouse a slight shake, "but it's...it's ruined...Amina, this is not nothing! What happened to you?!" Dyna cried, whirling around to face her daughter. "I want the truth! Now, Girl!"

"Mama please, alright?!" Amina snapped, shoving the drawer closed. "It's my business. Mine!"

Dyna watched Amina as though the girl were a stranger. "I guess I'll have a talk with your Italian friend, then."

"Leave Nikos out of it." Amina groaned, burying her face in her hands.

"I saw him drop you off. Amina?"

"I don't wanna talk about it."

"Fine." Dyna replied in a perky tone, as she turned to leave the room. "I'll get Chick to take me into town for a talk with your friend and we'll pick up the police on the way."

"Mama wait!" Amina demanded, racing to the door before Dyna could pull it open. "Don't!" She cried.

Dyna grabbed Amina's shoulders and shook her. "You tell me, then. You tell me what happened to you last night!"

"Mama!" Amina hissed, pain flashing across her lovely face.

Dyna's dark eyes narrowed in realization and she reached down to push up the sleeves of the sweatshirt Amina still wore.

"What is this?" She gasped, seeing the bruises. "Baby talk to me!" She pleaded, her eyes tearing when Amina began to cry against her shoulder.

"I want him locked up for what he did, dammit!"

"Dyna-"

"Hold it, Fe. Now, she's my daughter and I want that bastard behind bars!" The woman raged, after she'd told the family what had happened. "If it hadn't been for that Nikos Cantone letting her sleep on his sofa last night, Lord knows where she'd be now. All thanks to that black son of a bitch!"

"Dyna, calm down." Chick urged, stepping to the middle of the kitchen with both hands raised. "Now everybody's upset and we all want Tav's blood, but-"

"Forget buts, Chick I'm goin' over there." Dyna decided the mauve housecoat whipping around her tall, slender form when she stomped toward the kitchen doorway.

"Dyna could you think about this before you go running over there? This family's been through a lot because of the Gwaltneys."

Dyna sent Chick a cold enraged look. "Well, we're about to go through a lot more. You can't shut me up the way you do Ophelia when it comes to those people."

Chick massaged his jaw and focused his dark eyes on the polished hardwood floor. "Dyna..."

"Now, you either come along to support me over what that nigga did to my child or you can stay here. Either way, I'm going."

The kitchen was silent as everyone watched Dyna leave.

Chick realized Dyna was right. He reached into the side pockets of his dark pants and found his keys. "Let's go." He called to CJ, realizing this was no time to give the Gwaltneys the benefit of the doubt.

***

"Are you absolutely positive?" Minerva whispered to the clinic's head physician.

"We're one-hundred percent certain." Dr. Harry Royale replied.

Minerva bowed her head, the thick dark curls slipping forth to shield her face. "When can we see her?" She sighed.

Dr. Royale handled the visiting arrangements and tried to reassure Minerva that her daughter was doing fine. The call ended just as Jason walked into the front room.

"Baby, you seen Tav? I checked his room and it don't look like he been there all night."

Minerva stood behind the long, cherry wood roll top desk. Before she could respond to her husband's question, the sound of screeching tires filled the air. She and Jason exchanged frowns before racing out to the front door.

Dyna arrived in her own car with Chick and CJ rolling behind in the truck. Dyna jumped out of the LTD and bounded up the brick steps to pound on the door.

Minerva whipped the door open and raked Dyna's frame with cold eyes. "Who the hell are you?!"

Dyna brought her face within inches of Minerva's face. "I'm Amina Davidson's mother and your bastard of a son just used her for a punching bag!"

"Dyna-"

"Shut up Chick!"

"You bitch, who the hell you supposed to be comin' to my house puttin' down my boy!" Minerva raged, her hands clenched into fists.

"He did this." Dyna declared, raising her index finger before Minerva's face. "I'm only telling you sista, so you won't be surprised when the cops come here to arrest his black ass."

"Arrest?" Minerva whispered, her big eyes growing wider when she looked over her shoulder. "Jason?" She called, stepping back into her husband's arms.

"What's this mess about, Chick?" Jason queried, his dark face twisted with anger. "How can you come up here like this after what we been through?"

"Sorry Jason." Chick responded, his voice very firm. "This ain't somethin' we can ignore. You should understand in light of what Demetria just went through."

Minerva wrenched herself out of Jason's hold. "You keep my child's name out of your mouth! Remember, she was raped on your property. That shit destroyed her and we've even had to send her away to have the babies."

"Babies?" CJ blurted, looking towards the ground as he struggled to contain his emotions.

Minerva turned to look back at Jason. "Our baby's having twins." She whispered.

CJ wanted to disappear. It was all he could do to stand there on the Gwaltney's front porch. He prayed no one noticed how on edge he was and he breathed a sigh of relief when another vehicle arrived in the driveway.

Tav brought his Impala to a screeching halt and stepped out onto the cobblestone drive. The scene on the front porch slowed his movements for an instant.

"Son of a bitch!" Dyna gasped, laying a loud slap to Tav's face when he stood before her.

"Jason let go of me!" Minerva demanded, her gray platform heels scraping the welcome mat as she struggled out of her husband's embrace.

Tav massaged his flaming cheek, a knowing look on his dark face. "Ms. Davidson, is she alright?" He asked.

"You jackass," Dyna sneered, prepared to lunge for the boy again. Chick held her back.

"Tav, go to your room, Boy." Jason coolly ordered his son.

Tav held out his hands toward Dyna. "I'm sorry." He whispered, biting his lower lip when Dyna looked away.

"Tav," Jason called again.

"I'm sorry." Tav repeated, sending apologetic looks to Chick and CJ before leaving the porch.

Jason loosened his hold around Minerva's waist, but kept her close to his side. "Ms. Davidson please let me talk to my boy before you bring the police into this."

Dyna pushed away from Chick. "Talk to him quick, Mr. Gwaltney," she advised, heading down the porch steps, "I go to the police in the morning."

AlTonya Washington

The Gwaltneys watched the Augustines make a regal exit. Then, Jason left his wife in the doorway and went upstairs to his son.

Tav was seated on the edge of his bed, one fist balled beneath his chin. He was in deep thought when his father walked into his room.

"Is Amina alright?" He asked his onyx gaze expectant.

"Any reason why she wouldn't be?" Jason countered, hiking up the legs of his overalls as he took a seat in the large, leather swivel next to the window.

"I..." Tav began, rubbing wet palms against the legs of his jeans. "I was rough with her Poppa. I know I hurt her."

"You force yourself on her?" Jason slowly queried, watching Tav closely.

"No Sir. No Sir, I didn't get that far, but..."

"But?"

Tav sighed, grimacing as he remembered his earlier actions. "I probably would've-would've done that too, if-if she hadn't got away."

Jason shook his head. "Son, how many times have I warned you 'bout givin' in to your strength and temper? They can be a deadly combination if you can't control 'em. You love this girl?"

"Yeah Poppa. A lot. So much, I get scared by it." Tav admitted, his weary expression making him appear far older than eighteen.

"Why didn't you tell us?" Jason asked, closing his eyes and nodding when Tav sent him a knowing look. "Son, if you love this girl, you should know you can't treat her like this."

"I know that Pop."

"You probably already ruined what you could've had by pullin' something so stupid." Jason predicted.

Tav held his head in his hands and massaged his soft, thick hair. "What do I do, Poppa?"

"Apologize." Jason advised, moving from the leather chair to pat his son's head. "Apologize son and, more important, show the girl you mean what you say."

***

"You up for this meeting?" Chick asked his son as he drove past the guard gate at Augustine Seams.

CJ finished straightening his red and navy striped tie and looked away from the rearview mirror. "Why you asking, Pop?"

Chick shrugged. "Been a wild morning, that's all."

"And this is just what I need to get my mind off all that." CJ decided, leaning against the headrest. "Plus, I'm ready to get this presentation done."

"Feel like giving your ole man a sneak preview?"

CJ returned his father's teasing grin. "No way. I'll be nervous enough with you being in the room."

Chick's deep laughter filled the Continental's interior as he eased the car into his reserved space. Three young women passing the car, stopped to give their boss dazzling smiles.

"Morning Mr. Augustine," They greeted in unison.

"Ladies," Chick replied, bowing his head slightly as he smiled. "How are you all this morning?"

The young women were distracted. Each had her eye on the devastatingly handsome man standing next to their equally handsome boss.

"Uh yes, yes Sir we're fine." Melissa Black finally answered for herself and her friends. "Good morning." She whispered, casting one last interested glance towards CJ.

"Easy, boy." Chick cautioned, noticing his son's reaction to the young woman. They headed into the main entrance of the five story rectangular building. Every employee who passed Charles Augustine Sr. greeted him with enthusiasm and respect. Female employees couldn't help but look twice at CJ. They marveled at how much the young man resembled his father.

Chick patted his son's back when they stepped off the executive floor elevator. "Good luck." He whispered, ushering CJ to the main conference room.

CJ watched his father greet the twelve men at the long, rectangular table. He closed his eyes briefly and prayed he could present his proposal and make his father proud. The meeting began promptly with more pressing issues being handled first. Then, everyone looked to the end of the table where CJ waited his turn.

CJ cleared his throat and stood with one hand in the pocket of his navy blue trousers. "Thank you." He said, offering a quick smile to the men but avoiding his father's eyes. "My proposal involves The Harrington Hotel. Construction is complete and it's scheduled to open this fall. They're recruiting now for staff and shopping for a company to handle production of uniforms-housekeeping, cafeteria, security, and so on." CJ took a moment to assess reaction from the executive staff and was pleased to see all eyes on him. "What gives us an edge," he said, passing out booklets which outlined the proposal, "is they want to deal with a local company. They'd like to have a more hands on relationship with the production of the uniforms which could also parlay into design and production of kitchen and bedroom linens. After you all read the proposal I passed around, we can arrange a meeting with the hotel's owners."

The group was obviously quite impressed by CJ's composure and professionalism. Not to mention, his prospecting skills.

Chick brushed invisible lint from his gray pin-striped suit and tried to hide his proud smile. Though he had no plans for retirement in the near future, he was more than confident the company he built would be in the best hands.

***

Stephanie's pretty face clouded with disgust, when she opened the door that evening. "What the hell do you want?"

Tav glanced at his father, then back at Steph. "Is Amina home?"

"Why?" Steph spat.

"I wanted to see her a minute."

Steph pushed both hands into the back pockets of her blue jeans. "You got to be crazy." She sighed, her mouth curved into a disapproving smile.

Dyna and Ophelia walked out into the living room. When they saw two men on the front porch, curiosity filled their eyes.

Jason pulled the tan Stetson from his head and stepped closer to the front door. "Good evening Ms. Davidson. Ophelia. My son has something to say to Amina...an apology. A much needed apology."

Dyna exchanged a quick glance with her cousin, before nodding. She tugged on the cuff of her black and green Dashiki and turned to head upstairs. She found her daughter already walking down the staircase.

"Amina." Tav called, wearing a humble expression on his handsome face. He waited for Stephanie to step aside and entered the house with his hands clasped before his chest. "I'm so sorry." He whispered, stopping just a few feet short of the stairway where Amina was standing. "I never should've touched you like that and I deserve anything you do to me. Your mother wants to call the police and I don't blame her." He said, sending Dyna a meek look. "I am sorry, though. I mean that."

Amina's expression remained closed as Tav spoke. She wanted to steel herself against his heartfelt words, but; combined with the sincerity on his face, the wall around her emotions slowly eroded.

Tav stopped speaking then and looked over his shoulder. Jason smiled proud of his son's composure and sincerity.

Dyna and Ophelia were also impressed. Only Stephanie appeared unaffected by Tav's actions. When he knelt before her cousin, she frowned.

"What in the world are you doin'?" She demanded, folding her arms over the front of her black sweater.

Tav reached into the front pocket of his gray and white striped shirt and extracted a black box. Inside, was a small, yet dazzling diamond ring.

"Will you marry me, Amina?"

FOURTEEN

The living room was so silent, Derric and Cameo could be heard in their playroom on the second floor. Everyone, including Jason Gwaltney, was stunned by Tav's gesture. Amina's mouth was agape, her wide eyes shifting from Tav's face to the gorgeous ring.

"What the hell are you up to, Tav Gwaltney?" Steph probed, her firm voice shattering the heavy silence.

"Son?..." Jason whispered, suddenly at a loss for more words.

"Amina?" Tav said, his dark eyes riveted on the girl standing before him.

She only shook her head. "Go home, Tav." She sighed, before ascending the staircase.

Tav watched Amina disappear up the maple staircase. After a while, he stood and; without a word, left the Augustine home.

"Goodnight, ladies." Jason bade, turning to follow his son out the door.

Dyna, Ophelia and Stephanie watched the men leave. Jason Gwaltney's shiny black Ford truck was pulling out onto the street, when Chick and CJ returned.

"We miss somethin'?" Chick asked when he walked in through the front door.

"Hmph, that's an understatement." Ophelia sighed, smiling when Chick kissed her mouth.

"What's happenin'?" CJ asked, his midnight eyes trained on his sister.

"Tav came over here with his Daddy and apologized to Amina. Then, he got down on his knees and proposed."

"Proposed?!" Chick and CJ responded in unison.

"Had a ring and everything," Ophelia shared.

Chick whistled. "Some apology."

"Hmph. I wonder if he meant it." Steph remarked.

Dyna took a seat on the hunter green chaise lounge. "His father seemed surprised too."

"You think the apology was sincere?" Ophelia asked her cousin.

Dyna looked down at the lounge's embroidered patterns and sighed. "I did, but this proposal has me... concerned."

Upstairs, Amina was still in shock. She wouldn't have believed what just took place had she not been there.

"Was he serious?" She asked herself, rubbing her hands across the sleeves of her fuzzy sweater. "No!" She cried, shaking her head frantically.

A knock on the door, interrupted her troubled thoughts. "Come in!" She responded brightly, though she was in no mood for conversation.

Stephanie stuck her head just inside the bedroom door. "Sorry, um...Nikos is downstairs. You feel like seeing him?"

Amina smoothed back a loose, wavy tendril and smiled. "I'll be down in a minute."

Nikos waited on the front porch. The sweet contentment on Amina's face did little to soothe his concern.

"You okay?" He asked, pulling her away from the bay window.

"Far from it," She admitted, closing her eyes resignedly.

Nikos' expression grew murderous. "What'd he do?"

Amina shook her head. "Nothing like that," She assured him, patting his smooth cheek.

Nikos pulled her into his arms and they shared a long hug. Unfortunately, the embrace did little to calm either of them. Moreover, it only reminded them of their night together. Amina's long lashes fluttered as the exquisite memories filled her mind.

Nikos was no less affected, but realized this was neither the time nor place for such emotion. "Talk to me." He ordered softly, pulling her back to look into his eyes.

Amina looked up at the night sky amass with stars. "Tav came over here and apologized. Then, he asked me to marry him."

Nikos couldn't have been more shocked. "Marriage?" He queried, in a hushed whisper. "What the hell is he up to?"

Amina toyed with a tassel dangling from the hem of Nikos' blue sweatshirt. "I don't think he was up to anything." She admitted, smiling a bit as she remembered how humble Tav seemed. "I think he meant it. He just looked so-so sincere and-"

"Hold up. Amina please don't tell me you fell for that shit? Not again?"

"Nikos, wait." Amina urged, raising both hands defensively. "Now I think Tav meant the apology-at least I thought he did. When he proposed...I know now that he was tryin' to buy my forgiveness. That threw me."

"You were surprised he'd try to do that?" Nikos asked, tilting his head and watching her closely. When she averted her gaze, he raked one hand through his onyx hair and turned away.

"Wise up, Girl. Before it's too late," He advised without looking back.

***

Life around the Augustine home seemed to return to normal over the next several weeks. 'Normal' however, had a rather surreal feel. CJ threw himself into learning more about his father's business, while preparing for college in the fall. While all the hard work paid off; by providing CJ with valuable experience, he was motivated by different reasons. Demetria and all that had happened between them constantly filled his thoughts. He hoped working would push the unsettling memories from his mind. It didn't. Every day he thought of Deme and their unborn children.

Meanwhile, Chick and Ophelia Augustine prepared for the arrival of the new baby. Everyone predicted the child would be a boy. Dyna Davidson left Virginia for Ohio and urged her daughter to do the same.

Amina had already received notification of her acceptance to Bennett. She found little joy in the fact. Her thoughts were filled by matters of a more delicate situation.

"Amina Celeste Davidson?"

Amina's heart lurched to her chest when her name was announced. Smoothing both hands across her green and blue plaid skirt, she stood and headed towards the long, chrome counter.

"Amina Davidson?" The nurse repeated, when Amina stood before her. When the girl nodded, she smiled and glanced down at the pad she held. "Right this way, Sweetie." She instructed, waving Amina along as she led the way down the hall.

"Wait right here. The doctor will be in to see you shortly."

Amina managed a shaky smile for the nurse before the woman left the room. Her hazel stare appeared weak as she gazed around the cramped, white space. Suddenly, what remained of her strength left. She leaned against the white, Formica counter and covered her face with both hands. "Please

Taboo Tree

don't cry. Please don't cry." She chanted, squeezing her eyes shut as they grew more pressured by tears.

"Miss Davidson?"

Amina cleared her throat and pretended to have been simply massaging her temples. "Yes?" She whispered, smiling at the brunette 30-something female doctor who had entered the room.

Dr. Angela Fredericks nodded satisfactorily as she scanned the contents of the manila folder. "Okay...let's see...you're here for the follow up on your tests."

"Yes. I um, wanted to ask you about that." Amina replied, clasping her hands as she watched the doctor with a steady gaze. "Couldn't I get the results by phone? I don't understand why I needed to come in."

Dr. Fredericks set the folder aside and met Amina's concerned gaze. "Well, in some cases, we like to see the patient in person to discuss options and...things of that sort."

"Options?" Amina parroted. "For what?"

Dr. Fredericks folded her arms across her chest. "Well Honey, you're pregnant by almost six weeks."

Amina stood leaning against the counter. She kept her eyes closed so long Dr. Fredericks thought she'd fainted. Once the news settled, Amina was able to tune into the doctor's words.

"This is a surprise I take it?"

Amina shook her head. "I thought I could be, but...I still couldn't believe it."

"Have you thought about what you'd do?"

"I don't know."

"Do you plan on telling your family?"

Amina didn't want to think about how her mother would handle the news. Not to mention another involved party.

"What about the father?" Dr. Fredericks asked when no response met the prior question.

Amina thought the woman was reading her thoughts. "What about him?" She snapped.

"Do you know who he-"

"Yes I know!"

"I'm sorry, Miss Davidson."

"Is there anything else?" Amina queried, clutching her purse and preparing to leave the room.

The doctor's blue eyes registered concern, but she kept her comments silent. "I'd like for you to take these," she said, gathering several pieces of literature regarding childbirth, adoption and abortion, "whatever you decide, I want you to come back and see me. Alright?"

Amina swept the pamphlets into her bag. "Thank you." She said, leaving the room without a backwards glance.

***

"Uncle G, you're as bad as Uncle Connie about getting me up there."

Giorgio Bellini chuckled at his nephew's perception. "Listen Nik, forget all the crap about the business. You are our little sister's only child and you know we never got to know you as a baby."

"Uncle-"

"Now, now, you know it's true. Carlos hovered worse than a mother hen."

Nikos massaged the bridge of his nose. "He was tryin' to do right by me. Make sure I didn't get caught up in all that, Uncle G."

"We know. We know." Giorgio sighed, and then chuckled a bit louder that time. "Look kid we all just want a chance with you. Especially your aunties. 'Los cut them out along with us wise guys too, you know?"

"I don't know what to do, Uncle." Nikos groaned, suddenly realizing just how important the decision was concerning his future.

"Just get your butt to Brooklyn, kid."

***

Amina flushed the toilet and leaned her head against the porcelain seat. The vomiting which started weeks ago had first prompted her to see a doctor. She repeatedly berated herself for behaving so carelessly-so foolishly with Nikos. Now she was carrying his child.

"No..." Amina groaned, gathering fistfuls of her brown tresses. No one could ever know about the baby's father, but there was no way she could raise it alone. She knew what that type of childhood was like. She spent a few more minutes in the bathroom, before summoning the strength to stand.

"Amina, you okay?"

Amina's eyes snapped open when she heard Stephanie's voice. "Oh no," She whispered, rushing out of the small, private bathroom. She found her cousin standing next to the bed.

"What the hell is all this?" Steph asked, waving the pregnancy pamphlets in the air.

Amina was shocked and speechless. She had no time to hide the material or think of an explanation should it be discovered. Instead, she stood there just inside the bedroom and waited for her cousin to figure it out.

"I would ask if you were working on a school project, but we're not in school." Steph mused, tossing the pamphlets to the bed. Smoothing damp palms across the seat of her snug light blue jeans, she stepped before her cousin. "You pregnant, Girl?"

The whispered question caused Amina's eyes to pool with tears. She fell into Steph's arms and the girls embraced for the longest time.

"Is that why Tav proposed?"

Amina's tears abated. Suddenly, as though a fluttering blanket had found a place to settle, a lie so perfect-so...potential explosive-came to mind. She felt her head bow once, as she accepted the deception.

"What are you gonna do?" Steph asked, looking back at the pamphlets.

"I don't know." Amina admitted, the lost tone in her soft voice prompting her cousin to pull her close once more.

***

"Are you sure that's all I can do?" Lila James asked Tav, taking the letters he'd asked her to file. Like every other woman who worked for Gwaltney Produce and Distributors, Lila was thoroughly enamored of the dark, sexy young man.

"Yeah, that's it and you can go on home when you're done." Tav replied, missing the disappointment on his secretary's pretty, vanilla-toned face. Unfortunately, for the company's female workers, Tav's strong sex drive did not carry over to his father's employees.

Lila was about to pull the office door shut, when Amina arrived. "Can I help you?" She asked.

Amina cleared her throat and prayed her nerves would settle. "Yes, I'm uh-is Tav Gwaltney here?"

Lila's dark eyes gazed distastefully at the lovely, petite young woman. "He's busy." She flatly replied.

Amina was too preoccupied to pay attention to the secretary's attitude. "Thank you." She whispered, pulling her purse strap snug across her shoulder.

"Amina!" Tav called, having heard her voice the moment she spoke. He waved her toward the office. "Lila you can go." He told the woman, without casting a moment's glance in her direction. He walked ahead of Amina when she stepped towards him. Deciding to keep his distance, he stood across the maple-paneled room.

Amina folded her arms over the front of the snug white blouse and forced herself to retain eye contact. "Sorry if I'm disturbing."

"You're not." He quickly assured her. "You look good." He complimented his dark stare narrowing as it raked her body.

Amina allowed her gaze to falter, lest he spot the coldness there. "Tav, I came here to ask if...your proposal was still open?"

"My...proposal?" Tav whispered, his expression changing as realization dawned. "Yeah, Amina. It's definitely open." He said, trying to hide his smile.

"Then your answer is yes. Yes I'll marry you." Amina sighed, sounding more resigned than excited.

Tav couldn't have been happier. He closed the distance between them and pulled Amina into his arms.

"I love you. I'm gonna give you everything." He vowed, raining kisses over her face. He never noticed his fiancée flinching and grimacing as he held her.

Amina's hazel eyes sparkled with tears of sorrow, and she lamented the mistake she was making. Her fingers shook terribly as they clutched the lapels of his tanned sport coat. She didn't correct him when he mistook the tears for happiness.

"We can tell my parents tonight." He decided, tightening his hold around Amina's small waist. "I ain't wasting no more time, now that I got you."

Amina nodded. "Mmm hmm. Time is important."

"We better tell your people soon, too." Tav suggested.

"Um Tav, you know, I think I'll tell 'em myself."

"Tonight?"

"Or tomorrow."

Tav nodded satisfied. "Alright, but I'll be over when you tell 'em. It's time for our people to get together. We're gonna be related, you know?"

The thought of telling the Augustines, her mother, or anyone about marrying Tav made Amina shudder. Tav felt her tremble and figured his fiancée's thoughts were on the same track as his.

Amina closed her eyes when she felt Tav's mouth against her neck. She knew it would be best to give in to him then, but could only stand his touch for an instant.

"I'll see you tonight." She said, easing out of the embrace. She left the office with the grace of a queen and did not lose her composure until the elevator doors closed behind her.

***

"Would you care for any more lemonade, Baby?"

"No. Thank you, Mrs. Gwaltney."

Minerva smiled and pressed her hand against Amina's shoulder. "I'm sorry for not having suitable servers. Everything was so sudden."

"I'm sorry." Amina whispered, setting her glass to the coffee table.

"Oh Baby, please." Minerva replied, folding her hands over the curve of her hips. "I'm so happy my boy is settling down. I was scared that child would spend his life flittin' from girl to girl."

"Mama don't be tellin' her nothing bad about me!" Tav called across the room.

Minerva waved her hand. "Aw hush Boy and come with me to the kitchen to freshen these drinks."

Tav winked at Amina when he crossed the living room. Inside the kitchen, he went over to Minerva and hugged her waist. "What'cha thinkin'?"

"She's lovely, Baby." Minerva whispered, smiling as she patted her son's hand reassuringly. "She's very well-mannered, very ladylike. Not a bit like those other fast things you use to run 'round with. But..." She sighed, turning to face Tav.

"What?" He asked, his heavy brows drawing closer.

Minerva's gaze was cool. "You just be careful not to hurt her again."

Tav's expression registered confusion, but Minerva was not convinced.

"You know what I mean, Tav. You treated that poor girl shamefully-"

"Ma-"

"Let me tell you something." Minerva snapped, her index finger inches from Tav's nose. "If I find out you touched Amina that way again, I'll help the Augustines put you in jail."

The firm threat brought shock to Tav's dark face. He blinked once and studied his mother closely. Then, he pressed a kiss to his cheek and left the kitchen.

"You're doing what?!" Ophelia cried, when Amina gathered the family in the living room the next evening and told them about the engagement.

"I don't believe this." CJ whispered, his feelings were shared by almost everyone in the room.

"Y'all please, don't make this into something." Amina begged. "I'm not changing my mind." She told them all. Her eyes met Steph's and Amina smiled when her cousin nodded as if to say she understood and was sorry.

Silence settled over the room, but only lasted a moment before someone rapped the front door knocker.

"That's probably Tav." Amina announced, turning to pull open the heavy, maple door.

No one offered a smile or a kind word when Tavares Gwaltney walked inside the house. No one even looked up, when the boy offered his most enthusiastic greeting.

Tav's smile grew a bit less bright, but he was determined to keep the evening civil. "I know we surprised y'all with this, but me and Amina are happy you accepted me into the family."

CJ uttered a brief, humorless laugh. "No choice, man." he practically sneered, before leaving the room.

Stephanie followed.

"Tav, how do Minerva and Jason feel about this?" Chick asked.

Tav rubbed his palms together and nodded. "They seemed real happy about it last night. We even talked about the wedding plans for a little while. Didn't we, Amina?"

Ophelia leaned forward in the armchair she occupied. "What about college?"

"Oh, I'll still be going to Hampton in the fall, Mrs. Augustine." Tav promptly replied.

Ophelia frowned and her gaze briefly shifted from the couple to her husband. "Well what about Amina? She'll be in North Carolina. How can a new marriage survive distance like that?"

Tav sent his fiancée a strange look. Obviously, he was surprised by the tidbit of information. The fact didn't go unnoticed by Ophelia and Chick. Without further comment, they excused themselves from the living room.

"North Carolina's out Amina." Tav coolly decided, once the Augustines had left the room.

Amina shrugged. "Fine." She coolly replied, though her hazel gaze was firm. "I don't have to go to North Carolina, but I *am* going to college. Nothing is gonna stop that."

Tav would have preferred Amina stay home and take care of him-the way his mother had done with his father. Before he could relay his feelings, bright lights flashed against the long cream drapes and the screen door. Amina jumped at the intrusion and went to see who the visitor was.

"What the hell?" Tav murmured when he saw Nikos Cantone pulling into the driveway.

"I'll be right back." Amina whispered, leaving her fiancé, standing in the doorway.

"Hey Girl." Nikos greeted, his gorgeous dark eyes thoroughly appraising, as they swept the cute, flowing light blue dress Amina wore. "You look nice." He complimented.

"Thanks." Amina sighed, her hazel stare shifting from Nikos to the front porch.

Nikos followed the movement and his expression grew murderous. "That Tav?" He whispered.

Amina nodded. "Mmm hmm."

Nikos shook his head. "He still trying to get you to fall for that proposal?"

Amina closed her eyes against the pain of her heart aching for Nikos. "I accepted." She finally replied, unable to look him in the face.

A sudden weakness overcame Nikos' entire body and he could only lean against the truck. His stunned gaze scanned Amina's face beneath the moonlight. What he saw in her eyes devastated him. "How could you do that? Amina? Didn't that night mean anything?"

"It did. I swear it did. It meant the world." Amina whispered fiercely, her hands clasped against her chest. "Nikos marrying Tav...it's for the best."

"How? Amina after what he did? Why the hell are you gonna do this?"

Amina's eyes streamed tears. "I knew you're confused..."

Nikos shrugged. "And that's it? I don't even get to know the reason why?"

Taboo Tree

Unable to speak further, Amina just stood there. She tried to tune out the sound of Nikos ragged breathing, hating herself for causing him such pain.

"Forget this." Nikos groaned, turning to wrench the truck's door open. His chest constricted as he suppressed the onslaught of tears begging for release. He heard Amina call his name, but ignored her as he got behind the wheel and sped away.

***

Everyone was caught up in a storm of activity during the next few weeks. Tav wanted the wedding quickly and, of course, Amina felt the same. Due to Amina's age, there were papers to be signed and the Gwaltneys arranged to have Dyna flown back to Virginia as part of their wedding gift to the couple. Eventually, all the plans came together and Amina Celeste Davidson was a pure vision when she walked down the aisle.

"I present to you Mr. and Mrs. Tavares Gwaltney." Reverend Joel Irons made the announcement amidst cheers and applause throughout the church.

The entire town attended the event, it seemed. Of course, the Gwaltney-Davidson wedding was hailed as the social gathering of the year. Despite everything, Amina felt like a princess. The ceremony was beautiful, the guests were wonderful and Tav looked and behaved like a dream. It was so easy to pretend the marriage and this man were all she ever wanted. Tav's kiss was passion personified and only enhanced the sweet emotions coursing through Amina's veins.

"Happy?" He whispered his handsome face alive with love and pride.

Amina nodded. "Mmm hmm," She confirmed, not wanting to hide her smile.

Tav kissed his new wife, and then the couple raced down the aisle. Confetti showered them, as they left the church.

Outside, family, friends and local news people snapped photos of the newlyweds. Across the street, away from the glee, Nikos stood in shadow. His expression was intent as he looked for some sign of despair on Amina's lovely cinnamon-toned face.

He could find none. She seemed completely happy and in love with her new...husband.

Slowly, he nodded his acceptance and turned away from the happy scene. His truck was parked a short distance away. Packed in the flatbed, was everything he owned. He chanced one last look across his shoulder and let the image of Amina's happy face burn into his mind. Then, settling inside the truck, he headed out of town on his way to New York.

***

The Newlyweds spent their wedding night at the town's best hotel. The honeymoon would last two weeks in the Florida Keys courtesy of Chick and Ophelia. Amina was eager to consummate the marriage, but her husband had other ideas. First, they danced he fed her strawberries and champagne. She reciprocated.

"I wanted you with me the first time I saw you." Tav whispered, as he dropped soft kisses to Amina's neck. "I'm gonna make you happy." He promised.

Amina had hoped to keep her emotions out of the way, but denying Tav's appeal was impossible. She shivered, when his fingers trailed the deep neckline of her pink see-through negligee. He caressed the soft swell of her buxom, before cupping the full mound in his large palm. His other hand eased about her waist and he held her close while suckling the soft flesh of her earlobe.

Amina moaned and unconsciously arched into Tav's muscular frame. Her eyes widened when she felt the devastating bulge of his manhood against the zipper of his black trousers. She moaned suddenly, when Tav moved his hand from her breast. It was only so he could unfasten the front ties on the negligee. The sheer gown fell silently to the plush carpet. Tav set Amina away in order to enjoy her nudity. If possible, he grew more aroused by the sight of her.

Amina wondered if she should appear a bit timid as a virgin bride should be. Unfortunately, the stimulating foreplay made it difficult to accomplish that fact. Tav was a master at lovemaking and most eager to try his considerable skills with his new wife.

Long moments passed once he had her on the huge canopied bed. His lips teased every inch of her body. He lavished her breasts with sweet strokes of his tongue, then journeyed lower, beneath the curve of her breasts, down her flat tummy, then on to more intimate places.

Amina's shocked yet excited reaction to the scandalous kiss brought an arrogant smirk to Tav's face. He pleasured her shamelessly, enjoying her gasps and the movements of her hips as she arched closer to the deep thrusts of his tongue.

Finally, Tav could no longer deny himself the full pleasure of his wife's body. He quickly removed his trousers and briefs and prepared to enter her. He whispered soft words of encouragement, warning her that she might feel a bit uncomfortable at first. When he entered her though, he realized she was no virgin. The realization occupied his thoughts briefly, before the feel of her body regained his full attention.

"Who was he?" Tav questioned later when Amina reached for her robe.

"What?" She queried her expression innocent.

Tav stroked his jaw and ordered himself to remain calm. "Who had you, before me?"

Surprise registered in Amina's clear hazel eyes, but she quickly dismissed it. "You're talkin' crazy." She laughingly replied.

Tav wasn't so amused. When Amina moved to leave the bed, he caught her arm and jerked her close. She managed to remain calm, laying her hands flat against his chest.

"Baby, does it matter if I'm not a virgin? Whatever happened was a long time ago." She lied, batting her long lashes with practiced innocence. "I'm sure you had a girl or two before me."

Of course, Tav couldn't deny that. "I'm sorry." He whispered, grinning as he kissed the spot where he'd squeezed her arm. The kiss heated and they made love the rest of the night.

AlTonya Washington

***

The Gwaltneys and Augustines managed a somewhat peaceful coexistence. Tav and Amina's marriage didn't draw them any closer, but a small truce did form as everyone went on with their lives. Ophelia and Chick celebrated the arrival of their son Huron Torrance Augustine. Demetria gave birth to twins Porter and Portia Gwaltney.

Stephanie and Sweet attended Howard University and married right after their junior year. CJ grew even more engrossed with his work and was a fine student at North Carolina A&T University.

Amina even settled in as wife and student at Hampton. The situation would've been better for the young bride had her husband not been such a monster. Tav's problems with jealousy only intensified. There was a brief respite when he discovered she was pregnant, but Amina knew she would soon have to leave him.

***

The years that passed were otherwise uneventful for the two clans. Of course, the silence only provided time for the hatred to simmer until it was ready to explode once more.

PART II

WHAT IS PRESENT

FIFTEEN

Virginia- 2012

"**G**irl, you need to slow up with that shit."

Melissa 'Missy' Kensie rolled her eyes towards the handsome young man who loomed above her. "Stop," She whined, slapping at his hand when he attempted to pull the rum bottle from her fingers.

Porter Gwaltney toyed with his shoulder-length dreadlocks. "You can't drink it away, Missy." He said, grimacing at the young woman who rested her head in his lap.

"I know that, Port. I know that. This will just help me deal with it, until we figure out what to do." Missy reasoned, her voluminous brown eyes sparkling as she taunted him with the bottle. "Sure you don't want a taste?"

"Positive." Porter replied with an overly dramatic sigh. Still, he understood his friend's reasoning. A drink would be a welcomed treat, especially then. Unfortunately, when the haze cleared, they would still be facing the reality of what had been discovered.

Porter and Missy grew close in grad school, despite the problems between their families. In fact, the hatred between the

Gwaltneys and Augustines pushed the kids closer and prompted them to retrace their respective family histories as a combined project for Porter's final doctoral and Missy's graduate theses. Over the weeks of research, they became close as brother and sister. As the only child of Stephanie and Samuel 'Sweet' Kensie, Missy savored the bond. Porter shared those feelings since he had never been close with his twin sister, Portia.

"I guess it's a good thing our relationship is platonic." Missy slurred. Her thick lashes fluttered as she tilted the bottle in mock toast.

Porter's dark gaze was soft as it caressed Missy's lovely face. The delicate beauty had a natural style he had found appealing from the moment they met. Missy's thick locks framed her round face like a soft black cloud. She wore little makeup, taking advantage of her flawless molasses complexion.

The sibling act had been hard on Porter in more ways than just the obvious. He had anticipated carrying the relationship further. Now, that was an impossible dream.

"Can we get the hell outta here?" Porter suggested, suddenly eager for fresh air.

Missy's smile was bright. "What you got in mind?"

Porter massaged his smooth jaw. "I got my bike." He suggested with a shrug.

Missy uttered a gleeful cry. "Let's go! I can drive!" She decided.

"You don't drive a motorcycle, you lush." Porter teased, pushing himself off the floor.

"Whateva," Missy drawled, before tilting back the bottle for another taste of the fruity rum. "Can we just go?"

The two friends left Missy's apartment around 1:20am. Porter had his share of drink that evening, but he was nowhere near as imbibed as Missy-she stumbled terribly and would have fallen more than once had it not been for Porter's hold around her waist.

"Easy." He whispered, as he helped Missy onto the polished, black leather seat.

"This is gonna be fun, even though I hate this damn thing..." Missy rambled as she clutched the bottle against her chest. "You know what, Porter? This whole mess is so crappy. I mean, how can this shit be true? I mean..."

Missy chattered so, she didn't realize Porter was unresponsive. Of course, he fully agreed with her drunken ramblings. The more preoccupied he became with his thoughts, the more Missy babbled. They had ridden quite a ways, when she lost her hold on the almost empty rum bottle.

Porter heard the shatter and turned to see what happened. Missy laughed at the fumble and shrugged at the mishap. The brief diversion took Porter's attention from the road too long. He turned and was met by the blaring horn of an eighteen-wheeler. Missy's piercing scream seemed to resound over the horn. Her cries were silenced when the motorcycle raced head on into the truck's grille.

***

The Gwaltneys and Augustines continued to prosper. Still, things had changed a great deal over the years. Jason and Minerva Gwaltney had both passed away, leaving their four children to carry on the business and estate. Chick Augustine had passed as well, leaving behind his wife and five children. Both clans thrived and were equally successful in business. Hatred, however, still ran deep between the families. Time and distance worked hand in hand keeping the foul emotions from erupting. The truce could only last for so long.

***

"By the time I saw 'em it was too late. It happened so fast...so fast." The truck driver's sunburned face grew redder as his tears returned.

The highway-nearly deserted less than 20 minutes ago, now teamed with police cars and emergency vehicles. Lights blazed and traffic was diverted to alternate routes. The shaken truck driver relayed the events of the night as best he could remember. His speech was slow at first, and then grew more rapid as he spoke. The coffee sloshed around the small paper cup within his shaking grasp until less than half remained.

"Mr. Dubose, take it easy. Please." Sgt. James Sterling urged as he tugged the cup from the driver's hand. "Get rid of this, will you?" He told one of the deputies. "Last thing the man needs is caffeine."

Several feet away, Porter was being strapped onto a stretcher. The young man was almost unconscious, but he was extremely talkative. The accident replayed itself with startling accuracy.

One of the EMS workers took Porter's hand and gave it a comforting squeeze. "Come on, buddy. You gotta calm down. You're gonna be fine."

"Where is she? Where is she?..." Porter chanted, moving his head from side to side.

"He's delirious." The ambulance driver told one of the deputies standing nearby.

"Son? Can you remember what happened?" The tall soft-spoken deputy asked Porter, his pen poised over a pad.

"Where is she? I only looked back a minute. Where is she?"

"Son? Son?"

"We better get goin'." One of the technicians decided, nodding to his partners as they prepared to load the stretcher into the ambulance.

"Hey get a stretcher over here!"

Porter's dark eyes widened when he heard the commotion. Across the darkened wheat field, another body had been discovered. Porter's eyelids grew heavy, but he managed to keep them open. In the distance, he could see the police, firemen and other workers shaking their heads. He knew they were looking at Missy's lovely young body, now torn and lifeless. The impact of the crash threw her against the truck. She bounced across the pavement and into a swampy field. Meanwhile, Porter had hit the edge of the truck's grille before he bounced into the field several feet away from Missy.

The vivid, horrible memories sent a scream rippling from Porter's throat. Convulsions began to wrack his body and he heard the EMS workers shouting that he was going into shock. Moments later, everything went black.

***

The three nurses at the 7th floor station of Richmond Regional turned to stare at their colleague. The woman, another RN, had just uttered a hushed, yet audible, 'goodness'. It didn't take long to realize what had the woman so captivated. Conversation at the nurses' station halted as the ladies focused on the man headed towards the round, white counter.

To say the exceptionally tall man was *fine* or *was to die for* would have grossly understated his features. Sanford Bay Gwaltney was built just as powerfully as his brother Tav and father Jason Gwaltney. His soft hair was close-cut and he wore a light beard that covered his gorgeous caramel-toned face. A silky mustache rested above the soft curve of his wide mouth and a lone dimple appeared when he smiled. Sanford was known to be less outspoken than his father or brother. However he was much more observant and far more thoughtful. His appeal to the opposite sex lay in ability to charm and fascinate a woman with seemingly very little effort.

The nurses exchanged glances and put their most dazzling smiles in place. Despite the situation, Sanford returned the smiles and made eye contact with each woman.

"Good evening, Ladies." He greeted in his soft, deep voice. "I'm Sanford Gwaltney. My nephew, Porter Gwaltney, was in an accident this morning. I'd like to see him."

Again, the women exchanged looks. This time, worry and concern filled their eyes. The terrible accident had been the talk of the hospital.

"They just moved him from Intensive Care, Mr. Gwaltney." One nurse explained, as she stepped around the desk. "He's in room 7019, they're still monitoring his condition. I'll show you."

"We'll phone the doctor and let him know you're here." One of the other nurses offered.

Sanford's usually unhurried stride was a bit more rapid now. The call to his Richmond condo regarding Porter had

215

AlTonya Washington

caused little shock at first. The boy had fallen victim to more than one scrape because of a motorcycle in the four years he'd been riding them. The fact that hospital personnel called; regarding the accident, raised more than a little concern.

The polite staff person had actually called with hopes of locating Porter's mother. However, he was authorized to handle any messages. Of course, this was true. Sanford and his younger sister Cecelia were more like parents to the twins than their own mother. In fact, Demetria had never expressed much interest in her beautiful, smart children. Because Porter and Portia were products of rape, no one-aside from Sanford and Cecelia, seemed to blame the woman for her cold approach to motherhood.

"Mr. Gwaltney? I'm Doctor Troy Morgenstern."

Sanford nodded and reached for the shorter man's extended hand. "Doctor. How's my nephew?"

Dr. Morgenstern's green eyes grew warm with understanding and he began to lead his patient's uncle down the silent, white hallway. "He's getting the best care. We've managed to stabilize him. He had some internal bleeding, but we got it stopped and moved him out of ICU."

"What happened, Doctor?"

"It appears that your nephew had a head on collision with an eighteen wheeler."

"Jesus." Sanford whispered.

"Mr. Gwaltney," Dr. Morgenstern called, stopping a few feet from Porter's room, "he was very lucky-despite his injuries. Aside from the bleeding, he has two fractured ribs and several bruises. Otherwise he's fine. He will fully recover."

The diagnosis was welcomed news, but Sanford couldn't fully enjoy it. "What about the young woman?" He asked.

Dr. Morgenstern hesitated before answering. "She was pronounced dead on the scene."

"May I see my nephew?" Sanford requested, filled with twin emotions of relief for Porter and grief for the young woman.

Dr. Morgenstern nodded and waved his hand before Sanford. "This way," He instructed. "He's been asleep for a while now. I'll give you a few moments, before sending in the nurse with more sedatives."

"Thank you, Doctor." Sanford whispered, when he stood just inside Porter's room. He slipped his keys in the front pocket of his saggy cream colored jeans and took a seat on the edge of the bed. "What the hell were you thinking?" He asked, staring at his nephew's features relaxed in sleep.

Suddenly, Porter frowned and, after a few seconds, he managed to open his eyes. The dark orbs were horror-filled when he grasped his uncle's Virginia Union sweatshirt. "She's dead, she's dead, Uncle. She's dead."

"Porter? Porter? Calm down, man. Shhh...it's okay." Sanford soothed, covering the boy's trembling hand with his own.

"It ain't okay." Porter sobbed, moving his head to and fro against the pillow. "Missy's gone. I'm the blame. I loved her and I killed her."

"Shhh...Porter, this ain't good for you, man."

"They always gonna hate us. They always gonna hate us, 'specially now."

Porter's rambling brought a frown to Sanford's face. Before he could probe any further, the nurse arrived with a sedative.

Sanford took advantage of the interruption, to leave the room. In the hallway, he leaned against the wall.

"Mr. Gwaltney? Are you alright?"

Sanford moved his hand from his face and found Dr. Morgenstern watching him with concerned eyes. "How long does he have to be here?" He asked, jerking his head towards the room door.

"Just a few days, but he'd need a soothing place to recover. Preferably outside the city."

"I got the perfect place in mind." Sanford said, making a mental note to call Tavares at the Gwaltney family home.
"Doctor, what can you tell me about the young woman who was with my nephew?"

Dr. Morgenstern appeared discouraged for the first time that morning. "We haven't located her parents yet, but we think we're on our way to finding them. We were able to locate her college ID from her purse among the wreckage."

"Any luck with that?"

"Well...we've contacted the University and it seems her parents live in Chicago. She does have family in Virginia, though. We thought it'd be best to inform them first. They live just outside Hampton."

"Outside...Hampton?" Sanford queried, his dark eyes narrowing further.

The doctor nodded. "That's right." He confirmed.

"What was her name?"

Dr. Morgenstern had a pad tucked beneath his arm. He scanned it briefly, before looking up at Sanford. "Melissa Kensie." He stated.

"Kensie..." Sanford repeated, not recognizing the name. "What about the family? Outside Hampton?"

"Oh yes, uh...Augustine. We're trying to contact Charles Augustine right now. I believe that's her uncle."

Sanford felt his throat constrict and bowed his head again. "Augustine...Jesus."

***

The Augustine estate had changed many times over the years. With Chick's death and Ophelia moving back up north with her family, the property had been left to the children. Only CJ had remained. He handled all immediate business from the executive floor which had been added to the stately mansion. His younger brother, Huron, conducted all national and international affairs of Augustine Seams. Huron stayed at the house whenever he visited Virginia. Still, despite all the changes, the original warmth and coziness of the estate had remained.

Martha Harvey rushed from her first floor bedroom. Her fuzzy blue house slippers brushed the polished hardwood floor as she headed down the employee wing and past the kitchen. She

Taboo Tree

whisked up the carpeted staircase leading to her boss's bedroom suite.

CJ pulled the door open several moments after he heard the knock.

"Mmm hmm," He greeted his head housekeeper, while rubbing sleep from his eyes.

"I'm sorry CJ, but there's a call for you on line two." Martha whispered, smiling up at the man before her.

"What time is it?" CJ mumbled.

"Just after six."

"AM?" CJ marveled, his long brows drawing close over his striking dark eyes. "Who the hell-"

"They say it has to do with Missy." Martha interrupted, her tiny wrinkled brown hands clasped before her chest.

CJ's sleepiness cleared and he headed back into the bedroom. "What line did you say?"

"Two." Martha called, waiting in the doorway while CJ answered the call. She pressed her hand against her heart when he uttered a hushed, shocked response to the caller's news. Her small, green eyes widened as the rest of his replies grew shorter and softer. Finally, he replaced the receiver.

"What is it?" Martha cried.

CJ massaged his tired eyes and took a seat on the edge of the oak night table. "Missy was in an accident. She's at Richmond Regional."

"Is she alright?"

CJ stood and headed for the walk-in closet across the room. "They only said I needed to come to the hospital right away."

"Oh Lord..."

"Hey..." CJ soothed, walking over to Marsha and squeezing her tiny hands in his large ones. "It's alright. Go see if Huron's in. If he is, get him up."

***

Porter awoke and found Sanford dozing in the chair next to his bed. "Uncle?" He called, after a moment.

Sanford opened his eyes. "How do you feel?" He asked.

"Like shit." Porter blurted his response carrying a double meaning.

Sanford smirked. "What the hell were you doin' with Melissa Augustine?"

"Kensie, Uncle. Melissa Kensie."

"Kensie," Sanford acknowledged with a slow nod. "But man, you had to know?"

"Hell yeah, I knew."

"And?"

Porter rolled his eyes towards the window where early morning sunlight was beginning to stream past the blinds. "You know, you and Aunt Cece always said that feud was tired and petty."

Sanford leaned forward. "I agree," he said, bracing his elbows on his knees, "but man, the girl is dead."

"I know." Porter moaned, closing his eyes as despair filled them. "I loved her anyway."

"What happened out on that highway?"

Porter hesitated, trying to decide on how to deliver the explanation without revealing too much. "We um, were celebrating. We'd just finished the project for our theses."

Sanford smoothed his hands across his close-cut hair. "They're gonna want your ass for this." He sighed.

Porter's grin revealed no trace of humor. He nodded and closed his eyes again. "They would deserve it."

SIXTEEN

CJ and Huron Augustine arrived at Richmond Regional later that morning. The devastating brothers drew as much female attention as Sanford Gwaltney had when he arrived the previous evening. CJ had grown into the image of his father. His handsome features had become a bit sharper with age, but his looks only improved. The silky black hair was still close cut and showed no signs of graying. His dark skin was still flawless.

The man next to CJ was no less striking. Huron Torrance Augustine was just as tall and gorgeous as his brother. The quick, outspoken businessman had often been mistaken for a young Jason or Tav Gwaltney. Everything about Huron was huge and dark. The onyx stare was deep set and slightly slanted. A set of dimples appeared on either side of his mouth. His hair was a silky mass of tight curls worn in a short afro. His dark, rugged appearance had long ago earned him the nickname "Blue". He wore his sex appeal on his sleeve and was well aware of his effect on the opposite sex. Though Huron was the youngest child, he was not spoiled. He played hard, but worked harder than anyone. Because of Huron's dedication to the company, Augustine Seams ventured into uniform manufacturing for companies all over the world.

CJ and Huron approached the emergency room desk and nodded toward the short, balding man who leaned against the counter.

CJ turned to one of the smiling nurses and nodded. "I received a call this morning about our niece Melissa Kensie."

"Mr. Augustine?"

CJ and Huron turned back to the short man who had spoken. They both nodded and watched him slip on a pair of glasses.

"Doctor Troy Morgenstern. I was here when they brought your niece in."

"Where is she?"

Dr. Morgenstern cleared his throat and motioned behind himself. "If you would follow me?" He requested.

"What happened to Melissa, Doctor?" Huron asked, once they were headed to the bay of elevators.

"Mr. Augustine, your niece was involved in a motorcycle accident, yesterday morning."

"Motorcycle accident?" CJ parroted, glancing at Huron. Melissa had never expressed the slightest interest in the things.

Dr. Morgenstern pushed the button, which to the car to the hospital's sublevel. "She was with a young man...the bike belonged to him." He explained when the car began its descent.

Huron pushed both hands into the pockets of his cream overcoat. He leaned against the rear wall of the elevator and frowned at his brother.

The doors opened and CJ noticed only one set of double doors on the hall. His questioning gaze turned more probing when he read the iron plaque above the chrome doors. He stopped mid-stride.

"What, Man?" Huron whispered, when he bumped into his brother. Following the line of CJ's gaze, a chill rushed over his body when he read the word: "Morgue".

"What happened to our niece?" CJ whispered.

Dr. Morgenstern clasped his hands tightly and stepped closer to the two intimidating-looking men. "She was pronounced dead on the scene. We need members of the family to make a positive id...if possible."

CJ felt faint. "Take us to her." He managed to keep a reign on his emotions. He'd believe nothing until he saw her.

The doctor nodded and led them through the cold, chrome and steel room. Huron squeezed his brother's shoulder and stiffened when Dr. Morgenstern's hands paused over one of the levers along the wall of drawers. When the drawer opened and the sheet whipped back, both men gasped and turned away. CJ stood with his fist balled against his mouth, while Huron nodded towards the doctor.

"It's Missy. It's our niece."

"There are a few papers to sign in order to have the body released to the family."

CJ slumped against the elevator as it began to climb back to the first floor. "My brother can handle it."

A gruesome expression made Huron appear more intimidating. His initial shock had passed and the anger began to wedge itself in his chest.

"Who did this?" He whispered. "You said she was with some guy?" He clarified, when the doctor appeared confused.

"He's recovering."

Huron towered over the man. "Who is he?"

Dr. Morgenstern squeezed the cold chrome of the stethoscope he carried. "His name is Porter Gwaltney." He slowly revealed, wincing when both men pinned him with hard stares.

"Gwaltney?" Huron pronounced the name as though it placed a foul taste in his mouth. "Not these muthafuckas..."

"Huron..." CJ whispered, patting his brother's shoulder.

Huron wasn't in the mood to be consoled. "Fuck that CJ. Now them bastards done killed somebody. Missy's dead."

CJ grabbed his brother's shoulders and gave him a little shake. "Listen to me. Blue? We gotta think about what's happening now. You need to go with the doctor and sign these papers. You hear me?"

Huron nodded and began to press the heel of his hand against his eyes. "Right. You're right. Come on, Doc." He said, motioning the man out of the elevator.

CJ went to the waiting room in a daze. He made a mental list of all the people that would need to be notified. Of course, Missy's parents were at the top of the list. Stephanie and her husband Sweet came to mind. CJ's unruffled demeanor vanished and tears filled his eyes. He covered his face with both hands and groaned. "Jesus, Steph how do I tell you your only child is dead because of my son?"

* * *

"Well how is he?!" Demetria Gwaltney cried. Her younger brother had called her home in Newport News, VA to deliver the news about Porter.

Sanford was almost stunned by his sister's reaction. The woman had never shown the slightest emotions regarding Porter or his twin sister Portia. "The doctor is sure he'll be out of the hospital in a day or two."

"Thank God." Deme sighed, bringing a hand to her chest. "I'll be there later today."

Sanford sighed, unsure of how to deliver the next bit of information. "There's something else you need to know."

"Well? Get on with it." Deme ordered, frowning at the strange chord in Sanford's voice.

"A girl was killed. She was on the back of Port's bike."

"Oh God."

"There's more, Deme."

"Lord, Sanford would you just say it?!"

"The girl was related to the Augustines."

"Augustine?" Demetria breathed, her hand going weak around the receiver. "What the hell?...What was Porter doing with-"

"They were in school together. It looks like Port had a thing for the girl."

"Jesus...Oh my God..."

"Deme? What is it?" Sanford probed, noticing his sister's reaction was more emotional than when he'd initially mentioned the accident.

Of course, Demetria was not prepared for any revelations. "San, I'll talk you later. Goodbye."

***

New York, NY

Princess Nandi Gwaltney was still rubbing sleep from her eyes, when she opened the door to her penthouse. A few seconds passed before she could clearly focus in on the huge man filling her doorway. "Daddy!" She cried, throwing her arms around Tavares Gwaltney's neck.

"Babygirl," Tav whispered, squeezing Princess's tiny form. A smile came to his handsome dark face as they hugged. He swore he could still smell her baby scent, though the girl was well into her twenties.

Father and daughter stood hugging for several minutes, before Princess pulled Tav inside.

"Why didn't you call and tell me you were coming up? Were you trying to surprise me or something?"

Tav patted his daughter's wavy brown locks and chuckled. "Nothin' like that. I had some business, so you know I had to see my girl before leaving."

Princess's bright smile made her even lovelier. She pressed a kiss to Tav's cheek and pulled him to one of the black suede armchairs in the living room. "Let me get you something. Have you had breakfast?"

"Now, babygirl don't go to all that trouble." Tav softly ordered, though his dark gaze warmed with the love he felt from his only child. "I know you must have to get to work." He said.

Princess placed a fluffed pillow behind her father's back and grinned. "I think I can be a little late since I do work for my mother."

225

AlTonya Washington

Tav's features softened and a smile triggered the double dimples in his still handsome face. "How is he?" He asked in his softest voice.

Princess gathered her long hair and twisted it into a thick braid. "In her element, as usual. Sometimes, I think Mommy's life started when she began Queen Cosmetics."

"And how is business?" Tav asked, folding his arms across the stylish hunter green and white football jersey he sported.

"Incredible...and hectic," Princess admitted, curling up on the cushiony black sofa. "We just snagged a contract from Nubian Entertainment to handle the makeup for their TV movies over the next three years."

Tav's sleek brows raised a few notches. "Impressive. Sounds like Amina's doin' well."

"Mommy's unbelievable, but sometimes I think she works too hard. You should always make time for play."

Tav's robust laughter burst forth. "Lil girl, you been 'round me too long!"

Princess shrugged. "Well, it's true where Mommy's concerned."

"So I guess she's at work now?"

Princess's champagne gaze twinkled. "I'd bet my life on it. Especially, since we're getting close to inventory time. There's a lot of number crunching and stock reports to get out. Mommy's sure to be in the thick of it. She never leaves it in the hands of the finance department."

Tav rubbed his fingers across his bald head. "That's what successful businesses are made of lil' girl."

Princess caught the soft look in her father's eyes. "She might like to know you're in town."

"Baby, I doubt that." Tav replied with a chuckle.

"I think she misses you sometimes."

Tav doubted that even more. Still, he loved his daughter for trying to give him hope. Unfortunately, he knew his ex-wife's hatred for him would never disappear.

Princess saw the light leaving her father's eyes and she jumped off the sofa. "So, are you free to spend the day with your favorite person?"

"Happy to oblige," Tav promptly replied, despite the slew of meetings he'd been asked to sit in on. He could never deny anything his only child requested.

***

Richmond, VA

Cecelia Lisette Gwaltney waded through the sea of newspaper and boxes to find her phone. She was practically out of breath when she located the navy blue cordless beneath a heap of blouses.

"C. Gwaltney."

"Dr. Gwaltney? Greg Holmes."

Cecelia went still, her heart slamming against her chest when she realized it was Richmond Regional's Chief of Staff. "Dr. Holmes, is anything wrong?"

"Nothing like that, Cecelia. Your assignment is still intact. I'm calling to let you know you'll be meeting your mentor at breakfast next Tuesday morning."

Cecelia released the breath she'd been holding and sat on the cluttered sofa. "So it's official?"

"It's official. The meeting was scheduled for this week, but he's had a family emergency."

Cecelia sighed and said a soft prayer of thanks for the opportunity to work closer to home. "So which doctor will I be working under?"

"One of our best. Doctor Derric Augustine."

Cece knew she would have fallen to the floor had she not been sitting. "Augustine?" She parroted. "He wouldn't be from Virginia, would he?"

"That's right, small town near Hampton." Dr. Holmes confirmed. "He's our top Pediatrician. You'll be in good hands."

Cece swallowed the urge to cry. "Thank you, Doctor Holmes." She managed.

"No problem. You enjoy the rest of your weekend."

"Oh..." Cece groaned, clutching fistfuls of her bouncy shoulder length hair. She didn't even want to speculate how badly this would turn out. Part of her believed they might be able to overlook the drama between their families and develop a thriving professional relationship.

"Hmph. I'll believe that when I see it." She said, just as the doorbell rang. Taking a quick look at her cluttered surroundings, she shrugged and went to answer the door.

"Hey, Girl."

"Sanford!" Cece cried, pulling her older brother inside the doorway and hugging him tightly. "You would show up here, now with my place in shambles." She playfully berated.

"Don't worry about it. I didn't have time to call." Sanford was saying, as he shrugged off the lightweight, black, bomber jacket he wore.

"Well, come in, come in. Lemme show you around." Cece whispered. Her lovely narrowed brown eyes were bright with excitement as she pulled her brother into the condo. "Like I said, it's a little bit messy around here, but-"

"Cece, hold up."

Something in Sanford's voice caused Cece to frown. "What's goin' on, San?" She asked, not liking the weary look on his handsome face.

Sanford took Cece's hands in his and focused on the thumb ring she always wore. "Porter was in an accident last night."

Cece blinked once, her eyes growing to the size of saucers. "An accident? Well...what happened? How is he? Is he in the hospital? Dammit San, why didn't you call me last night?"

"Shh...Shh Cece. Baby? He's alright." Sanford cupped his sister's round face in his hands and forced her to look into his eyes. "He's fine. You hear me? He's fine. The doctor says he should be out this week."

Cece blinked tears from her wet lashes. "Is there more to the story? Port's never been in much more than a scrape with his damn bikes."

Taboo Tree

Sanford couldn't help but smile at his younger sister's keen perception. Only a few short years separated their births; however, they had always been close as twins. As the last two Gwaltney children, that closeness was a lifesaver many times.

"So, what happened?" Cece probed, strolling down the short stairway which led to the sunken living room.

Sanford tossed his jacket onto the sofa and ran both hands across his head. He decided to just come out with it. "A girl named Melissa Kensie was with Porter. She died. Melissa's related to the Augustines."

Cece stood frozen to her spot. "I'm having lunch next Tuesday with Derric Augustine," she finally announced, "He'll be my mentor at the hospital. I thought I could get past that, but now I can truly imagine what my great job will be like."

Sanford bowed his head. "Cece..."

"Nah, nah...don't say it." She pleaded. "I should've known this was too good to be true."

"I don't think it'll be so bad." Sanford predicted, chuckling at the sharp look his sister sent him. "Think about it, Cece. The man has to be a pro. Otherwise he wouldn't be mentoring anybody, right?"

Cece was far from convinced. "Right," She managed.

Derric Montague Augustine's fierce-looking, black leather hiking boots hit the driveway with a dull thud. His handsome, angular dark face appeared uncharacteristically hard. Almost the splitting image of his father Chick and his brother CJ, the man never failed to turn a female head. He wore his coarse, black hair in a close fade with long sideburns and a neat mustache. Derric was usually soft-spoken like his older brother. Unlike CJ, he exuded an aura that forewarned others that he was not an easily approachable man. In fact, many found it shocking that such a silent, intense man could have such a wonderful relationship with children.

Derric was the most popular Pediatrician at Richmond Regional. He had been off duty the night before and was informed of his niece's death just that morning. Stunned, only

AlTonya Washington

began to describe his reaction when he heard that his only niece had been the victim of a fatal crash. The news that it was at the hands of a Gwaltney, enraged him. Once Martha Harvey told Derric his brothers were in Huron's study, he headed down the maze of hallways leading to the office portion of the mansion. Both men were there making the necessary calls-to save their sister and brother-in-law the trouble. When CJ and Huron saw their brother walk in, they forgot the calls.

"What the hell happened?" Derric asked, after he and his brothers shared a tight embrace. "Why was Missy on the back of Porter Gwaltney's bike?"

CJ patted Derric's shoulder and took a seat on the edge of the big, walnut desk in the corner of the study. "It seems they had a friendship going in school. That's how they met."

"Jesus." Derric hissed, rubbing his palm back and forth across his forehead. Where the Gwaltneys were involved, he harbored a hatred only rivaled by Huron, Stephanie and his little sister Cameo. *And on top of this, I have to work with one of 'em,* he silently bemoaned. "I want his head." He stated.

"You ain't said nothin'." Huron replied, fully agreeing with his brother.

CJ shuddered from the hatred he saw in both men's eyes. His reaction was intensified by the fact that the resentment was directed at his only son. He became so affected, he remained silent, while Huron and Derric discussed the legalities of the situation. A knock on the study door, interrupted the conversation.

Martha Harvey stuck her head inside the room. "Your sister Stephanie and her husband are here."

SEVENTEEN

Stephanie and Samuel Kensie stood before the living room fireplace warming their bodies chilled from the sudden nip in the air. The couple had changed little over the last twenty plus years. Stephanie was still just as lovely. She'd let her beautiful hair return to its natural waist length, but usually styled the silky, onyx mass in some elaborate up do. Sweet's love of athletics landed him a high profile coaching job for one of Chicago's top recruited high-schools. He was just as handsome as ever and possessed the body of a well-built man in a much younger age bracket.

"Jeez, it's almost as cool down here as it is Chicago." Sweet remarked, as he pulled the black toboggan from his bald head.

"I know that's right." Steph agreed, flexing her fingers towards the ferocious flames.

A lone knock sounded in the room and the couple turned. Steph screamed and ran to meet her brothers, favoring their handsome faces with kisses. Sweet followed with handshakes and hugs for his brothers-in-law.

"So, how's Missy? There isn't any permanent damage, is there?" Steph rattled the questions off to the three men who watched her stone-faced. No one had informed the Kensie's about the extent of their daughter's accident. When silence answered her question, she winced as though something foul had just passed beneath her nose.

"Sweet, why don't y'all sit down?" Huron suggested.

Stephanie raised one hand. Her lovely almond-shaped eyes narrowed as she focused on CJ. "Where's my baby?" She asked.

CJ pressed her fingers flat against his chest. "Honey, let's sit-"

"Dammit CJ! What the hell is goin' on?!" Stephanie demanded, her hands curling into fists against her brother's dark suit.

CJ pressed his lips together. Bowing his head, he began to speak. "Missy was on a friend's motorcycle-a boy. She...she didn't...she'd dead Steph."

The wind that had been howling and whipping the leaves on the ground, silenced. Inside the house, even the sound of the pots rattling in the kitchen, quieted. Slowly, the reality of the situation hit the two parents.

"Misseeeey!...." Stephanie cried, her fists pounding CJ's chest. All four men had to hold onto her, lest she reel into the raging fire. Sweet cried just as hard, even as he tried to console his wife.

"Who did this?" Sweet demanded, his usually mellow deep voice, now shaking with emotion.

"Those damn Gwaltneys." Huron revealed.

"Porter Gwaltney." Derric clarified.

If possible, Stephanie's expression grew more horrified. Her eyes snapped to CJ's face. A moment later, she fainted.

When Stephanie opened her eyes, she realized she was in her old bedroom and snuggled into the thick warm covers. Of course, the room was no longer the girlish boudoir she remembered. It was now a large suite with a grand king sized canopied bed and decorated in warm, classy earth tones. It felt wonderful to be home until she looked at CJ who sat perched on the edge of the bed. Her eyes filled with water.

"Shh...Baby. Shh..it's alright." He soothed, brushing her tears with his thumb.

"How could you just let this happen? How could you..."

CJ was just as distraught. "Honey, I'm so sorry."

"What were they doing together?" Steph asked, shaking her head at the distant look on her brother's face. "Have you ever been to see him?"

"I've never seen either of them."

The response triggered Steph's temper and she sat up in bed. "You've never seen them? Their your children. You have a daughter and a son."

CJ rolled his eyes and braced his elbows on his knees. "Steph, it's not that easy to go see a boy-a man after thirty years and tell him you're his father."

"I am so sick of this," Steph snapped, whipping back the covers and getting out of bed. "It's always poor CJ, isn't it?" She sneered, pinning him with a fierce glare. "Well, let me tell you something brotha of mine, you go see that boy before I do. It's time for all this mess to come out. I want him to know what he'd done. I want him to pay."

CJ's brows drew close. "Pay?"

Steph folded her arms over her chest. "He killed my child. You don't think I'll just let him get away with it, do you? I don't care whose son he is."

CJ shook his head. "Honey, you're upset-"

"I'm serious." She assured him, her stare unwavering.

***

Princess threw the front door open expecting to see her father. "I overslept. Sorry." She said, finding her mother at her door.

Amina Davidson's knowing smile remained intact, as she strolled inside the condo. She waved her hand with the grace of a queen. She was a woman who still turned heads. The adorable plumpness of her younger face had changed to become a bit sharper. The effect only enhanced her stunning beauty.

"Baby, hush. I'm not here for that."

"What's wrong, Mommy?" Princess asked, frowning as she propped one hand on her hip.

Amina tossed her leather tote to the sofa and smoothed her hands across the long sleeves of her plum dress. "I got a call from Virginia today. Melissa was killed in an accident."

"Missy!" Princess gasped, her light eyes sparkling with tears. "When do we go home?" She asked.

Amina smiled. "The funeral is day after tomorrow. I'd like to be on a plane tomorrow afternoon."

Princess nodded. "I'll be ready."

"Baby, I'm not interrupting anything, am I?" Amina whispered, unable to ignore her daughter's tousled hair and unbuttoned blouse.

Princess couldn't help but chuckle at the playfully suggestive tone of her mother's soft voice. "I was getting ready for a lunch date when you rang the bell."

Amina's arched brows raised a notch. "Anyone I know?" She asked.

The question was answered by the ringing doorbell. "That's him now. Can you get that for me? Thanks, Mommy!" Princess called, hustling from the room.

Amina was still smiling when she opened the front door. Her inviting expression vanished the instant she saw her daughter's lunch date.

"What the hell are you doing here?"

Tav grimaced. He expected a cold reception where his ex-wife was concerned. Still, he always hoped they could get back what they had when they first met. "I'm taking our babygirl to lunch."

Amina rolled her eyes. "What are you doing in New York?"

Tav sighed. "Relax Amina. I'm only here for a few days on business."

"Good."

"You're welcome to join us."

The offer was met by a humorless laugh. "You're crazy if you think I'd come."

Tav's dark eyes were trained on Amina's petite form as she sauntered into the living room. "You look good." He complimented, when she caught him staring.

Amina smoothed her hands over the figure-flattering dress and sent him a wicked smile. "I know." She agreed.

Suddenly, Tav chuckled and scratched his brow. "Does it always have to be this way?"

"Damn right, it does."

"Princess wants us back together." He said, pushing his hands into the pockets of his nylon wind suit.

Amina shrugged. "That's natural, but she's a grown woman now. She knows I'd never put myself in a position to suffer you again."

Tav turned away to hide the hurt in his eyes.

"Besides," Amina sighed, getting her bag off the sofa, "I have to get packed. I'm taking Princess with me to Virginia tomorrow."

"What's goin' on there?"

Suspicious, Amina watched Tav closely. She couldn't believe he knew nothing about what happened. "My cousin's daughter. She was killed in an accident early yesterday morning."

Tav eased down to the arm of the sofa. "What happened?" He asked.

"Haven't you talked to your family?"

"Amina would you please tell me what's goin' on?"

Amina finally snapped. "The Gwaltneys strike again. Steph's only child was killed riding on the back of your nephew's bike!"

Tav was stunned. "My nephew? Porter?"

Amina could stomach the sight of her ex-husband no longer. She headed out the living room. "Enjoy your lunch."

*****

"CJ Augustine."

Silence met the abrupt greeting.

"Hello CJ." A soft female voice finally replied.

Taken aback by the unexpected response, CJ braced his elbows on his desk and held the phone close to his ear. "Demetria?" He whispered.

Again, a brief silence met the greeting.

"You remember my voice?"

CJ closed his eyes. "It's been a long time, but I could never forget. How are you?"

"You should know the answer to that."

CJ nodded. He could not speak.

"How are we going to handle this, CJ?"

"I've been asking myself that very question ever since they told me about my niece. They want his head."

The words didn't upset Deme. "I figured as much." She told him. "This is why I want to come to the funeral and see Stephanie in person."

CJ swiveled his chair around to face the back lawn of the estate. "Deme, nobody knows. Nobody knows they're mine."

Tears began to pressure Demetria's eyes. "You never told your family about Portia and Porter?" She asked, hurt he hadn't cared enough to tell his family.

CJ could hear the despair in her voice. "Stephanie knows. I wanted to tell her."

"Thank you."

"Demetria...Love, the funeral isn't the place to have this out."

"What about the wake? It's tomorrow evening, right?"

"You're determined to do this?"

"CJ I only want to talk to Steph. I grieve for her loss, but I don't want to lose my son."

CJ knew he couldn't stop the inevitable. Besides, he would give anything to see Demetria Gwaltney again. He told her the time and place of the wake and they ended the call.

***

Porter stood staring out his bedroom window when Cece walked in. She watched him there, her heart breaking at the sorrow on his face. After a moment, she cleared her throat and shut the door behind her.

Porter's handsome face lit up when he saw his aunt. "Cece." He whispered, pulling her close for a hug.

"How are you?" Cece asked after they'd embraced a while.

Porter pulled away, the darkness returning to his handsome face. "Physically, I'm fine. My conscience should still be in Intensive Care."

"How in the world did you get involved with one of the Augustines?" Cece asked, pulling a bit of lint from Porter's burgundy terry robe.

"School," Porter recalled, smiling as he remembered the first time he met Melissa Kensie. "Missy came to the cafe late and couldn't find her friends. It was lunch hour and the place was packed. She asked me and my boys if she could eat her soup at the table. Hmph, she sat right across from me and we talked the whole time."

Cece ran a hand through her thick curls. "And y'all have been friends ever since?"

Porter nodded. "Yeah. It takes a special friendship to weather a working relationship. But Missy and me...we managed to finish that project...we finished way before the deadline."

"And you were celebrating?"

"Hmph. Trying to forget."

"Forget? Why?"

Porter pushed both hands through his dreads and frowned. "Aunt Ce, if you don't mind, I don't think I can talk about it now."

Cece smoothed her hands across the close-fitting gray cotton pants she wore and took a seat on Porter's bed. "Baby, I don't want to upset you, but people are going to want answers about what happened that night. Her family's not gonna take no for an answer."

Porter's dark stare was probing. "Have y'all talked to them?"

Cece traced the streaks of hunter green in the amber comforter. "We haven't talked to them, but I can imagine how they're taking it. I just want you to realize this may not just fade away."

Porter slammed his fists against the back lacquered dresser. "Damn Ce, I didn't want this to happen. I loved Missy! I'll make anyone who doubts that...I'll make them believe it."

Cece pushed herself off the bed and went to hug her nephew.

"I'm goin' to the funeral, Aunt Ce. I just made up my mind."

"Baby, no..." Cecelia sighed, pulling away to search Porter's face with worried eyes.

"I'm going." Porter stubbornly replied.

Cece squeezed her hands around Porter's upper arms. "Sweetie, Missy might not be dead if she hadn't gone out on your bike."

"I know that."

"Then you also know that to go to that funeral will be like walking into a den of hungry lions."

Porter remained steadfast. "I have to do it. For Missy. I have to say goodbye."

Cece patted her nephew's cheek.

"Aunt Cece I'm not crazy. I know the Augustines hate me for this. That's why it would help if you were there- somebody in my corner, you know?"

Cecelia pulled Porter into another hug. "Course I'll be there, Baby." She promised. At the same time, she prayed she and Derric Augustine would not cross paths.

EIGHTEEN

Melissa Kensie's wake was held at Bradfern Funeral Parlor, locally owned by James Bradfern and his family. James was a friend to both the Augustines and Gwaltneys. He had witnessed many dramatic episodes between the two clans during his sixty years. Still, the outspoken, humorous, mortician had a feeling he hadn't seen it all.

The elegant, classically designed peach and gold parlor had almost filled to capacity. The Augustine family was in full attendance. Friends and relatives flew in from all over the country to pay their respects to the bereaved parents. Strong emotions filled the room as people walked by the closed casket. Despite the sadness tugging at everyone's heart, the wake passed quite smoothly. Smooth, until Demetria Gwaltney arrived, with her brother Sanford.

The two Gwaltneys received lukewarm greetings from several people. Of course, most of the local residents were already aware of Porter Gwaltney's involvement in Missy's death. They all wanted to witness the scene that was sure to take place.

CJ's dark eyes followed Demetria's every move from the moment she walked in on her brother's arm.

Deme's lovely brown gaze located CJ's face through the crowd. "Excuse me a minute, San." She whispered, nodding towards CJ. A moment later, she was gone from the main room.
CJ wasn't far behind.

Sharon Sams' crooked, dimpled smile grew brighter as she hugged the tall, dark woman who had tapped her shoulder. "I don't believe you got here so soon."
Cameo Cherelle Augustine shrugged, her slanted almond-brown eyes roaming the crowd. "I had to be here. Besides, it helps to have a job where you basically set your own schedule."
"That's right. You're a big time journalist." Sharon sighed, propping her chin against her palm. "How's the magazine work doing?"
Cameo tossed a lock of her waist-length straight black hair and sent her old classmate a smug look. "Pretty well in spite of the economy." She proudly announced in reference to her work as a freelance writer for many monthly entertainment publications.
Sharon's small, narrowed hazel stare registered unease. "How are y'all holding up?"
"Those damn Gwaltneys." Cameo sneered, her easy expression growing dark. "Somebody's head is gonna roll for this, you can bet on that."
"They say it was an accident."
"Yeah, an accident that could've been prevented. But you can bet that if the shoe was on the other foot, they would've already had the cops beating down our door."
"Cameo..." Sharon warned, glancing at the devastating, caramel-toned male standing behind her friend.
"What?" Cameo retorted, propping both hands on her round hips. "Sharon you know it's true. Those slimy bastards are probably hiding the lil' Gwaltney nigga who did this."
Cameo was so incensed she couldn't catch the pointed looks Sharon shot across her shoulder. Despite the fact that the lovely, chocolate beauty was running his family into the ground,

a soft smirk lifted the corners of Sanford's mouth. When the two women moved on, he turned to study her graceful, unhurried stride.

"Cameo..." He whispered.

CJ followed Deme to one of the secluded back rooms in the parlor. He closed and locked the door, then waited for Demetria to turn. When she did, it was as though all the years passed between them had never existed.

"CJ." Deme whispered, rushing forward until barely a few inches separated their bodies.

"You're a brave lady." CJ whispered, his striking dark eyes wandering across her lovely face and lustrous hair.

Deme shook her head. "No, I'm not. I never would've made it inside if I didn't have my brother to lean on."

CJ's mouth curved into a soft, warm smile. "It's good to see you."

"You too." Was the soft reply. Deme's mahogany brown stare, clashed with CJ's penetrating obsidian gaze, and a flurry of suppressed emotion rushed to the surface.

Deme's parted lips and lovely face were CJ's undoing. His fingers tightened around hers and he pulled her into a deep, savage kiss. A helpless moan left his mouth as his tongue thrust against hers. Demetria could barely breathe, but she didn't care and met the pressure of his mouth with wild abandon. CJ's hands were everywhere. He backed Demetria against one of the room's paneled walls and cupped her breasts through the chic satiny material of her lavender blouse.

"Deme..." He breathed, breaking the kiss to trail his lips along the fragrant column of her neck.

Demetria arched her body, seeking more of his incredible touch. "Don't stop." She moaned, her fingers stroking the silky crisp darkness of his hair.

"I need more than this." He growled into the base of her throat. "Meet me." He ordered, pulling her into his arousal.

AlTonya Washington

"Anywhere," Deme obliged, her hand disappearing beneath the lapel of his black suit. She gasped at the feel of the hard, wide chest she encountered.

CJ smoothed his hands against the black suede skirt she wore. "Let's go." He ordered, caressing her temple with his nose.

Demetria was already nodding in submission, when she remembered the reason for being there. CJ began to pull her close again, but she managed to resist.

"Wait...CJ please. I have to talk to your sister. I need to see Steph."

CJ couldn't hide his frustration. "This isn't a good idea."

Deme nodded. "Maybe not. But I have to try."

"I don't want this to get messy."

"Hmph." She replied, stroking CJ's flawless dark cheek with the back of her hand. "It's the nature of our families, Love."

"Deme..."

"I'll do my best to keep it non-violent." She promised, her expression softening. "I missed you." She whispered, snuggling her face into his neck. "Where do you want to meet?"

CJ's deep laughter filled the room. In spite of all that was happening, he couldn't remember the last time he'd felt so at ease. "Muncie's Bed and Breakfast. It's still in town. Be there at four. Ask for Cliff. He's very discreet and will bring you to me."

"I'll be there." Deme assured him, offering her mouth for another kiss.

CJ didn't disappoint her.

"How could this happen?!" Ophelia Augustine cried. The beautiful matriarch of the family hugged her daughters close as they sat encircled by friends and family.

"Someone needs to pay, that's for sure." Dyna Davidson blurted, nodding as words of agreement followed her statement.

"Now, ain't the time for Demetria Gwaltney to ease her conscience," Sweet whispered to CJ who had just informed him of the woman's desire to talk.

"It's not about that, Man." CJ tried to assure his brother-in-law. "Could you and Steph just spare her a few minutes? She's waiting in Mr. Bradfern's office with her brother."

***

Forest Hills, NY

A stately, brick mansion sat not far off the main dirt road. A cobblestone drive led from the imposing iron gate and encircled the huge home. The immaculately manicured lawn was filled with massive pine trees which loomed overhead. The cool breeze lifted the pine needles in the air. Far off; out in the huge expanse of property behind the house, seven, tall, middle-aged Italian men stood laughing. Each man held a golf club. Two carts in the distance carried other equipment.

Nikos Cantone's rich laughter had to be the loudest. The joke he'd relayed to his 'co-workers' sent each man into peals of helpless chuckles.

"So how's that boy of your, Nik? You still trying to pull the kid into the business?"

Nikos ran one hand through his full head of dark hair. With a slight grin, he regarded Lou Terci comically. "You're getting me confused with Uncle Connie. He's tryin' to get that boy to come in, just like he did me."

"How you feel about that?"

Nikos shrugged and practiced his golf swing. "My kid is doing exactly what I want him to. He's making a good living doing something totally legit and I want to keep it that way." He said, growing quiet as a thoughtful expression came to his handsome, bronzed face. "I had the chance for a completely different life once and I let it slip right through my fingers."

"Hey you deadbeats! It's time to move on!"

Nikos and Lou waved to their golf partners. Then, Nikos patted Lou's shoulder and they left the heavy conversation behind.

***

Demetria turned in the chair which sat before James Bradfern's wide, pine desk. Her expression remained cool when CJ, Stephanie and Sweet stepped into the office.

"What's this about?" Steph demanded her gaze cold.

Demetria glanced at Sanford, who nodded. "Stephanie, I only wanted to tell you how sorry I am for your loss. I'm so sorry."

The kind words triggered Steph's tears. She turned and buried her face in her husband's chest.

Demetria stood and held her hands clasped tightly against her chest. "Porter's sorry too. He and Melissa were close friends."

Steph slapped her tears away and whirled around to face Deme. "Close friends?" She inquired. "That's surprising Demetria, considering the fact that he didn't bother to show up here today."

Sanford stepped forward. "He was just released from the hospital. They have him on bed rest."

"Oh I'm so happy for him." Steph replied, sarcasm almost dripping from the words.

"Steph-"

"Don't CJ." She ordered, never taking her eyes off Deme. "I want that boy in jail for what he did."

Demetria's eyes widened. "Jail?" She gasped.

"Yes and don't you dare stand there tryin' to look surprised." Steph hissed, slicing the air with her index finger. "You never tried to raise those kids and now one of 'em has killed my only child."

Deme tried to stifle her sobs, but failed miserably. "That's so unfair Stephanie. It would be useless to ruin my child's life by throwing him in jail. It won't bring Melissa back."

"You selfish bitch," Cameo called across the room. She had just walked in, accompanied by her brother Derric.

"Cam..." CJ called, warning his youngest sister to silence herself.

Cameo ignored him. "I can't believe you would come here on the day of my niece's wake to plead for your son who's still alive and recovering so he can get back on his bike and kill someone else's daughter!" She ranted, silencing when Derric pulled her back.

Deme covered her face in her hands and cried. CJ's heart ached as he watched Sanford pull her close.

"Augustine. I suggest you put a muzzle on that one." Sanford advised, his deep-set eyes pinned on Cameo.

"You people got some nerve," Derric spoke before Cameo could reiterate, "but then y'all have always had a lot of nerve. Tomorrow we're burying a young woman whose life was just getting started and you come in here to talk about Porter? Porter who's alive and well and walking around, while Missy's going in the ground." Derric's handsome features, twisted into a sinister scowl. "No, Gwaltney. It's your sister who needs the muzzle." He finished.

Sanford patted his sister's shoulder and urged her forward. "Let's go, Deme."

"Best thing I've heard since I walked in here." Cameo grumbled, only to earn a sharp look from Sanford and a sharp tug from Derric.

The Gwaltneys left the room without looking back. Cameo went to Steph and escorted her out with Sweet's assistance. Derric and CJ were about to leave, when Jason Bradfern returned.

"Is my office in shambles?" The man teased.

CJ managed a brief smile. "Not quite, Mr. B."

James watched the group leave and shook his head. He wondered if the two families would ever call a truce.

Porter winced at the pain in his back. He waved off his mother's assistance and propped himself against the pillows on the headboard. "What are you sayin', Uncle San?" He asked, wondering why his uncle suddenly felt it important that he speak with Cornell Alan, the family attorney.

Sanford pushed his hands into the deep pockets of his black trousers. "Port, I'm not tryin' to upset you but in light of what happened at the wake, I think you should talk to Corn."

Porter slammed his fist to the bed. "Talk to him about what?!"

"They are trying to have you thrown in jail for murder!" Deme blurted.

Porter was stunned. "What did y'all do?"

Deme took a seat on the edge of the bed. "We went to the wake and tried to reason with those people. They're determined to make you pay for that girl's death."

Porter leaned his head back and closed his eyes. "I can hear you talkin' to them now. You probably made it sound like I was tryin' to save my own ass and cared nothin' about Missy."

Deme was incensed. "You little-I go over there and put up with all kinds of insults and you want to get upset with me?"

Porter raised his hand. "Mama cool it, alright? You've never been there for me before. I really don't need you now."

Deme turned away just as a tear slid down her cheek. "Fine." She said and left the bedroom without looking back.

"She *is* trying to help, you know?" Sanford was saying as he moved into the spot his sister had just vacated.

"I can't deal with her now, Uncle San."

Sanford patted his nephew's knee through the heavy covers. "I agree. You got more important stuff to think about."

Porter understood his uncle's meaning and looked over at the tall, stout middle-aged man who sat waiting silently behind the desk across the room. "What can we do, Corn?"

Cornell leaned forward, bracing his elbows against the cluttered desk. "The fact that Melissa's blood alcohol level was very high, while yours was non-existent makes you look very good. If you'd been drinking..."

Porter didn't need clarification and closed his eyes briefly. "She was so crazy that night...She hardly ever drank and she couldn't handle it. I was trying to settle her down..." he remembered, "...I must've been busy with her, so my attention wasn't on the road."

"Well, rest assured," Cornell sighed, "there's no way you'll be on trial for murder. The most they could go for is reckless endangerment and even that's a stretch."

"Reckless Endangerment?" Porter repeated, obviously shaken by the term.

Cornell scratched his balding head. "Porter this is all speculation for the most part. I doubt this'll go beyond a few fevered arguments."

Porter leaned forward and pressed his fingers against his forehead. He knew those fevered arguments had the potential to explode into a situation out of control. Especially where the Augustines and Gwaltneys were concerned. He knew there was no way he could miss that funeral.

***

Deme held her breath after she rapped the brass knocker against the room door. The more sensible side of her brain screamed that she was a fool. CJ probably hadn't bothered to show. Still, something made her take the chance. After such a day, she needed something-anything to relax her. She couldn't think of a better way to relax, than spending the evening with CJ Augustine.

What would this mean? Deme asked herself, closing her eyes as she shook off the question. It was not the time for such heavy thoughts. The door had opened and CJ was leaning against the doorjamb.

Deme stood speechless as her uneasy gaze grew wanton with desire. The man was impossibly sexy as he stood there with his tie loose around his open collar. The crisp, white shirt hung outside his dark trousers.

"I didn't think you'd be here." Deme whispered, as CJ's hand grasped her wrist and he pulled her into the room.

The door shut behind them and CJ pressed her high against it. His lips tugged her soft lobe between his teeth and he suckled gently.

"CJ..." Deme gasped, her long nails curving into his neck. She kicked off the stylish lavender pumps and flexed her feet, before rubbing them against his long legs.

CJ allowed Demetria to slide down the door and he began to unbutton her blouse. His dark gaze was intense as it devoured every inch of exposed skin. When the last button came undone, his hands encircled her bare waist. A jolt of electricity surged through him at the realization that her skin was as taut and silky as he remembered.

Deme pulled her hands away from CJ's shoulders and eased out of the blouse. Then, she was arching against his chest. Her haunting brown eyes were full of wonder as they roamed the build of his body. She marveled at the unleashed power that rested beneath her fingertips. The years had only made him more incredible.

CJ's hands moved to Deme's waist where he unzipped the black suede skirt and let it slip to her feet. Effortlessly, he lifted her against him and waited for her eyes to meet his. When they did, his mouth crashed down upon hers. Helpless moans filled the dimly lit, Victorian-styled bedroom.

CJ laid Deme in the center of the bed and indulged in the opportunity to savor the great beauty before his eyes. His fingers moved with a mind of their own, undoing the front snap of her bra and slipping lower to remove the garter and panty hose.

Deme arched herself into the sweet kisses CJ rained across her collarbone. When his tongue trailed the valley of her breasts before disappearing beneath one lacy cup, she almost screamed his name. Her eyes snapped open when she felt him move away. She saw him removing his clothes and pushed herself to her knees and assisted him. Her lips parted when the shirt fell away to reveal the sleek darkness of his wide chest. She favored the area with her lips, then her tongue. She probed his navel lightly, while undoing the fastening of his trousers and easing him down his muscular thighs and legs. When he was nude before her, she pulled him back to bed, eager to feel him against her.

"Deme..." CJ groaned against her mouth, before nuzzling the dark cavern with his tongue. His hands whipped the bra from her chest and cupped one of her breasts in his palm.

Deme threw her arms above her head as CJ's mouth worked over the softness of one dark mound. His tongue traced the rigid nipple before suckling so lightly, she could barely stand it.

Taboo Tree

"CJ please..." She whispered, pulling his head closer to her chest.

A purely arrogant smirk tugged at CJ's lips when the soft request reached his ears. In response, he added pressure to the suckling motions and helped Deme out of the remainder of her under things.

At last, they were both naked and rolling across the king sized four poster. CJ pulled Deme across his tall, agile form and settled her down onto his pulsing length. Through narrowed eyes, he watched her head fall back, the thick curls bouncing with a life of their own.

Deme's hips moved back and forth in reckless abandon. She took all CJ had to give and ached for more. The remaining hours of the afternoon passed in a splendid blur.

Much later, the two lovers lounged in each other's arms beneath warm covers. They reveled in the delight they had not experienced in years. They whispered sweet words of desire and spoke on the past.

"What is it?" CJ questioned, spying the sadness on Demetria's face.

Deme propped her chin on the back of her hand which rested flat against CJ's chest. "Why didn't you step in and stop your family from saying those things?"

The concern on CJ's handsome dark face slowly turned pensive. "I'm sorry." He said, but offered no explanation.

Deme didn't probe. "And that's why it could never work between us." She decided.

The solemn realization frustrated CJ and he shook his head. "I won't accept that, Deme. Too much time has passed for us not to be together."

"There was a reason for that, CJ."

"We were kids, Deme. Reasons that were good enough back then are irrelevant now."

Deme sat up. "How can you say that? You don't even have a relationship with the kids. They don't even know about you. Hell, my relationship with them leaves a lot to be desired. Porter doesn't even want me defending him and Portia..."

"Tell me about Portia." CJ asked, intrigued by the far off look in Deme's eyes when she spoke the girl's name.

"She feels the same way about me that Porter does. I wasn't there for them-not like I should've been." She said, shrugging. There was nothing she could say to explain her attitude towards the two children who were conceived in love. Besides, there was no way she could ever tell CJ the truth about his daughter's life.

CJ watched the solemn look cloud Deme's face. That look alone, convinced him that following his heart would only hurt her even more now. So, as he did all those years ago, he indulged himself in the pleasures of her body and decided he would be content with whatever she could give.

NINETEEN

"Thanks, Dark Chocolate."

The devastating, petite, dark beauty smiled as she handed the pad back to the young man who practically beamed as he spoke to her.

"You have a good day, alright?" She said her expression a tad uneasy as she prayed the young man would be on his way.

The young man had other ideas. "I just wanna tell you how big a fan I am." He said, his vibrant blue eyes almost sparkling as he watched her in awe.

"I appreciate that, but if you'll excuse-"

"I have every movie you ever made, some I bought and some I record."

"How nice."

The young man glanced at the pad he held and grinned. "I'm gonna frame this. Thanks, Dark Chocolate."

Portia Renette Gwaltney smiled as she nodded. When the avid fan went about his business, she closed her eyes and sighed reverently. She could've imagined all the questions Lewis would have if he'd seen her giving out autographs in the airport.

"Dark Chocolate."

Portia grimaced at the low, bass-filled voice behind her. She took a deep breath and prepared to greet another fan. "And

AlTonya Washington

what can I sign for you today?" She asked, in the midst of turning around.

Huron Augustine's mischievous, white grin grew wider. "Can't an old friend just speak?" He asked.

Portia's cool, mahogany brown eyes narrowed as her interest peaked. She began a leisurely appraisal of the man who stood before her and hoped she didn't appear too awed. "I don't think I know you." She finally told him.

"Huron Augustine," He replied, stepping closer to take her hand in his.

Intrigued, Portia leaned back and studied the gorgeous, dark giant. "Now, I'm suspicious." She admitted.

"Why suspicious?" Huron queried, keeping her hand enclosed in his.

Portia forced herself to ignore the tingles stemming from his fingers stroking her palms. "They told me about my brother's accident. That's why I'm here." She explained, her expression softening. "I was sorry to hear about your niece."

Huron's handsome features hardened momentarily. "Thank you." He managed.

For a moment, Portia allowed herself to be mesmerized by the striking intensity of his gaze. "Anyway," She sighed, after a while, "I figured that was just another bucket of fuel added to the fire of the feud between our families."

Huron shrugged. "It's got nothing to do with us."

"You really feel that way." Portia asked, surprised by his attitude.

Huron's grip around Portia's hand tightened, as he pulled her closer. "I wouldn't want us to get started on the wrong foot." He whispered.

"Get started?" Portia parroted, her heart thundering against her chest. "Get started with what?"

Huron shook his head. His cool, confident smirk made him appear even sexier. "Whatever." He told her, studying her face in a manner that said he was more than pleased by what he saw.

Portia felt herself falling deeper beneath whatever web the man was weaving. They were interrupted before Huron could work his considerable charm. They both turned, when someone called Portia's name.

"Lewis." She breathed, quickly extracting her hand from Huron's.

Lewis Hines's handsome vanilla-toned face was made brighter by his big grin. He rushed over, his hands outstretched. "Huron Augustine!" He bellowed. "What's up Blue?!"

Huron chuckled, recognizing his old college football teammate. "What's goin' on Lew?!" He said, while the two shook hands.

"I see you already found my girl?"

Huron's expression grew guarded. "Your girl?" He repeated, watching Lewis pull Portia close.

"Portia Gwaltney, this is Huron Augustine. We played ball together in college." Lewis explained.

"Is that right?" Portia sighed, her eyes returning to Huron's probing dark gaze. She tuned out Lewis's babbling about their college days, as she took in the man's purely sensual features.

"So how did you two meet?" Huron asked, studying the couple before him. He was obviously curious to discover how a dull, homebody like Lewis Hines had latched on to one of the most popular adult film stars in the country.

Portia Gwaltney was an exact replica of her grandmother Minerva Gwaltney. She had the same rich, chocolate skin and thick jet black hair that used to bounce over her head before she had it cut into a chic, boyish style. Portia was extremely voluptuous and overtly sensual. She had always been the 'black sheep', so to speak, of the Gwaltney family. Tired of withering in the shadow of her smart twin brother, Portia left Virginia at eighteen determined to make a name for herself. That name was in the world of pornography and she was never ashamed of the fact. Unlike her family, who kept a close eye on Portia's success-determined that it not reflect on them.

As Lewis relayed the story of their 'love affair', Portia grew more uneasy. She doted on keeping their relationship private. Especially since she hadn't told him how she really earned her living.

Everyone involved with the industry, including the fans, knew Portia only by her stage name "Dark Chocolate". Unless one was an avid adult movie enthusiast, she would never be taken as an adult actress.

Suddenly, Portia tightened her hold around Lewis's arm and regained his attention. "Baby, we really need to get going. Huron it was nice meeting you." She said, without so much as a glance in his direction.

Huron waved them off, smiling as he watched Portia hustle Lewis through the crowd. A devious smile tugged at his mouth.

***

Derric massaged the bridge of his nose and sighed. "Is there any way around this, Greg? I mean, I'm gonna be even more backed up with work after taking all this time off to be with my family."

Greg nodded, feeling sympathy for the young man they were grooming to become head of Pediatrics. "We were all very sorry to hear about your niece, D. I still think you'll be very pleased. Between the two of us, she is a real beauty. Tall, curvaceous, soft-spoken, intelligent...I could go on all day. I promise, you'll thoroughly enjoy being around a woman like Cecelia Gwaltney."

Derric believed the man was exaggerating and was still disinterested. Besides, he had no desire to work around any Gwaltney, regardless of her looks.

"She's counting on meeting you Tuesday morning, D."

Derric smothered his frustration realizing he had no choice. "I'll be there." He promised, cringing as he spoke the words.

Taboo Tree

Cecelia walked into the huge black and burgundy tiled kitchen and smiled at the warm memories the room evoked. She found her big sister there, making coffee for the house.

"Girl, there're plenty of people here to do that for you, you know?"

Demetria shook her head, but didn't turn. "I'm not having it. I need to do something to keep me occupied."

Cece smiled. "Well, I'm glad to hear that, 'cause no one can match your coffee."

Deme looked back and smiled. "I'm surprised you remember. It's been a long time."

"You never forget good coffee." Cece teased, dropping an arm around her sister's shoulders. She watched Deme prepare two steaming, creamy mugs of the brew.

"Is Porter up yet?" Deme asked when they took their seats at the big round table near the fireplace.

Cece nodded. "He's getting dressed."

Deme stirred her coffee and grimaced. "I wish he wouldn't go to that thing."

Cece leaned back against the packed, high-backed chairs. "So do I and that's not sayin' much for me."

"What's that supposed to mean?"

"I've got my own selfish reasons for not wanting Porter to go to that funeral." Cece admitted, smiling at Deme's probing look. "I'm supposed to be working under Derric Augustine."

"Oooo," Deme stated, feigning a pained look.

Cece sighed and pulled both hands through her bouncy bob. "Oooo is right. I was so excited about this, too."

Deme waved across the table and pinned her sister with a stern look. "Don't sit there expecting the worst. You'll have yourself all upset for nothing. Derric Augustine wouldn't have anyone working under him if he weren't a professional."

Cece frowned, even as a smile came to her face. "You're mighty level headed today. What happened?"

Deme shrugged and raised the green mug to her lips. "Sometimes you have to give the past a rest and move on." She said, blowing the coffee before taking a tiny sip. "You worked hard to get your degree and you shouldn't let anybody mess with you making the most of it."

"You're right." Cece said, sounding as though the reality had just claimed her.

"And besides, I've seen Doctor Derric Augustine. It should be sheer Heaven working around him-if only to look at him."

Cece burst into laughter. "I hope you're right!"

"I am."

"Thanks Deme..." Cecelia sighed, reaching across the table for her sister's hand.

Portia walked into the kitchen and found her mother and aunt hugging. "Well, well this is cozy." She noted, smiling brightly when they pulled apart.

"Girl!" Cece cried, moving from the table and running over to envelope her niece in a tight hug.

Across her aunt's shoulder, Portia's eyes met her mother's in a meaningful look. "Mama." She said when Cece pulled away. Then she glanced behind her. "Demetria and Cecelia Gwaltney, this is Lewis Hines. My fiancé."

Twin looks of surprise froze on the sisters' faces. Slowly, they stepped forward to greet the tall, smiling young man who waited patiently just inside the kitchen.

"Where are you from, Lewis?" Cece was asking.

"Just outside Norfolk."

Cece nodded. "Really?" She whispered, noticing the set look on Deme's face. "Would you like some coffee?" She asked Lewis, knowing her sister had a lot to say to her daughter.

"Why would you marry this man?" Deme asked when Cece had pulled Lewis to the other side of the kitchen.

Portia blinked and took a step back from her mother. "I'm marrying him because I love him."

"Bull."

"What is it with you?" Portia whispered, furious at her mother's reaction.

"What is it with *me*? Does the man you love have any idea his wife-to-be is a porn star?"

Portia crossed her arms over the front of the clinging blue sweater and fought the urge to cry. "I'll tell him soon."

"When? On your honeymoon?"

Portia threw her hands in the air and stomped away from her mother.

Demetria watched her daughter through worried eyes.

***

The happy chirping of the birds nestled within the heights of the towering magnolias was a distinct contrast to the solemn, silence below. Christman Memorial Gardens was the site for Melissa Kensie's funeral. The reverend's voice reverberated through the air as he delivered a stirring eulogy. Afterwards, he stepped aside to allow the attendants an opportunity to come forth and place their roses on the silver, chrome casket.

Stephanie squeezed her husband's hand and barely smothered her gasp when Porter Gwaltney stepped up to leave his rose. Sweet patted his wife's gloved hand, knowing she was close to attacking the boy. Stephanie remained calm and the rest of the funeral passed calmly.

Much later, people milled about the yard speaking with members of the family and one another. Stephanie stood in a huddle with Ophelia, Cameo and Amina. Stephanie was practically dazed over the reality of burying her only child. Cameo and Amina rubbed her back while Ophelia held her hands and hummed a soft tuned from the service.

Porter watched the four, lovely women for several moments, before working up the nerve to approach them. Ophelia, her daughters and cousin tensed while watching the young man step towards them.

"Mrs. Kensie?" Porter spoke his tall frame a bit slumped in an effort to appear humble. "I only wanted to tell you how very sorry I am, Ma'am. Melissa was my best friend and I will think of her every day. I loved her so much."

The words were delivered so beautifully, despite the tears streaming Porter's handsome face. Still, they made

AlTonya Washington

Stephanie sick inside. The relationship should never have existed, let alone rise to such a level where Porter believed he loved her daughter. Feeling more depressed now, she couldn't bring herself to look at the boy.

"Excuse me." Stephanie whispered, covering her mouth as a sob rose in her throat. Amina followed her.

Cameo held her fists clenched as she watched her sister. Unable to hold her tongue, she turned hate-filled eyes toward Porter. "You know, it's strange how the Augustines outnumber the Gwaltneys but still, you people always manage to strike a mighty blow."

Across the yard, Sanford saw the tiny huddle and walked over. He wasn't surprised to hear Cameo Augustine's voice loud and clear.

"...I mean, first your bastard uncle marries our cousin and beats the crap out of her for years, then you kill our Missy on the back of your damned bike and you have nerve to come here and speak to us, knowing how we feel about you?" She shook her head, mock disbelief on her face. "You got it goin' on in the arrogance department, my man."

Porter could not respond. Cameo's words cut deep. She said nothing more and walked away with her mother.

Sanford watched his nephew standing there with his head hung low and he couldn't stand by a moment longer. Porter turned when he felt the hard clap against his shoulder. He didn't resist when his uncle pulled him into a tight hug.

"I gotta get out of here." Porter said, shutting his eyes against the tears filling them.

Sanford laid a playful slap against his nephew's cheek. "I'll see you at home." He said.

When Porter walked off, the hard glare returned to Sanford's face. His eyes narrowed as he looked in Cameo Augustine's direction.

"So, are the rumors true?"

Portia smiled at her old high school friend as they held hands. "Rumors?" She queried.

Sheila McWhite's lovely, round, caramel-toned face grew animated. "Are you really getting married?" She asked.

Portia closed her eyes. Her long lashes swept her cheeks when she smiled. "It's true." She confirmed.

Sheila let out a tiny scream. "Is it true he's from Virginia?"

"Mmm hmm. Norfolk."

"How in the world did y'all meet?" Sheila inquired, always interested in a love story.

Portia glanced up at the sky as she remembered. "Well, his name is Lewis Hines and he's an art buyer for a brokerage firm out of Richmond. We met at an art show out in LA."

Sheila nudged her shoulder against Portia's. "I know he's gorgeous."

"He is."

"Getting cold feet yet?"

Portia shrugged, guilt coming to her face. "I'll admit I have had a few second thoughts, here and there. Especially when I see a man who pushes those buttons."

"Mmm...and when was the last time that happened?"

"This morning," Portia replied, without hesitation, joining Sheila who had burst into laughter.

Sheila propped both hands to her wide hips encased in a black blazer dress. "Anyone I know?" She asked.

Portia glanced across her shoulder. "Huron Augustine?"

"Blue?..." Sheila drawled, appearing both surprised and intrigued by the news.

Portia shrugged. "I didn't even know who he was. I don't think I've ever forgotten meeting a man so fine."

"I hear you, Girl. He is one incredible looking thing."

Portia smoothed her hands across her fitted black skirt. "So what's his story? Is he living the life of a playboy as the youngest Augustine?"

"Far from it, Portia. He runs the family business with his brother CJ. His dad's uniform business is now an international organization. Most of that is because of Blue."

AlTonya Washington

"Is that right?" Portia whispered, her arched brows raising a notch.

"Mmm hmm and I should know. I work out of the marketing department of their Chicago office."

Portia and Sheila launched a conversation about their respective careers. Of course, Portia had already decided to tell everyone she was personal assistant to the director of one of the popular prime time medical shows on TV. They were discussing the poor state of quality African-American programming, when Portia spotted her fiancé, talking with Huron Augustine.

People were beginning to leave the cemetery and head out to their cars. Cameo was among them. She reached the dirt road where many vehicles were parked and found Sanford Gwaltney leaning against her cream Porsche. Her steps slowed at the sight of his tall, athletic frame perched against the driver's side of the car. The glare on the man's handsome face told Cameo, his mood was far from friendly. Unfortunately, that fact did little to warn her from taunting him.

"What the hell do you think you're doing?" She demanded, pushing one hand into the side pocket of her black swing dress.

Sanford pushed himself off the car. "Trash talkin' lil' wench, aren't you?" He sneered.

Cameo's almond-browns grew more narrowed. "Excuse me?" She whispered.

"I could excuse the rest of your family." He returned, coming to tower over her slender form. "They lost Melissa too. But, you...all I've heard is you accusing and tearing down my family. Talking about *our* nerve, when it's your shit talkin' that's the real disgrace."

"You bastard."

"And you little snobbish bitch. You're more interested in being heard, no matter how ignorant you sound. You rather shoot off your big mouth about how we're responsible for this, instead of mourning the loss of your niece."

"You son of a bitch!" Cameo spat, slamming her leather clutch against the side of the car. Before she could utter another word, Sanford grabbed her upper arm and jerked her close.

"The next time I so much as hear you breathe wrong around my family, I'll be in your face." He whispered, his long brows meeting to form a fierce frown. "Unlike you, I back up my talk with action. I almost want you to step out of line. The thought of really tearing into you again makes me feel so good, I can almost taste it."

Cameo stumbled on her high, black pumps when Sanford suddenly released her. She swallowed past the lump which had lodged in her throat and watched him with wary eyes.

Sanford kept his expression hard, though inwardly, he cursed losing his temper. He was well aware how fierce he could be and hated people to see that side of his character. He especially hated for a woman to be the recipient of the evil side of his personality.

"You have a good day, Ms. Augustine." He told the stunning beauty. His deep voice had returned to its usual soft tone.

Cameo stood rooted to her spot several seconds after Sanford walked away. Finally, she found courage enough to move. Inside, her car, she buried her face in her hands and took several deep breaths. When she looked up, the hard glare had returned to her face.

CJ escorted his mother to the Limo with Stephanie and Sweet walking alongside them.

Stephanie snuggled closer to her husband and bowed her head. "Baby, I want to get to the police before another day passes."

CJ heard his sister and stopped a couple of feet from the car. "How can you think about that today? How can you think about it at all?"

Steph's expression was murderous. "It's all that's keeping me going CJ so don't even think you're gonna talk me out of it."

"Would you be so hell bent on doing this if a Gwaltney weren't involved?" CJ challenged.

Silence settled as Steph smarted from the question. Slowly, she closed the short distance between herself and CJ. The cracking slap she laid to the side of his face seemed to echo against the wind.

CJ watched his sister walk on to the limo. When Sweet passed, he touched the man's shoulder.

"Talk to her Sweet." He urged.

Sweet shook his head. "Why? I fully agree with her."

CJ clenched his fists, fighting the urge to show his frustration. "I'll see you at home, Ma." He told Ophelia, pressing a kiss to her cheek.

Ophelia's lovely eyes narrowed. Her suspicious gaze followed her son as he walked away.

***

Portia lost sight of her fiancé, but spotted Huron Augustine at the driver's side of his black Navigator. She rushed over before he could settle into the SUV.

Huron heard his name and smiled when he saw Portia headed his way. The lazy, dimpled smile he wore belied his intense curiosity.

"Do you know where Lewis went?" She asked, when only a few inches separated them.

Huron's shoulder rose. "Haven't seen him since we talked 'bout half an hour ago."

Portia let her eyes trail Huron's powerful form and she lost herself in the devilish thoughts racing through her mind. "And just what did you talk to him about?" She finally queried.

Huron pretended to be confused. "Portia...whatever do you mean?" He drawled.

"Don't even try it."

"Try what?"

Portia smoothed her palms across her short, glossy cut and fought the desire to scream. "Listen, it's obvious that you and I aren't going to be friends. So let me be blunt, stay away from Lewis."

Taboo Tree

"Why?" Huron called, when Portia began to walk away. "You afraid I'll tell him what you really do out in Cali, Dark Chocolate?"

Portia turned and retraced her steps, until she stood extremely close. "What do you want?" She sneered.

Huron smiled and placed his index finger beneath her chin. "You."

TWENTY

Dr. Cecelia Gwaltney ducked into the ladies washroom of La
Nouveau and took a moment to work up her confidence for the
meeting.

"Please don't let this man curse me out and spit in my
face." She prayed. Shaking the notion from her mind, she gave a
quick toss of her bouncy bob and headed out. With a smile, she
greeted the breakfast hostess who stepped from behind the
walnut stand. "Good morning. I'm here to meet Doctor Derric
Augustine. Has he arrived yet?"

The hostess's green eyes scanned the large, flat book
lying open on the booth. "Yes ma'am, he arrived about ten
minutes ago. I'll take you to the table."

Cece smoothed her hands across the professional, yet
feminine suit she'd chosen. The two piece turquoise outfit
accentuated her 5'10" hourglass frame. The shirtwaist blazer had
a stylish butterfly collar and long sleeves that hugged her wrists.
The row of tiny, gold buttons stopped at the cleft of her breasts
and offered a slight yet enticing view of ample cleavage. The
matching skirt reached her knee and emphasized her full bottom.
Wedge-heeled turquoise pumps clicked upon the hardwood floor
as she followed the hostess through the sunlight dining room.
Although the popular restaurant boasted very busy morning

hours, the place was not crowded. It was easy for Cece to spot Derric Augustine across the room; arranged with oak-trimmed, glass-topped tables and cushioned oak-backed chairs.

Derric Augustine; however, was the type of man who would stand out in any size crowd. Cece thought she would know him anywhere. She realized he was exceptionally tall, making her feel short for the first time in her life around any man who wasn't her brother.

"Cecelia Gwaltney." She said, extending her hand. "Doctor Cecelia Gwaltney." She clarified.

Derric's cool, brown eyes quickly appraised Cece as he took her hand in his. "Good to meet you." He said.

"I'll send the waiter to your table." The hostess told them, leaving menus before she walked away.

"Have a seat." Derric was saying as he resumed his own place at the round glass table.

"What's good here?" Cece asked, opening the purple gold embossed menu.

Derric tugged at the cuff of his olive green suit coat. "I have no idea." He said, leaning back to regard her with a coolly pensive stare.

Cece cleared her throat and scanned the menu. Beneath the table, she smoothed her damp palms across her skirt. When the waiter arrived, she was thankful for the interruption.

"Uh yes. I'll have your pancake platter with apple syrup, um...hash browns and two eggs-hard scrambled."

The waiter jotted the order and nodded. "And to drink?"

"Coffee-cream and four sugars and a glass of milk."

"And for you, Sir?" The young man asked, turning to Derric.

Derric had been listening to Cece order-amazed by the extent of her appetite. "Yes, um I'll have the hash browns, toast and two eggs-over easy. Black coffee."

Again, the waiter nodded. "Thank you both."

"Big eater," Derric noted, propping an index finger along one sideburn.

Cece's trademark sunny smile made her even lovelier. "I never know when I'll have the chance to eat, so when I sit down for a meal, I make sure it's a big one."

For an instant, Derric's stern, guarded expression softened. He quickly caught himself, though.

"So, tell me what you think of our pediatric wing. Any goals or ideas for anything there?"

Grateful for Derric's change in the subject, Cece nodded. "I think Richmond Regional has a wonderful program, first off. I was very impressed by the tour as well as the portfolio I read regarding recent programs you've implemented. My main goals and ideas for the wing; however, center mostly around the kids themselves. If possible, I'd like to incorporate a more interactive structure in conjunction with the treatment being administered. Give the kids the opportunity to feel as though they're playing an active role in their recovery."

Derric found himself nodding as he listened to Cecelia Gwaltney relay her opinions for the Pediatrics department. Her ideas were well-planned and extremely thought provoking. Then, like a cloud moving across sunny skies, his mood blackened and he reminded himself who Cecelia was.

Cece stopped her words mid-sentence, when she glimpsed the hard look on Derric's face. Thankfully, there was no time to question it. Their breakfast orders had arrived and several moments passed as they enjoyed the meal in silence.

"So why did you leave such a good hospital in Delaware to come back to Virginia?"

Cece cleared her throat and pondered her response to Derric's question. "Well, being from Virginia, I missed the area. I guess my coming back is a testament to my hopes of having it all...a home and a family of my own."

Derric's dark handsome features registered surprise. "You don't strike me as the type who cares about that."

"What do you mean?" Cece queried in a soft voice though her brown eyes narrowed in suspicion.

Derric's shrug was flippant as he turned back to his partially eaten hash browns. "You strike me as the type who

AlTonya Washington

prefers the club scene and single life to taking the kids to the park on weekends."

Cece commended herself on remaining cool when she wanted to dash the rest of her coffee in the man's face. "You really don't know me to make an assumption like that."

Derric lifted a forkful of the delicious browns to his lips. "Obviously." He quickly replied.

A short, soft laugh passed Cece's mouth, but she felt far from amused. Instead, she gently placed her napkin on the table and eased her chair away from the table. "I know this breakfast was arranged by our boss, Doctor Augustine, but I think it'll be better if we end it now. Maybe we can meet in your office, before I actually come aboard." She said, reaching for her black leather tote. "I'm sorry if this causes you inconvenience, but I think it's best that I leave while we're still being civil."

Derric's stare followed Cece's every move as she spoke. He said nothing, but inwardly regretted what he'd said. Especially when Cecelia still managed to remain so polite. His dark gaze was riveted on her as she left the dining room.

***

Judy Canters smoothed her fuchsia skirt beneath her bottom and perched her full-figured frame against Euletta Michaels's desk. "Is he here yet?" She asked.

Amina Davidson's assistant shook her head. "He's here." She confirmed her pretty, caramel-toned face bright with a smile. "Every woman in this building should know the date and time of the man's weekly meeting."

Judy nodded towards the hall leading to Amina's office. "Is *she* here yet?"

"No..." Euletta sighed, standing behind her desk in order to reach for the shipping package slips atop the mahogany file cabinets. "Her office door is open and he's in there all alone going over some paperwork. Help yourself to peek if you like."

"And you know I will." Judy replied, with a devilish giggle.

Taboo Tree

Several women inside the lavender painted halls of Queen Cosmetics found a reason to stroll by the boss's office that day. Each hoped to catch a glimpse of Adonis Mason. From his spot at the round conference table, he provided a source of pleasure to all who peered inside.

Anytime the gorgeous investment banker made an appearance, every woman on Amina's payroll had to see him. The tall, intense-looking god surpassed even the male models whose jobs were to be handsome and irresistible.

Still, Adonis carried himself professionally and only spoke with Amina. No matter to the female employees, though. The man was just incredible to look at. Silky, close-cut black hair lay in waves over his head. His eyes were pitch-black and striking, his nose was long and wide and his full mouth was enhanced by a deep cleft in his chin. Adonis's brownish-bronzed features were so chiseled and refined, it was often stated that he truly lived up to his first name.

"Mommy, I got that meeting set up with the advertising team. Now if I could just get you-"

Princess bounded into the office, fully expecting to find her mother there. Instead, she realized the room was occupied by a man seated at the round conference table on the other side of the office.

She couldn't stop herself from staring. Though the man's head was bowed and his eyes were focused on the papers before him, Princess could easily assess that he was handsome. Extremely handsome.

Suddenly, Adonis raised his head. His obsidian stare narrowed, before he turned and looked directly at Princess.

"Good morning." He said.

Amina walked in as Princess stood staring dumbfounded at the man who had just greeted her. "I'm so sorry I had to keep you waiting like-oh, Princess? Baby what a surprise." She said, laughing as she approached her daughter with open arms.

"Hey Mommy." Princess absently replied, as she kissed her mother's cheek.

Amina pulled back and glanced across her shoulder. "Have you met Adonis?"

"What?" Princess blurted, not realizing 'Adonis' was the man's name and not some reference to his features.

Amina was already waving the man close. "Adonis Mason, this is my daughter Princess Gwaltney. Princess, Adonis is my investment banker."

"I see." Princess whispered, extending her hand. She had always pictured her mother's personal banker as someone stodgy and much older.

"It's nice to meet you." Adonis replied, his strong deep voice going soft. He prided himself on always remaining professional during business, but he allowed his gaze to slide over Princess's extraordinary face and form. He thought the name suited her to a tee.

Princess could feel her palms moisten as her hand lay snuggled within his. "Nice to meet you too," She managed, slowly extracting her hand before turning to face Amina. "Um, Mommy, I only came by to tell you the ad department can meet with us tonight. I arranged a small dinner party at my place. The group can bounce some ideas off you about the Christmas campaign and vice versa. What do you say? Can you make it?"

Amina shrugged and leaned against her glass-topped desk. "Should I bring anything? Is there anything else they'll want to discuss?"

Princess folded her arms across her snug red T-shirt. "Nope. This is gonna be really informal. Just a little get together to see where we stand. What sort of direction we're heading in."

Amina went to check her schedule for the evening. Meanwhile, Adonis watched his favorite client's daughter, studying her petite, hour-glass figure through dark eyes. Princess was the virtual image of her mother, whom he'd had a crush on for years. Still, Adonis could sense Princess possessed a harder streak than her mother. He believed she had a no-nonsense personality and doubted she would gush over any compliments.

Mother and daughter finished their conversation and promised to see each other that night. When Princess turned and saw Adonis standing near the conference table, she was again struck by his height and incredible looks.

"It was nice meeting you Mr. Mason." Princess said. Then, she blew a kiss to her mother and hurried from the office.

Amina saw the look Adonis sent her daughter. She had often wondered which of her lovely female employees would draw the attention of the pensive young man. A smug expression came to her face over the fact that he'd been smitten by her own daughter.

"You know," Amina sighed, as she strolled across the office, "I'd love to have someone take me to this dinner-an escort. It wouldn't look right for a woman my age to walk into a party without a gorgeous man on my arm, you know?" She taunted, tapping her nails against the gold chain belt around her waist.

Adonis's laughter was the complete opposite of his cool, observant personality. It was boisterous and infectious. "I accept." He told Amina, amidst his rumbling chuckles.

***

Portia took another sip of the Amaretto coffee she'd ordered from room service. The doorbell rang as the flavorful brew warmed her tummy.

"Who in the...?" She grimaced as she padded barefoot across the furry beige carpet. "I'm coming..." She called, smoothing both hands across her floor-length peach silk robe. She looked through the peephole and gasped when she saw who was outside. Slowly, she pulled the door open. "What do you want?" She demanded, frowning up into Huron Augustine's smiling face.

"I already told you what I wanted, Dark Chocolate."

Portia was set on standing her ground; but had no choice but to back away, when Huron walked inside. "Are you having trouble finding your own woman?" She asked, forcing herself to act hard and unaffected by his tremendous sex appeal.

Huron massaged the back of his neck and turned. "That's not the case." He assured her.

"Really?"

"You don't believe me?"

"Hmph." Portia gestured, smoothing her fingers along her collarbone as she stepped further into the living room. "It's hard to believe when you come on to me and know I already have a man."

Huron dimples appeared. "A man, Portia? From what I've seen, you got several men."

"Bastard," Portia hissed, her palm aching to slap him. "Don't you care that I'm engaged?"

"Engaged ain't married."

Portia's brown eyes narrowed. "Engaged may not be married, but it is a promise to marry."

Huron stroked his jaw. "Is that so?"

Portia propped both hands on her hips and walked right up to the huge dark man who ravished her with his eyes. "That is very so and it also means that whatever it is you want from me is out of the question."

Boldly, Huron reached out and trailed his index finger down Portia's cheek and along her neck. "So, I guess you won't mind my telling Lew about your real job?"

Enraged, Portia shoved her small hands against Huron's chest. She became angrier when he didn't so much as budge from the blow. "Son of a bitch." She breathed. "You get out!" She ordered, slapping his hand away from her neck.

"Portia-"

"I don't take kindly to blackmail or threats."

Huron extended his hand again this time, cupping Portia's breast in a light hold. "I believe in being honest, Miss Gwaltney. When I see something I want, I'm up front about it and I'll do whatever it takes to get it."

"That include backstabbing your best friend?" Portia challenged, wincing when she felt her body respond to Huron's hand on her chest.

He shrugged. "We weren't that close."

Portia rolled her eyes and started to turn away. Huron caught her upper arms in his massive hands and forced her to face him. Before she realized what was happening, he'd pulled her close and his mouth was against hers.

Initially, Portia tried to fight. Then, she stomped her foot-becoming frustrated because she had allowed Huron to excite her with nothing more than a kiss. His hands eased down her arms to curve around her hips and hold her against his powerful frame.

His tongue massaged hers with maddening thoroughness. He broke the kiss and trailed quick, wet pecks against her cheeks and chin. Then, he was back to pamper the dark softness of her mouth.

Soon, Portia was responding eagerly, matching the slow deep thrusts of Huron's tongue with her own. In minutes, Huron cupped her bottom and lifted her high against him.

Portia lost herself and her inhibitions. She threw her head back and moaned when he suckled her earlobe while squeezing her buttocks as he carried her to bed. Silently, Portia cursed herself. She knew this was wrong, but she couldn't stop herself or Huron.

Determined to enjoy the beauty in his arms, Huron's hands found their way beneath the folds of Portia's robe. He lowered her to the bed and pulled her thighs apart. The lusty kiss resumed and he moaned into her mouth when his fingers touched her femininity.

Portia arched toward the fiery caress, rotating her hips when Huron's fingers were inside her. She pushed her hands into his soft hair and begged him not to stop.

Huron played with Portia a while longer, before he released her. Smiling devilishly, he pressed a kiss next to her ear and spoke gently. "Think about my offer. I think you'll enjoy yourself."

The words were like a bucket of ice being tossed into a steamy bath. Portia's lashes fluttered open and she saw Huron leaving the bed. She felt a sob rising in her throat and turned away from him. "Get out." She demanded, her voice partially muffled in the pillow.

272

AlTonya Washington

The smug confidence on Huron's face faded. The look
was replaced by something more solemn-more thoughtful. He
pushed one hand into the side pocket of his saggy indigo blue
jeans and left the room.

When the door closed, Portia looked down at her
engagement ring. She watched it grow blurred through her tears.
Just then, the phone began to ring. It took several seconds for her
to work up the nerve to answer. "Please don't let this be Lewis."
She prayed, before lifting the receiver. "Hello?"

"Portia?"

"Hey Cece." Portia sighed, a relieved smile coming to
her lips.

"Listen, can we meet? Today. Maybe for lunch? I need
to talk."

Portia closed her eyes and fell back onto bed. "I can't
think of a better idea. Why don't you come over here to my
hotel? They have a nice cafe."

"Sounds good," Cece said, marking the date on her
electronic calendar. "You have no idea how much I need this."

"Hmph. Not half as much as I do."

"Something wrong?"

"Let's just wait 'til we meet."

"Alright. I'll see you then."

Portia pressed the phone to her chest when the
connection broke. "Cece'll know what's wrong with me." She
whispered.

***

That afternoon, Stephanie met with three young women
who had attended school with Melissa. The visit was lovely and
Steph enjoyed hearing the girls say such wonderful things about
her daughter.

"What do you all know about Porter Gwaltney?" Steph
asked, after one of the maids brought in a tray of hot tea.

Deandra Cafrey eyed Steph thoughtfully. "Porter...mmm.
Fine."

"Very fine," Joyce Shellars concurred.

"They were friends." Deandra continued. "Everybody swore they were more than that. They were so cute together and all."

"Especially after they started the project." Joyce recalled.

"Project?" Steph queried.

"Yeah, um...for the African Studies candidates. The graduating students were given final projects. Topic choices were very broad as long as it was culturally and historically related to the African Diaspora."

Steph strolled a lemon slice in her tea as she nodded. "Missy and Porter were partners on this?"

Joyce nodded, her Chinese bob shining beneath the noonday sun filling the sitting room. "Porter was a doctoral candidate and they collaborated on it. The thing seemed to consume them. They spent all their time working."

"Was Melissa stressed out over it?" Steph asked.

"Not at first," Deandra replied, her large brown eyes staring out across the room, "but then we could tell it was starting to get to her."

Stephanie began to withdraw from the conversation as her mind absorbed the information. The girls sensed her mood change and soon decided to leave the woman with her thoughts. When she was alone, Steph allowed her worry to show.

***

Aunt and niece drew scores of male stares as they hugged each other in the restaurant.

"I like this." Portia said, complimenting the gray silk scarf which coordinated with Cecelia's cream pantsuit.

"Thanks." Cece replied, nodding at the waitress. "Scotch and soda."

"Same." Portia complied.

Cece's almond-shaped stare narrowed sharply as she leaned close. "So, was that nervousness I heard in your voice earlier? You getting fidgety over the upcoming nuptials?"

Portia smoothed one hand across her sleek cut and smiled. "If only that were it."

"What's goin' on?" Cece queried, not liking the distress in her niece's voice.

"This morning. I got a visit from Huron Augustine."

"Huron Augustine? I didn't know you knew him like that."

"I didn't. We went to high school together, but we didn't know each other that well. Huron's um...a fan, shall we say?"

Cece closed her eyes. "Ah-ha." She realized. "So what happened?"

"In a nutshell he wants to have sex with me whether I'm engaged or not."

Cece was both amused and stunned. "He told you this?"

Portia nodded, taking a quick sip from her glass. "He told me just before he picked me up and took me to the bedroom."

"Portia!"

She waved he hands. "Nothing happened. I mean, something happened but...it didn't go that far."

"You stopped him?"

"He stopped himself. I was too busy moaning and-dammit Cece! What the hell is wrong with me? Am I a nympho or something?"

Cece burst into laughter. "Girl, stop! I've seen Huron. He's a magnificent looking man. You're entitled to be tempted."

"Cece..." Portia groaned, covering her head with her hands. "I'm serious. I mean, I knew it was wrong, but I couldn't stop it. I would've let Huron...if he hadn't stopped-"

"But he did." Cecelia reminded her niece, patting the center of the table. "He stopped and you just have to make sure you don't let it happen again."

"Easier said than done, Auntie."

"Don't sell yourself short."

Portia's weary expression drew even more distressed. "I never mean to Cece, it just always works out that way. Anyway," she sighed, forcing a smile to her face, "I am not gonna bring you down with me. Let's talk about your new job. How are you settling in?"

"Hmph." Cecelia replied, with a grimace. "I just don't know, Portia."

"What?"

"The chief of staff set up a breakfast meeting between me and...Derric. God, that man...I tell you, the men in that family do have their share of good looks."

Portia's brown eyes twinkled. "Gorgeous, huh?"

"Gorgeous, sexy and incredibly intense. In a sensual, intelligent, probing kind of way." Cece clarified, her almond-shaped gaze taking on a faraway look.

"Hmm...sounds like someone was impressed." Portia sensed.

"Very impressed. It was all I could do to concentrate on the purpose for my being there...I've never been attracted to a man at first sight, you know?"

Portia shrugged and browsed through her menu. "I hear it still happens."

"Well it happened. We were having a decent conversation and then, then it was like he reminded himself who I was-who my family was."

"And the magic ended?"

Cecelia smiled at Portia's choice of words. "I left before it could disappear completely. I was so damned polite to him. Any other man I would've told to go straight to hell no matter who he was."

Portia propped her chin in her palm. "What is it about those Augustine men?" She said, adding a distinct, playful twang to her words.

The discussion continued and was quite enlightening and often times, extremely naughty. Portia and Cecelia felt much better as they released pent up anxieties through talk and laughter.

***

Simone Frakas counted the stack of memos she held, before looking up at her boss with an expectant gaze. "Do you want these to go out today or after the meeting tomorrow?"

A knock sounded on the office door before Sanford could respond to his assistant's question. He blinked, surprised to see Cameo Augustine standing in his doorway.

"I didn't see anyone out front." She said, tapping leather gloves against her palms as she focused on the gorgeous man behind the desk. "Can I talk to you a minute? In private?" She asked, removing her black leather trench.

Sanford nodded towards Simone and waved Cameo inside. She waited until the door closed, then walked over to his desk and leaned against it.

"You have some nerve." She sneered, her eyes shining with disapproval. "Tell me, do you make a habit out of harassing people at the funerals of their loved ones? I mean, if you have a problem with me, that's fine. Your friendship is not something I desire, but to say those things to me on a day like that...I guess I know what kind of upbringing you had."

The words should have unleashed another tongue lashing, but Sanford was barely paying attention to Cameo's words. He was too taken by her appearance. As she leaned across his desk, her silky black hair hung straight and frequently brushed his fingers. She was beautiful and close enough to touch, yet he resisted.

"I'm serious, Mr. Gwaltney." Cameo told him, becoming aware of the 'look' he was sending her way. After all, she couldn't resist appreciating his smooth, handsome caramel features either. The mustache and neat beard with the lone dimple beneath held her lovely gaze for several seconds.

"I'm sure you are serious." Sanford finally responded. "I do want to apologize for the way I behaved that day. You're right, I could have picked a better time to tell you how I felt and I guess I could have used different words to get the same point across."

Cameo stood straight and propped one hand against her hip. "What are you saying?" She asked, clearly suspicious.

Sanford leaned back in his gray leather chair and braced his elbows against the arms.

"What do you mean?" He innocently queried, his probing deep-set stare raking Cameo's figure eight frame encased beneath the clinging baby blue wool dress.

"You say that as though you meant what you said, but only regret the words you used."

Sanford's serene smile told Cameo she had judged correctly. Before any more of his considerable subtlety and charm could work on her defenses, she decided to leave.

"I better get out of here." She grumbled, snatching the leather coat from a chair.

"Let me take you to lunch."

Cameo stopped. "It's not necessary." She told him, without bothering to look around.

Sanford propped his index finger along the side of his face and silently appraised her round bottom. "I insist." He replied. "Besides, it's the way I apologize and I won't accept a refusal."

Slowly, Cameo turned. She expected to see a look of cocky certainty on his face. Instead, his expression was serious and void of any amusement. She slapped both hands to her sides. "Where should I meet you?"

"No need to meet there," Sanford was saying as he stood, "I'm ready now."

"But, my car-"

"Will be here when you get back." He assured her, as he walked closer.

"Where're we going?"

Sanford shook his head, pulling a mocha-colored overcoat across his matching three piece suit. "That'll take the fun out of it." He said, slipping both hands around her hips and giving her waist a soft pat. Then, keeping his hand in its possessive location, he escorted her from the dimly lit, corner office.

They made their way down the halls of Gwaltney Products' corporate headquarters. Cameo could see that Sanford had his male staff just as charmed as his female employees.

"Sanford where are you taking me?" Cameo asked, once they were descending in the elevator. When he began to walk towards her, she backed away.

"To the parking garage," he replied, trapping her in one corner of the elevator, "my car's down there."

"I meant where are we going to have lunch?"

Sanford massaged his beard and smiled. "I can't tell you that, but it's someplace very nice."

Cameo leaned her head against the paneled car. "I didn't come over here for this. I hadn't planned on interrupting your day."

"I see," Sanford whispered, leaning against the wall as well, "you just came over to tell me off, then leave?"

Guilty, Cameo focused on the floor. "Something like that."

"Mmm hmm...well, you know I can't have that, right? Besides, I don't know when I'll have another chance to be with you, not with everything that happens between our families."

"Amen." Cameo sighed, deciding to enjoy lunch and the intriguing man in her company.

"What the...? The executive airport?"

Sanford had already exited the car and was walking around to open Cameo's door.

"I can't." She told him, when he reached for her.

Sanford smiled, triggering the lone dimple in his cheek. "Cameo-"

"I want to know where you expect to take me?"

Sanford shrugged and covered Cameo's hand with his. "Come with me and find out."

"Sanford..."

"Please, Cameo? You won't be disappointed, I promise."

The soft, persuasive voice combined with the heavenly face and smooth charm, gradually wore down Cameo's defenses and she took Sanford's hand.

"I don't suppose it's gonna just sit here while we eat, huh?"

Sanford slipped his arm around her waist. "Uh-uh." He replied with a slight shake of his head.

A petite, brunette flight attendant greeted them when they stepped inside the cabin. She offered to bring in their drinks after instructing them to settle in for take-off.

Meanwhile, Cameo was reminding herself that she was an award-winning journalist and was always prepared for the unexpected. This time; however, she was at the mercy of a charming, intelligent, sexy man and he was making all the rules.

"How is it?" Sanford asked, referring to the dish Cameo ordered.

"A great French restaurant, not far from your office serves this very thing, you know?"

"But tell me this isn't better?" Sanford dared, tapping his fingers against his mustache.

"Canada, Sanford?" Cameo pointed out. She looked out at the pristine, snowy view and couldn't help but be struck by its beauty.

Sanford shrugged as he stared out the bay window next to the table. "It's the way I like to do things. If I can."

Cameo swirled her spoon in the deliciously thick seafood chowder and smiled. "The ladies must love you." She noted.

"Hmph. Well, you'll be a lot tougher than any of them." Sanford predicted, slicing the flaky trout with the side of his fork.

Cameo crossed her long legs beneath the cozy round table. "Meaning?" She asked.

"Our families hate each other," he spoke without looking up, "you hate me..."

Laughing softly, Cameo buttered a slice of the warm rye bread. "I don't hate you...that much." She added, when he sent her a doubtful look.

"Thank you for trying to be honest." Sanford teased.

"So then tell me why you decided I'm worthy of this elaborate lunch?"

"Because you don't like me, or at the very *least* you don't like me. I can't have that."

"Is it important for me to like you?"

"Mmm hmm."

"And why is that?" Cameo asked, her spoon stilling in her soup as she waited for his response.

Sanford set his fork aside and leaned forward. "There's a lot I want to know about you. Even more I want to do with you. For that, I think you need to like me first."

Cameo could only sit across from Sanford. Suspicion and excitement played havoc with her emotions.

TWENTY-ONE

"Hi Baby, I hope we're not too late?...Honey?"

With some effort, Princess managed to pull her eyes away from the tall, bronzed god standing next to her mother.

"Ahem."

"I'm sorry Mommy." Princess whispered, leaning close to kiss the woman's cheek.

Amina smiled, noticing the awed look on her daughter's lovely face. "Sweetie, you remember Adonis?"

Nodding, Princess smiled and extended her hand. "Of course. It's nice to see you again Mr. Mason."

"Please use my first name." Adonis requested, his onyx stare penetrating the delicate fabric of the clinging olive green dress she wore. "Your mother asked me to escort her. I hope my being here isn't an inconvenience?"

"No, not at all." Princess promptly responded, cringing inwardly at the husky soft quality of her voice. With a quick toss of her head, she motioned behind her. "Please come on in. Everyone hasn't arrived yet."

Amina strolled in ahead of Adonis and headed towards the cluster of bodies in the middle of the living room.

AlTonya Washington

Princess stood near the front door and watched as Amina greeted the advertising team and introduced them to her investment banker. She stole secret glances at Adonis as he shook hands and conversed with the small group. When he looked up and caught her staring, the intensity of his midnight eyes held her captive. It took sometime before she even heard the doorbell buzzing. She criticized herself for behaving like some love struck school girl and turned to greet the rest of her guests. She was the perfect hostess and mediator for the dinner meeting, despite Adonis Mason's probing gaze following her every move.

"Since everybody's here we can head out to the dining room if you people are hungry!"

"Don't ask stupid questions, Princess." Someone teased.

Amidst all the conversation, Princess set out the meal. She tried to remain busy as long as possible. Adonis had chosen his place between his client and her daughter. Since Amina was involved in business talk, Princess wondered if she was to be his conversation partner. She didn't have long to ponder the situation, with everyone reaching across the table to fill their plates.

Everyone complimented their hostess on the delicious feast set out for them. Sourdough bread with a spicy butter spread, spinach quiche, lemon pepper roasted chicken with steamed greens and fragrant white wine.

"This is incredible."

Princess's fork paused over the thick slice of quiche when she heard Adonis speak. She looked up and saw him smiling in her direction.

"Excuse me?" She whispered.

"The food." He clarified, spreading his hands as he looked down into the plate. "I can't remember the last time I had a home cooked dinner."

"Stop."

"I'm serious."

Princess propped her elbow on the table and toyed with a curly tendril dangling from the high chignon. "I just can't believe that."

"Why not?"

Because no one could look as good as you only eating fast food and frozen dinners. "You strike me as a big eater." Princess said instead, taking in the breadth of his shoulders.

Adonis pretended to be offended. "You tryin' to call me fat?"

Princess laughed. "Not at all."

"Stout?"

"No, I didn't mean it that way." Princess assured him, her laughter just below the surface.

Adonis continued to probe. "Dumpy? Pudgy?"

Princess pressed one hand to her forehead. "Please stop." She begged, almost hysterical with laughter.

Adonis began to chuckle. The sound was rich and soft. It had a dazzling effect on Princess and she could have swooned at the sound.

"I apologize, but I'm very sensitive about my appearance."

Princess's eyes widened. "You are?"

Adonis leaned back. "Aren't you?"

"Forget I said anything," Princess groaned, dissolving into a fit of soft giggles.

Adonis's unsettling black stare softened as he watched Princess laughing. His eyes caressed her profile and the smattering of baby hair against her temple.

"So, have you always worked for your mother?" He asked.

Princess savored the tender seasoned morsel of chicken and nodded. "Since college."

"She's quite a lady."

"She is that."

"You two could be twins."

Princess smiled. "I can only hope I'm half as beautiful when I'm her age."

Adonis's deep midnight gaze narrowed. "I don't think you need to worry about that."

"Thank you."

Adonis shrugged. "It's the truth." He said, turning back to his dinner.

Princess said nothing more. She felt strangely giddy over the subtle compliment.

The dinner guests began to trickle out after cake and coffee. Everyone complimented Princess on a wonderful meal. The gathering gave them all the opportunity to make productive decisions regarding the upcoming fall and winter seasons.

"I'll get it!" Princess called to her mother and Adonis-the only remaining guests. When she pulled the front door open, a scream flew past her lips. "What are you doing here?!" She squealed.

Adonis's tall frame tensed as he watched Princess hug the huge dark man in the doorway. When he heard her say 'Daddy', he breathed an unconscious sigh of relief.

"What are you doing back here so soon?" Princess was asking again, as she pulled her father inside.

"I was looking for your mother. Have you seen her?" Tav asked, pulling heavy leather gloves from his hands.

Princess brows rose and she looked across her shoulder. She almost shuddered at the cold glare on her mother's face.

Tav saw his ex-wife and nodded. "I need to talk to you. Alone. Could I give you a ride home or something?"

If possible, Princess arched brows rose even higher. She knew 'alone' with Tavares Gwaltney, was the last place her mother wanted to be.

Amina; however, was not afraid of her Ex any longer. She simply despised him for everything he had put her through. "Alright Tav." She replied, almost bursting into laughter at his stunned expression. She had already planned to get home on her own in order for Adonis and Princess to have time to talk privately.

"Mommy," Princess whispered concern evident on her face.

"It's alright, Baby." Amina sighed, patting Princess's arm. "I'll call you. Adonis, I'll see you later this week."

Adonis squeezed Amina's hand and smiled. "Good night."

Princess watched in speechless fascination as her mother walked out the door with her father. She knew she would never have believed it, had she not been there to witness it.

"It's hard to believe they were married."

Princess shrugged and shook her head. "Yeah, sometimes I can't believe it either."

Adonis's slight smile triggered a pair of dimples. "You say that like it was a bad thing."

"My parents...they've had a very um...tension-filled relationship."

Adonis nodded. "Passionate tension?" He playfully queried.

"Dangerous tension," Princess corrected, smoothing down the soft clinging material of her dress. "I can't believe she agreed to be alone with him."

Adonis followed Princess back to the dining room. "You act like he'd hurt her or something."

Princess began stacking the dessert saucers. "He wouldn't do anything like that now."

Adonis prided himself on keeping a business-like relationship with all his clients. Amina Davidson was different. She always reminded him of his mother and something in Princess's comment concerned him.

Princess felt Adonis staring, but didn't look up. "He used to beat her." She said, hearing the unspoken question.

"What?"

"It was a long time ago. He hasn't touched her in years. Not since I was a baby. I don't even remember it."

"Hmph. I'll bet she does." Adonis guessed, grimacing at what he'd just discovered.

Princess took a seat at the table. "I'm sure she remembers it. But, she's done everything to put it behind her."

"I'd say she's done a good job. Success is the best revenge, you know?"

Princess returned Adonis's smug smile. "You're right. If anyone deserved success, it would be my Mom." Princess sighed, shaking her head as she thought of her mother.

Adonis propped his chin against his fist and regarded Princess with a thoughtful stare. He could tell the conversation had triggered her emotionally and understood.

"Sorry." Princess whispered, realizing that she had allowed her thoughts to carry her away.

"How about some help with this mess?" Adonis offered, already removing the beige cashmere jacket he wore over a cream crew cut T-shirt.

"You'd actually want to help with the dishes?" Princess asked, stunned.

Adonis shrugged. "I don't want to help, but I don't mind." He replied, with an exaggerated sigh.

The two worked dutifully as the conversation moved to lighter topics. Neither seemed to realize just how comfortable they were around each other.

Not until later; when they both collapsed on the cushiony living room sofa, did Princess take note of the situation. Alone, with a man who was virtually a stranger, regardless of how gorgeous he was. No words had been uttered, but Adonis could sense the change in Princess. He figured she may be growing a bit edgy and refused to do anything to make her wary of him.

Princess watched him collect his jacket from the arm chair. "You're leaving?"

"I think I better." Adonis replied, his expression a bit regretful.

"Did I say something?" Princess asked, watching him pull the jacket over his powerful, leanly muscled upper body.

"I have a lot to do tomorrow. Will you show me out?"

"Yes." Princess quickly obliged, scooting off the sofa. Her nostrils flared as the cool scent of his cologne filled the air.

At the door, Adonis hesitated a moment before turning. "Have dinner with me tomorrow?" He asked.

Princess stared up into his incredible face, aching to stroke his flawless bronzed skin. After a while, she nodded. "I'd like that." She accepted.

Adonis leaned against the doorjamb and lowered his striking stare. "I'll pick you up about eight? Here?" He asked.

Princess tapped her long nails against the oak wood door and nodded. "I'll be ready."

"Alright," He whispered, taking another moment to study the woman before him. Then, without another word, he was gone.

Princess closed the door softly, and then leaned back against it. Suddenly, she covered her face in her hands and groaned. "Oh Princess girl what are you doing?"

***

"I want you to know I carry pepper spray and I have no problems using it."

Tav chuckled. "Damn, was I that bad?" He teased, watching Amina open the front door to her five bed room Brownstone.

Amina tossed her keys to the glass and brass message stand. "I don't have enough time to tell you how bad you've been." She dryly replied.

"Amina, I'm sorry." Tav said after a while, his amusement fading.

Amina leaned back on the heels of her leather pumps. "What the hell are you up to?" She whispered, feeling her temper heat at the soft-spoken apology.

"I miss you."

Amina's hazel gaze narrowed and she searched for some sign of insincerity on his handsome face.

"I know what I put you through in the past is unforgivable," he said as he walked further into the house, "but I still want to make it up to you...somehow."

"What's wrong with you?" Amina breathed, hoping to catch a glimpse of something dishonest in his eyes.

Tav Gwaltney; however, was completely honest. "I know I've hurt you. Badly. But, I do love you. I have ever since the first time I saw you. There's no one else I want, but you."

Amina's lashes fluttered as a wave of shock washed over her body. "Tav..."

He raised his hands. "I know how this sounds. You've got no reason to believe a word I say, but I swear to you I mean it all."

For an instant, Amina allowed her hatred to clear and she swore she could see the man she fell in love with-the man she thought she was falling in love with. Then, before her emotions got the better of her, she shook her head.

"Tav, you know it's too late." She whispered.

"Are you sure?" He whispered back.

Amina turned away, balling her fist against her mouth to keep her lips from trembling.

Tav hesitated only briefly, before he walked over to her. "Are you sure, it's too late?" He murmured against her hair. The soft scent in his nostrils brought back memories of them together. "Do you remember what it felt like to make love with each other? Do you remember, Amina?"

"Oh Tav, I remember a lot." She retorted, her body stiffening beneath his touch. "I remember things I don't even want to remember. And why are you saying this to me? I'm sure you've had plenty of women over the years. I'm willing to bet any one of them would love to be the next Mrs. Tavares Gwaltney."

Tav pressed one hand against the front of his navy wind suit jacket. "I'm not interested in that. You're the one I want."

"Why Tav?! Why?!" Amina snapped, whirling around. She could feel tears of frustration pressure her eyes. "Do you just love the sound your palm makes when it hits my cheek, what?!"

Tav stepped back, the outburst robbing him of all argument. "Amina..." he groaned, taking a seat on the gray suede overstuffed sofa. "God, you have every right to hate me after all the shit I did. I've hated myself ever since I took a good look at myself. I tell you Amina, you can't even begin to hate me as much as I do."

"It's been so long, Tav. What-what happened? Why this sudden change?"

Tav massaged his fingers against his bald head. "You know, they say kids grow up to mimic what they see. I guess I'm the exception to that rule, because I never grew up seeing that. My father treated my mother like a queen-despite all the things she put him through at times. I guess that's why I never took a good look at what I was doing to you. I was too scared to ask why."

Amina kept her hands folded across her chest as she slowly shortened the distance between them. "And you know why, now?"

Tav leaned back against the sofa and shook his head. "It was staring me in the face all the time. Jealousy. Pure, stupid jealousy."

"Jealousy?" Amina gasped her hazel eyes wide. "Of what? You knew how I felt about you."

"Mmm...and I also knew how Nikos Cantone felt about you."

"Nikos?" Amina whispered, her gaze faltering as she let her memories drift back to the man she hadn't allowed herself to think of in years.

"He was in love with you." Tav stated, his deep-set midnight eyes caressing her lovely cinnamon-toned face. "He was in love with you and; though I know you loved me, I know you felt something for him. Something I couldn't begin to understand."

Amina bowed her head and prayed her heart would slow its frantic beating.

"But then, I realized it wasn't just Nikos. I had a problem with any man who even glanced your way. Unfortunately, I took it out on you."

"You shouldn't have felt the need to take it out on anyone." Amina admonished, circling the sofa like a cat stalking her prey.

290

AlTonya Washington

Tav nodded, his handsome face appearing weary with
sorrow. "I know that now. Even when I accepted the fact that
Princess wasn't mine, I-"
"What did you say?"
Tav's smile was soft and not at all cold or accusing. "I
know she's not mine. I think I've known since she was a baby.
She's got your looks and my stubborn streak. But...there was
always something...else...She belongs to Nikos, doesn't she?"
Amina sat on the sofa, her legs as unstable as water.
"How did you?..."
Tav shrugged. "I went back-piecing together a lot of
stuff, but I didn't care. My babygirl is mine and I'm hers. Hell, if
it weren't for Princess, I never would've started therapy."
"Therapy?" Amina parroted, shocked again.
"For the last four years...Thanks to our girl."
"I can't believe it." Amina said, more to herself than to
Tav. She felt as though she were looking at him through new
eyes.
"I'm not trying to tell you I'm a changed man, but I am
trying to turn around."
Tav was about to stand, when Amina pressed her hand
against his thigh. "I believe you." She said, leaning close to kiss
his cheek. He turned and their lips met.
Amina gasped, allowing Tav the entrance he craved.
Missed sensations of pleasure rose between them as the kiss
grew deeper. Amina shivered when she felt Tav's ragged groan
against her mouth. Slowly, she inched closer to his massive
frame, eager for his touch.

***

Derric Augustine's handsome, dark face was set in a
stony mask as he listened to Greg Holmes greet Cecelia
Gwaltney. While the two doctors conversed, Derric allowed
himself to appreciate Cece's face and form. There was no
denying she was incredible to look at. Unfortunately...
"...and I think we'll be putting those plans into motion as
soon as we run the budget past the board."

Cece pulled one hand from her white coat pocket and pressed it to her chest. "Well please let me know the moment it passes. I think this could be so helpful to the kids and the functioning of the Pediatrics wing as a whole."

"Will do." Greg promised, his blue eyes contrasting vibrantly against his tanned face.

Cece allowed herself a brief glance in Derric's direction. In the two weeks they had worked together, he had treated her lukewarmly, coolly and coldly. Finally, Cece decided to concentrate on work and tried to push the man's devastating image from her mind.

"Derric." She muttered, as she hurried past him.

Greg frowned and turned to Derric. "Man, how in the world can you treat that sweet beauty so coldly?"

Derric's expression turned weary. "It's a long story. Suffice it to say our families have been feuding since before our parents were born. We were raised not to like each other."

Greg's eyes crinkled at the corners, when he began to chuckle. "Isn't it time to grow up, then?" He asked, clapping Derric's back before walking away.

"Dinner tonight sounds great. With the way this day is turning out, a nice quiet meal will be just what I need."

Porter chuckled at his aunt's exaggerated sigh. "So, I'll meet you later and we'll head out?"

"It's a plan." Cece replied. "Talk to you later." She said, replacing the receiver just as a knock sounded on her office door. "Come in!" She called. Her heart leapt to her throat when Derric Augustine stepped inside.

"Sorry to interrupt," he began noticing the expectant look on her face, "I wanted to compliment you on those proposals for the wing."

Though shocked and rather pleased, Cece couldn't accept his words so smoothly. "Was there some reason you couldn't tell me that out in the hall with Greg?"

"Meanness and stupidity." He promptly replied, almost laughing at the surprise on Cece's face. "I'm sorry." He added.

Cecelia didn't want to soften at the apology, but she did. "You're sorry?" She repeated, her vibrant brown gaze seeming dazed.

"You're a good, caring doctor. The kids love you and I shouldn't have let issues with the families get in the way of my treating you with anything but respect."

Cece was almost afraid to move, thinking it would shatter the sweetness of the moment. "Thank you." She whispered.

Derric waved his hand. "No need for that." He said, and then left the office.

***

Male and female heads turned, when Princess and Adonis entered the dining room of the cozy Caribbean restaurant. The gorgeous couple coolly acknowledged the interested looks, but were more preoccupied with what the evening would hold.

"Is this alright?" Adonis asked, once the host had escorted them to an intimate round table in a private corner.

"It's fine." Princess managed, hoping he couldn't feel the goose bumps riddling her skin where his thumb brushed her spine.

Adonis nodded, accepting a menu from the smiling red haired host. "What looks good to you?" He asked.

"Well," Princess sighed, scanning the colorful laminated menu, "I have to admit I've never really eaten Caribbean food."

"Get out."

"I'm serious."

Adonis rested his cheek against his palm and pretended to be amazed. "The daughter of a world renowned cosmetics magnate and you've never eaten Caribbean? Haven't you ever been to the islands?"

Princess smoothed her hands across her bare arms. "Afraid not. It's something I'd love to do, but haven't gotten around to."

"Alright then, I guess I can forgive you. This time," He teased.

Taboo Tree

Princess smiled and looked back at the menu. "So, I guess I should be asking what looks good to you."

Adonis's searing charcoal stare rose from the menu and he looked across the table. Slowly, he studied the flawless line of her arms, bared by the clinging spaghetti strapped gown. He hoped she hadn't realized how hard it had been for him not to brush his hands against her. "Would you trust me to order for you?"

Princess dropped her menu to the table. "I would love for you to order for me."

Adonis was happy to introduce his dinner date to his favorite cuisine. By the time he was done giving the waiter their selection, Princess wondered where she would put all the food.

"Now," Adonis sighed, tapping his fingers against the table, "I want to know everything about you."

"No, you don't."

Adonis would not be dissuaded. "I want to know it all."

Princess leaned back against the cushioned burgundy and navy blue chair. "If you knew it all, you'd probably run screaming."

"Try me." He challenged.

Shrugging, Princess toyed with the mouth of her wine glass. "Where would I start?"

"Tell me what you do for Queen Cosmetics. It must be something pretty top secret, I've never run into you before the other day."

"Well...I suppose you could say I'm my mother's PR Rep. I handle all the meetings with outside clients, employees, radio and TV people, etcetera."

"Isn't that what her assistant is for?"

"Euletta is more a liaison between Mommy and me. I'm usually traveling up and down the coast taking care of concerns from our employees in the plants, models, photographers. When Mommy needs to be there, I make the arrangements and get the info to Euletta who contacts Mom."

Adonis nodded, his mouth curving into a knowing smile. "It's an interesting system."

"Well, it works for us and with Mom who's always so busy."

"So you've never wanted to do anything but work with Amina?"

"Well Mommy and Daddy divorced when I was little. I remember the day she closed on the building in New York for Queen Cosmetics. I wouldn't think of working anywhere else, but when I first started I believe I thought she was lonely and scared, but couldn't admit it, you know?"

"Must've been rough?"

"You have no idea."

"Actually, I do." Adonis corrected his expression hardening for just an instant. "My parents divorced when I was young too."

"How old were you?"

"Eight."

Princess winced. "That must've hit you so hard."

Adonis tugged on the sleeve of his gray suede jacket. "My parents were so cool about it. They always made sure I knew it wasn't my fault and we still went out just like a real family, so..."

Although Adonis spoke lightly on the subject, Princess could tell it still hurt. Reaching across the table, she patted his hand. After a while, the discussion moved to lighter topics. Still, it was nice knowing they had something so emotional in common. The huge, delicious looking meal arrived and they ate heartily. Dinner passed easily, but far too quickly.

***

"How long do you plan on keeping me here?" Cameo asked when she and Sanford shared a table overlooking the grounds of a Canadian inn.

Sanford sank the marshmallows in his mug of creamy cocoa. "Are you in a hurry to leave?" He asked, without making eye contact.

Cameo surveyed her surroundings. Her slanting dark eyes traced the trail of the horse drawn carriages dotting the thick snow. "I'm having the best time." She admitted.

"Well, enjoy it, then."

"For how long?"

"Does it matter?"

Cameo met Sanford's challenging stare with one of her own. "It may become an issue if you don't get what you want."

Sanford's mustache twitched above his lips. "And what would that be?"

Cameo leaned closer across the table. "If you expect me to sleep with you, you'll be disappointed."

"Will I?" He asked, his fantastic stare tracing the outline of Cameo's breasts beneath the fuzzy, mocha sweater. "You shouldn't be so hard on yourself. I'm not a very demanding man."

The suggestive remark forced a smile to Cameo's face. She tossed her napkin across the table and laughed at his unmatched confidence.

***

Portia called Lewis at his office and dropped a few hints that she "needed" him. She waltzed through her hotel room, lighting candles and incense. Though it wasn't dark outside-all the drapes were pulled and the seduction scene was set.

The doorbell rang and Portia gave herself the once over-smiling at the naughty piece of lingerie that barely covered her body. She clasped her hands and prayed the night would purge all thoughts of Huron Augustine.

Portia could have stumbled back on her 4" black platforms when she whipped the door open and found Huron in her hallway. Before she could say anything-including "come in", he was walking inside, forcing her back.

Portia finally found her voice. "What are you doing?"

Huron favored her with a crooked smile. "I'm...coming inside."

The response sent Portia's heart thundering in her throat. "What are you doing here? Now?" She coolly rephrased.

"Interrupting something from the looks of things." He said, his dark eyes studying the romantic transformation of the room.

"Well, since you're aware of that, why don't you leave?" Portia suggested unaware that she was still retreating from Huron's advancing body.

"I get the feeling we're alone." He said, becoming more interested in the lacy black and fuchsia corset and matching string number she wore.

Portia was determined not to let Huron see how unnerved she was. "I'm expecting my fiancé, so if you could please get the hell out!" She ordered, frowning up into his extremely handsome face.

"You're waiting here like this for Lew and he ain't here yet? Hmph, that don't look too good for the brotha."

"Huron please go."

"Or does he really know what he's missing? Or maybe you're keepin' him on hold 'til the big night?"

Portia's almond eyes narrowed sharply. "Bastard. For your information, Lew knows exactly what he's getting."

One sinewy shoulder rose beneath the dark purple sweatshirt Huron wore. He continued to stalk Portia until she was trapped against the back of the sofa. "I wouldn't expect anything less of you, Dark Chocolate." He told her, using his softest voice.

Portia landed a cracking slap to the side of Huron's face. To her further unease, he only smiled at the gesture. His fingers began a leisurely trail through her glossy, short crop of hair.

Portia's long lashes fluttered and then closed over her eyes as her desires took control. She felt Huron's fingers leave her hair to caress the sensitive flesh behind her earlobe. He massaged the column of her neck, and then his middle fingers traced a line from the base of her throat to the cleft of her breast.

Portia's nails curled into the sofa. She almost melted into the cushiony forest green material when Huron's fingers disappeared beneath the lacy cups of the corset.

"Stop me." He whispered, his fingers finding a hardened nipple and circling it scandalously.

Portia's mouth opened, but she could barely find her voice. "I..." She began, only to moan instead. She wanted Huron so badly, even her palms ached. "Lewis-Lewis is gonna be here soon."

"Let him wait." Huron groaned, his arm slipping around Portia's tiny waist as he hauled her against his chest.

Portia was grateful for the hold, since she had no strength left to stand. When Huron's mouth crashed down on hers, she met the punishing kiss with her own fire. Huron cupped her bottom in his wide palms and held her even closer. Portia locked her legs around his back when he rocked her against his stiff arousal.

The kiss grew deeper. Huron's fingers left imprints against Portia's satiny, dark skin. He carried her to the sofa and covered her lithe frame with his massive body. Slowly, his hands encircled her thighs and he pulled them apart to settle between.

"Huron..." Portia sighed, her fingers sliding through his soft dark hair. She arched her neck as his mouth tugged her earlobe before easing down her neck to press his tongue against her racing pulse.

A muffled groan rose when Huron buried his face in Portia's ample cleavage. His hands constricted around her thighs, while his strong teeth tugged the front ties on the corset. A shudder suddenly wracked his body as he took stock of the situation. Not one of the hundreds of fantasies he'd had about Portia came even marginally close to actually having her in his arms.

Portia ignored the voice which screamed that she was making a terrible mistake. All that mattered then was the way Huron was making her feel. She arched into his hard body, when he pulled the corset away. His hands held her breasts as though they were precious jewels, his thumbs brushing the rigid nipples repeatedly. He teased her, suckling the firm buds alternately. Portia wanted to scream in frustration, when his lips closed over one peak to pay it special attention.

Portia snuggled into the sofa, her entire body alive with sensation. She kneaded Huron's wide shoulders, marveling at the unleashed power beneath her fingertips. She smoothed her hands down the front of his sweatshirt and ventured beneath the hem.

Her eyes opened when her nails grazed the wide plane of his chest chiseled with unyielding muscles. She urged Huron to remove the clothing, eager to see what she touched.

Huron stood and stripped naked. Portia's mouth went dry when she viewed the uncovered beauty of his dark body. She didn't have long to admire, though. Huron was covering her on the sofa. His kisses were feverish and fell across her chest and flat stomach. He eased the G-string off her hips, worshipping the shapeliness of her long legs as he tugged them down across the heels she wore.

Soon, they were both naked and being pleasured by the feel of their skin touching. Huron pressed kisses to the undersides of Portia's taut breasts as his fingers delved past the folds of her womanhood. When they sank into a well of moisture, he knew he could no longer resist. In one movement, his arousal sank deep within her body.

Portia's breathless cries filled the living room of the hotel suite. Her hips writhed as she struggled to take all Huron had to give. At first, his thrusts were so slow, she screamed that he be more forceful. She didn't have long to wait. The lunges gradually grew more rapid and urgent.

Huron caught her wrists and pressed them to the sofa. He rose up a bit, his eyes closing as he savored the tightness of her body. Sweat fell from his face, but Portia didn't mind the moisture when she was just as drenched. They spent hours in the living room. Just before dusk, they fell asleep.

Later, Portia, lay sprawled on her stomach in the king sized brass bed. She had never felt so ravaged on or off the camera and cursed herself for being so weak. However, Huron Augustine possessed an appeal, impossible to ignore.

The phone began to ring. Portia answered quickly before the shrill sound woke Huron.

"Portia? Why are you whispering?"

"Lewis?"

"Listen Baby. I'm sorry about this afternoon. I've been in meetings all day and I just got your message."

Portia lay back down, snuggling her head into the cool pillow. "Don't worry about it."

"Everything alright? You sounded like it was urgent."

Portia ran her fingers through her short hair. "Everything's fine. I just wanted to see you."

"Well, I'm finishing up here so I'll be over to your hotel as soon as-"

"Oh no Lewis, don't!"

"Excuse me?"

Portia closed her eyes and uttered a silent curse. "I'm sorry, but I already made plans with my aunt tonight."

"Oh. Well, I'll just see you in the morning then. We'll have breakfast, okay?"

Huron had awakened and rolled over to Portia. His hand closed around her upper arm and he favored her shoulder and back with soft wet kisses.

"Portia?"

"Hmm?"

"I was asking about breakfast."

"Yeah, yes Lewis breakfast is fine. I'll talk to you in the morning." She called, already sending the phone back to its cradle. She and Huron made love for the rest of the evening.

***

CJ gathered Deme close and pressed a kiss to the thick curls covering her head. They were unable to honor the mutual decisions to end their relationship and enjoyed many intimate afternoons.

Soft, suggestive conversation gradually turned to talk of the children. Deme knew CJ wanted to know more about his daughter, especially about her life in California. She realized it was a subject they couldn't avoid forever and it would be best if she told him herself.

"Portia always wanted to act." Deme began, bracing herself on her elbows as she looked down into CJ's face. "What?" She asked, seeing the smile cross his lips.

"You tryin' to tell me she ran out to Hollywood seeking fame and fortune?" He teased.

Deme was not so amused. "She sought it and she got it."

"Say what?"

"Your baby is a big Hollywood star."

CJ sat up in bed. "You're kidding? I've never seen her in anything."

"I'm sure you haven't." Deme sighed.

CJ's expression turned weary. "Hell, I probably wouldn't know if I had. I've never even seen her."

"Hmph. Even if you had seen her, you've probably never seen any of her movies."

"Why not?"

Deme pulled a corner of the sheet over her shoulder which was suddenly covered with goose bumps. "I don't know what your movie tastes are, but unless you're an avid adult film viewer, I doubt you've seen Portia's work."

Realization moved across CJ's face like the moon eclipsing the sun. His hands weakened and he leaned forward. "Adult film?"

"Mmm hmm."

"Portia...Portia she-she acts in those things?"

"Acting, hmph. I think that's what she calls it."

"What?" CJ snapped his temper heating.

Deme couldn't look at him. "The only thing that got me through this when I found out was the idea that she was trying to break into acting and this was the only road in. It was killing me to think a porn star was something she aspired to be-that the things she was doing were-were enjoyable to her. I pray every night she'll get out of it."

CJ was frowning murderously. "You pray? You pray? Dammit woman, why the hell didn't you make her get out of it?!"

Deme slammed her hand to the bed. "She wasn't going to listen to me. For God's sake, CJ she was an eighteen year old woman and I certainly hadn't been there much any of the years before. Why in the world would she have listened to anything I had to say?!" She cried, her brown eyes shining with unshed tears.

CJ covered his face with his hands and groaned. "Jesus, Deme what have we done to those kids?"

"I ask myself that every day. After I curse myself for not being a mother to them. And I wanted to, CJ." She swore, looking up at him as the tears slid down her cheeks. "Oh God, how I wanted to be a mother to them. But, every time I looked at them-especially Porter-all I could think of was you and how sad our situation was and always would be."

"Shhh..." CJ urged, leaning down to bury his face in her soft curls.

"Our babies were made from love, CJ and they don't even know it." Deme sobbed, causing her entire body to shudder. "We should have raised them together. We should all be together now."

CJ kissed her shoulder. "We should, but it would take a miracle for that to happen and both those kids are gonna hate me when they find out how differently their lives could have been."

Deme sniffled and looked into his dark eyes. "Well, at least you and I would be in the same boat."

CJ couldn't contain his laughter. "I love you, Deme."

A rush of sensation covered Demetria's body and she practically glowed. "I love you." She whispered.

***

"...so when I asked why she wanted Jose's cast, she said she needed a place to put her dolly's clothes. So I said, 'well Layla can't you wait 'til he takes the cast off, first?'"

Cecelia burst into laughter and Derric joined in shortly. Their meeting regarding the patients turned into an amusing discussion of the kid's crazy antics. Neither realized how much time had passed while they talked and laughed.

"It's interesting to know you want kids."

Derric smoothed his fingers along his sideburns as he regarded Cece closely. "Why so surprised?" He asked.

Cece shrugged. "Most people I've worked around in Pediatrics love their patients dearly, but cringe at the idea of having their own kids."

AlTonya Washington

"Well, I can understand that." Derric replied. "When you have ringside seats to all the crap out there that can harm kids, you're afraid to even think of it touching your own."

"It only makes me want 'em more." Cece argued, her bob bouncing when she shook her head. "Knowing what's out there makes you better prepared, right?"

"Not really. Especially when you can't be with them every minute." He pointed out, his expression growing guarded. "Then, one day you get a call that they're gone. For good."

Cece re-crossed her trouser clad legs and let her eyes drift around Derric's spacious oak paneled office. "You know, I was thinking that maybe we should have the kids put on some kind of play or talent show-they're all so creative."

Derric's mood didn't improve. "Yeah, they are creative. Lots of kids are, until someone takes all that away."

"Dammit, Derric." Cece snapped, bolting from her chair so quickly, it inched back. "Are you ever gonna let this go? How long will you keep throwing it up in my face.?"

Derric stood as well. His dark angular face carried an expression which spoke volumes. "My niece is dead, Cecelia. She's never coming back. Now I'm sorry if you're tired of hearing about that, but don't snap at me. Talk to your nephew."

"You people are never gonna let Porter forget this, are you?"

"Forget?!" Derric roared his black stare murderous.

Cece wasn't fazed. She walked right up to him and pointed her index finger against his chest. "He is hurting and he is grieving. He loved Melissa and never told her that. He hates himself so much he can't even look in the mirror. He doesn't see that truck or his own motorcycle as the cause of Missy's death. He sees himself. You think Porter's not suffering? You think he's not paying? Think again."

Derric's eyes followed Cece as she stormed out of his office. When the door slammed shut behind her, he pounded his fist against his palm. "Damn." He whispered.

Cece found Porter waiting in her office and uttered a prayer of thanks.

Porter smiled, watching his aunt whip the white coat from her back. "Are you that hungry?" He teased.

"I'm that ready to get the hell out of here." She grumbled, tossing the coat to the suede tan sofa. Smoothing invisible wrinkles from her tailored black pin-striped suit, she grabbed her leather tote from atop the oak file cabinet and headed back out the door.

Porter followed.

In the hall, Cecelia saw Derric headed towards her. Her expression grew colder the closer she got. When they met, she brushed past him and didn't look back.

***

Chicago, IL

"Oooo, my feet!" Cameo drawled, when she walked into her condo that night.

"Hope you had a good time." Sanford was saying as he followed her into the sunken living room.

Cameo collapsed to the overstuffed red sofa and spread her jet black hair around her head. "I had the best time and I wouldn't mind doing it again." She admitted, groaning as she kicked the powder blue wedge heels from her feet. "I'd just like to be more prepared next time."

Sanford's mustache twitched when he smiled. It pleased him to hear that she was thinking of a 'next time'.

Cameo saw him leaning against the back of the sofa and swung her long legs off the couch. "Make yourself comfortable while I go hunt down a pair of sweats." She instructed, already headed to the spiral staircase at the back of the dim living room.

Sanford did as he was told, unbuttoning the casual charcoal/navy blue jacket. He took a seat on one of the matching armchairs and surveyed his surroundings. The coziness of the condo was so pronounced it was almost tangible. Sanford could tell that Cameo loved to spend time there. Huge throw pillows filled every corner just as paintings and photos decorated the earth-tone painted walls.

When Cameo returned to the living room, she found Sanford engrossed with an article from one of the many magazines she free-lanced for.

Sanford knew she was there without looking around. "Would you ever consider moving back to Virginia?" He asked, waiting for an answer to the question he had put off asking.

Cameo was a bit taken aback by the question and took a moment to answer. "That would depend on quite a few things." She said, resuming a seat on the sofa.

Sanford kept his eyes focused on the magazine. "Such as?"

"Well," Cameo sighed, folding her legs beneath her, "where, for one thing. After living in Chicago for so long, I don't think I'm cut out yet for country life."

"Richmond?"

Cameo nodded slowly. "I could live there."

"So what else would it take?" He promised, tossing the magazine to the coffee table.

Cameo wound her hair into a loose ponytail. "Sanford, what is this? Why all these questions about where I live?"

Sanford tapped his fingers to his mustache and shrugged. "I'd just like to know. Would your job keep you here?"

Cameo waved her hand. "Oh nah, no I can work from anywhere."

"Then what?"

"Sanford...I don't know, alright?"

Sanford smiled at her flustered expression and stood. "I think it's time for me to say goodnight." He told her, bending to kiss her.

Cameo's lashes fluttered as the kiss sparked electricity along every pleasure point on her body. "So when are you going back to Virginia?"

Sanford's dimpled smile was mischievous. "When I have you," He said, kissing the tip of her nose, before he headed out.

Cameo sat speechless as she watched him leave.

TWENTY-TWO

Almost a week had passed since Portia's evening with Huron. During that time, she was sure to have dinner with Lewis in places she didn't think Huron Augustine frequented. It worked...for a while, until Lewis decided he wanted to spend an evening club hopping.

"Well, look who's here."

Portia squeezed her fiancés' shoulder and leaned close. "Who, Baby?" She asked, following the line of Lewis's gaze. When she saw Huron across the bar area, her heart jumped to her throat. She tried to think of a quick excuse to leave the bar, but to her despair Lewis was already waving towards the man.

Huron returned the wave, but his dark eyes were focused on Portia. He arrived at the club with a woman on each arm. They were promptly forgotten though, when he caught sight of Portia.

Sandy Jensen exchanged a glance with her twin sister Sharon, before nudging Huron with her shoulder. "Hey, boy are you even listening to us?"

Huron's attention was held captive by the slinky black dress Portia wore. The frilly, uneven hemline flared just above her knees, accentuating her long, shapely legs. The bodice dipped low in front, while the spaghetti straps called notice to her toned dark arms and graceful neck.

"'Scuse me, y'all," Huron left the flamboyantly dressed sisters staring after him in stunned amazement.

"What's goin' on, man?" Lewis shook hands with Huron when they met in the middle of the bar floor.

"Not much," Huron stared at Portia as he shook hands with her fiancé.

Lewis didn't seem to notice the heated stares between the two. "You out on the town alone?" He slyly queried.

Huron smirked and cast a quick glance across his shoulder. "Nah, I got a couple of twins with me."

Lewis chuckled, while Portia tensed. She tried to keep her expression closed, but Huron saw everything she was trying to conceal.

"We're waiting on a table, if y'all want to join us." Lewis was saying.

Huron's black brows rose as he surveyed Portia's reaction. Clearly, she was less than thrilled by Lewis's offer.

Nervously, she eased her fingers through her short, glossy hair and stepped away from Lewis. "Baby, I see someone I know. I'll catch up with you later."

"Um, Lew man, I'm gonna pass on that offer." Huron was saying, his onyx gaze following the path Portia took through the crowded club.

"You sure, man?" Lewis was asking.

Huron clapped Lewis's shoulder. "Thanks man, but I'm gonna find my ladies and get up outta here. I'll talk to you later." He was saying, already turning to walk away.

Jeran Croswell's brown eyes gleamed when he smiled. "So, when's the big day?" He asked.

Portia eased her arms around her dance partner's neck and giggled. "We haven't set a date yet."

Jeran was shocked. "Stop playin' Girl, what the hell is that brotha waiting on? Every cat I know would jump to marry you." He declared.

Portia leaned close and kissed Jeran's cheek. "You're so sweet."

Jeran rubbed his fingers along the light beard he sported. "Aw, stop it." He drawled, joining Portia when she burst into laughter.

Jeran's animated expression grew brighter then. "What's up, Blue?!" he greeted.

Huron clapped Jeran's shoulder. "What's goin' on, kid?"

"Hell man, what it look like?" Jeran teased, his brows rising when he jerked his head toward Portia. "I got this fine sista in my arms."

Huron pushed one hand into his wine trousers. "Lonette know 'bout this?"

Jeran pretended to be on edge. "Why? You seen her?"

Huron chuckled at Jeran's reaction to the question. "I saw her a minute ago and she asked if I'd seen you."

"Damn." Jeran hissed, though he was completely in love with his girlfriend of eight years.

"I'll just take this fine sista off your hands." Huron decided, already slipping his arm around Portia's waist.

"Mmm hmm." Jeran gestured, seeing through his friend's sly act. "She better be lookin' for me, Blue."

Huron only chuckled at the warning. Portia only had a chance to wave at Jeran before he was blocked from view by Huron's wide body. "What are you doing?" She asked, pushing against his chest.

Huron pretended to be confused. "You didn't expect me to leave you alone on the dance floor, did you?"

Portia gave up trying to escape the snug embrace and scowled up at Huron. "We shouldn't be doing this."

Huron's innocent smile belied the intense emotion coursing through him. "We're just dancing. What's wrong with that?" He asked, fighting to keep his voice light.

Portia's gaze faltered as she thought of endless replies to the simple question. The dance was anything but innocent. Huron's wide hands moved over her body with the familiarity of a lover. His fingers massaged her hips and back. Portia could feel the heat from his touch penetrating the silky fabric of the dress. When he pulled her into his iron frame, she gasped at the pronounced bulge against her belly.

"Huron, don't." She pleaded, losing the feather hold she had on herself control.

In response, Huron slid his nose along Portia's temple and inhaled the soft cool scent of her perfume. The pressure of his fingers against her hips increased, when his lips brushed her cheek.

"We can't do this here." Portia warned, even as her lashes fluttered close.

"Why?" He challenged.

"Lewis-"

"Would never be able to see us in this crowd and in the dark," He pointed out, just before his lips pressed against hers.

"Still..." Portia replied, losing herself in the man's masterful touch. Her entire body was alive with need and; unconsciously, she rubbed herself against him in a purely wanton fashion.

"I want this." Huron groaned into her mouth. His hands reached down to cup her bottom, indicating that it was the part of her anatomy he was referring to.

"No..."

"You want it. Tell me you don't." Huron dared, pulling Portia against the stiff ridge beneath his trouser front.

"Mmm..." She moaned, her fingers curling tightly around the lapels of his stylish wine-colored jacket. "Lewis..."

"I don't give a damn about him." Huron growled, thrusting his tongue deep in a punishing kiss. "You don't care about him either, so stop lying." He ordered, once he'd released her mouth.

"Huron-"

"Come home with me."

***

Chicago, IL

"I thought you were taking me home?"

"I will. Later."

Cameo cleared her throat and ran her hand over the tight chignon she sported.

Sanford headed up the curving driveway, leading to the hotel he used while in Chicago. His relaxed stance behind the wheel camouflaged the tension surging through him.

Cameo had enjoyed the extravagant feast at the Japanese steakhouse and the jazz session they'd sat in on at a popular club afterward. She was exhausted and planned to turn in and head to the magazine early the next morning. Sanford's sudden change in plan concerned her but she remained silent even when he handed the keys to the valet and escorted her into the high rise.

Inside the elevator, Sanford kept to his side of the car. He leaned against the paneled wall and watched Cameo with a hooded gaze. Nervous, Cameo switched the strap of her leather tote to the other shoulder and pretended to be fascinated by a string hanging from the cuff of her roseblush pantsuit.

"I got to get back to Richmond soon." Sanford announced, his soft deep voice seeming to boom in the confines of the car.

"Alright," Cameo coolly responded, though her heart dropped when she heard the words.

'Alright' was the last thing Sanford wanted to hear. The lid he kept on his temper snapped off like a twig against the wind. "I want you with me." He said, his voice growing firmer.

Cameo kept her almond-brown gaze on the floor. "I can't." She whispered.

"Why?"

"Well Sanford, for one thing, I need to work."

"Try again-you told me you can work from anywhere."

Cameo's mouth fell open and she turned to watch him with wide eyes. "Do I have to justify my work schedule to you?"

"All I want from you is the truth."

Cameo couldn't stand the accusing look in his fantastic dark gaze and looked away. "You calling me a liar?" She finally challenged.

"Do you feel like one?" Sanford challenged, massaging his beard as his eyes raked the length of her hour glass frame.

Cameo pounded her fist against the elevator doors. "Dammit, don't you ever get turned down? Why is this so hard for you to accept?!"

The chrome doors swished open, before Sanford could respond. They exited and walked toward his penthouse suite. Sanford unlocked the door and let Cameo precede him. He slammed the door shut and caught her arm before she could get too far.

"San-" Cameo argued, but never had to chance to complete the sentence. He was kissing her-harshly at first, then with gentler more intense passion. Cameo wanted to melt in the embrace.

"I can't let you go." He whispered, during the devastating kiss.

"San..." Cameo arched her neck when his lips trailed the soft skin below her earlobe. "I have a life here. My work...I-I love living here."

"Don't you ever think about what we could be like?" He asked, stepping away from her.

Cameo clasped her hands to her chest. "You know I do, but I've lived here for years. I can't just pick up and leave just like that."

Sanford jerked out of the quarter length brown leather jacket and hurled it to the sofa. Cameo could see his chest heaving beneath his olive green knit top. She knew he had reached his breaking point.

"What's the real reason, Cam?"

"Excuse me?"

The granite expression on Sanford's deep brown face, spoke volumes. "You won't come to Virginia, because you don't want anyone to know we're together."

"Sanford! That's not-"

"Cameo if you say 'that's not true', I'm really gonna lose it with you."

"I'm not ashamed of us, Sanford."

"What the hell is it, then? What the hell do you expect me to think?"

"Alright!" Cameo snapped, throwing her hands in the air. "Dammit, maybe, on some small level my family might have something to do with it."

"I knew it."

"But that's not all of it!"

"Save it, Cameo."

"Sanford."

"I don't want to hear it."

Cameo had never seen Sanford so angry. The roar of his voice wasn't nearly as vicious as the expression he wore. She watched him a moment longer, then left him alone and went to the other side of the living room to fix herself a drink.

Sanford pretended to go through some files on his desk. As he stood there, he followed Cameo's every move. When she took a seat on the sofa, he tossed the folder aside. "Will this mess between our families always be an issue?" He asked, folding his arms across his chest.

Cameo tucked a loose tendril behind her ear and shook her head. "I don't want it to be, but...I'm afraid it'll always come up." She admitted.

"What do we do about it?"

Cameo set her glass to the coffee table and patted the spot next to her. "We could stay away from each other." She suggested when he sat down.

Sanford's laughter only lasted a few short moments. His demeanor quickly sobered and he leaned over to stroke her cheek. "I'm sorry." He whispered.

"Me too," Cameo whispered back. Her fingers tightened against his and she pulled him close.

***

Princess and Adonis had been seeing each other since the dinner party. They had enjoyed several evenings together and, in the process, became much acquainted. Through it all, Adonis had remained a perfect gentleman. It was extremely difficult considering how much he wanted Princess. Really wanted her. He had been grateful for their evenings out-they helped him keep control over his urges.

When Adonis arrived at Princess' door for their dinner date, that evening, he was pleasantly surprised by her appearance.

Wearing a snug orange T-shirt with a wispy multi colored wrap skirt, Princess looked casual and unknowingly seductive.

"Hey, I hope you won't mind staying in tonight?" She asked, clasping her hands against her chest.

Adonis's charcoal gaze slid from the top of Princess' tousled hair to her small, bare feet. "Sounds good to me," He sighed, knowing he should've pressed for dinner away from the cozy apartment.

Princess's smile brightened. "Great. I have dinner all ready, so..."

"It's a good thing I said 'yes'?" Adonis guessed, chuckling when she looked across her shoulder and sent him a cunning look.

Princess waved in the direction of the living room. "You can relax in here. I'll start bringing everything out." She called, already rushing towards the kitchen.

Adonis pulled off the casual jacket and set it across the back of the sofa. The living room was lit by only two of the six glass lamps in the room. The soft golden glow gave the large room a warm, more intimate feel. Soft jazz sounded from the built in speakers and filled the apartment with soothing brass and woodwind pieces.

"Are you sure you don't mind eating in?" Princess asked, returning to the living room with a casserole dish filled with a spicy, tender beef and vegetable stir fry.

Adonis sat with his elbow propped along the arm of the sofa and stroked the line of his temple. His black eyes were warmed by desire as they trailed Princess's shapely dark legs. "I don't mind staying in at all." He assured her.

Princess didn't catch the double meaning behind the words. She set the dish to the coffee table which was already set with dinnerware, silverware and a pitcher of lemon-iced tea. "I hope you'll enjoy this." She whispered.

"I'm sure I will." He replied, his dark gaze growing more intense.

For the next forty-five minutes, Princess and Adonis indulged in the delicious meal. Besides the stir fry, Princess had also prepared sweet, golden cornbread with bits of broccoli and cheese baked into the batter. As usual, conversation was abundant and the meal disappeared in record time.

"No you didn't make dessert too?" Adonis marveled, when Princess returned to the living room with a blueberry pie in hand.

"Just a lil' somethin' somethin'," Princess drawled, cutting into the rich pie and placing a slice on a dessert plate.

Adonis shook his head and accepted the plate. "You're too much."

Princess began to chuckle. "Well, that's true, but I need to confess. I bought this from the market."

"It's the thought that counts." Adonis remarked between mouthfuls of the succulent treat.

"I agree." Princess sighed, taking a napkin before moving back. When she swung her legs onto the sofa, her feet rested innocently against Adonis's thigh.

The fork was poised to cut another morsel of pie, but Adonis hesitated. He reached out and slowly traced her small feet and the perfectly polished toes. His midnight stare followed the path of his fingers as they slid higher along her legs and thighs.

"Adonis?" Princess whispered, when his hand disappeared beneath the hem of her skirt. "Adonis?" She called again.

"Damn." He muttered, setting the half eaten pie back to the coffee table. "I need to get the hell out of here."

Princess set her plate aside as well and pressed her hand to his thigh, before he could leave. "What is it?" She whispered.

Adonis squeezed his eyes shut tightly and debated on whether to respond.

"Adonis?"

"I can't act like this is just a friendly dinner, Princess."

"Why?"

He uttered a short laugh. "Because I want more than friendship from you. Being alone with you is murder on my self-restraint."

Princess fiddled with a lock of her hair. "Are you tired of seeing me?" She asked, her sparkling champagne stare lowering to the embroidered pattern on the black sofa.

"That's not it." He quickly assured her, his gaze narrowing sharply. "I'm half out of my mind thinking about what it'd be like to take you to bed. This private dinner only makes me more aware of how much I want you."

"Oh."

The hushed response brought a look of uncertainty to Adonis's face. He and Princess had never discussed where their relationship was headed. He realized he didn't know whether Princess regarded their relationship as platonic or, worse, sisterly.

"I hope I'm not making you uncomfortable?" He said, his deep voice whisper-soft, his dark gaze downcast.

Princess managed a quick nod and grimaced when her hair flew into her face. "It's just a surprise. Um...I mean, we haven't-you haven't even kissed me." She quietly noted, smoothing her damp palms across her bare legs.

Adonis looked up, his eyes narrowing as a slow smile came to his face. "Well, I can definitely change that." He assured her, and leaned across the small space separating them.

Princess's bright eyes traced the sensuous curve of Adonis's mouth, before her lashes fluttered close. She moaned when his lips brushed hers; softly at first, then with increased pressure. Slowly, his tongue traced the even ridge of her teeth, before delving inside to taste the sweetness of her mouth. Princess' soft moans grew louder as her fingers crept over the designer's emblem on the crew shirt he wore.

Suddenly, Adonis slipped his long arms around Princess's waist and held her against his chest. The kiss deepened, growing wetter in its intensity. Whispered words of desire flowed between them as their hands explored, fondled and caressed. The kiss, so slow in coming, was well worth the wait.

***

By the time Huron had taken Portia back to his condo, she was having second thoughts. She remembered Lewis and the fact that she'd left him behind with no word that she had even left the club. She had little time left to dwell on her actions, though. Huron had already parked the shiny, navy blue Navigator and was walking around to the passenger's side.

Huron held Portia in an unconsciously possessive embrace as they walked through the lobby. He could feel the stares of several men who watched him escort the voluptuous dark beauty.

"Evening, Mr. Augustine."

Huron smiled, but didn't look up as he signed the security log. "What's goin' on Henry?"

The guard tipped his black cap. "Not much." He absently replied. "You look so familiar." He told Portia, his small blue eyes sparkling with curiosity.

"She hears that a lot." Huron replied, slipping his arm back around Portia's waist as they headed toward the elevators.

"I have to tell him." Portia blurted, once they were alone in the car and ascending to the top floor. "Sooner or later somebody's really gonna recognize me."

Huron appeared to be fascinated by the face of his gold watch. "You ready to break up with the man?" He lightly probed.

"It wouldn't come to that." She retorted, smoothing her palm against the back of her glossy cut. "I have to tell him, though. Before someone else does."

The maple paneled elevator doors opened with a quiet swoosh. Portia lagged behind when Huron stepped out into the carpeted corridor.

"I shouldn't be here with you." She whispered, smoothing both hands across the red cashmere wrap covering her shoulders. "Lewis doesn't deserve this."

Huron gnawed the inside of his jaw for a moment. Then, he stepped back into the car and hit the elevator's stop button. "You mean that?" He challenged his coal-colored gaze intense as he watched her expression change.

Portia leaned her head against the wall. "I have to mean it. We never should've started this."

Huron walked further into the car, until he stood right before Portia. "That doesn't mean you have to leave."

"Huron..."

"Hmm?"

Portia banged her clenched fists against her thighs and turned away from Huron's seeking lips. His mouth traced the pulse point below her ear as his hand cupped the generous swell of her breast. Portia's resistance weakened, and then vanished all together, when she felt his thumb brush the firm nipple.

"Come with me." Huron commanded softly. His mouth found hers, his tongue tracing the curve of her full lips. His satisfied grunt filled the car, when he felt her lithe body arch against him. Portia's slender fingers disappeared into the mass of dark hair atop his head. She became an eager participant, her tongue dueling madly with his. Huron's long muscular arms slid around Portia's waist and effortlessly carried her from the elevator to his condo.

Hours later, Huron watched Portia sleeping peacefully in his bed. He traced her flawlessly beautiful face and shook his head. A stuffed shirt like Lewis Hines could never overlook what she was, he thought to himself. He didn't like her career choice either, but he could tolerate it. Partly because he truly believed she would stop for the right man.

"Huron, man what are you saying?" He whispered, his long brows drawing close to form a confused frown.

The doorbell sounded, the shrill noise breaking into his thoughts. He left the bed and went to answer the door before Portia woke.

"Who the hell...?" He grumbled, slipping an ankle length black and gray silk robe over matching boxers. His frown cleared, when he saw Lewis Hines through the small privacy window.

"Have you seen Portia?" Lewis asked, the moment the door opened. His handsome vanilla-toned face appeared haggard, his worried expression making him seem older.

"Have I seen her?" Huron parroted, managing to appear confused.

Lewis threw his hands up. "She just disappeared from the club. I thought maybe you might've seen her leave."

"Sorry man." Huron was saying, as he tried to stifle a yawn.

Lewis shrugged. "I'm the one who's sorry for interrupting you so late or so early I should say."

Huron waved off the apology. "Don't sweat that shit, man. You know women. She probably hooked up with one of her girls and they got to cacklin' about this and that and, you know..."

The explanation didn't sit well with Lewis. "I wouldn't be surprised if she did somethin' that flaky." He retorted, his expression a cross between worry and anger. "That girl's gonna have to learn to be a little more responsible if she's going to be my wife."

"Well, man...she is a big girl." Huron noted, trying to keep the edge from his voice.

"That's right. She's a big girl. She should know better."

Huron had to bite his tongue in order not to laugh. He couldn't believe Lewis Hines was so self-righteous. Huron remembered several less than responsible situations the man had been part of when they were in college.

"Anyway," Lewis sighed, feeling around inside the tanned trench coat pocket for keys. "I'll hook up with you later, man."

Huron reached out and shook hands with Lewis. He watched the man head towards the elevator.

"I should go." Portia said when Huron closed the front door.

"He'll be alright." Huron assured her, pushing both hands into the robe's deep pockets as he walked towards her.

Portia shook her head. "I have to go. Now would be as good a time as any to get into this."

Huron didn't want to hear that. "You know, it's too late to go anywhere tonight." He whispered, his fingers curling around the sheet Portia held around her body. "Let's go back to bed. I'll get you home in the morning." He promised, discarding his robe and wrapping the sheet around both their bodies.

A tiny giggle escaped Portia's lips when she stumbled against Huron. They headed back to the bedroom encased in the flowing dark green sheet. In bed, Huron pulled her into a spoon embrace and pressed his face into her hair. Portia fell asleep right away. Huron continued to think. He finally admitted to himself that he wanted something real-beyond sexual-from Portia Gwaltney. He wanted her with him and he wanted Lewis Hines out of the way.

***

The Augustine mansion was quiet. Family and friends present for the funeral had long since returned to their homes. Only Sweet and Stephanie remained a while longer. Despite the earlier tension, CJ was happy to see his sister becoming her old self. He even began to think Stephanie's preoccupation; with seeing Porter pay for Melissa's death, had passed. He prayed he wasn't mistaken.

"CJ!" Sweet called, when he walked into the dining room and headed for the buffet.

CJ looked up from his newspaper and smiled at his brother-in-law. "What's goin' on, man?"

"Hangin' in there." Sweet sighed, as he heaped fluffy scrambled eggs and sausage links to his plate.

"How's she doing?" CJ asked, his dark eyes filling with concern for his sister.

Taboo Tree

Sweet took a few slices of toast from the warmer and turned away from the buffet. "She seems fine. I think she'll be a lot better when I get her out of the country."

CJ frowned, his coffee mug poised a few inches above the table. "Out of the country?" He probed.

"I want to take her on a long vacation. Maybe someplace warm." Sweet was saying.

"Sounds good." CJ told his brother-in-law, a satisfied smile coming to his brown face. "When do y'all leave?"

Sweet didn't look up as he sliced the juicy, hot sausage link. "As soon as we leave Richmond, Steph wants to find out about the investigation and talk with some of Missy's friends on campus."

"Dammit!" CJ muttered his expression suddenly fierce. He left the dining table so quickly, the newspaper fluttered to the floor in his wake.

CJ stormed up the curving back staircase. Outraged curses filled the air as he headed to the second floor.

"Steph!" He roared, pounding his fist upon the heavy mahogany door until it rattled. "Steph!"

Several seconds passed before the door opened. Stephanie's lovely caramel-toned face was a picture of aggravation.

"What the hell is it?" She almost whispered.

CJ brushed past his sister and grimaced at the open suitcases on the bed. "What the hell is gonna make you give this mess up?"

"This about Porter?" Steph calmly queried, placing a navy scarf into a Louis Vuitton overnight case.

"You know it is." CJ muttered.

"Get over it, then."

Steph's calm, unruffled demeanor only made her brother more enraged. CJ stomped over to the bed and pushed the open case shut. "Going after that boy won't bring Missy back."

"I know that." Steph hissed, her temper slowly rising. "But, I get nauseous when I think of my only baby dead and that boy walkin' around without a care in the world."

"I'm sure he doesn't feel that way, Steph."

Stephanie propped her hands to her hips. "You're sure? How can you be sure of anything where your kids are concern? They didn't even know you exist."

The grim, true reality of Stephanie's words rendered CJ speechless. He lost his strength for arguing and sat in the corner of the bed. "You have to know nothing will come of this." He finally said his tone hollow and solemn.

"Some girlfriends of Missy's came to visit me some weeks ago. They told me she was working on something with Porter. Something for a class."

CJ shrugged. "So?"

"So, it made me think about something Missy asked me earlier this year, I remembered it involved one of her classes, but I can't remember exactly what she asked. The girls who visited, told me Missy and Porter were working on something really heavy."

CJ folded his arms over the Virginia Union sweatshirt he wore. "You think it's connected to the accident?"

Steph's brown eyes misted with unshed tears. "I don't know, but maybe...it could explain why she was drinking."

"Steph, you know this could've been a case of college angst that got out of hand?"

"I don't buy that and I have to know why."

"What if you don't find anything?"

Steph looked down and smoothed her hands across her thighs. "I guess I'll have to go to the source. Porter Gwaltney."

"Dammit Steph." CJ whispered, running one hand across his face. "Can't you leave the boy alone?"

"Can't you go see your son?" Stephanie challenged. "If not for yourself, then for me and your only niece. I have to know what happened, why it happened. Something-anything to give me peace or some closure about this. CJ, if you can't do it for those reasons, then think about Demetria, the woman you love."

CJ's dark eyes snapped to his sister's face, but Steph had already left the bed and resumed her packing. He held his head in his hands. Heavy thoughts filled his mind.

***

"Thanks for seeing me, Greg. I know how hectic your schedule is."

Greg Holmes's vibrant blue gaze sparkled as he eyed the stunning beauty taking a seat before his desk. "I always have time for my new doctors. Especially the very good ones."

Cece leaned her leather tote against the leg of her chair and sat back. "I appreciate you saying that."

Greg waved his hands. "It's true. I want to keep you all happy so you'll stay and from the looks of you, you don't seem too happy." He noted, his expression becoming less animated.

"You're too perceptive." Cece sighed, toying with a heavy curl dangling from her high ponytail.

"What's the trouble?" He inquired, perching his slender frame on the edge of the neat oak desk.

"Well I-um...Goodness." Cece muttered, suddenly finding it difficult to explain her dilemma. "Um I-I'd like to have a different mentor." She blurted, wringing her hands as she judged his reaction. "You're disappointed." She guessed.

Greg massaged his jaw and smiled. "I'm not disappointed Cecelia and I can't say I'm surprised by your request."

Worry clouded Cece's face. "Don't get me wrong Greg, please! Derric's a great doctor and he'd be a fantastic mentor. For someone else. I just can't work with him."

Greg leaned forward and patted Cece's hand. "I understand. Derric confides in me from time to time. He's told me about the problems between your families."

Cece shook her head. "I don't think we'll ever get past all that."

Greg eased off the desk and brushed the wrinkles from his khaki trousers. "Well, I'll try to work on getting you teamed with another doctor, but I'll be honest. You couldn't have a better mentor than Derric Augustine."

"I know that." Cece admitted, her lovely brown face shadowed with regret. "Greg, you just don't know what it's like working so closely with all this tension." She said. Of course, the unbearable tension had little to do with family matters and more to do with her growing attraction for the man.

"I suppose you won't want to be here when I tell him?"

Cece's brown eyes filled with unease. "I was hoping you wouldn't have to tell him."

Greg chuckled. "Don't you think he'd miss you?" He teased. "Besides, it's only fair, you know?"

"I know." Cece groaned, grabbing her purse as she stood. "Well, thanks for the offer but I think I'll decline on being present."

"I tried." Greg replied, stepping close to shake hands with his newest doctor. "You take care and I'll be in touch."

"Thanks Greg." Cece said, managing a small smile before she turned and walked out of the office.

In the corridor, Cece spotted Derric. Her heart dipped to her stomach and she couldn't believe how attracted she'd become to the man. She felt such elation when he was just the least bit civil to her, but hated herself for acknowledging that fact. Before he could notice her, Cece ducked down another hallway.

Derric had noticed Cece the moment she stepped out of Greg's office. When she retreated down a side corridor, his dark eyes narrowed with curiosity.

***

The glass countertop was cluttered by at least twenty magazines. Amina had decided to leave home late that morning and used the time to check out her advertisements in the entertainment and fashion periodicals. She was making notes regarding one of the ads when the doorbell rang. She eased off the white, cushioned stool and went to answer. Surprise and a hint of suspicion filled her sparkling hazel gaze when she opened the door to Tav.

"What are you doing here?" She pointedly queried, hoping he hadn't come to finish what started during their last private meeting. She'd commended herself for turning him away before, but silently admitted she'd never be able to resist him again.

Tav pushed himself from the doorjamb and cleared his throat. "We didn't finish our conversation."

"I was sure we had." Amina whispered, folding her arms across the snug green T-shirt she wore. "What more do we have to talk about?"

"May I come in?" Tav asked, his deep-set gaze drifting past Amina's shoulder and into the spacious top floor condo.

Amina hesitated, her suspicion obvious as her eyes studied Tav's handsome molasses-toned face. Every instinct told her this would not end on a friendly note, but she stepped aside and allowed him into her home.

"Okay." She said, once the front door was closed. The expectancy on her face, matched the tone of her voice.

Tav watched her closely. "The last time we talked, I told you I wanted you back."

Amina nodded and strolled around the side of the sofa. "I remember."

Tav chuckled. "And do you remember what happened after that?"

"We kissed." Amina said, taking a deep breath as she recalled the sweet moment. "Things might've gone further, but..."

"You told me to stop." Tav finished the statement, using his softest tone of voice.

Amina pushed her hands into the side pockets of her brown Capri pants. "I didn't think we needed to become involved in something we weren't ready for."

"And how do you feel about it now?"

Amina shook her head, her brows rose as she struggled to find the right words. "Tav..."

"I was serious about wanting you back."

Damn, now I've done it, Amina told herself as Tav's admission hung in the air, waiting to be claimed. "Tav...I don't know how to say this without there being hurt feelings, so...It would be hard-no, no that's not right...It would impossible for me to forget all the years. All the hurt and start fresh with you. We had a very sweet moment a few weeks ago. I could never deny that, but it's not enough to make me want you back in my life."

Tav let Amina speak without interrupting her. He kept searching for some sign. Something to help him believe she wasn't admitting her true feelings. Unfortunately, he saw no such signs. She appeared confident and sure of herself. He realized she had no desire to come back to him, that the 'sweet moment' they shared was only a stolen pleasure-nothing more. He could feel the rage slowly, very slowly beginning to build. He turned away from Amina, so she could not see him struggling to keep the anger from his face.

"There's someone else." He guessed.

"No." Amina told him, not realizing how her blatant honesty was affecting him. "I just really enjoy being single and; more importantly, unafraid."

"You can cool it with the 'new woman routine'."

"Excuse me?" Amina replied, pretending to have missed the grumbled remark.

"What is this?" Tav whispered, whirling around to face his ex-wife. "When we talked that night, I thought we were both thinking on the same track."

"Well, you were mistaken."

Tav pushed one hand into the deep pocket of his tan trousers. "So, you're one of those now, huh?"

Amina smoothed a loose tendril back into her ponytail. "One of those?" She retorted, frowning deeply.

"You don't mind a man bringing you home and staying a while as long as he don't start thinkin' he's the only one."

Amina stepped closer to Tav. "What the hell are you saying?"

"We might not have had sex that night, but we came damn close. You let me believe-"

"Now you hold it right there!" Amina demanded, one hand poised in the air. "I never let you believe anything. You were the one who walked in here with all these preconceived notions about us getting back together. I let you believe..." She repeated, as though the statement made her sick inside. "You know Tav, you ain't changed a bit. You don't know how to be anything other than what you are: a self-involved, violent, controlling son of a bitch!"

"Who the fuck do you think you are, speaking to me like that?!" Tav roared, allowing his anger to show. "I'm your-"

"Nothing! You are nothing to me!" Amina finished her suppressed anger gathering like a heavy ball in her chest. "What you were was a source of fear, aggravation and self-loathing. Not one good thing came from that sham of a marriage!"

Tav was shaking with anger he ran one hand across his bald head. "You forget our daughter." He softly reminded her.

Amina's smile was hate-filled. "I never forget my daughter, Tav. I thank God every day of my life that she is not yours and that I got away from you before she could be scarred by all the shit you put me through."

"Bitch." Tav sneered, his mouth almost curling into a vicious snarl. "You lied to me all those years about Princess. Lied 'cause you were ashamed of letting that Italian muthafucka screw you. You knew them high and mighty Augustines would kick you out on your ass if they ever found out. You played me for a fool and I had every right to whip your ass for that shit!"

"Get out." Amina breathed, turning to leave the room.

Tav lost what little control he had over his emotions, when Amina turned her back on him. His heavy steps were muffled on the thick carpet as he bolted across the room with clenched fists.

Amina turned just before Tav reached her. Momentary surprise registered on her face, before she flinched just out of his grasp. She ran to the edge of the glass counter top and gathered the thick fashion and entertainment magazines.

Tav caught Amina's arm and he jerked her back. Amina flexed her hands around the stack of magazines, before swinging them across her shoulder. She hit Tav square in the face and smiled when she heard his surprised grunt. Something snapped, then and she raised the stack of books again. This time, she slammed into the side of his neck sending him reeling backwards.

"Amina-" Tav gushed, his voice barely audible. He raised one hand, only to have it smacked away by another swing of the magazines.

Amina's aim was dead on as the heavy blows landed against Tav's back, chest and ribcage. At one point, she uttered an enraged cry and increased the speed of the blows. Tav fell to the floor, the look in his onyx eyes a mixture of shock...and fear. After a while, the hits lost their intensity and Amina let the magazines spill from her fingers. She pinned Tav with a scathing glare, her body shaking with anger.

"We are finished." She announced her voice raspy and cold. "Don't call me, don't come by here and don't ever try to use my daughter against me."

Slowly, Tav pushed himself from the floor. He still watched her warily as he spoke. "She'll always be between us." He managed to whisper.

"That may be, but you and I are done." She assured him, her thick wavy brown hair now a wild disarray as she stood glaring at him.

"Amina-"

"Get out of my sight before I kill you."

Tav couldn't stand straight without wincing at the pain in his back. He regarded Amina as though she were a different person. He limped from the room, flinching when the door slammed behind him.

***

Cece finished massaging the rich lotion into the soles of her feet and sighed at the relaxing sensation. She'd come right home, indulged in a long bath and a few glasses of wine, before venturing into the living room with the lotion. She had just set the bottle aside, when the doorbell rang.

"Derric." She whispered, upon opening the door. Unconsciously, she tightened the belt on her burgundy silk robe.

Derric's humble expression belied his true emotions. His hand curled into a fist, which he hid in the deep pocket of his sagging blue jeans. "Can I come in?" He asked.

"Oh yes, please." Cece invited, stepping aside as he entered.

Derric stopped just inside the foyer and turned to wait for Cece to precede him.

Cece felt slightly self-conscious beneath his probing, dark eyes. Still, she managed to walk past him and into the living room without tripping over the hem of her robe.

"Please, have a seat." She offered, waving one hand toward the turquoise-gray overstuffed living room furnishings.

Derric settled onto one of the armchairs near the brick fireplace. He cleared his throat and looked as though he were debating. "Greg told me you asked for a new mentor." He blurted after a few silent moments.

Cece walked over to the fireplace and extended her fingers toward the flame. "Derric..."

"You don't have to say anything. I do understand."

"It's nothing against you." Cece spoke suddenly, her brown eyes wide and pleading.

Derric waved his hand. "Don't explain to me Cece, please. You had every right to do what you did."

"I did?" Cece replied, surprise registering on her brown caramel-toned face. "So, you're not upset with me for making you look bad in front of Greg?" She slowly questioned. Tiny bumps appeared along her arms when Derric's soft laughter reached her ears.

"You didn't make me look bad in front of Greg, Cece. Believe me lately I've been doing that on my own."

Cece shook her head slightly. "I don't understand."

"I'm not so cold-hearted that I don't know when I'm being an ass."

"Well, not to add fuel to the flame, Derric, but you um- you must like being an ass around me because you've played the part with a lot of enthusiasm."

Cece's soft spoken reply brought another smile to Derric's lips. "I don't want you to have another mentor."

"What?"

"I told Greg to forget it."

Cece perched on the arm of one of the chairs and regarded Derric suspiciously. "Why would you do that? I thought-"

"I know what you thought and I'm sorry."

"Why? Was I mistaken?" Cece queried, her cheeks beginning to burn. "Are you trying to tell me you didn't mean it?"

Derric could see the pain flashing in Cece's warm gaze and wanted to kick himself for hurting her. "I'm sorry for the way I treated you. I was mean and petty to you when you had nothing to do with it."

"You've been so cold and now...all of a sudden you're apologizing?"

Derric leaned forward, bracing his elbows on his knees. "I don't expect you to believe a damn thing I say. Just know that I am sorry. I never should have treated you that way. Especially when..."

"What?"

Derric cleared his throat, and then met her soft stare with his penetrating one. "Especially when you've been nothing but professional, accommodating and very, very sweet."

Cece clutched her hands, to stop their shaking. Though Derric spoke and appeared sincere, she hesitated to take him at his word. Emotional and confused, she went to stand before the fireplace. Derric watched her staring blankly into the flames. "Listen Cece," he sighed, standing from the armchair, "I said everything I came to say. If you still don't think we should work together. I won't stand in your way if you still want another mentor."

"A different mentor won't solve the problem."

The barely audible comment prompted Derric to take a step closer. "What problem?"

"Just go Derric. Please?" Cece whispered, bringing her hands to her face.

Derric shook his head. "What did you mean by that? Cece?" He persisted.

Taboo Tree

Finally, Cece worked up the nerve to face him. "Your attitude isn't the only reason I want a new mentor."

"What then?"

"I um, I can't tell you this." Cece whispered, pressing her fingers to her brow. She tried to turn away but Derric stopped her.

"Talk to me." He gently commanded, his fingers massaging her upper arms.

Cece felt her eyes water and pressed her lips together. She read the look on Derric's handsome face and knew he would persist until she came clean.

"Cece," Derric called again. This time his tone was unyielding.

"I think I'm falling in love with you." She whispered, staring at the floor through a blurred gaze.

Derric was struck speechless for a moment. Then slowly he shook his head as his hands tightened on her arms. "Cece-"

"Would you just go now? Please go?" She begged, wrenching out of his grasp.

Derric followed Cece to the other side of the living room. When he stood behind her, he could hear her sobbing. "Hey." He soothed, pulling her back into his chest.

Cece's shoulders shook beneath the force of her soft cries. The tears flowed harder when Derric enfolded her in a comforting hold and pressed his face against the nape of her neck.

Derric didn't know how long he and Cecelia stood there in the simple, yet telling embrace. He could have cares less, though. Several long, relaxing moments passed and; in that time, Cece's sobs subsided.

"Cece?"

"Hmm?"

"Honey how in the hell could you possibly fall in love with me?"

Cece studied the question a moment before realizing how funny it was. Her laughter was mixed with sobs as she turned to Derric. "It surprises me too." She admitted, smiling as he used his thumbs to brush tears from her cheeks. "I don't know how or when it happened," she continued, "at first it was purely superficial. My girlish, shallow side saw a gorgeous sexy man and I was hooked. Then, as we started working together, I was um, intrigued by your intelligence and slowly I found myself more attracted to you."

Derric's heart softened more as he listened to Cece reveal her feelings. His hand curved around her neck and he pulled her closer. His lips traced the line of her brow and temple.

"...I just couldn't keep working so closely with you. Feeling this way and knowing how you feel about me, I just couldn't keep it up."

"Shh..." Derric soothed against her forehead. He reached for her hand and pulled her to the sofa. "I don't know what to say." He told Cece, once they'd settled onto the overstuffed cushions. "I think when you asked for a new mentor, I knew I didn't want to lose the time I got to spend with you, even if I did spend most of the time acting like a damned fool. I like being around you and I'd like to know what it's like to be around you away from the hospital."

"Are you serious?" Cece asked, disbelief filling her eyes.

Derric's grin made him appear adorably boyish. "I'm very serious, but I don't expect you to just take my word for it."

"Thanks."

Derric tugged on one of Cece's curls and chuckled. "What I'm trying to say is that I want to know you. *You*, Cece. Not Doctor Cecelia Gwaltney. Just Cecelia Gwaltney. Just Cece."

Tentatively, Cece reached up to stroke Derric's sideburns. "I think I can arrange that." She whispered.

Derric took her hand and kissed the tips of her fingers. "Maybe in the process, you'll see I'm not such a bad guy."

"I can't wait." She said, her brown eyes focused on his mouth.

Derric's midnight stare traced Cece's lovely face with striking intensity. Slowly, he leaned forward. His thumb followed the outline of her full lips. Next, his tongue mimicked the action before delving into the sweet dark cavern of her mouth. He felt her shiver in his arms and smiled at the reaction.

"Derric..."

"Shh..." He urged, delighting in the taste and smell of her body.

The kiss intensified as pent up desires escaped. In that moment all labels fell away, who they were and the discontent between their families become unimportant and nonexistent.

Much later, Derric and Cece were still cuddled on the sofa. Their long-awaited kiss awakened an intense passion. They both wanted to act upon it, but decided to wait. Instead, they talked of the drama between the Gwaltneys and Augustines.

"I honestly believe our families are destined to hate each other forever." Derric mused, though his expression was serious.

Cece rubbed her hands across her thighs. "I hate to agree with that, but I think it's true. Nothing short of a miracle would change the way things are."

"Especially now. After what happened to Missy..."

Cece turned to face Derric. She pressed her hand against his cheek and could almost feel the pain she saw in his eyes. "I'm so sorry for your family. I know it's small consolation when Porter has fully recovered and-"

"Hold it." Derric softly interrupted. "You know, a lot of what I said was pain talking. Missy was my only niece, my parents' only grandchild. What happened to her hurt us all. The fact that a Gwaltney was involved, added to the hurt."

Cece took Derric's hand and squeezed it gently. She easily could imagine the pain the family had endured.

"...I think Stephanie's past wanting Porter behind bars," Derric was saying. His thumb stroking her fingers absently as he spoke. "She really wants to know about that night. What happened? What was Missy thinking? What made her drink? Was she happy, upset, scared, what?"

Though Derric's clear, deep voice held no trace of anger, Cece felt tears pressuring her eyes. She truly felt for Stephanie Kensie's loss. In that moment, Cece knew she would do anything

332

AlTonya Washington

in her power to give the woman the peace she so desperately sought.
***

"Have y'all set a date yet?" Kimberly Swiggins asked, as she inspected the dazzling diamond.

Portia smiled at the woman's awed expression. "Not yet, everyone's schedule is so crazy, we haven't been able to decide on a time that's right for the main people we want to invite."

"I hear ya, Girl. When Jamil and me had our wedding, we wound up setting the date way in advance so our families could arrange to have the time free."

Portia clasped her fingers together when Kimberly let go of her hand. "We'll probably end up doing that too." She sighed.

"Well, I can't wait." Kim was saying, heading behind her neat desk. "You call me if you need help with anything."

"Thanks Kim." Portia replied with a smile. When the woman excused herself to take a call, Portia allowed the happy expression to fade. She wished she could feel as enthusiastic about her upcoming nuptials, but admitted that it was a hopeless wish. People like her brought sadness on themselves, she decided. Her only prayer was that she not lose the best man she'd ever had, because of the terrible choices she'd made.

Huron Augustine came to mind. Portia felt her cheeks burn as images of their time together flooded her memory. If only Lewis could make her feel that way, she thought. Sadly, sex with her fiancé, was at most...tolerable.

"Stop it, Portia." She ordered, shaking her head quickly. She was there to have an honest discussion with Lewis. He was the first man who had ever made her feel worthy of respect. She prayed he would still be her fiancé, when their discussion was complete.

"It's good to see you, man." Lewis was saying as he refilled Huron Augustine's cognac glass.

"I was in the area." Huron said, swirling the burgundy liquid in the stout snifter. "I really wanted to know if you and Portia ever hooked up?"

Lewis grimaced, setting the cognac back to the bar in the corner of his spacious office. "We talked on the phone. She wandered off with one of her girls. They were out in the parking lot when I left."

"Mmm," Huron replied, his deep-set gaze lowering briefly. "How was it that you two met anyway?"

Finally, Lewis smiled. "I had a meeting with one of the art galleries in downtown LA. She was there, we started talking about one of the pieces...I don't think I've ever been able to talk so easily to any woman."

"What does she do out in LA?" Huron asked, setting his glass to the coffee table.

"She's a director's assistant to one of the medical dramas on TV."

"Mmm, which one?"

Lewis smoothed one hand across his bald head. "I can never remember."

Huron wasn't surprised to hear that. Anyone who talked with Lewis would realize he had a rather vague idea of how his fiancée earned her living.

"Lewis man, you know I consider you a close friend." Huron remarked, his expression and tone of voice were laced with just a tint of foreboding. "I've always thought of you as one of my boys," he continued, though he couldn't remember a single conversation the two of them may have shared alone during college. "Anyway, I think you have a right to know it all."

Lewis shook her head. His green eyes registered confusion. "Know it all?"

"I hate to see anyone I know being made a fool of."

"Man, what the hell are you talkin' about?" Lewis demanded, bracing his fists a top the desk.

Huron massaged his jaw, then reached into the inside pocket of his tanned jacket. "Maybe I should show you." He said, pulling out a DVD package.

Lewis stood straight and watched Huron walk to the entertainment case. He pushed the tape into the machine and grabbed the remote. When the fuzz cleared, the title: DARK

AlTonya Washington

CHOCOLATE appeared in pink neon letters. When that screen faded, a young woman was shown wearing a rather revealing business skirt suit.

"Portia," Lewis breathed, his green gaze narrowing as he sat on the edge of his desk.

It didn't take long to realize what type of movie he was watching. Lewis sat motionless and watched his fiancée. By now, she was bent over a desk being ravaged by one man as she performed oral sex on another.

Huron grew angered as he watched the screen. Unlike the other fifteen times he watched the flick, this time seeing it enraged him. Still, he let it play. Lewis appeared to be shocked by the antics of the on-screen threesome.

After a while Huron cleared his throat and headed towards the entertainment center.

"No." Lewis called, raising his hand when Huron moved to turn off the TV.

Huron's brows drew close and he wondered if his plan might backfire.

"Hellooo?" Portia called, knocking lightly as she stepped into the office. She was about to call Lewis's name, when she saw Huron Augustine perched on the arm of the sofa. Lewis was watching the TV screen with a fixed stare. It was then she heard the sounds of high-pitched moans mingled with deep groans.

Slowly, Portia stepped forward. Her eyes grew wide, when they focused on the screen. The blood rushed to her head and she felt faint at the sight of herself having sex now with the three white actors who passed her around like a toy.

With a start, she hurried to shut off the TV. Lewis jumped from the desk and caught Portia, jerking her back against his chest.

"Is this you?" He whispered against her ear. His voice shook with emotion.

"Lewis-"

"Is it?!"

"Yes, yes."

Lewis shoved Portia, then. He looked completely disgusted and even wiped his palms together as though they had been dirtied. "Freaky bitch," He sneered.

"Please, Lewis-"

"What the fuck, Portia!" Lewis raged, rubbing his hands across his head as he paced the room like a caged lion.

"I can explain." Portia cried, her hands clasped against her chest as she followed her fiancé around the office.

Lewis whirled around. "Explain what?! Explain what, Bitch?! I can see the fuckin' shit right here in full color!"

Portia's gaze was totally blurred by tears. "I-I was going to tell you." She shuddered.

"When?!"

"There was never time-"

"Bullshit!"

"Lewis, please-"

"Please what?! You tryin' to tell me I shouldn't be pissed about this shit?!"

"No."

"Then what?!"

Portia's palms were so damp she only succeeded in wrinkling her powder blue satin dress when she wiped them across the alluring frock. "It's just my job. It doesn't mean I'm a..."

"Ho? Slut?" Lewis nastily supplied.

Portia broke into sobs and stood there with her head bowed.

"All the time we were seeing each other and you never told me," Lewis reflected, sounding as though he were speaking to himself.

"I just-"

"Shut up!" Lewis snapped, his vicious tone drawing the attention of several people.

The degrading names and foul language Lewis barked at his fiancée drew increased interest. Gradually, the onlookers noticed what was playing on the television. Soon, many people gasped and some pointed at the graphic flick. The doorway cleared when Huron walked over and closed the door.

Tears streamed Portia's face and ruined her perfect makeup. Lewis's heavy breathing came in rapid pants as he struggled to control his actions.

"I came here today to tell you about all of this." Portia explained, her words almost impossible to decipher due to her crying.

"Portia, don't." Lewis urged, raising one hand to silence her excuse.

Portia wouldn't listen. "Lewis, you can't do this. Not now. Not when we're getting married and-"

"I said, shut up!" He roared, whirling around to send a backhand slap to her face.

The force of the blow sent Portia to her knees. She had to clutch the edge of the desk, lest she fall on her face.

"Rank Bitch. You can forget meeting me at the altar. I'll be getting checked at the health clinic." Lewis muttered. He stepped over his ex-fiancée on his way out of the office.

Portia's body shook against the force of her sobs. Across the room, Huron watched her, his dark gaze registered pain. Deep in his subconscious, he knew he had done wrong, but it was too late to change things now. Dismissing the heavy thoughts, he went and closed the door behind Lewis. Then, he shut off the TV and went over to Portia.

"Come on, Baby." He whispered, leaning down to help her up.

Portia retaliated. "Get off! Get off!" She snapped, waving her fist towards his legs. "You did this?" She breathed, glaring up at him from the floor. Her lovely brown eyes were red and watery. Her lips trembled and her breathing came in soft shuddery gasps. "You did this, didn't you?" She asked again.

"Portia-"

"Why? Why would you do something so cruel?"

Huron couldn't find his voice. He had never felt so powerless to stop a situation from spiraling out of control.

Taboo Tree

Portia braced against the desk and pushed himself up. She brushed wrinkles and lint from her dress and acted as though every movement pained her. "Did you enjoy the show? I mean the live one?" She clarified, glancing at the DVD Huron carried.

He glanced at the disc and threw it onto the sofa.

"Well, don't you have anything to say? Or are you here today purely as a spectator?"

Huron reached out with intentions of wiping Portia's fresh tears. When his fingers brushed her face, she reared back and slapped him hard. Then, despite her hysterical state she strolled out of the office.

***

Porter laughed when he found Cece outside his door. He pulled his aunt inside the spacious off-campus apartment.

"What you doin' here, woman?" Porter teased as they hugged.

Cece couldn't hold her smile for long. "What were you and Melissa Kensie involved in the night she died?"

Porter's easy expression faded. In its place, appeared a drawn, haunted look that made him appear far older than his twenty-two years.

"Porter?"

"Cece, I can't talk about-"

"No. I don't want to hear that. Now, I could understand you not wanting to talk just after the accident, but the time for that has passed."

Porter paced the living room. He toyed with the twists in his thick black hair. Cece pressed her lips together and prayed she could remain calm. The pain on her nephew's face tore her apart, but she had to have some answers.

"Every time I think about that night I feel like I'm livin' through it all over again." Porter sighed, rubbing one hand across the front of his white T-shirt as though his chest ached. "All I hear is Missy screamin'..."

Cece felt a sudden chill and began to smooth her hands across the fuzzy red turtleneck she wore. "Were y'all just foolin' around or what?"

"Damn Cece!" Porter snapped, pounding a fist against his jean-clad thigh. "Why you gotta know this?!"

Cece folded her arms across her chest and walked over to her nephew. "You know I work with Derric Augustine?" She asked, watching Porter nod. "Since we've been working together, we've become very close. Do you understand what I'm trying to tell you?"

If possible, Porter's expression grew even wearier. "Oh Lord." He groaned.

"Boy what is wrong with you?!" Cece snapped, tiring of his nervous behavior. "Dammit Porter, that girl's mother is about to lose her mind. Missy was her only child and all of a sudden she's dead! All she wants is to know her daughter's state of mind that last night. Was she happy, sad...Honey, you were the last one to see her."

"I know that!"

"Well talk to me, then!"

"You should leave Derric Augustine alone."

"Excuse me?" Cece queried, missing Porter's grumbled remark.

Porter shook his head and took a seat on the window sill. "If you're interested in Missy's uncle, then what I know could seriously affect your life and not for the better."

"Affect my life?" Cece blurted, her almond shaped stare narrowing sharply as she stepped closer to Porter. "Now, I know you better tell me what's going on."

Massaging the bridge of his nose, Porter tried to ignore the sudden pain pressuring his eyes. "Missy was working with me on our final degree projects. It was an involved assignment but in a nutshell, we each decided to trace our family trees."

"Mmm hmm," Cece said, with a nod as she took a seat on the short leather sofa which faced the window.

The reason we wound up working together was because during our research, we discovered our families were related."

"Excuse me?"

Porter bowed his head and sighed. "The Gwaltneys and the Augustines share the same blood." He clarified, then grew silent and waited for his aunt to absorb what he'd said.

Finally, Cece waved her hand urging Porter to continue. He relayed everything he and Missy had discovered and how it affected the feelings he was beginning to have for his friend. After the story was finished, Cece could not move. Porter called her name several times to regain her attention.

Slowly, Cece eased off the sofa and brushed her hands across the long, black wool skirt. "I think we need to take a trip to the Augustines."

TWENTY-THREE

Over the next several weeks, Princess Gwaltney found herself falling more in love with Adonis Mason. The relationship had not been consummated, but they felt just as close. Still, the sexual tension between them was strong, almost tangible. Neither knew how long they could resist the need-or why they should even try.

"I want you to meet my family."

Princess looked across her small round kitchen table. "So soon?" She blurted, her heart beating in her throat.

Adonis's smirk triggered a deep dimple. "We've been seeing each other a while, you know?"

"Doesn't seem that long," Princess sighed, reaching for another blueberry muffin.

Adonis leaned back in his chair. "That a good thing?" He asked.

Princess's smile was almost as sunny as the decorative blue and yellow terry robe she wore. "It's very good. It's only..."

"Only?..." Adonis encouraged, his attention focused on his breakfast.

Princess tried to choose her words carefully. "Adonis, it's um...obvious that you're not black and my um, concern is

AlTonya Washington

how your family will react when they meet your black girlfriend."

Long, deep male laughter filled the room. The sound was so infectious, Princess had to smile.

"I'm serious!" She cried, tossing a linen napkin at him.

"I'm sorry. Sorry." Adonis said, through softer chuckles. "Prin, you'd be treated like a queen. The queen that you are." He assured her.

"Thanks." Princess replied, though it was obvious she didn't believe him.

Adonis reached across the table and took her hand in his. "Hey," he whispered, waiting for her to meet his dark gaze, "most of the people in my family are men. Trust me, they'll love you. Besides, my mother is a black woman." He coolly added, as he picked up his fork.

The muffin slipped from Princess's hand. "Your mother is black?" She replied.

"Mmm hmm."

"Why didn't you ever tell me that?"

Adonis shrugged. "I thought it was obvious at least one of my parents was black."

"You still should have told me." Princess softly scolded. "Sometimes I feel this connection with you, like I've known you all my life."

Adonis's smile and his devastating onyx eyes crinkled just slightly. "I know what you mean." He said, reaching over to squeeze her hand. "I think I felt that way shortly after we met."

"Mmm..." Princess reminisced. "And then I find out something else about you."

"Well, speaking of mother's, I'd like for Ms. Davidson to be there."

"My mother?" Princess squeaked, her translucent champagne stare widening. "You want my mother to meet your family?"

Adonis shrugged. "I want them to meet the mother of the woman I'm in love with."

Taboo Tree

Princess blinked and her mouth fell open at the simple admission. Adonis had returned his attention to the hearty breakfast, while Princess watched him incessantly. When she reached across the table to trail her fingers through his silky black hair, he caught her hand and pressed a kiss into her palm.

***

After weeks of nagging, Cece finally convinced her nephew to talk with the Augustines. Porter would only speak with CJ, since he remembered Missy telling him her uncle had helped her mother with a similar project when they were in school.

"Mr. Gwaltney has to know what's up with this." Porter decided.

"Well, he didn't slam the phone down in my ear, when I called, so maybe that's a good sign." Cece mused, glancing over her shoulder as she took the off ramp.

"Good thing he's in Richmond, so we don't have to go all the way home." Porter mentioned, rubbing his palms against his jeans in an unconsciously nervous gesture.

Cece noticed, but knew this had been put off too long. "We're here." She announced, as she turned her pearl white Lexus into the complex of high rise condominiums.

"He'll probably kick us out, you know?" Porter forewarned as his dark eyes scanned the posh outlay of the complex.

Cece dropped her keys into her purse. "This has to be done, Baby."

"No matter how many lives it screws up?" Porter challenged, his expression darkened by thoughts of what lay ahead.

Cece could offer no response. She closed and locked her car, then headed towards the main building. In silence, she and Porter made their way to the 30th floor.

CJ Augustine answered the door about ten seconds after Porter rang the bell. When Cece looked up at the tall, undeniably gorgeous dark man, she couldn't help but think how much he

AlTonya Washington

favored her nephew. Deciding it was simply the circumstances of the moment she shook her head and smiled at their host.

"Mr. Augustine, I'm Cecelia Gwaltney. We spoke on the phone and, this is my nephew Porter."

"I remember speaking with you," CJ was saying as he stepped aside, "and please call me CJ. I was glad to get your call."

"You were?" Cece remarked, as they walked through the quiet, dimly lit living room to the spacious dark study.

"Mmm..." CJ replied, his attention focused on the young man next to Cece. "I'll um...I'll be able to tell Missy's parents something. They've been having a hard time-at least I can tell them I followed through talking with someone who knew Melissa." He said, his eyes fixed on the young stranger who was his son.

Cece tugged on the hem of her olive green top and cleared her throat. "I want to thank you for agreeing to see us. I was so vague on the phone."

"That's no problem." CJ assured the lovely young woman who was the image of her sister Demetria. "Please, speak as freely as you need to." He urged.

Cece looked over and nodded. Porter offered a quick smile, before he stepped forward and extended his hand.

"Porter Gwaltney, Sir."

"Good to meet you, Son." CJ replied, his deep voice shaking on the last word.

"Mr. Augustine, I know there have been a lot of questions about the night Missy...I wanted to try and explain-or talk about what happened. I'm not trying to excuse what I did, but I need you to understand. I loved Missy, she was my best friend."

Cece stepped closer and took Porter's hand in hers. He looked to her and what he saw in her eyes urged him to continue.

As Porter spoke on his relationship with Melissa, CJ studied his face. *Sweet Lord, he looks just like me!* he silently marveled. A sharp curse ripped through his head then and he clenched his fists. He hated himself for not knowing his own children and swore that was about to change.

"...that's when we decided on our family trees."

"What?" CJ blurted, his body temperature dropping at the sound of the two words.

Porter shook his head. "We thought it'd be fun to trace back the families. Since our properties have always joined, we figured tracing the trees could segue into an interesting history report based on how certain members of each family coexisted. We never expected to find what we did. We got pretty far in our research, but we knew there was a lot more to find."

"And this is what had the two of you in such a frenzy that night?" CJ asked, watching his son nod.

"I had planned to tell Missy...I planned to tell her how I felt, but then we found all this mess." Porter revealed, squeezing his eyes shut when tears formed there.

CJ clenched his fists again in order to restrain himself. He wanted to comfort the boy, but watched as Cece hugged him.

"...we were feeling so good that whole week," Porter continued, wiping away the tears with the back of his hand, "we were about to finish the project and then we find we're all somehow related...I was too shocked to say much. Missy was all talk, but I think that was just her way of dealing with it."

"Porter I appreciate you coming here and telling me this," CJ said, after silence had settled across the room for several minutes. "My sister will be interested in knowing what you had to say. She's been so on edge not knowing Missy's state of mind at the end."

"That's why I called." Cece said, while rubbing Porter's shoulder. "I knew how Stephanie was still hurting."

CJ pushed his hands into the deep pockets of his khaki trousers. "How do you know that?" He whispered, in a polite tone.

Cece's gaze faltered a moment. "I've been seeing Derric. He confided in me."

Smiling mischievously, CJ nodded. "So, you're the doctor?"

345

AlTonya Washington

"That's me." Cece confirmed, with a laugh as she slapped her hands to her black, fitted pants.

"My little brother is so in love with you." CJ remarked, with a teasing grin. The grin widened when he saw Cece's eyes lower. "How's all this going to affect your relationship?" He had to ask.

Cece became serious. "That would depend." She softly, yet firmly replied.

CJ understood. "Depending on whether we breathe a word of this, right?"

Suddenly, the study doors opened and everyone watched Deme rush into the room. She didn't notice that CJ had company.

"Baby, do you have any special place you'd like to eat tonight?"

"Ma?"

Deme almost stumbled over the claw foot of one of the arm chairs. Her brown eyes widened to the size of small moons and she clutched her hands to the center of her chest. "Cece?...Porter? What-"

"What's going on Deme?" Cece asked, stepping closer to her sister.

"Cece..." Deme sighed, slowly turning her eyes to her son.

Porter appeared just as puzzled. "What are you doing here, Ma?" He whispered, as though he already knew.

Nervous and unable to form an explanation, Deme looked across the room. "CJ?" She whispered, the urgency in her voice matching the look in her eyes.

CJ quickly closed the distance between himself and Deme. He kissed her temple and squeezed her shoulders. "I think it's time for some revelations. What do you think?"

Deme pressed her lips together and nodded. "I agree." She told him.

Porter and Cece shared the sentiment.

"So, how long have y'all been seeing each other?"

Deme looked at CJ and smiled. "We started back after the funeral." She told her son.

"Started back?" Porter queried, toying with his thick twists as he listened.

CJ scratched his eyebrow and patted Deme's knee. "Porter, your mother and I started seeing each other a long time ago. Before you or your sister were born. I was in high school, she was about to start."

Cece leaned forward then. "Y'all were high school sweethearts? Well, how did that work?"

"We kept it a secret, Cece." Deme told her sister. "No one knew."

"What happened?" Porter asked.

Deme and CJ exchanged worried glances.

"We decided to end it." CJ said. "With the way things were between our families...we knew it'd never work. Time never seemed to be right." He recalled. "Things always seemed to work against us." He added, his dark gaze becoming more solemn.

"Like the rape?"

"What?" Deme said, her eyes snapping to Porter's handsome face.

"Well it's obvious y'all still love each other." He noted. "Even after things were cut off, my mom's rape had to hit you hard Mr. Augustine."

Deme patted CJ's hand to keep him quiet. "Baby um, oh God..." She sighed, realizing the significance of her next words and the devastating effect they could have.

Porter was concerned. "Ma? What is it?"

"Baby...I wasn't raped."

Demetria spoke the phrase in a voice so low it seemed softer than a whisper. Still, no one misheard her.

"Deme what are you saying?" Cece questioned. "Daddy had everybody out searching for this man. You were...pregnant."

"I wasn't raped Cece." Deme firmly stated, watching her sister steadily.

Cecelia's luminous grown gaze shifted from Deme to CJ. Only a second passed before her lashes fluttered. "Oh my God,"

She breathed, bringing one hand to her mouth. "I should leave." She murmured, about to stand.

"Cece please!" Deme called, extending a hand towards her sister. "Please stay."

"What the hell is going on?!" Porter snapped, confused and angered by his aunt's behavior and his mother's sudden revelation.

"Baby-"

"You weren't raped?" Porter interjected. "Why didn't you tell us?"

Deme reached for CJ's hand. "Because telling that would have made things even more difficult."

"Mama what are you talkin' about?!"

"Dammit Deme, just tell the child!" Cece ordered.

"CJ's your father! He's...your father."

A long sigh from Cece pierced the otherwise silent room. Porter appeared to be frozen. His horrified expression was the only indication that he'd heard his mother's outburst.

Deme eased out of her seat and knelt before her son. "Baby?" She whispered.

"Don't." Porter said, flinching when Deme touched his cheek. "I said, 'don't'!" He snapped and jumped from his chair.

"Porter-"

"You stay the fuck away from me, man!" Porter exploded, when CJ moved towards him. Tears streamed down his handsome face and his head ached from all he'd been told. "You," He sneered, sending his mother a scathing look. "You let me and Porti think we came from something dirty and violent. All these years..."

"Baby I was so young!" Deme cried, the mascara she wore streaked her face with black marks. She was still on her knees before Porter's vacated chair. "I didn't know what else to do! Jason Gwaltney wanted blood when he found out I was pregnant. He would've killed your father if he knew!"

"Don't call him that!" Porter raged, through harsh tears. He had cried so hard, his voice was hoarse.

Taboo Tree

Cece was crying as well. She couldn't stand to see Porter so upset. Eventually, she had to leave the room.

"Porter, I know-"

"You don't know shit!" Porter spat, watching CJ through a murderous glare.

"I know this is hard to hear!" CJ countered, his bellow clearly outweighing his son's. Even Demetria looked up, when she heard his uncharacteristic outburst. "From the day I discovered your mother was pregnant, I've been living in hell. Letting her carry a shameful lie like that and knowing she'd only feel more shame if I stepped forward and told the truth! Hell boy, we're related. You and your sister would've surely been outcasts if it ever came out that I got my cousin pregnant!"

"Y'all coulda told us!" Porter argued, his slender frame shaking with anger.

CJ massaged his chin. "You're right." He conceded. "We should have. I suppose time and distance made it easier for us to put off telling you and Portia something so unbelievable."

"Hmph, Portia." Porter spoke his sister's name almost mournfully. "When we found out we were products of...rape, I think she took it the hardest. I guess that's why she turned out the way she did. She never stopped feeling dirty."

CJ thought about his daughter and the way she earned her living. The anger renewed itself and he buried his face in his hands. "God..." He groaned. "I still don't understand how this could have happened to her."

Deme pushed herself from the floor. "She ran away at eighteen. We did everything to find her, but when we did it was too late..."

"Aw Ma, cut it please." Porter drawled, his mouth turned into a distasteful curl. "Porti didn't just run away, she gave you plenty of clues 'bout what she was plannin' to do. You never gave a damn about us!"

"That's not true!"

"It is, dammit!"

"Porter!"

"Look, *Dad*, lemme tell you somethin' about the love of your life," Porter sneered, using anger to mask his hurt, "she never raised us. Cecelia and Sanford Gwaltney were more like parents than she ever was. You didn't want to know us, lady." He told Deme, pointing his index finger in direction. "You never came to our school plays, never met our teachers...Portia tried to act like she didn't care, but I tried to do everything to make you proud." He admitted, his voice breaking on the last word, as the tears returned. "I always figured you hated us because of the rape. But now...to know we were born out of love...why would you treat us that way, like we didn't exist, like you hated us?"

"I never hated you or Portia." Demetria swore. Her hands clutched her cream silk blouse so tightly it was a mass of wrinkles. "Porter, I love you and your sister so much...but when I had you I was young, very young, very...naive. By the time I was old enough to realize what a special gift my two babies were, y'all didn't know me." She shared, weeping softly as she remembered. "Credit my reaction to you both as a mixture of guilt, remorse and sadness, but not hate. Never hate."

CJ walked over to pull Deme close. Porter watched his parents embrace.

"You really love her, don't you?" He queried.

"I always have." CJ said his smile fading as he looked into his son's dark eyes. "Porter, I don't expect you to accept me now. I only hope you let me and your mother try to give you some of the love we've kept inside all these years. Please." CJ urged, his face wet with tears.

Porter let his own tears escape, then. Tentatively, his parents stepped forward and reached out to pull him close. The family cried heavily as they shared a tight, meaningful hug.

***

"I'll knock this thing down! I mean it, dammit!"

Huron had resorted to pounding on Portia's door when ringing the bell produced no results. He knew she was inside the hotel suite and he was determined to stay until she answered.

Just then, the jingle of the chain lock scratched against the door. Huron waited and stepped back when the door opened.

His dark eyes narrowed when he saw Portia. She looked weary and withdrawn. The dark bruise beneath her right eye, roused Huron's concern, but not his curiosity. He knew how she'd received it. Instinctively, he stepped forward to comfort her.

"Don't." She spoke in a voice that was surprisingly firm considering how weak she felt. "Go away, Huron."

"I can't." He told her, slamming the door and following her into the living room suite. "I let you avoid me long enough. I'm not going anywhere until we talk."

"Talk about what, Huron?" Portia snapped, her sobs rising when she began to speak. "Why'd you do this? Did you just set out on hurting me time you met me? I mean, was this your way of getting revenge for what happened with Porter and Missy?"

"Stop, stop Portia." Huron soothed, as he pulled her against his hard chest. "Baby, revenge never entered my mind."

Portia's eyes ached from all the tears she'd shed. "You ruin my life and then you expect me to believe this had nothing to do with what happened?"

Huron pushed Portia away, but kept his hands around her arms. "Baby, stop this." He ordered, massaging his fingers into the silky material of her black robe. "Now, when I say revenge is not what I had in mind, I mean it."

"Then why did you do it?" She whispered, wiping the back of her hand across her eyes. "Why would you do something so cruel? I told you I was going to explain everything to Lewis. I was gonna make him understand-"

"He didn't need to understand!" Huron snapped, his hands flexing around her arms. When she gasped at the pressure, he let her go. "You didn't need Lewis Hines."

Portia ran her fingers through her short, dark hair and massaged her neck. "What are you talking about? Of course, I needed him. He was my fiancé."

"He was your fiancé, but you were sleeping with me." Huron reminded her. He folded his arms over the hooded cream and black sweatshirt that he wore and coolly waited for her to respond.

"It was just sex. A very good fuck." Portia sneered, her scathing glare unwavering as she watched him steadily.

Huron chuckled. "I thought it was more than that. I think you did too."

Portia turned away. "I can't talk to you about this."

"I want you with me, Portia." Huron continued, speaking softly but with fierce conviction. "I want to see you everyday."

Portia wasn't touched by the soft confession. "Well, you have all my greatest hits, so why don't you go home and pretend!" She cried.

"Port-"

"This ain't about feelings, you jackass. It's about sex! That's all you ever wanted from me!"

Huron was fighting not to explode. "Portia," He called more firmly.

"Lewis was the first man who wanted more." She quietly added, then covered her face with both hands.

Huron stopped himself from going to comfort her. "You're right." He said, as he watched her from across the room. "Sex was all I wanted...at first."

Portia pulled her hands from her face as a knowing smirk lifted the corner of her mouth. "Please don't say you're in love with me." She tiredly pleaded.

Huron smiled in spite of himself. "I care about you...a lot." He said, beginning to walk towards her. "I want you with me. I don't want anyone else but you."

"Hmph," Portia gestured, gathering the hem of her robe as she sat on the sofa. "Guess you don't meet many porn queens, huh? You wanna hold onto this one."

A sharp curse slipped past Huron's lips, but he managed to maintain control of his temper. "Are you gonna give me a break, here?"

"Fuck you."

"Listen Portia, I can't blame you for hating me right now." He said, the sincerity on his face mirrored the honesty in his voice. "I had my own reasons for doing what I did and none of them had to do with revenge. But, you were still hurt and humiliated. I know everything you're going through is my fault."

Portia curled her fists beneath her chin and looked up at him. "Then maybe you can understand why I can't talk to you, why I just want you to go."

Huron couldn't ignore the feeling of helplessness washing over him. "Will I see you again?" He asked, clenching his fists as he awaited her reply.

"I'm going home for a while, then back to California." Portia finally shared, her voice monotone and soft.

"Back to California," Huron repeated, ignoring the subconscious warnings to keep his opinions to himself. "Back to your job," He guessed.

"That's right." Portia sang as she stood from the sofa.

The muscle twitching in Huron's jaw cast a more threatening element to his intimidating features.

"What?" Portia queried, noticing the murderous expression on his handsome face.

"You know you're too good for that shit?"

"You have a point." Portia admitted, folding her arms across her chest as she watched him. "I was beginning to think that very thing, but your little show made me think twice."

The simple admission robbed Huron of any further argument. He knew there was nothing more he could say or; for that matter, should say. He left quickly and quietly. The sound of Portia's soft weeping rang in his ear as he closed the front door.

***

"Thank you." Princess whispered, when Adonis told her he'd only invited his father to dinner.

Adonis's dark eyes followed the path of Princess's hands as she smoothed them across her arms left bare by the clinging black spaghetti strapped gown. "I knew you weren't ready to meet the entire clan."

A bright smile graced Princess's lovely cinnamon-toned face. "It's cozier this way." She said, looking around the candle lit dining room. "I hope our parents hit it off. Mommy's been so edgy lately. I think she and my dad had some kind of argument."

AlTonya Washington

"Well, Poppa has a weakness for beautiful women. It'd be nice for him to find one his own age for a change." Adonis was saying, his dimples flashing deep at the corners of his mouth when he laughed.

The couple was still chuckling, when Amina returned from the ladies room. "Has your family gotten here yet?" She asked, smoothing her hands across the elegant, ocean-blue pantsuit.

"Not yet, but I just told Prin I only invited my father tonight."

Amina frowned. "Nothing wrong, I hope?" She inquired, her hazel gaze marred by concern.

Adonis shook his head. "I thought it'd be better to make it a small gathering." He explained, winking at Princess. "That group can get pretty wild."

"So I take it you're the calm one?" Amina asked, realizing just how little she knew about her banker.

Adonis sent her a devilish look. "You don't know me." He said, reading her thoughts.

The threesome was still laughing when the waiter walked over to ask about refreshing their drinks. The lively conversation continued and was only interrupted when Adonis was paged.

"There he is." Adonis whispered.

Amina and Princess turned to look, but couldn't see the man across the crowded dining room.

"Be right back." He said, smoothing one hand across the front of the casual white crewneck he wore with a stylish charcoal gray jacket and matching trousers.

Princess reached for her mother's hand and squeezed it tightly. Adonis went to greet his father and soon the two men were walking towards the table.

"Princess Gwaltney, Amina Davidson this is my father Nikos Cantone."

Amina's expressive dark gaze seemed to widen and her hand connected with the water glass to her left. Princess caught the stem before the clear liquid soaked the embroidered white tablecloth. She saw the stunned look on her mother's face. "Mommy?" She called.

Nikos appeared just as stunned. His dark, deep-set gaze was narrowed in wonder. He looked like a man viewing ghost. He left his son's side and walked around the small table as though he were in a daze.

"Amina," He breathed, going to his knees before the chair she occupied. When her hand touched his cheek, he closed his eyes and smiled.

"Where did you go?" Amina whispered, her eyes wandering his face.

Nikos knew what she meant. "After you married Tav, I couldn't handle it. I packed my truck and took my uncle's offer to come up here."

"You've been living in New York all this time?" She asked, amazed by the change of his features. He was even more handsome than she remembered.

"I try to keep a low profile." He said, sending her a mischievous wink. "God Amina, you haven't changed." He marveled, his smoldering dark eyes immensely flattering in its intensity.

Princess and Adonis exchanged inquisitive looks as they listened to the content of their parent's conversation. When Amina and Nikos stopped talking and just stared at one another, Princess frowned.

"Mommy?" She called.

To Amina, her daughter's soft voice was like a cymbal crashing during the midst of a quiet lullaby. The soft look in her eyes turned horrific. She turned back to Nikos.

"He's my son." He replied, answering the unspoken question. He stood then and extended his hand toward Princess. "Young lady, I'm Nikos Cantone. I've known your mother since before you were born. I don't know you, Bella, but I can't think of a better woman for my son to have in his life. If you're anything like your mother," He added, casting another soft look in Amina's direction.

"Thank you." Princess beamed, in awe of the tall, handsome, powerfully built man. Her smile faded when she noticed her mother's strange expression. "Mommy, what is it?"

"You can't." Amina blurted and began to tremble noticeably. "You can't do this."

Princess sat down and rubbed her mother's arm. "What are you talking about? Can't do what?"

Amina shook her head. Her eyes had begun to tear and she was fidgeting with the buttons on her pantsuit.

"Mommy you're scaring me." Princess whispered, glancing toward her boyfriend who appeared just as concerned.

"You have to stop seeing him. You and Adonis have to end this. You have to."

"Mommy-"

"Princess, just do it!"

Princess stood. She was completely confused and felt tears pressuring her eyes as well. Her shoulders rose slightly as she turned to Adonis. "I don't know..." She whispered, laying her head on his chest.

Adonis held Princess tightly as he frowned at her mother. "Amina what are you saying? Until now, you've been all for us."

Amina remained steadfast. "The two of you must stop seeing each other. You must."

Princess whirled around. "Why?!" She cried.

"He's your brother!"

Amina's whispered words were fierce. Nikos felt the strength leave his legs and reached for the nearest chair.

"Amina," he whispered, "Amina." He called more firmly, taking her by the arms and forcing her to face him. "What the hell are you talking about?"

Amina's long lashes fluttered as she inhaled deeply. "That night-the night we...were together. I got pregnant. That's why I married Tav."

"Dammit, why didn't you tell me?"

"I couldn't! I couldn't tell you and have everyone how I'd done something so...careless."

"But, why Tav, Amina? How could you marry that monster and let him raise our child?"

"It was the only choice I thought I had at the time aside from...I wanted to have your baby, Nikos."

Princess stood, watching the scene unfold. After a while, she realized she'd been holding her breath. Her breath was expelled in a long shudder and; a moment later, she ran from the dining room.

"Prin!" Adonis called, but was unable to stop her. He left after Princess and caught her out in the lobby. She was pushing the dark mahogany door open, when his hand closed around her arm.

"Let go." She demanded, straining against his grasp. "Let go." She insisted.

"No."

"I can't." Princess whispered, tugging and twisting against his hold. "I can't breathe. I have to get out of here."

Adonis ignored the pain in his chest. His expression was a picture of apprehension. He could feel her slipping away. "Look at me." He softly persisted. When her eyes met his, he cupped her face in his hands. "Let's go back in there and get the rest of the story. Maybe your mom is mistaken-"

"No, no, no..." Princess repeated as she shook her head. "I heard enough. This is true. I always knew there was something..."

"Baby, come on." Adonis tried to convince Princess, using his softest tone of voice. He tugged gently on her arm and attempted to pull her close.

"No, Adonis." Princess resisted, straining against his hold. When he kissed her temple, her lashes closed over her eyes and she leaned into the pressure of his mouth next to her skin.

"Come back inside." He tried to urge her.

Princess wrenched herself out of his grasp. "I said no!" She cried, then turned and ran out the door.

Adonis hesitated a moment before leaving after her. Princess had already hailed a cab and rode away.

"Adonis seemed to handle it well."

Amina sent Nikos a skeptical look. "How could you tell? He barely said a word." She recalled.

Nikos tossed his keys to the message desk in Amina's foyer. "Could you blame him?"

"His whole world has gone crazy." Amina groaned, burying her face in her hands. "No. I certainly can't blame him."

"Jesus." Nikos whispered, massaging his jaw absently as he walked over to the French doors leading to the balcony.

Amina watched him warily. She took in his appearance. Of course, he was older now, but his attractiveness was not diminished. "How are you handling this?" She asked when he turned and found her staring.

"Hmph. That's the question of the year." He remarked, and then stepped onto the balcony.

Amina followed. For a while, she enjoyed the view of the New York City skyline and pretended everything was completely different. "You have every right to hate me."

Nikos smiled, causing a dimple to flash. "I could never hate you, but I am angry." He admitted, looking at her. "How could you keep this from me? Marrying Tav, when you knew how I felt about you? That night wasn't about just sex for me."

"I know." Amina assured him, her hazel eyes wide with sincerity. "But you know how it was, how it still is."

"What?" Nikos retorted, his black stare questioning.

"Nikos, please. You know what I mean. I'm a black woman, you're a white man."

"Italian," Nikos corrected.

Amina raised her hand. "I'm sorry. But, regardless...a relationship like ours would've been so tough. Impossible."

"Never. I would've never treated you that way."

"Baby are you forgetting your family?" Amina was saying, her hands spread as she tried to reason with him. "Just because your father lived, worked and was friendly with black folks didn't mean the rest of your family would've been so open-minded. I know my family wouldn't have been, no matter how close you were to CJ and Steph."

"But why'd you have to marry Tav? Of all the men who would've cut off an arm to get you, why Tavares Gwaltney?"

Amina's smile was a mixture of regret and amusement. "Chalk it up to fear and the dumbness of youth." She said, slapping her hands to her thighs she turned to lean against the iron railing. "I knew that my mother would've been so disappointed in me if she found out. So...I accepted Tav's proposal. I was stupid enough to think this was such an ideal plan. I'd marry Tav, everyone would think Princess was his, Mommy would be so happy because I'd married into this socially elite family and...Nikos I paid dearly, so dearly for ever agreeing to become his wife."

Nikos grimaced and silently prayed he wouldn't lose his temper when he heard the answer to his next question. "I take it fatherhood didn't soften him any?"

Amina shook her head. "Oh no. He was-is a fantastic father. Princess was lucky to have him. Tav chose that name for her and he's always treated her that way. Like a little Princess."

"And you? Did he treat you like a queen?"

Amina's bright gaze seemed to cloud as unwanted memories of her marriage moved to the forefront of her mind. "You remember how he was," Amina was saying to Nikos as he nodded, "he didn't change." She said her voice dropping to a whisper.

"Son of a bitch," Nikos breathed, his handsome bronzed features drawing into a tight mask. "Why didn't you leave him?"

"I did." Amina promptly told him. "I bided my time, until I graduated college. It was easier after Princess-he never...hit me *much* when she came. When I graduated, I went straight to New York."

"New York?" Nikos parroted, his expression brightening.

Amina strolled over to take a seat on one of the wrought iron arm chairs. "Mmm hmm. I told you I wouldn't mind living here one day."

Nikos chuckled. "I didn't think you were serious."

AlTonya Washington

"Well, I was." Amina sang, her lovely oval face glowing as she remembered. "I left that negro right in Virginia and didn't look back. I'm my own boss and I don't answer to anyone but myself."

Nikos whistled. His long brows rose and he was obviously impressed. "Don, really didn't tell me a lot about either of you-obviously. So, you own your own business?"

"Mmm hmm. Queen Cosmetics. We're going into our twentieth year." Amina announced. Her voice was filled with pride.

"Well, you said you'd do it and you did." Nikos was saying, as he took a seat on the chair opposite the long iron bench.

Amina turned to face him more fully. "I assume you did what you set out to do as well?"

"It's not necessarily what I set out to do. I would've preferred a different path. I guess now I know why my father was so hell bent on keepin' me away from my mother's family."

"So, um are you one of those 'high powered' figures I hear talk of? One of the untouchables?" Amina pried in a teasing tone.

Nikos smiled. "You could say that. I tried to stay out of it. Even thought I could go to college, get a degree and live the American dream, but...that's where I met Don's mother. She was a journalism student."

"Really? Is that what she does now?" Amina asked, fascinated by all that happened since they'd last seen each other.

"When Don began to make money in his field, he demanded she stop working. Now she's a professional traveler." Nikos said, with a laugh.

"Mmm that sounds like a life." Amina sighed, resting her elbow along the back of her chair. "Adonis is a wonderful man. You should be proud."

"I am." Nikos replied, his expression turning serious. "When he was born I swore I would not let him know a life like mine. That's one reason why his name is Mason. It's his mother's name. I didn't want him to have that stigma."

"That must've been a tough decision. He is your child."

"It wasn't tough at all. I've done some things...I'd never want him to be touched by."

Amina nodded, her hazel stare taking on a faraway look. "That's why I left Tav right away. I couldn't let my baby, my baby girl see her mother living that kind of life. I wanted to be someone she could look up to."

Nikos' penetrating dark gaze softened as it wondered over Amina's wavy tresses wound into the classy French roll, her flawless, still smooth skin and her glowing eyes. "I'd say you did an incredible job."

"Hmph. Now I wonder...she might hate me now."

"No..." Nikos soothed, moving closer when he saw tears sparkling in her eyes. "Amina," he called, pulling her head to his shoulder.

"She was so in love with him." Amina whispered, through soft sobs. Her tears disappeared into the fine, dark material of Nikos dinner jacket.

"Honey, even if you had told her about me, do you know how slim the chances are that all this would've come out any sooner than it did?"

"Still..."

"Hey," Nikos called, cupping Amina's face in his big hands, "don't do this to yourself. It won't solve a thing."

"But what will happen?"

"Amina listen to me. Nobody knows about this, but the four of us. I say we do whatever the kids ask."

"But how could they stay together knowing they're blood?"

Nikos could only shake his head. Amina's tears flowed more freely as the weight of the situation burdened her. They held each other for a long time that night.

Princess whipped open the front door expecting to find the airline messenger outside. Instead, she found Adonis standing in the hall.

AlTonya Washington

"I don't want to talk." She said. She could barely look at him.

Adonis leaned one shoulder against the doorjamb. "May I come in?" He asked.

Princess pulled one hand through her tangled hair. "I can't see you." She muttered.

"Over this?" Adonis questioned, a glare clouded his face over the exasperated look she sent him.

"Yes over this." Princess hissed. She couldn't believe he was as unfazed as he appeared.

"Are you going to let me in?"

Princess raised her hand. Before she could say a thing, the messenger arrived.

Adonis frowned when as he watched the stout, young man hand Princess the envelope embossed with an airline logo.

"Princess Gwaltney?" The man queried, his small brown gaze shifting nervously toward the tall, stern-faced man who stood just inside the door. "Your tickets, ma'am," He said, when Princess nodded.

Before she could accept the envelope, Adonis intercepted. The messenger tipped his hat and hurried off. Adonis brushed past Princess and stormed into the condo.

"Don't." She said when he held the tickets out of her reach. "Adonis, don't do this."

"Let me get this straight," he whispered, as he pulled one hand through his thick hair, "you were going to just leave?" He asked, in a tone laced with steel. His onyx gaze glinted with anger.

Princess threw her hands up and walked away. "I have to get out of here." She groaned.

"I can't believe you." Adonis whispered, tension clouding his bronze face. "No one knows about this, but the four of us. No one would ever suspect that-"

"What are you saying?" Princess interjected, her hazel eyes narrowing sharply. "You're not suggesting we forget about this, are you?"

"I love you and this shit..." Adonis was so angry, he could not speak. "I won't lose you over this." He finally said.

Princess was shaking her head. "I understand you being upset, but this is pain and shock that's making you say this."

"Prin-"

"You have to know it's wrong. It would be wrong for us to do this."

Adonis leaned against the wall and bowed his head. "I love you. That's not wrong."

"You're my brother."

"Half brother."

"Adonis..."

"Damn!" He raged, suddenly overwhelmed by the reality of the situation.

Princess wrung her hands when Adonis threw the tickets to the floor. She watched him pace the living room-his expression growing darker every second. Her eyes widened when he picked up a heavy beaded glass vase and hefted it in one hand. A quick scream flew past her lips and she jumped when he smashed it against the wall.

Adonis took several deep breaths, struggling to control his raging temper. He could hear Princess crying softly. After a while, he turned to face her. She appeared blurred to him and it was then that he realized his own eyes were filled with tears.

"Prin..." He whispered, his long strides bringing his right in front of her.

Princess ached to reach out and touch him, but she restrained herself.

Adonis turned the tables and pulled her hands into one of his. "Do you know this is killing me?" He asked, his voice a raspy whisper.

Princess offered a sob in response.

"I just found you and now I'm supposed to give you up, just like that?"

"You know we can't keep seeing each other." Princess told him, her voice thick as she watched him through red eyes.

AlTonya Washington

Adonis's long brows drew close as he pressed his face against her temple. "I'm not ready to let you go." He whispered, his words sounding closer to a growl.

Princess turned her face into Adonis's neck and inhaled the sharp, sexy aroma of the cologne he always wore. Realizing that she would have to be the one to remain steadfast, she pushed against his chest. "You have to." She said when his hands tightened on her arms. "We can't do this. You know that. The sooner we accept it, the better."

"You don't mean that." He decided.

Princess could feel Adonis's fingers massaging her upper arm and she shivered from the intense sensation the touch ignited. Another sob filled her throat and she turned away before he could see the tears spill from her eyes. "Go home." She asked her voice surprisingly firm. "Go home." She insisted, when he held her tightly against his chest.

Adonis buried his handsome face in Princess's thick hair and inhaled its honey fragrance. He let her go suddenly and left the room without a backwards glance.

The front door closed with a resounding slam. Princess fell to the floor and laid there crying. The harsh sobs caused her small frame to convulse.

***

Cece closed her eyes and pressed her fingers to her temples. She had begged Derric to let her meet him at the restaurant. He agreed, reluctantly, but she was glad. In light of all the 'revelations' she was in a state of upheaval. Her life, once so stable, was now in a state of chaos.

"Oh, get me through this dinner, please." She prayed. Taking a deep breath, she left her Lexus and headed towards the tiny, brick steakhouse.

The hostess offered to escort Cece to her table located in a cozy corner of the quiet dining room. Derric stood when he saw them approaching and Cece could feel the electricity sizzle up her spine. Derric Augustine was too incredible, too gorgeous a man to let slip away. The last weeks had brought them closer than she ever thought possible. Now, she was facing the possibility of losing something that had the potential to be so very special.

Cece tossed her head, sending a slew of heavy curls bouncing. She managed to brighten her smile by the time she was taking Derric's hand.

"What's going on?" He softly greeted, his dark eyes sweeping the long-sleeved black off-shoulder dress in one heated look.

"Hi." Cece whispered, giving his hand a tight squeeze as she kissed his cheek. She managed to sit on the opposite end of the suede booth, but Derric would not release her hand. "What?" She asked.

"Stay next to me." He requested.

Cece cleared her throat and abided his request. She pressed the flaring hemline of the dress beneath her knees and settled in next to him.

The hostess nodded and left them with a menu.

Cece re-crossed her long legs as unwanted sensations began to tease her senses. The pleasure began at the center of her palm where Derric caressed the sensitive flesh with his fingertips.

"So what's good here?" Cece asked, hoping to move Derric's interest away from her body.

He shrugged. "I have no idea. This is my first time coming here."

"Oh." She replied, in a hushed tone that held a twinge of disappointment. "Well, shouldn't we go on and order?" She suggested, already reaching for one of the menus.

Derric placed his hand across hers. "We have time." He assured her.

The seductive, dark atmosphere of the restaurant; combined with Derric's overwhelming sex appeal were murder on Cece's resistance. When he cupped her chin and pulled her into a deep kiss, she eagerly responded.

The kiss was heat and desire in action. A low savage growl rumbled within Derric's chest. His large hand almost completely encircled Cece's neck as he held her still.

AlTonya Washington

"Derric..." Cece whispered, whenever he released her lips. It was no use. Each time his mouth returned to hers, his tongue thrust deeper and longer.

"Mmm..." Cece moaned, and began to press against the worsted material of Derric's Herringbone jacket. "Wait!" She gasped, jerking away suddenly.

"What?" Derric queried, a frown coming to his face. "What's wrong?" He asked again, when she moved to the other end of the booth.

Cece pressed one hand against her hot cheek and grimaced. "It's nothing. I'm just ready to eat."

"Long day?" Derric asked. His onyx stare was as probing as the tone of his voice.

Cece didn't look up from the menu. "Hectic." She replied.

"Anything I should know about?" He asked, resting his chin against his fist.

"No." Cece sighed, still focused on the menu.

Derric stamped down the frustration welling inside him. He decided to overlook his suspicions and turned his attention to his own menu. The waiter arrived shortly to take their orders for New York Strips, sour cream and onion baked potatoes, steamed broccoli, rolls and red wine.

"Let's dance." Derric decided. He didn't wait for Cece to accept his request.

Cece kept a serene expression plastered to her face as they walked out to the dance floor. Inside, she was a mass of nerves.

"...we could make a long weekend out of it."

"What?" Cece muttered, catching the end of Derric's sentence.

"This weekend? I said I want to take you somewhere."

"Take me away?" Cece repeated, her warm brown eyes clouded by confusion.

Derric laughed shortly as he tapped Cece's waist. "I want you to go away with me this weekend." He rephrased, purposefully speaking in a slow teasing manner. "Maybe we could go to the mountains or something."

"I can't."

"'Scuse me?"

"Derric I can't go with you."

"Why not?"

Cece watched Derric in disbelief. Then, she began shaking her head. "I can't just pick up and leave town on a long weekend. Not when I just started. I have so much on my plate already."

Derric smiled, delighted by the way her nose crinkled when she was frustrated. "Cece, I am your boss. I know how much you have on your plate."

Cece decided to keep her comments silent on that subject. Instead, she lost herself in the soft jazz and enjoyed Derric's hands caressing her back.

The waiter was setting out the salads when Derric and Cece returned to their table. The meal began in silence. There was the occasional request to pass the salt or butter. Beyond that, however, almost forty-five minutes passed with no conversation.

Derric's mood had grown more sour with the passing of each minute. He was only halfway through the thick, tender steak when he slammed his fork to the table.

Cece held her sterling silver fork poised over a stuffed potato. She met Derric's dark glaring eyes with an innocent look.

"What the hell is wrong with you?" He asked his voice raspy with aggravation. "Most of the time, I can hardly get a word in, you're such a chatterbox."

"I told you my day was hectic."

The excuse did not soothe Derric's mood. "So this has nothing to do with me wanting to take you out of town this weekend?"

"No, no Derric I swear."

"So you'll go?"

"I can't. Please understand."

Derric leaned back in his chair. "How can I do that when you won't tell me anything?"

"Derric..."

"I'm listening."

"Damn, I don't want to talk about this." Cece snapped. The fact that she whispered did nothing to diminish the fierce tone of her words.

Derric refused to beg, but he couldn't sit there and continue to eat in silence. He could feel Cece's wide eyes follow him as he stood and pulled a few bills from his wallet.

"Dinner's on me," He said, tossing the money to the table. "Enjoy it." He added and left her alone at the table.

***

"And there's no way this could be a mistake?" Princess asked. The weak feeling in her hands and arms returned when Amina shook her head. For the hundredth time in the last two days, she felt the urge to cry.

Amina wanted to kill herself for bringing her only child such grief. "Baby, I-"

"Stop." Princess ordered, when she saw her mother coming to comfort her.

"Baby, I've talked to Nikos and we agree not to say a thing about this. If you and Adonis want to..."

"Mommy..." Princess sighed, briefly burying her face in her palms. "You know that wouldn't solve it. We can't pretend this isn't happening. I can't forget he's...my brother."

Amina knew that. She didn't know what to say to ease Princess's mind. Sadly, she realized there was nothing to say that would ease the hurt. "How long will you be away?" She asked.

Princess shrugged and pulled her car keys from her purse. "I'm not sure. Right now, I just want to get out of here."

"I understand how you feel Baby, but it won't do any good to run away from the problem."

"Why not? It worked for you, didn't it?" Princess challenged. She saw the glimmer of hurt flash in her mother's light eyes and smothered a curse. "Mommy..." She groaned, rushing forward to pull Amina into a tight hug. "I'm sorry and I do understand. But right now I have to face the fact that I can't have Adonis and that's killing me."

"Baby..." Amina whispered, toying with a thick wavy lock of hair that had fallen from her daughter's high ponytail.

Princess managed a tiny smile, then kissed Amina's cheek and left the condo. She went out the way she'd come; using all rear exits and back elevators. Her car was parked in the private executive lot and she entered the well-lit area directly from the elevator. Her fingers had just brushed the handle to the polished, burgundy Infinity, when someone grabbed her from behind. The man's arms slipped around her waist and she was enveloped in an iron embrace. Princess struggled earnestly and was opening her mouth to scream, when her attacker whirled her around to face him.

"Adonis?" She cried, her eyes practically bulging from her face. She felt faint even as a flood of relief washed over her. "What are you doing here?" She asked, while massaging her aching chest.

Adonis offered no reply. It was then that Princess took note of his appearance. He wore a wrinkled denim shirt over an equally wrinkled white T-shirt. Dark blue jeans hung low on his hips and his black Gortex boots were unlaced. The uncharacteristically unshaven, disheveled appearance only enhanced his bronzed gorgeous looks.

Despite Adonis's handsome face, Princess could tell his mood was sour.

"I have a plane to catch." She softly reminded him as she continued to strain against his hold.

Still, there was no response. Adonis held Princess by the elbow and pulled her behind him.

Princess ceased her struggles when she saw his silver SUV parked in the distance. Adonis opened the door and waited for her to precede him.

Princess was past uneasy, but remained silent. She was grateful for the oversized magenta cashmere sweater and jeans she wore. She had been freezing since she turned and looked into Adonis's eyes. The pitch black stare seemed blank-as though he were void of any emotion. It unnerved her more than she cared to admit.

Adonis drove only a couple of blocks before he turned into a hotel parking lot.

"What are you doing?" Princess whispered, as she looked out at the high rise.

Of course, there was no reply and Adonis left the truck. He pulled Princess from the SUV and accepted a parking stub from the attendant.

"Adonis what is going on?" Princess demanded to know. She managed to keep her voice firm, in spite of her unease.

The hotel staff didn't seem to think there was anything out of the ordinary. They greeted Adonis as though he were royalty. He signed in, and then carried his softly protesting guest to the elevators.

"Adonis, whatever you're thinking of doing...don't."

Adonis leaned against the maple siding of the elevator. He kept his dark gaze trained on the panel of lighted numbers which charted their ascension to the top floor.

Princess kicked her booted foot back against the wall. "What is wrong with you? Why are you doing this?" She cried, tears spurting from her eyes as her frustration mounted.

The elevator car finally reached the 39th floor. Again, Adonis took Princess by the arm and led her out to the hallway. She watched him unlock the room door and push it open. When she refused to step inside, he simply carried her across the threshold. He kicked the heavy door shut with the heel of his boot.

The sound filled Princess with a sense of dread and she pounded Adonis's chest with renewed enthusiasm. They were heading towards the back of the plush, dark suite-headed towards the bedroom.

"Don't do this." She whispered, clutching the lapel of his shirt as though it were a life line.

Adonis covered the distance from the doorway to the bed in only a few strides. He tossed Princes to the middle like a bundle of clothes. He removed his denim shirt and was about to pull the T-shirt over his head, when Princess scrambled to get off the bed. He foiled the attempt, by catching her wrist and pulling her back. Then, he straddled her wriggling body.

"Stop." She ordered, though her voice shook terribly.

Adonis grabbed the neckline of her sweater and eased it over her head. Despite her struggles, he undressed her easily and was undoing the front hooks of her bra. Princess slapped his hands, her heart racing as she grew more unnerved by the set look on his face.

The bra opened and her breasts were bared to his gaze. Adonis's smoldering midnight eyes narrowed as he leaned close to her chest. Princess clutched fistfuls of his thick hair to keep his mouth off her body. It was no use. His lips closed over the peak of one breast and a helpless moan escaped him when he felt the hard bud next to his tongue. Princess shivered as the forbidden caress sent delicious sensations to the core of her femininity.

"Wait." She whispered, even as her body arched into his touch.

"No." He growled and tugged the nipple between his strong teeth, then soothed it with his tongue. He teased the curve of her hips with his fingertips and switched his attention from one breast to the other.

Princess pressed her head deeper into the pillow and allowed herself to indulge in the forbidden treat. Her fingers played in his luxurious dark hair and she moaned softly. Her lashes fluttered open when she felt him tugging at the fastening of her jeans. His mouth left her breast to rain kisses over and beneath the soft, caramel-colored mound. His insistent, wet kisses traveled the flat plane of her stomach. His mouth skirted the lace edge of her white panties...

"Stop Adonis...I said stop!" Princess snapped, finally wrenching herself from his loose hold. She snatched her sweater from the bed and fixed her bra as she ran out of the bedroom.

Adonis caught her in the hall and they tripped over one another. Princess began to cry as they lay on the floor sprawled in the tangle of arms and legs.

"I can't take this, Adonis."

"You love me."

"Yes, but you know this is impossible."

Adonis pressed his nose to her temple and shook his head. "I can't accept that."

Princess gathered all her strength and pushed Adonis away. "Don't do this again." She told him and stood. "I don't want you calling me. I don't want you trying to see me. I mean that. Don't press me about this. I'd hate for things to turn ugly between us." With those words, she left him there in the hallway and walked out of the suite without looking back.

TWENTY-FOUR

"**D**o you know anything about this, Cece?"

"Just that we need to be there."

Portia sighed and switched the red cordless phone from one ear to the other. For the fifth time, she scanned the card. "Why are we being invited to our own home?"

"I don't know Honey. I'm as much in the dark as you are." Cece replied, silently commending her ability to keep the secret.

"Hmph. It is intriguing, mysterious." Portia admitted, her dark eyes twinkling mischievously. "I guess I'll be there. I certainly have nothing else to do."

"Honey, I am so sorry about the wedding." Cece consoled.

Portia managed a quick, humorless smile. "I'm not so sorry about the wedding being called off. I don't think I was ready for that, you know?"

Cece chuckled. "I suspected as much." She said.

"The way things happened with Lewis, though...I never wanted to hurt him."

"Well, he had to be told."

"But the way he found out, Auntie." Portia clarified. She ran one hand through her short hair as her frustration mounted. "Damn, that jackass!" She snapped.

Cece frowned. "Lewis?"

"No, that damned black bastard Huron Augustine."

"Ah."

"I mean, of all the low, dirty, backstabbing things to do..."

"Well...he did do you a favor, right? I mean, you weren't making much headway explaining things to Lewis."

Portia curled her legs beneath her when she sat on the sofa. "Are you defending that fool?"

"I'm not defending him." Cece assured her niece hesitating a bit as she chose her words. "I don't approve of the way he handled things, but I can see what motivated him to do what he did."

"What motivated him?"

"I think his feelings for you may be more than sexual, Honey."

"You'll forgive me if I don't share that sentiment?"

"Have you even asked him how he feels about you? How he really feels?"

"I already know how he feels."

"I think you're selling yourself short."

"And I think you feel this way because you're in love with Huron's brother." Portia guessed.

Cece hesitated a moment. She felt her cheeks burn at her niece's keen assessment. "That's not true."

"It is true. You're in love with Derric Augustine." Portia insisted.

"We're talking about you."

Portia waved her hand. "I'm too depressing. So how is it? I haven't seen much of you, so he must be keeping you pretty busy?"

"Portia..." Cece groaned. Her romantic involvement with Derric was the last thing she wanted to discuss.

"Fine, fine." Portia finally took the hint. "I guess I'll have to grill you in person when I see you tomorrow night."

"Make sure you're there." Cece warned.

"I promise. See you then."

When the connection broke, Cece let out a long sigh.

***

"Do I really need to be there? I mean, I don't really have anything to do with those people anymore."

"Amina, baby it's important." Ophelia told her cousin. "At least that's what CJ says." She added.

CJ could hear the doubt and concern in his mother's voice. He tightened his grip around the receiver. "It is important and that's all I can say."

"Or all you will say." Amina retorted. "CJ what's this really about?"

"It's best if we get into this when we all meet tomorrow night." He decided.

"But why are we meeting at the Gwaltneys?" Dyna Davidson asked from her phone line. "What does this have to do with them?"

"Ladies please, just say you'll be there."

"I'll be there, Baby." Ophelia promised her son.

"So will I." Dyna added, after a few seconds of silence.

CJ sighed and leaned back in his suede desk chair. "Thank you both...Amina?"

"I don't feel good about this." She admitted, her lovely cinnamon-toned face darkened by a worried frown. "I'm curious, though...I guess I'll be there to find out what the devil this is about."

"I appreciate that." CJ whispered, realizing how difficult this would be for his cousin.

"Baby?"

"Yeah, Ma?"

"Will I need to bring protection to this lil' shindig?"

CJ burst into laughter. "No Ma. I promise you won't need protection. Just don't go up in there with an attitude." He cautioned, shaking his head at the muttered remarks that met his request.

"So what do you think?" Princess asked, once the conference call had ended.

Amina was already focused on work. "You know Honey I really don't care as long as it takes your mind off Adonis Mason for a few hours."

A quiet minute passed, before she realized what she'd said. Princess had just returned home after being away for a week. She seemed rested, but Amina could tell her daughter was not in the best frame of mind.

"I'm sorry, Sweetie." She whispered.

Princess shrugged and moved from her perch on the corner of her mother's desk. "Don't apologize. I'm fine." She lied, pushing her hands into the side pockets of her black, cotton Capri pants. "I'm gonna have to deal with this and move on." She decided.

Amina propped her hand against the side of her face. Her eyes sparkled with wonder as she watched her daughter. "My hat's off to you Babe. Not many women could put on such a brave front when they're losing the man they love."

Princess allowed her uneasiness to show. "It's an act." She confided, with a smile.

Amina returned the smile. "No one could ever tell."

"Well, speaking of brave," Princess began, rubbing her hands together as she stood facing her mother. "I think Daddy's been noticing how brave and confident a woman you've become. He's impressed. Very impressed. Is there anything going on that I might need to know about?"

"Hmph." Amina returned. "Baby, I know you've wanted us back together since we split up. But, the truth is that will never happen again."

"Even if he's trying to change?"

Amina was touched by the childlike manner clinging to Princess's words. "He told me about the therapy, Baby. Said that you were the reason he started going."

"No Mommy. He wanted to get help." Princess insisted, moving folders aside on the desk so she could sit crossed-legged on the corner. "I only...suggested."

"Mmm. Well...that's wonderful. For your father. For me, it makes no difference. If that hurts you, I'm sorry."

Princess lowered her light gaze. "I understand."

Amina leaned back in her chair and fingered a strand of her wavy hair. "There are things that have happened between your father and I...I could never forget them. I don't like the way I see myself when I remember how it was between us. I could never give him a fair chance. I would always be expecting him to relapse, I guess."

"I know what you mean." Princess said, and reached across the desk to clutch her mother's hand. "I haven't even seen Daddy since I found out..."

"He loves you. In spite of anything regarding-"

"Oh Mommy I know that. He raised me and treated me more wonderful than any other man could have. He'll always be my father. I've never questioned that. Even when you two broke up I just wish my parents could've made it, you know?"

Amina stood and walked around her desk. "Me too, Baby. Me too," She sighed and pulled Princess into a tight hug.

***

Warm, golden light beamed from each window of the Gwaltney mansion. The dark, brick structure exuded an inviting appeal that seemed to say all were welcome.

Unfortunately, that fact offered little solace to the approaching guests. The guarded looks and suspicion added to the thick silence hovering around the estate. The invitation called for formal attire and everyone obliged. Stylish tuxedoed gentlemen and devastating evening gown clad ladies filed into the house.

The evening began with a round of cocktails provided by the house staff. Everyone requested the stiffest drinks in hopes of dispelling the overabundance of nervous tension.

"Baby!" Tav called, when he saw his daughter arriving with her mother.

"Daddy," Princess whispered, enjoying her father's warm embrace.

Tav pressed a kiss to the side of Princess's glossy French roll that complimented the peach silk off-shoulder gown with its empire waist. Then, he looked over the top of her head. "Could I talk to you a minute?" He asked Amina, watching her nod.

Princess clutched the lapels of Tav's tux. "I need to talk to you too, but later, okay?" She said, then kissed his cheek and walked off.

Amina's expression revealed nothing. She folded her arms over the black silk spaghetti strapped evening dress and waited.

"I wanted to apologize for what happened the last time we talked."

"Apologize?"

Tav chuckled at Amina's surprise. "I guess I'm not as in control as I thought. I want you to know I'm not the beast you think I man, but I know I have problems. Some day, I'll try to make everything up to you, but for now just know that I am sorry and I regret every time I've ever touched you in anger."

Amina clutched her hands and watched Tav walk away. For the first time, she truly believed he was finally on the road to change.

Sanford saw Cameo enter the living room. His brown deep-set eyes narrowed as he appraised her in the straight black and gray gown with its upturned collar. She wore her long hair in two thick braids entwined across the back of her head. He made himself look away and hoped she would come to him. Since they had parted ways in Chicago, there had been no contact between them.

Cameo spotted Sanford the moment she walked into the room. She'd seen him turn away and knew what he wanted.

"Oh well." She sighed, tugging in the cuffs of the gown's long sleeves. "One of us has to make the first move." She decided.

Sanford felt the faint brush against his shoulder and turned. "Glad you came." He said.

Cameo nodded and glanced around the room. "Do you know what's going on?"

"I don't have a clue." Sanford replied, his probing stare never leaving her face. "I'm glad you came because I missed you."

"Oh." Cameo managed. The unexpected admission had rendered her speechless beyond that word. "Sanford, I-"

"I know." He interjected, pressing his index finger against her lips. "We can get into it later, alright?"

Cameo nodded and stood on her toes to press a kiss to his mouth. She laughed when his mustache tickled her skin.

Cecelia nursed her Vodka Twist and waited. Her brown gaze was unusually troubled as she looked around the room. The glass she held shook between her hands as she conjured images of how the evening would end. Someone brushed against her back and she turned. Seeing Derric standing there, she wanted to laugh and cry at once. Before she could say a word, he leaned down and kissed her.

Cece traced the side of his handsome, dark face with her fingertips. The kiss deepened and would have become more heated, had Derric not pulled away. Cece threw herself against his chest and hugged him tightly.

Derric chuckled. "What's this?" He asked, caressing her back beneath the severe, red tailored pantsuit she wore.

"Just keep your arms around me." Cece whispered, resting her face against his stylish black silk tie. "Just keep your arms around me." She repeated.

Portia decided to enjoy herself that evening. She took advantage of the gathering to wear one of her most glamorous frocks. The ankle length mauve gown was adorned with rows of black tassels that circled the form-fitting dress. The neckline sloped off one shoulder, but the sleeves were long and fitted at the wrists. A deep split revealed one long, shapely leg and thigh.

AlTonya Washington

The back dipped low to reveal the small of her back. Despite all that had happened, she was determined to keep her spirits high. She enjoyed a few drinks and mingled with family and speculated on what prompted the evening's unusual gathering. She was doing quite well, until Huron Augustine arrived. His dark, penetrating stare found her mahogany brown one. The meaningful looks held for several seconds. They never closed the distance separating them.

Stephanie and Sweet were among the last guests to arrive. With them, were Ophelia and Dyna. The two older women wore guarded expressions on their lovely faces and entered the living room as though they expected to be attacked.

"I got a strange feeling about all this." Ophelia whispered to her cousin.

Of course, everyone in the room shared Ophelia's worries.

Porter Gwaltney walked in some ten minutes later. Conversation ceased as all eyes turned to the young man near the front of the living room.

"I want to thank everybody for being so patient. We'll get started here, soon." Porter was saying as he stood looking out over the group. His expression was cool, but his hands shook terribly. He kept them hidden in the pockets of his black tuxedo trousers. "Portia, if I could get you to come with me and Mr. Kensie, if you and Mrs. Kensie would follow us, too."

Soft conversation rose as the four people left the room.
***
Almost half an hour had passed and the guests were growing restless. No one seemed to notice, but during the wait, they all began to converse without the usual suspicion and snide tones coloring their words. Despite the easy flow of the various discussions throughout the room, silence resumed when Steph, Sweet, Porter, Portia, Deme and CJ returned. Everyone watched as the six took places on the extra long cream sofa near the front of the room.

"If everyone would find a seat, we can begin." CJ instructed.

Portia fidgeted in her spot next to her mother. She kept her eyes downcast, but it was clear she wasn't at her best.

"Baby?" Deme whispered and placed a hand across her daughter's knee.

"I have to get out of here." Portia muttered. She ran from the living room with her hand covering her mouth.

"Don't, Blue." CJ called, when his brother stood.

"What the hell is going on here, CJ?" Huron snapped, losing what patience he had left..

Porter cleared his throat and stood. "This is about Missy and me. It's about a project we worked on and what we discovered."

Huron returned to his seat. He, like everyone else in the room, waited for more answers.

"The project we decided on was to trace our family tree. Because of the feuding...we thought it'd be interesting to trace our history. See who the original feuders were, you know?" Porter said, smiling as he remembered how eager they were at the beginning. "Anyway...the night Missy...the night of the accident, we had collected an important piece of information. It put everything in place for us. We discovered that a relationship had developed between an Augustine woman and a Gwaltney man-a romantic relationship. They had a son together."

Someone gasped and glances were exchanged. A few people began to fidget in their seats.

Porter felt his eyes ache as his tear ducts filled. "Missy was so out of it. I guess it was just finding out something like this through research instead of hearing it, sort of threw her. For me...I was stunned and angry. I loved Melissa. I would've-I was going to ask her to marry her." He said, just before losing control of his emotions.

CJ stood and walked over to console Porter. "This is my son." He announced, nodding at the devastated looks he received. "Deme and I had a relationship many years ago. We had two children. She wasn't raped, but said she was because of this damned feud."

"But, how could this be?" Cameo asked her confusion as evident in her voice as it was on her face. "Who was this Augustine and Gwaltney that had this relationship and how could the two of you keep the truth about your kids a secret because of some petty squabbles?"

"Cam-"

"No Derric, it's alright." CJ said, turning to Demetria who wasted no time coming to his side. "The feud wasn't the only reason, Cam. Deme was underage. I could've gone to jail for having sex with her. That scared me enough, but then I already knew about the blood shared between our families."

"You knew?" Ophelia blurted.

"Ma, CJ and I worked on the same project in school, remember?" Steph explained. "When we realized...well, that's why we started acting so weird and told you and Daddy we couldn't finish the work."

Ophelia was speechless. It seemed that only yesterday she and Chick were hit with the news that their children would not be turning in the all-important senior project.

"Who else knew about this?" Sanford asked.

"My father knew." CJ replied. "He wanted to know why, at the last minute, we decided not to turn in our report. We couldn't believe it when he started filling in the blanks on our family tree."

"Well, did *our* father know?" Tav was asking.

CJ looked back at his sister. "Dad told us Mr. Gwaltney knew, right Steph?"

"I think I remember him saying that. Our father and yours were definitely brothers."

Tav muttered a curse. "How did this happen?"

CJ stepped away from Deme, a smile coming to his face. "Pop told us a story about one of his aunts who reminded him of Steph. Her name was Lulabay Augustine. He told us how she got hurt when she fell in love with the wrong man."

"Josiah Gwaltney." Steph supplied.

"Gwaltney?" Princess blurted.

CJ nodded. "In the old days, the Augustines and Gwaltneys only fought over land. When Lulabay and Josiah got together, they had to hide it. My aunt was way younger than Josiah."

"Then she got pregnant and that caused even more problems." Steph added, re-crossing her legs as she leaned back on the sofa. "She wanted to keep her son, but...Josiah took the boy-James and gave him the Gwaltney name. No one knew the mother."

"Well, then how does that make our dad and Jason Gwaltney brothers?"

"Grandma Ressie, Pop's mama, she fell in love with a man she didn't know was her own cousin."

"James." Sanford said, watching CJ nod.

"Like my aunt, she got pregnant with my father. James knew he had a son, but he never owned up to it." CJ explained.

Steph cleared her throat. "Then he married your grandmother Lauranetta." She told Sanford. "They had Jason."

Suddenly, Derric lost control of his temper and kicked over the heavy armchair he'd just vacated. "Shit, CJ! What the hell were you and Stephanie thinkin' keeping this from us? From me, when you know how I feel about Cece."

"Derric-"

"Didn't either of you think about how this would affect a relationship?!"

CJ looked over at Deme, then reached for her hand and pulled her close to his side. "I know Derric. Believe me, I know."

Huron uttered a disgusted sound and bolted from the living room. His angry expression warned everyone to think against dissuading him from leaving.

"I told you we should've tried avoiding our families." Cameo managed to tease.

Sanford's arms tightened around her small waistline. "What's this mean for us?"

Cameo couldn't hold her tears for long. "I don't want to stop seeing you." She whispered.

Sanford could see the concern in her gaze. They mirrored the look in his own eyes. Conversation seemed out of place, then and he simply pulled her close.

"I know Daddy. About... Nikos Cantone. I know."

Tav couldn't have been more devastated. "How? Did your mother-"

"It's a long story." Princess sighed. The tired expression she wore made her seem older than she was. "But I know it all."

"Nikos Cantone." Tav repeated the name as old memories resurfaced. "I hated him with a passion." He admitted, with a soft laugh. "There was never any real reason for it. He was a likeable guy. Everybody liked him. Especially your mother."

Princess pressed her hand against the white handkerchief peeking out of Tav's breast pocket. "Daddy, you don't have to say anything."

Tav covered Princess's hand with his. "Yes, Babygirl, I do. Amina had strong feelings for me, but they were nothing compared to what she felt for Nikos. I could see that, but I didn't want to admit to it. They had something special. Some kind of connection I could never understand. He was a good man, Princess. You should be proud."

Princess brushed her fingers against Tav's brow. She wanted to wipe away the pain there. "A good man is responsible for bringing me into this world. But another good man is responsible for my surviving-for helping to make me the woman I am. That man is you, Daddy." She told him, her champagne stare sparkling with tears.

Tav kissed her forehead. "I love you and I tried to do right by you, but I am no saint. The way I treated your mother-"

"Was wrong. Wrong and disgusting," Princess answered, watching Tav's dark eyes cloud with regret. "Despite that, all I've ever known from you has been sweetness, gentleness and love. I don't care whose blood runs through my veins. You are my father."

"Babygirl," Tav whispered, pressing a kiss to Princess's bare shoulder when they hugged.

"Is this why you've been acting so nervous?" Derric asked Cece later, as they shared a private corner in the back of the living room. He smothered a curse and grimaced when she nodded. "How long have you known and why didn't you tell me?"

Cece's mahogany eyes glistened with tears as she searched his striking dark gaze. "I never expected to hear something like this when I went to see Porter. I felt so terrible for your sister when you told me what she was going through." She explained, absently toying with Derric's crisp tie. "My plan was to go to Porter and make him talk to me about what happened that night. When he finally confided, I could scarcely face it myself. Talking about it…even to you…it was out of the question."

"And now?" He asked, tilting his head just slightly as he watched her closely.

"All I know is I am scared." Cece admitted, rubbing her hands against the sleeves of her pantsuit. A sudden chill sent a deep shudder through her body. "I don't know what to think of all this, what's going to happen…"

"Shh…" Derric urged, burying his fingers in her thick hair as he kissed her temple. "Shh…I'm not going to lose you over this, you can believe that."

Cece closed her eyes and cried.

Ophelia met her son and Demetria Gwaltney in the middle of the cream Persian carpet covering the living room floor. Minutes seemed to pass as the three of them stood motionless and speechless. At last, Ophelia took Deme's hand in hers and squeezed it gently. Tears sprang from Demetria's warm, brown eyes she bowed her head.

"Mrs. Augustine-"

AlTonya Washington

"Hush, child." Ophelia soothed, pulling Deme into a tight hug. She reached for CJ's hand and kissed the tops of his fingers. "I will know my grandchildren. I will know my grandchildren and their mother." She vowed.

Huron left the living room in search of Portia. He feared she'd left the estate until he caught sight of her on an isolated terrace just off from the den on the east wing of the house.

Portia straightened off the iron railing and frowned in the direction she heard her name called. She rolled her eyes when Huron came into view.

"You should've waited until tonight, before revealing your little tape," she said, her voice shaky with emotion, "Lewis would've thought even less of me."

Huron unbuttoned his tuxedo jacket and slipped his hand into a trouser pocket. "When I think I'm doing what's best...that I have everything under control, I don't always think about the consequences."

"Would you just stop? Huron now is not the time." Portia snapped, her index finger poised in the air. "Your attempt at explaining yourself is falling on deaf ears right about now."

Huron leaned against one of the tall, iron posts several feet away from the railing. "You may not want to hear me, but since this seems to be the night for getting things off your chest, now is as good a time as any to say this."

Portia shrugged and sent a flippant wave in Huron's direction.

"I tried to get you to believe I told Lewis about those movies, because it was for your own good and he had to be told. The truth was I did it for my own good, because I wanted you. Having you in my bed, made me selfish and mean. I guess I was trippin' over the fact of having a porn queen in my bed. I knew Lewis wouldn't overlook you being in those films. He'd dump you and you wouldn't have to feel like you were betraying him with me. I realized how wrong I was when I saw what that did to you. I never set out to hurt you, Portia. But in my quest to get what I wanted, hurting you was exactly what I did." He admitted,

Taboo Tree

his black stare lingering on Portia standing alone, huddled against the railing. He pushed himself off the iron post and began to walk away.

"People with less than reputable jobs always say they never planned on doing that when they were growing up." Portia said, her voice sounding faint.

Huron could hear her perfectly. He turned and waited for her to continue.

"Well, I guess I can say I may be the first person who did set out to be something less than reputable." She admitted, leaning over the railing as she gazed up at the stars. "Oh, I won't be a cliché, and say it was my troubled childhood and the lack of love from my mother that drove me to it, hmph. I never felt like I was worth much. I could always sense I was…I don't know… dirty…unworthy. I used to always get different lotions and soaps and perfumes to use, thinking I could wash away the nastiness. It didn't work. Porter never seemed to have that problem. He could rise above and everyone loved him. I never felt that, but it was there. I had the same love Porter did, but it didn't do anything for me, I guess."

Huron was standing right behind Portia, when she finished speaking. He hesitated before pulling her back against his chest. "Why do you always put yourself down this way?"

"Huron," Portia drawled, turning to face him, "haven't you been listening? This is who I am."

"You don't believe that." Huron argued, his gorgeous dark face hardened by a glare. "If you did, you wouldn't have felt bad about telling Lewis Hines what you really do for a living. You'd be big and bold and Miss Billie Badass about it."

"You don't-"

"You're better than this. You know that. Look at me." He softly commanded, leaning close to peer into her face. "You know that."

Portia's hard stare faltered, and then she began to shake her head. The tears started to rush forward uncontrollably and soon she was slumped over in Huron's arms.

"My father's my second cousin and I've slept with my uncle." She said, with a cynical laugh.

Huron used his thumbs to wipe the tears from her cheeks. "I don't think anybody in this group could look down on you for it."

The simple statement managed to break through the wall of sorrow surrounding Portia's heart. Slowly, the laughter began to swell inside her, until it tickled her stomach and chest.

Huron felt her body shaking against his and pulled her back to make sure she wasn't crying. When he saw the amusement brightening her face, he smiled. Seconds later, their laughter resounded free and loud.

***

Everyone eventually trickled back into the living room. CJ was standing near the front, where he requested that everyone settle down.

"I wanna thank you all for comin' out here tonight. I know this hasn't been the most fun party-considering the topic of conversation and all." He acknowledged with a laugh. "But, I want you to understand no one else knows about this. The staff that was here earlier, we sent home before we got started. No one else knows, but us. We can leave all this behind and bury it." CJ pressed his lips together and looked towards Ophelia. "Ma, since you're the oldest person here, I'll ask you. Do you want things to change or keep on the way they are?"

Ophelia stood and cleared her throat. She looked out over the crowd and smoothed her hands demurely across her cream silk bellbottomed pantsuit. "No." She announced, and then smiled when she saw confusion register on everyone's faces. "I want this feuding to end and from what I see here in this room tonight-all these beautiful relationships in bloom, this mess is on its way out. Now, if keeping this thing a secret will end the feud and make these romances stronger-make our families stronger and end the hate… by all means, end it. It's what Chick always wanted and it's what I want. I think we deserve it."

A collective sigh filled the room. No words were spoken, as everyone thought over all that had been revealed.

Taboo Tree

Silently and firmly, they agreed that it was finally time for the Augustine-Gwaltney feud to end.

EPILOGUE

One year later...

The forbidden pond had regained its old splendor. Gone were all traces of the fire that had once ravaged its startling beauty. Gorgeous brush and flowers decorated the land with splashes of vibrant color. The Augustine pond was no longer a quiet, secluded place. Now, sounds of laughter, love and family further enhanced its devastating beauty.

Ophelia Augustine relaxed on one of the chaise lounges which skirted the pond. She smiled and raised her glass of lemonade for another sip. "I never thought I'd see the day when the Gwaltneys and Augustines would be partying *here* of all places! And at a wedding reception on top of that!"

Dyna smiled at her cousin's acknowledgement. "Change is definitely in the air, Girl." She agreed, laughing as she looked at the crowd across the yard. The gathering had been touted as the event of the year. Business associates as well as relatives from both families had traveled great distances to be part of the historic social event. Neighbors marveled at the love flowing between the two clans. Many of the older attendants never thought they'd live to see such a time.

Happiness, in fact, touched the entire group as everyone bestowed well wishes to Mr. and Mrs. Huron and Portia Augustine. The couple shared a long, loving kiss, only breaking apart when they were showered by a slew of confetti. The wedding attendants cheered and dancing resumed in the clearing that had been sectioned off by chains of pink carnations.

"Happy?" Huron whispered and kissed the tip of his bride's nose.

Portia closed her eyes and smiled. "Actually I am. Very."

Huron pretended to be offended. "Well you don't have to sound so surprised."

"Well it took us a long time to get here." Portia reminded him, sending a playful slap to the side of her husband's handsome face. "If I sound surprised it's because I never expected to be this happy. This blissful."

Huron pressed his forehead against hers. "I love you." He whispered.

"And you know I love you." Portia whispered back, fierce conviction in her soft voice.

While friends and associates celebrated the end of the Gwaltney-Augustine feud, others looked forward to the future. Sanford and Cameo managed to sustain a long distance romance, until Cameo took a different freelance assignment. She headed right to Richmond and into Sanford's waiting arms. Porter was back in school and doing well. He maintained frequent contact with Stephanie and Sweet. The couple had taken a much needed vacation circling the globe for the last month and a half. The doctors: Derric and Cecelia were more in love than ever. Everyone predicted they would be exchanging vows in less than a year.

Adonis walked up behind Princess and pulled her back against him. He knew what thoughts ran through her mind as she stared at the bride and groom. He had been shocked when she called and asked him to attend the wedding with her and hoped she would keep communication open between them.

"Talk to me." He whispered against her ear.

Princess snuggled back into his strong embrace. "I wanted this for us."

Adonis striking dark eyes narrowed. "So did I. I still do. Sorry." He whispered.

Princess turned in his arms. "Don't be sorry. I feel the same way."

"So?" Adonis prompted.

"Hmph. You know I've witnessed so many unbelievable things this year, nothing would surprise me."

"And I won't even ask what the hell that means." Adonis teased, his dimples appearing.

Princess laughed. "It means I don't want to lose our friendship. That was going strong before anything else."

Adonis tugged his bottom lip between his perfect teeth and debated. "And what about everything else?"

Princess smoothed her hand against the glossy chignon she wore. "Like I said, nothing would surprise me."

Adonis leaned back to look into her face. He saw the sparkle coming to her eyes and pressed a kiss to her cheek.

The sound of silverware clinging to the crystal glasses caught everyone's ears. They gathered around CJ who stood under the gazebo where the jazz band performed. His fiancée, Demetria stood at his side. Since more than immediate family was celebrating the happy day, he had to be creative with his toast. "First, let me thank all of you for celebrating today with us. I'm sure you'll all agree when I say we've come a long way." He chuckled, when everyone teasingly agreed. "Anyway, as I look forward to becoming Portia's father as well as her brother-in-law," he said, winking at his daughter who blew him a kiss, "I want to say that over all this pain, loss and anger we triumphed. When we thought too many heavy blows would make us bow down, we fought back and won. We'll do anything to prevent the past from ever repeating itself because we believe power rests in being united over divided. To the bride and groom!" He shouted.

"To the bride and groom!" The crowd replied.

"To family!" CJ shouted again.

"To family!"

AlTonya Washington

A myriad of glasses were raised. The amber color of the champagne caught the sunlight and rays of color beamed through the cut crystal. Family and friends all raised their glasses to celebrate the beginning of a new time.

Dear Reader,

Thank you for spending time with the Gwaltneys and Augustines of Virginia. I was visited by the idea for this story many years ago. The story woke me actually and I immediately reached for pad and pen to begin a furious scribbling of what I could remember from the dream I'd had about the characters whose lives you have just dropped in on. I knew the storyline was one of taboo, hence the title, yet I was compelled to write it. The characters and their haunting dilemma was a tale I had to tell, had to get out of my head. It has sat completed for some time, only being pulled out to be tweaked, revised, strengthened and then set aside again until I felt ready to share it.

My love for family sagas is well known among those who are familiar with my work. Of course, this particular saga is far different than any title I've penned about a family thus far. Shock would be an apt descriptor for one of the many emotions I'm sure *Taboo Tree* evoked. Additionally, I hope you experienced some of the reactions I had to the characters and their journey towards a devastating revelation. Heartbreak and anger visited me many times during the course of crafting this story. I was also visited by a sense of curiosity, curiosity to discover how anyone could survive the truths uncovered about these families and what it meant for their futures and for the lives they thought they were on their way to having. There are no plans for a sequel at this time- the Gwaltney and Augustine 'affair' is at last settled in my mind.

I would enjoy your feedback. Thank you for allowing me to present *Taboo Tree*.

Sincerely,
AlTonya Washington
altonya@lovealtonya.com

ALTONYA'S TITLE LIST

Remember Love
Guarded Love
Finding Love Again
Love Scheme
Wild Ravens (Historical)
In The Midst of Passion
A Lover's Dream (Ramsey I)
A Lover's Pretense (Ramsey II)
Pride and Consequence
A Lover's Mask (Ramsey III)
A Lover's Regret (Ramsey IV)
A Lover's Worth (Ramsey V)
Soul's Desire (Ebook/Short Story)
Through It All (Ebook/Novella)
Rival's Desire
Hudson's Crossing
Passion's Furies (Historical)
A Lover's Beauty (Ramsey VI)
A Lover's Soul (Ramsey VII)
Lover's Allure (Ramsey Romance Novella)
A Ramsey Wedding (Novella)
Book of Scandal- The Ramsey Elders
Layers
Another Love
Expectation of Beauty (YA Romance)
Truth In Sensuality (Erotica)
Ruler of Perfection (Erotica)
Pleasure's Powerhouse (Erotica)
The Doctor's Private Visit
As Good As The First Time
Lover's Origin (Ramsey/Tesano Novella)
A Lover's Shame (Ramsey/Tesano I)
Every Chance I Get
What the Heart Wants
Private Melody
Pleasure After Hours
A Lover's Hate (Ramsey/Tesano II)
Texas Love Song
His Texas Touch

<u>FIND ALTONYA ON THE WEB</u>

www.lovealtonya.com
www.facebook.com/altonyaw
www.shelfari.com/novelgurl
www.goodreads.com
www.twitter.com/#!/ramseysgirl

An AlTonya Exclusive

5814121R00233

Printed in Great Britain
by Amazon.co.uk, Ltd.,
Marston Gate.